Shattered Illusions

A Bear Shifter Paranormal Romance

Annie Rae

Rae of Romance

Lovers of Love

Rae of Romance, LLC

ISBN: 978-1-7370057-0-4

ASIN: B091MC56G2

Cover design by: Graphics by Stacy

Printed in the United States of America

Dedicated to my own fated mate and the reason I smile every day.
Your love and support make this crazy life the best in every way.
I am so glad I picked you all those years ago. ;)
Me & You against the world!

Contents

♥

Chapter 1

♥

Evie

I'm a glutton for punishment.

Volunteering to work late for the second night this week. It's only Wednesday. How can I ever expect to have a life if I can't learn the word no?

I eyeball the wiggly Jack Russell under my hands. Poor little guy destroyed a bag of trash while his owner was at work today causing her to bring him in minutes before closing time. Giant crocodile tears streamed down her face because Pickles was the last gift from her dad before he died. Someone to love so she wouldn't be alone. Unfortunately, the mischievous pup had the woman as frazzled as her bleached hair, worrying about what trouble we'd find in his stomach.

"You little devil," I tease, scuffling the fur on the tiny dog's head while I run the ultrasound wand over his lower tummy.

As far as I can tell, the worst things inside Pickles' stomach are some coffee grounds and leftover chicken bones. They won't be fun to pass, but he'll be good as new in a few days. The little stinker can even go home with Miss Rodriguez tomorrow. She just needs to lock up the trashcan with this food thief.

I turn off the ultrasound machine, realizing I've zoned out on Pickles' exam. The entire building has gone dark.

"Guess everyone left for the day. Huh, Pickles." I carry him over to snuggle the baby blanket inside his carrier. Poor guy's so bloated, he doesn't argue when I lock the door. Just curls his body into a ball to rest off his excitement.

Times like these, I feel like a loon for talking to myself, but it's the only remedy when you work late and not a single coworker cares enough to say goodbye. Hell, if they invited me to happy hour now and then, I'd be ecstatic. But I can't exactly get miffed when I don't have time for drinks, anyway.

"That's probably why no one ever asks you, Eveline." Great! Now, I'm giving my own self sass. But I can't exactly argue about loneliness when I'm essentially a recluse in the city, anyway.

I'm perfectly happy to spend my Wednesday night taking care of Pickles; someone needs to make sure the little dude's ok after his trashcan snack.

Sighing, I grab my purse from the cabinet, needing to let Dr. Michaels know I'm taking Pickles home with me before I go. No one will be here for over-night monitoring, so it's the best option I have. Except, I haven't seen Michaels for an at least an hour. Then again, Pickles' barfing was so distracting, I didn't notice the office had shut down either.

It's eerie back here. Having no patients in the clinic besides Pickles means no purring or barking, no scratching at cages or whimpering. There's no sound at all... like the eye of a hurricane. As a matter of fact, the only light, other than in my back room, is under the boss's door. And since the doctor has a closed-door policy, I tiptoe over on quiet feet.

Thank you, rubber-soled shoes, for discretion.

Sometimes I want to ask other people if they have to tip-toe around their bosses, but I haven't wanted to rock that boat yet. Dr. Michaels might be a little weird, but since I'm the only other veterinarian in this office, I'm building a great client base. The old guy rarely puts in face time with his patients... that's all me.

When I get my own clinic one day, these clients are going to remember who gave their precious babies all the love.

Me.

Still... I cringe the closer I get to the doc's door. What sort of weirdness goes on in that office? Why can't trusted staff enter without an invitation? Imagining that pot-bellied, gray-haired grandpa getting up to naughtiness on his computer is not palatable on an empty stomach. *Ick.*

The thought alone makes me hesitate outside his closed door, shaking off a chill that rolls down my spine. Except, it doesn't sound like the doc's alone. Deep voices talk fast in there, but I can't make out words through the wood.

Are they bickering? Should I just leave a note instead of interrupting?

Torn, I wave off the split second of guilt and press my ear against the door to listen, knowing I should just turn around and leave. The doctor's hushed whisper is at odds with the other gruff voices. They all grow louder, more agitated, as I stand here eavesdropping.

Somebody's pissed. Their heated tones spike the hair on the back of my neck. Is it an unhappy client? I haven't heard of any issues, but if someone went straight to the doc...

Straining my ear, I press harder at the door, chewing on my thumbnail. I have to know if it's one of my clients that's dissatisfied.

"The boss ain't happy, Michaels!" The visitor's deep voice booms through the flimsy door. *Boss?* Michaels owns the clinic; he doesn't have a boss.

"Yeah," pipes a nasally one. *OK, so two visitors.* "You remember what happened to Ray at the pawnshop, right? He thought he could get over on us." An evil cackle cuts off the sentence before a violent thud slams the door, shaking the space I just had my ear.

I jump farther from the opening, praying the angry visitors don't walk out and catch me snooping. Self-preservation is the only thing keeping me quiet when another impact rattles the hinges of Dr. Michaels' door.

The moan that follows churns my stomach. What the hell is happening in there? Should I get help? This doesn't sound like a disgruntled client anymore.

The doctor talks frantically, his whiny voice speaking so fast that I can barely catch a word through that thick Tennessee twang. "No, no... you don't understand," his muffled cry echoes through the door, followed by another thump, a pop, and a scream of pain.

Oh, my God! I cover my mouth, so I don't scream myself, and press tight against the painted cinder block hallway. *What do I do? What do I do?*

I can't convince my feet run. My gut's twisted with morbid fascination, terrified to move but terrified someone's going to walk out and find me stalking the hallways.

"Last warning, Michaels," the gravelly voice warns. "Look... ya either clean more money through this here sham of an office, or our next visit will end a little diff'rent. Hear me?" *Thwack.*

The sound of bone crunching pops me out of my daze. I know the agonizing groan on the other side of the door is the doc... so are the muted sobs that follow.

That last slap of skin is the gun powder shooting me into motion, my feet picking up steam as I dart to the back room. I barely clear the corner when the boss's office door smacks the wall, the thump reverberating down the hallway. My breath catches.

Shit, shit, shit.

It feels like my lungs are on fire as the panic sets in, moving my feet fast to Pickles' cage. I grab the thing quick, trying to minimize the rattle so we can slide through the back exit before the doc's guests realize they have company.

Unfortunately, before I get the door closed, my eyes catch a motion in the hallway. Glowing yellow eyes sear themselves into my memory, their unnatural shade sending chills down my spine.

As quick as I can, I race toward my car. Running with the cumbersome cage and an upset dog is hard but I get Pickles loaded in my backseat, nearly missing the sidestep in my hurry to climb in the driver's seat.

When I crank my Jeep and jerk the car from the parking lot, I glance one last time at the rear entrance of the clinic, dread flooding my system.

A buzzed-hair meat head stands in the open door, veins bulging in his tattooed arms. His beady eyes take on a reddish glow as scary as the daggers he's glaring. *What the actual fuck?*

In the back of my mind, those eyes solidify the niggling fear that I'll never see this building again.

·♥·♥·♥·♥·♥·

I double check my deadbolt, the lock on the patio door, and close the curtains. After I'm certain my apartment is secure, I inhale the deepest breath I can and start pacing my tiny kitchen.

For the last thirty minutes, I've tried to stave off my impending panic attack with busy activities... sorting the mail, washing a bowl. Fidgeting. None of it helps. My hands still shake, my heart still thunders in my ears. Every single breath I take feels like pulling a pineapple through a tiny straw. If I didn't know better, I'd swear actual fireworks are blasting under my skin like the Fourth of July.

I need time. Time to figure out what the hell happened tonight.

Glancing down at Pickles, I sigh. He's whimpering to come out, so I slide the ottoman from my favorite chair to the kitchen doorway. It creates a large bulky, fabulous blockade to quarantine the whiny pup to a tiled area—just in case those coffee grounds decide to reappear.

At least focusing on the puppy solves my temporary problem. It keeps me moving. I have a hunch that if I sit down, I'll self-combust, so distraction it is.

For the next few minutes, I work on a kitchen fort. A jump-free barrier that can hold a Jack Russell's energy.

Until now, the little guy has effectively been a dog with the 'man flu,' but the second I open his door, the white ball of fur launches from his crate. Tiny legs darting circles around my kitchen, not letting his stomach ailment put a damper on his newfound freedom.

After placing a bowl of water on the floor, I realize I need dinner for both of us. Since Pickles is on a restricted diet, I can't give him much, but the grilled chicken in my fridge will work for both of us.

"Alright Pickles, you're going to help me figure out my problem while we eat."

Pickles' only response is the comical slant of his head while I warm up our dinner in the microwave. He either thinks I've lost my mind or couldn't care less about my problems and only wants food.

When the microwave dings, my scruffy friend nearly trips my feet with his happy dance. It makes me laugh despite this awful night while I divide his part of the chicken into a plastic bowl. "Come on, Pickles. Help a girl out." I watch the little guy dive into his bowl like it's the best food in the world and wish I could be that way.

God, the ridiculousness of seeking advice from a dog sinks in. *I must be really freaking lonely!*

"I didn't hear what I thought I heard, right?" I ask Pickles, not expecting an answer. We both focus on our chicken, but the pounding headache that's settled into my brain makes it hard.

I choke back tears and stab at my salad. All the fear I shoved down with busy activities is bubbling back up and I can't stop it.

How did my life go from slightly structured boredom to an episode of Law & Order with no effort on my part?

My vision blurs and I sink to the floor beside Pickles, my salad forgotten. The maple cabinets I loved two years ago when I moved in are no comfort now. They were cute when my life was on the upswing... fresh out of vet school, new job, new town...

I hug my knees in front of me, trying to calm my raging thoughts. Shaking fingers massage my temples, knowing I can't sit on the floor forever. I have a dog who isn't mine, a criminal boss, and the solar system of issues that come with that. I need a plan.

"I have to call the cops, Pickles." The dog yips, and I wonder if he knows I'm talking to him. "If Dr. Michaels is laundering money, the clinic's in trouble. I can't work there anyway. Oh my God! I'm unemployed."

My heart is two steps from climbing out of my chest. There are too many ways this could turn south. "What if the cops think I'm involved too?" Pickles, who's done with his dinner, walks over and climbs in my lap for a scratch. He doesn't care that I'm too distracted to do more than a small rub behind the ears. The little snuggler actually seems to want to help console me.

At least his scruffy fur is something to focus on besides the hard cabinet behind my back. My nerves rattle when the phone buzzes on the countertop. A million dollars wouldn't make me answer the damn thing, I don't care who's calling. I've had enough of people today.

Pickles finally tires of my half-hearted ear rub and takes to sniffing the corners of my kitchen... *uh oh.*

When I stand, thinking the little guy needs a relief walk, my legs are the equivalent of room temperature Jell-O. I need to wiggle the tingle away fast because Pickles is starting that tale-tell circling. If I want his messes to stay outside and not in my kitchen, I need to move.

My mad dash to the dog crate sends Pickles into a fit. When I pull out his leash, those pint-sized legs spring him near hip height, creating a bundle of energy that makes it hard to snap a leash.

"OK, boy. I got it. You must feel better." His answering sneeze is either an excited agreement or frustration with my unnecessary commentary. Sighing, I relent and pick up the cellphone before following the incredibly motivated puppy out the door.

In the dark breezeway, I have to pause, anxiety settling in my stomach that makes me want to stay locked in my apartment. Those beady eyes from the clinic flash in my head for a second. I hope I never have to see those creepy eyes again. *Something was wrong with that guy!*

Pickles, unlike myself, is impatient for the unknown, for whatever hides in the darkness. His leash drags me behind him until the silly dog is almost choking himself. "Dude, slow down." The last thing I need is a patient hurting themselves in my care. Especially because I'm too freaked out to walk at a normal human pace.

Problem is, the farther from my apartment we get, the more my chest hurts. Sweat's trickling down my neck at this point. I just don't like being out in the open like this. At least Pickles doesn't complain too much when I keep him restricted to the lit walkway close to my apartment. Being within earshot of a few patios gives me a small amount of comfort.

"God! I hate this feeling!" My grumble falls of deaf puppy ears, but I just can't shake the needles tickling my skin. Pickles couldn't care less that my eyes scan the parking lot like a paranoid mad woman. As far as I can tell, nothing's out of place. That doesn't stop my feet from wanting to hundred-yard dash it to the safety of my triple deadbolt.

Unfortunately, Pickles is showing extreme dedication to marking every bush within reach. "Come on, little guy, help a girl out."

From my pocket, the ring tone programmed for the clinic chimes and that's it. I can't talk to Dr. Michaels tonight without cracking and all things considered, Pickles has had plenty of time for his business. *This potty break's over!*

The whole way back to my apartment, I'm looking over my shoulder. With my heart in my throat, I manage to tug my defiant companion back to the safety of my four-walled security blanket, flip the locks, and get Pickles' collar unlatched before I drop into my kitchen chair with an odd combination washing over me... relief and dejection.

"All the work I put in that office, Pickles! I thought I was building something. I had a ten-year plan." *It's all gone!*

The little guy ambles over like he senses my distress. With his chin digging into my foot, I could almost feel the dog giving his pitiful house-mate a hug. That sweetness threatens to release a full barrage of tears but somehow, I manage to stifle them all... except one. That stubborn tear fights past my anger, falling on the back of my hand when I don't try to wipe it away.

Annoyed with my pity party, I slam my palm on the table, welcoming the sting as I stand. The pain helps me not become basket-case over the loss of my dreams. Especially when I'm in the place I sit every night, with no plans like every night. No friends to call when I feel like this.

Like a sign, my eyes fall to the invitation my mother mailed for the Great New Moon Festival next week. I stuck it on my fridge between the cutesy magnets and pictures of home.

Invitations to tribal ceremonies are my mother's greatest mission. Gather all the young Cherokees that have spread across the eastern states and guilt them home to honor our heritage.

It works. I'm always too guilty to throw it away.

"Only my mother."

The funny thing is, after today, getting out-of-town, even if it's for a large family celebration, is just what the doctor ordered.

One of my favorite photos from home catches my attention. It's me and my sisters hugging when I graduated. Before we grew distant with time… and actual distance.

Standing alone in my quiet kitchen, the thought of going back to simpler times with my family, where there are people to lean on and talk to, sounds perfect. Maybe it would help me work out a plan, since apparently, I'm starting my professional life over again.

A sweet relief washes over me. At least I've made one decision tonight. With renewed stamina, I practically jog to my bedroom and pack a bag.

Big Paw Mountain, I'm coming home.

Chapter 2

♥

Evie

Last night, after I dropped off Pickles with his surprised owner, I drove the hour and a half home, my Jeep packed with a week's worth of clothes.

Not a single person questioned my arrival, even though I only texted my baby sister, Kayah, about the impromptu trip home. She was the first person out of the house to wrap me in a bear hug. Tight on Kayah's tail were Mom and Dad, happy shock written all over their faces.

"Punkin,' what are you doing here?" Dad asked as his shock slowly wore off.

"She's here for the festival, Kota." I didn't argue with my mom's assessment, just kept my smile light as my family opened their door to me, no questions asked. Like any good southern family.

They led me to the kitchen for hot cocoa and night cookies, since apparently showing my face at home is treat worthy.

"Gran's already in bed," Mom admitted, keeping her voice low.

"She moved in I guess?"

"Yeah." Mom looked at my dad, a silent communication passing between them. "Ama got her own place closer to work so Gran could have her room."

The assumption that I should already know that was implied, so I kept the rest of the conversation topical, which was hard considering the night I had.

While the four of us caught up, Mom updated me on the progress for the New Moon and what we still needed to do. I let her keep the assumption that I was here to help with prep.

It was all extremely welcoming and inclusive.

That was last night...

This morning, a weird vibe clouds the house. Could be the two missed calls and slew of texts I woke up with on my phone. It immediately soured my mood.

Downstairs, everyone has already left for the day, except Ma and Gran, who're cutting vegetables at the kitchen table.

"Mornin'." I bend over and hug my grandmother's bony shoulders. "You guys prepping stew?"

"You know it, little lady," Gran winks with a sweet smile. "You are certainly a sweet surprise to wake up to."

It's impossible not to smile at Gran as I pour myself a coffee, but the pile of vegetables she's working worries me. I don't want my grandmother chopping a mountain of veggies with her gnarled fingers just so I can have my favorite meal, my first day home.

I grab one of Ma's homemade danishes and sit beside Gran at their massive kitchen table. The rustic top is showing its age after all the years of family dinners and holiday prep. But for the first time, I see that aging in Gran, as well. More white streaks thread her traditional braid. The lines have deepened around her expressive eyes. Still, those high cheekbones and strong Cherokee features create a regal beauty that's all Gran.

I just hate how the changes highlight the time I've been away. "Let me help, Gran." I wiggle my fingers playfully, ignoring my breakfast plate in favor of helping Gran chop.

Despite the woman's seventy years and arthritic fingers, she'll refuse help if I treat her like an old lady. She's been our tribe's wise-woman, or seer, since her own mother's passing, and is still one of the smartest people I know.

She gives me a hard look. "Mm-hmm. If you insist," she says, sliding me the chopping board warily. Of course, the smile in her eyes says she knows my game. Gran and I have always been close, so it's hard to sneak anything by her. Hell, I spent most of my childhood at my grandparents' house, following Gramps around... two animal lovers doing well-checks on the tribal herd. Let's say anything that gets by Gran is only what she lets by.

Those days with Gran and Gramps are some my best memories.

After every work call with Gramps, we'd join Gran on their porch for homemade lemonade and cookies. The two of them rocking in their favorite chairs while I played on the floor with my animal figurines and Lincoln Logs.

Their house was old-fashioned that way, and I loved it.

Gran entertained us with fables of Big Paw Mountain—amusing stories of magical heroes and protectors. Men who were mightier and more honorable than most.

Those days of playing Gramp's assistant gave me the bug to become a veterinarian. "I would just like to point out that I was doing just fine before you sat down," Gran says, and I laugh at her huff of annoyance. Our of the corner of my eye, I catch my mother's smile of approval so at least I feel like I'm not overstepping.

"I gotcha, Gran. I just want to help while I'm here."

Mom joins us at the table, love shining from her eyes as she squeezes my non-knife wielding hand. "I am so glad you came home, baby girl. We missed you 'round here."

I smile past the guilt of not being honest about my trip home. Luckily, Mom takes over the conversation while I chop. She and Gran chat about dinner, about services last weekend, about the festival. Eventually, my brain glazes over until one dubious sentence stands out from Mom.

"So, Eveline. Ash has been coming round askin' about you. The last year or so, right Gran?" Mom tries to rally my grandmother's input, but Gran knows better. Her smirk almost cracks me. She's heard my complaints about my mom and Ash's trying to push us together over the years. Ash is—and will only ever be—my best friend.

At least we were when I lived at home.

He was the boy who taught me to shoot a bow when Dad wouldn't. He taught me how to string the best fishing lure, and how to execute a perfect arc when skipping rocks.

Thankfully, neither mom knows twelve-year-old Ash got the bright idea we should practice our first kisses on each other. They'd go crazy. That kiss was awkward and weird and stiff. And then we pinkie promised never to speak of it again.

"I'll drive by his house today, Ma." Of course, I didn't tell Ash I was coming home either, but I can't let that guilt sink in right now.

Just when I'm about to tap dance on my mother's matchmaking efforts, my middle sister strolls into the kitchen, stopping short when she sees me sitting at the table. "Well, this is a surprise."

"Hey, Ama." I offer a smile, hoping she's outgrown the competition and jealousy that's fueled our rivalry these last few years… pretty much since I left for college.

No matter what I do, Ama assumes the worst intentions. We're only three years apart. We used to share clothes and whisper secrets about our crushes. Looking at my sister now, I can't believe we once covered for missed curfews, or that time I broke the barn door and all of Dad's goats got out.

She seems to have forgotten all of that now. The glower she aims my way is cold enough to frost a layer of ice over the Caribbean Sea. "So, what brings the prodigal daughter home?" Ama ask, grabbing a plate of Mom's breakfast leftovers.

Mom and I both sigh. So much for growing up.

"Behave, Ama," Mom chastises, squeezing my shoulder sympathetically. "Evelyn got home late last night. She doesn't need your sarcasm when she's tired."

"Well, if Eveline graced us with her presence more often…"

"Ama!" Mom hisses.

Ama lifts her eyebrow at me—a challenge. Somehow, she manages a bite of her sausage around the disdain curling her lip. *The girl's got talent.*

I admit—only to myself—that part of my annoyance with Ama is the fact that my sister can drive across town in her pajamas, a messy knot of hair piled on her head, and walk in here looking completely gorgeous. Despite routinely working until two a.m. managing the casino.

"I'm just joking, Ma," Ama says, pouting.

"Doesn't matter… behave." Mom is her typical middleman, wanting all her daughters to get along, even if we haven't for years. But it does stop this argument before it gets off the ground.

Mom stands with an apologetic look and starts to clean the morning dishes, leaving me with Ama "the sour-puss."

"Sure thing," Ama says, feigning innocence as she walks her plate to the sink and without another word heads for the front door.

"Where're you going, young lady?" Mama wipes her hands on the towel tucked perpetually in her apron.

"I got plans." Ama raises her chin snottily and then she's gone. All while I still have a half-eaten Danish beside me, and a cutting board of vegetables only partially chopped.

Gran's wrinkled hand pats my arm, easing some of the sadness in my heart. "It's alright, Bug. She'll come 'round."

I sigh, not having the energy to argue with Gran, but Mom interrupts anyway before I have the chance. "Alright ladies, time to exit the kitchen." She grabs my shoulders, ushering me from the table even though I didn't agree to whatever timetable my mom is holding too.

Gran chuckles under her breath but gathers her water cup and threads her arm with mine so I can help her to the porch—not that my feisty Gran needs it. I smell a ruse. Gran nearly spits out a mouthful when my mom pats her hand on my bottom like I'm a kid she needs to get moving off to school.

"Ma…" I whine, giving her my most put out look.

Ma and Gran aren't as slick as they think they are. I saw that cagey side-eye over my shoulder. That was Mom's not-so-subtle request for Gran to work me for gossip. No one denies Gran—especially me—and mom knows it.

Gran's fast as a whip when she wants to be—*sneaky Cherokee woman.*

I paste on probably the first fake smile I've ever used with Gran and get her settled in her favorite chair on the front porch. The one with the light blue tropical flowers on the cushion that she's mended about twenty times before I plop myself in the matching rocker beside her.

Gran rocks leisurely, like she doesn't have a care in the world while I wait for that Cheshire grin to say what it wants to say.

"So, what brings our little Evie home after all this time?" Her eyes pin me, brooking no nonsense. I'm expected to woman up here and I know it.

"Gran, it hasn't been that long." I stop when the guilt hits. It's been close to a year. "OK. Work's been crazy, but I do miss you guys. The New Moon Festival was a good reason to visit."

"You don't need a reason, young lady," Gran says, and I feel like an eight-year-old who got caught snatching a cookie. "And FYI, I can read a map. I know you're only two hours away, kiddo."

"OK. It feels weird sometimes, Gran." That's hard to admit to one of my favorite people in this world. Instead of meeting her eye, I watch our barn cat stalking a stray duck in the yard. "Sometimes I feel like I don't belong, you know. You saw it, Gran. Ama hates when I come home."

"No, she doesn't." Gran stops rocking. "That's ridiculous, Bug. Ama loves you."

"Did you hear her, Gran? She couldn't get out of the room fast enough." I shrug, hoping Gran can't see how bad that hurts. "After a while, I came back less so I don't rock the boat."

"Well, stop it!" Gran huffs, her tiny hand slapping the arm of her rocker. The sound surprises me with its sharpness. "We'd love to see you more often. Every. One. Of. Us." Gran's bony finger pokes my arm, emphasizing each word. "I know you've got your life in Tennessee. Your mom and dad understand that." She pauses until I meet her eyes. Until I read the sincerity. "This," she flicks her finger through the air, spanning our land, "this will always be your home, Bug."

"Thanks, Gran." A lump settles in my throat.

"You know... your granddad would be so proud of you, Eveline." I look over, surprised at the change of conversation. Gran's gaze shifts to the sky with a wistful smile, like she can hear her late husband's voice in her mind.

"I wish Gramp's could've seen me become a veterinarian," I confess, hating that I never got to show him I followed in his footsteps. Although... "Gran, would he have wanted me on the homeland? He devoted his life to helping our people keep their animals healthy. Would I have disappointed him?"

"Bug, no!" Gran shakes her head emphatically. At least she didn't pause for her answer. "Your grandfather loved you. He would love who you are, too. He didn't expect you to be the same person he was... that's not right." I smile, a piece of my heart appeased by her words. "Your grandfather knew that life has twisted roads, Evie. Every one of us has a different path but we all end up where we're supposed to be in the end. I promise."

If I imagine my road curvy—like Gran said—maybe I didn't hit a dead end this week. Maybe things just got a little twisted. "Do you think about Gramps a lot?" I ask.

"Every day!" Gran rests her head against the rocker, her lips tugging down briefly. "That man was my best friend. I've always wanted you to find that kind of love. The best kind," she says way with a knowing smile. "Whenever you're ready."

I do remember my grandparents taking care of each other. Gramps would bring her coffee in the morning. She'd bring him lunch out to the barn. I want that kind of devotion for myself, it just doesn't seem to be out there for me.

"I don't know, Gran. I haven't found it yet. Too busy working, I guess."

Her throaty-laugh washes over me. "Well, work won't give me great-grandbabies, will it?" I shake my head at my grandmother's sass. She's never been a shy one.

"You never know... maybe you'll find someone here," she offers, making me squirm. "Change of scenery. Change of environment. I can help you out, Bug." She laughs harder at my skeptical look. "There're some very hunk-a-licious men on this mountain, Evelyn." Gran winks and I'm left staring in shock.

God, please don't let me be desperate enough to let my grandmother set me up.

She continues as if reading my mind. "I play bingo with a lot of grandmothers, you know."

"OK, Mooom," I drawl sarcastically, stopping Gran from anymore matchmaking talk. "Maybe I'm not looking for anything hunk-a-licious right now," I say, standing. "I think I'll go surprise Ash. They on fall break this week?"

"Think so, Bug. Tell him hi for me."

"Will do, Gran." I kiss her wrinkly cheek, before heading in the house for my purse.

When I walk back by her, I catch a soft mumble under Gran. "You may not be looking for love, Bug, but that doesn't mean you won't find it." Her words send a zing of electricity down my spine.

I'd love to find love… I'm just not holding my breath.

Chapter 3

♥

Evie

When I pull up to Ash's house, five or so minutes later, a flood of high school memories hit me like a sledgehammer. Sure, my car was a beat-up piece of crap back then, but I still picked Ash up every Saturday to cruise the one-and-only Wal-Mart parking lot.

Just like back then, Ash bounds out of his front door before I get the car into park. "Eve!"

Grinning, I throw my door wide and run into Ash's open arms. "Ash! My God! I missed you so much." Ash's slightly taller frame swings my shoulders side-to-side, the sweet greeting of friends who miss the contact of old times.

When Ash pulls back, his eyes glimmer with happiness. It warms my heart. "So, what are you doing here? Am I daydreaming?"

"*Ha. Ha.* Alright, smart ass. I can come home without it being an ordeal."

"But you don't."

Annoyed, I jab my fingers in Ash's ribs, maybe a little too hard, but I'm surprised when I hit muscle instead of bone. "Ouch, workout much?" I ask, shaking my fingers. My old buddy's t-shirt is a lot tighter than he used to wear. It clings to muscles he certainly did not have in high school.

Holy cow, my friend grew into a man.

At least he still has that same boyish smirk. I'm just under a lot more lean muscle when he tucks me under his shoulder, now. "What are you actually doing here?" His tease isn't as playful as we walk in his house. The one he inherited after his parents' death a few years ago.

"*Come on*! Offer a girl some coffee before the third degree," I whine, smacking his hand from my shoulder, since he won't drop the extra scrutiny. "Didn't your mama teach you nothing?"

Prodding Ash's manners is a distraction—a small one—but something to shake the feeling I've let down everyone. The downward cast of his mouth reaffirms my need to smooth over our friendship... my neglect.

"Noted," Ash says, his voice dimming for a moment before the humor picks up again. "Well, my long-lost friend... would you prefer a cup or an IV drip for your caffeine hit?"

The joke softens the awkwardness; our long running caffeine joke setting a bit of normalcy into our reunion.

In Ash's living room, I notice the old green carpet gone we used to make fun of, so the room doesn't look like deranged soccer turf anymore. Now, the distressed hardwoods and fresh paint give the home a more modern vibe... or at least a vibe-in-progress.

"This place looks incredible, Ash." I have to raise my voice because Ash is already on coffee retrieval in the kitchen. But I have to say something so I'm not just standing her twisting my fingers like a nervous toddler.

It sucks to feel uncomfortable in a place that used to feel like my second home, but it is, what it is.

"There's a lot to do still," he yells back over the fizz of that little coffee maker heating our water.

Distracted, I walk over to the stone fireplace where our 'friend-date' prom picture still sits beside his parents' wedding photo on the mantle. There's a picture of me and Ash with my sisters at our high school graduation and I'm not sure if I feel flattered that Ash still honors our younger days, or guilty that our most recent picture was ten years ago.

On the opposite side, a few candid photos of Ash with people I don't know is another blatant reminder that I haven't kept in contact like I should have. I've got no idea what goes on in his life, if he's dating, or anything. I feel like the underside of a pond-rock, covered in scum... and tossed in the mud.

Thankfully, before I can beat myself up too much, those telltale spittling bubbles from the kitchen means our coffee's almost ready. Ash's coffee may taste close to tar, but if Ash dressed it up the way I like, I won't argue with his taste buds too much. Today.

Needing to clear my head, I take my own liberties to pull back the thick floral curtains Ash's mom sewed. A little light will go a long way brighten the room and my mood.

By the time Ash walks in with those thick as molasses single cups, I feel like I can breathe again. Although, my plop on the couch is a little too obvious in the *fake it, til you make it* category. At least the smirk on Ash's face when he extends the cup says he doesn't mind and if anything, he'll laugh at me for it later.

When Ash gets situated with his back against the other side of the couch, legs extended in my direction, I take the hint and bring mine up beside his. This was our position in high school, the place we'd talk for hours on end about teenage drama.

The only thing different is the secretive twist of his lips. I almost ask him 'what's up,' but on my sip of warm cinnamon-y goodness in my hand, I get it. "Holy crap! Lightened up your taste in coffee, huh?"

Ash beams. "I have some date-pleasing coffee on hand. Figured I'd pick a pod you like since you're here." He sticks out his tongue, teasing. "Not my fault you never had good taste in coffee."

Our laughter cracks through the air, releasing the last bit of uneasy tension from my shoulders.

"So... how have you been? What's new? How's life?" My rapid-fire questions are an effort to keep the conversation on Ash and away from my distance these last few years or the reason for my return.

Ash lets me get away with my evasive tactics, like a true friend, and hits me with a cheesy grin over the lip of his coffee mug. "I'm good. Started my master's finally. Life is... busy." Chuckling, he asks, "did that hit them all?"

"Smart ass!" I smack his foot that's propped beside my hip, relishing the easy acceptance from my childhood best friend. I didn't know how healing this visit would be after my last hellish forty-eight hours. "It does. But, more about the master's... are you leaving teaching?"

"No way, E. You know I love teaching." He sighs, his head falling to the couch pillow under the weight of this topic. "Those kids are amazing, but our school has significant issues." He pauses... "An interesting administration, I guess."

I take a sip of coffee, waiting for my friend to formulate his thought without pushing. Finally, Ash pulls himself from a memory, fire storming in his eyes.

"I just thought that rather than complain, I'd finish my master's, so in a year or two, when Principal Granger retires, I'll be ready to take over. Unless I kick his butt out first, because I would be way better for that school." At least the mischievous smile that lights up Ash's face is better than that brooding expression.

The sad thing is, I don't know the ins and outs of Ash's life enough to comment on his situation. When I open my mouth, nothing comes out.

Ash notices and continues with a light-hearted shrug. "Hey, if you can't beat them, take them over, right?"

That sounds good and all but... "What's going on there over there? Is Granger giving Kayah crap too? Maybe he's losing touch in his old age."

The determination hardening Ash's features makes me worry for my baby sister. She's student teaching at the same school we attended growing up, the same school where Ash has been teaching for five or so years.

Another notch in my guilt. Everyone is helping our community but me.

He waves a hand dismissively. "Too much to get into right now. What's going on with you?"

Taking a fortifying breath, I dive into the basics with a large gulp of coffee for motivation. "So... recently, I had some issues at work—very recently, actually. And, well... the gist is, I'm not going back to the clinic. But no one knows that yet," I hurry to push in that last part and almost laugh when Ash chokes on my words. He's as surprised to hear them as I am to say them.

With worry in his dark eyes, Ash leans forward, squeezing my knee for support. "Are you staying?" he asks, and his hopeful tone immediately guts me.

I have to be honest though.

"I'm not sure what I'm doing. Except requesting a temporary leave of absence. That's definite." The tight coil in my chest loosens, having only made that decision as the words left my mouth. It's just hard to explain to my best friend that I made a huge mistake in the path of my life. "I-I just need a break. To, uh, reevaluate."

At Ash's nod, I set my coffee cup on the table and hold out my pinkie for one of our childish promises. "This stays between us for now."

His head cocks with a 'really' expression, but Ash still can't resist our tradition and he links my finger with a little shake. The silliness and his promise relieves a touch of the nauseousness turning my stomach over the current state of my life.

Finally, Ash's leans back on the couch, his eyes searching mine... for what, I don't know. I can't give the man answers I don't have myself. And I damn sure don't want to talk about the scariest night of my life.

Though his brow is still furrowed, Ash agrees to my request for temporary discretion. "Eve, I get it. But if you need anything, I'm here, OK."

I nod, feeling the weight of our friendship wrap me in a warm hug. How did I not realize how much Ash's support means? Or how good it would feel to have someone in your corner, even when you're doing something stupid, like not immediately running to the cops and joining witness protection.

"I will." I salute jovially just to crack the tension. "But let's talk about something else."

"Alright, fine. How about how much I've missed you? I have nobody to get in trouble with anymore." Ash's pout immediately shifts into a mischievous grin. "What if we go on an adventure tomorrow?"

"What sort of adventure?" I ask skeptically.

"Well, there's a new company doing mountain tours, exotic exploration stuff."

"Why would we pay money for a tour when you know this mountain like the back of your hand?"

"I know, I know." He shakes his head. "But these guys are different. Real wilderness and hidden trails—unique stuff, you know." He looks more excited by the minute. "They cater to adventure. And... they take locals to remote areas tourists don't go."

"OK." I hedge, wondering if I should be going off on a fun day instead of getting my life in order. *What the hell?* Screw it... "I'm game if you are." I honestly don't care what we, but this could be a nice way to forget my worries for a while.

"Nice!" Ash pumps his fist to the ceiling, hopping off the couch before I've even finished my sentence. "This is the best ending to fall-break I could imagine, E."

Before I can say anything else, Ash grabs his dinosaur of a laptop and pulls up the adventure website. "I'll book the waterfall tour. I heard these guys know the most romantic spots." He winks at me with a glint in his eye.

"Planning a hot date?"

He pauses, a hint of pain reflected when he meets my eye, but just as quickly, it's gone. As if it was never there. "You know how it is, E. Gotta find a romantic spot for all those ladies chasing me?"

A laugh bubbles up that I immediately tamp down on when Ash's excitement dims. He's never been much of a lady's man, but I don't want to hurt his feelings, either. Ash has always been a good friend.

Plus, this is the first time since I left work on Wednesday that I'm not thinking about lies and drama and what-ifs.

Chapter 4

♥

Wyatt

Mornings suck!

No matter how many times I wake up at the butt-crack of dawn, it doesn't get any easier. The one—and only—thing making mornings bearable around here is the Green Beret Coffee wafting from my kitchen.

That rich scent is what I live for after a late night. Maybe I'd be happier if I was exhausted because of a woman instead of accounting books.

God, how I wish we could afford outside help for this crap.

I started Smokey Mountain Rugged Tours so my brother and I could work outside, not hung over a computer for hours on end.

Too bad Caleb's stuck in his middle child, rebel phase and is usually too hungover to be much help before ten a.m.

My youngest brother would never be that irresponsible, but Seth's on deployment. For another eighteen months! Which is a whole other kind of hell sitting on my shoulders. It's a lot of stress worrying about someone you love, not that I'd hold that against him. I admire my baby brother's sacrifice for his country more than he'll ever know. *I just miss the shit out of him!*

And it leaves me with Caleb as my backup to keep our fledgling tourism company alive.

Maybe that's why Seth ships me my supply of coffee every month. *Guilt.* The custom grind is diesel enough for those military rangers, so it has no problem keeping up with my overly tired, grumpy ass. I couldn't function at six a.m without it.

I fix myself a murky cup while plating a piece of toast with some grape jelly. Not a great breakfast to head into the day, but I'll deal. At my table, I wait for the slow as hell computer to load our online scheduling system.

When the screen finally populates, I almost swallow my coffee down the wrong pipe.

Holy hell! Nearly all my tours are booked up today.

It's deeply gratifying to see our website and online booking system prove their worth. Those were my decisions, my investments. And probably the best ones I've made since starting *Rugged Tours*. I'm embarrassingly close to doing a happy dance—albeit an extremely manly one—in my kitchen.

Nearly!

But these programs have taken so much pressure off managing my time, that it feels wrong not to celebrate. I guess going out today and doing what I do best is its own reward. Even if it's going to be an absolute crazy day—and exhausting—but so far, this technology is a huge win.

One more step in securing a future for my family. All this stress *will* be worth it in the long run.

I glance around my quiet kitchen, momentarily feeling the emptiness of having no one to celebrate with. After years of tweaking and renovating, I've finally gotten my cabin the way I want it. I have close friends and a community standing behind me. Everything a man needs, except one thing. Is that why I'm always so frustrated with my life?

I want my mate!

My bear steers my head to the main issue unsettling my life and driving me crazy. What is success worth if I don't have anyone to share it with? I'd like someone to curl up with after a long day or meet for a beer after a painful tour.

What the hell am I supposed to do about it? I argue, getting frustrated with the growling in my head. I don't need that this early in the morning. *I can't conjure a mate out of thin air. Chill out!*

Knowing I don't have time to sit around licking my wounds, I carry my plate to the sink and rinse it. *There's no use in running a dishwasher for one person. Is there?*

With that depressing thought, I head off to shower and get ready for the day. I can't reek of stale man for my nine-a.m. tour. That would definitely not earn repeat customers.

·❤·❤·❤·❤·❤·

Once cleaned up, I toss my lunch and a cooler of water bottles and sodas in the bed of my truck. The extra supplies go far toward client satisfaction, and the water itself could prevents unnecessary liabilities— like a heat stroke during one of the tours. Win-win.

On my way to the pass—where I greet new tours—I drop a call to Caleb, mentally pleading with him to be out of bed at this hour.

"Yea," my brother's deep voice answers, fuzzy with sleep.

"What the hell, Cale? You still in bed?"

"*Ugh.*" I hear rustling through the phone that sounds like Caleb trying to get himself out of bed. My sensitive shifter ears cringe from his clumsiness banging through the truck speakers. "Wyatt. Man! It's only 8:00. Why would I be out of bed?"

"Because I need you at the office at nine," I explode, trying and failing to rein in my temper. Caleb's curses fill the phone. "Dammit, I told you to set your alarm in case we get any walk-ins. I'm booked the entire day, man!"

"Yeah, yeah. I remember." His grumble is barely audible over his banging through the house as he wakes up.

"Caleb!" My shout reverberates through the phone just as I pull into the trail's parking lot. "Dude wake your ass up! I need you this morning. You can message me if you have any issues, but I can't do everything by myself, man."

"Yes, sir," Caleb snaps, his voice dripping with sarcasm before he hangs up, leaving the cab of my truck at a dead silence.

A growl rumbles deep in my chest, venting my frustrations over being the one always left holding the bag, the one solely responsible for my family. Yes, I'm future Alpha of our clan, and the oldest, but my brother's a grown ass man, too. He shouldn't need a babysitter.

Thirty minutes later, when the first tourist arrives, I'm still trying to cool my temper. It's hard to plaster on a fake smile when my bear's irritation is like wearing a coat made out of porcupine quills. But I square my shoulders and do it anyway.

I'm scanning the crowd that's gathered and ready to go. Our thirty-pound cooler doubling as my backpack weighs peanuts, but I'm getting more and more irritable waiting for the last two people to show up.

This won't work for today. These people signed up for a guide to secret oases, romantic hideaways, and impressive waterfalls. Not a pissed off bear that's gonna bite someone's head off because they show up late.

I'm about to give up and start the tour when the last stragglers pull in, parking their candy-apple red Jeep Cherokee a few spaces away. On the bright side, they're running, cognizant of being late so I don't want to blow up too hard.

Call me neurotic, but I keep a tight schedule to keep my life organized. It saves my sanity. Especially when most people nowadays go through life thinking *their* time's the only one worth respecting.

I turn to the group for my opening speech about my expectations on the mountain, saving the safety portion for when my last adventurers catch up.

Behind me, the tell-tale crunch of gravel tells me they're ready to go. Before my brain can process rolling through our safety protocols, I'm distracted by the most fascinating aroma—something sweet mixed with... honey. It warms my insides, enticing my bear to the surface in search of the smell.

The closeness of my animal spirit puts me on high-alert and when a male strolls into our circle, blocking sight of the gorgeous source of my temptation, my bear doesn't handle it very well.

"You Mr. McAllister?"

"I am." My answer is curt, immediately put off by this guy. It could be the striking female he dragged up behind him by the elbow. For some reason I don't like his hands on her.

"Good. Yeah, we uh—we're on your tour this morning," annoying guy says, shifting his feet.

"Kinda gathered that by you standing here." It's hard to crack a smile, to pretend to joke, when my bear's having a visceral reaction to this guy.

Forcibly, I cross my arms, gripping my own biceps so I don't reach out and pull the sweet-smelling female away from him.

Smell her. She smells good.

"Umm, hi." The beauty steps forward, offering her hand, which I grasp immediately. "I'm Evie. This is my friend, Ash. We're excited about our hike this morning."

My spine tingles in response to her silken voice, from the electricity of holding her soft hand in mine... so tiny. Even her smile lights up her face, despite the apology in her tone.

When she realizes the group is watching our interaction—including the dude she came with—my cute trail-walker shifts her feet like she's got ants in her pants. It's apparent this one doesn't enjoy being the center of attention. I sense that easily and have to fight my grin. She should be front row, center with Broadway lights shining on her.

I keep my mouth shut, letting the current flow between myself and this enticing new stranger. Evie drops her eyes to where our hands lock in a slow burn handshake, almost as if she's just realized that we're now basically holding hands, no shake about it.

It takes actual restraint to school my face so I don't show disappointment when she rips her hand away. Those lithe, little fingers move to the strap of that bulky backpack, twisting it awkwardly. I can't tell if the backpack is uncomfortable or if she is. Every ounce of my self-control goes into not pulling this woman in and bury my nose in her hair.

Yes! Let's do that!

My bear's quick agreement startles me away from the goddess with her caramel skin and dark, smoked eyelashes rimming her eyes. "Can I take your bag?" I offer. *What the hell am I doing? People hike with their own bags—I'm not a Sherpa!*

Before she can answer, the scrawny male beside Evie wraps her elbow and drags her into his body. "We got it, man." He's placating me with a smile, the victor of our first round over the beguiling Evie. With stumbling feet, she's quickly pulled toward the entrance where the rest of our group waits.

Frustrated, I stride through the circle of tourists, past two barely dressed girls in the front who've been giggling since they arrived. *Focus, man... gotta concentrate here. This is your legacy you're building.*

"Alright, ladies and gentlemen. It's a beautiful day, but we'll be hiking a decent clip so we can make it to all three waterfalls. If you need extra water, I have it. I've got protein bars and a first aid kit, too."

Jealousy burns in my gut when Evie giggles at something her friend whispered in her ear. I clear my throat... loudly and lock eyes on my enchantress. That snaps her lips close immediately. Before I return to the group, I send her a sly wink, loving her gasp of air and the light pink tinting her cheeks when she sees I'm joking in my reprimand.

Feeling rewarded by the couple of extra inches separating those two now, I continue my opening spiel. "We'll stop often for some nature lovin' and to learn about the animals native to our forest in these areas. Where they live. What they eat. And the most critical, how to protect them."

I lay a dimpled smile—the one that wins dates—on the pretty Evie, admiring how the tint of her cheeks darkens. It's a good thing a tittering giggle beside me breaks my trance before my hormones do something stupid. Like toss Miss Sweet Honey over my shoulder and run away.

An hour and ten mental talk-downs with my bear later, the six hikers follow me into our second clearing deep in the mountain. Standing tall, I clap with exaggeration, both to teach my group and to scare away bears that might drink at the waterfall.

In reality, I smell no bears here and I never take my tours into areas where there are, but if these people ever venture out of their own, they need to know the ins and outs of animal safety. And it's a heck of a lot easier for it to sink in by me showing them, than telling.

The group gathers around where my hand rests on the 'NO HUNTING' sign while I give the hikers history and facts on the cascading waterfall that reaches above our heads.

"If you notice the berry bushes along the water's edge, here. These are prime attraction to the local bears, so be alert. Although, you should always be alert near streams and food sources."

Stunned nods blend with the terrified awe looking back at me after that practiced speech. I pat the sign of wildlife safety tips. "My conservation group petitioned to have these signs installed along the trail last year. Basic tips for how to avoid surprising wildlife, inciting attacks, or acting aggressively toward the animals."

"Are we in danger?" A small voice asks beside me, her hands gripping my arm like I'm her personal bear repellent.

If she only knew.

The laughter in my head echoes, but as sensitively as I can, I unwrap jailbait's fingers from my bicep, hating her over-perfumed scent interfering with the freshness outside and Evie's deliciousness that's been heating my blood. "Don't stress too hard. We preach caution and preparedness. Black bears don't *hunt* humans, but it wouldn't be great to accidentally surprise a mama with her cub, or interrupt a feeding bear."

My group looks a little uneasy as they spread out, but I draw their attention to the majesty of the waterfall so they'll focus on the beauty instead of their fear. Even the two young girls who've been tight on my heels the whole trek venture out to take selfies and amateur model shots in front of the waterfall.

Immediately, my eyes find Evie whispering something in her preppy friend's ear. His laughter flares my temper, moving my feet in their direction before I can stop myself.

"Caution as you step, guys. These rocks gather moss like no one's business." The tanned ass-hat grabs Evie's arm to help her climb to a higher elevation.

That should be you, my bear complains, surprising me. He's never had so much to say about a female on one of my tours.

Finally, I agree with my bear and move closer to Evie on the giant rock she's perched on above me.

Looking up at the waterfall spritzing the fringe of her braid is like heaven shining a light on my future, creating a halo from the sunlight streaming through the canopy. It calls to my hands.

When Evie's head turns my way, her eyes questioning, I'm overwhelmed with the urge to smooth those stray edges from her face tickles my fingertips. The sudden sensation of being shocked with a cattle prod hits me like a stray bullet. Pure force of nature. I'm locked in this exact moment, unable to move or even to care about finishing the tour.

"Mr. McAllister, should we expect to run into bears today?" she asks, her melodic voice hypnotizing me in her spell.

"Wyatt. Please." I grin up at this angle, desperate to feel close to her, for some reason. "You don't have to worry, though. Bears visit this waterway to munch foliage, but they'll go for insect or small game if they can't peacefully hunt fish."

Evie chuckles under her breath. The sound draws me in until my arms rest on the rim of her rock, curious to what she finds funny.

"So, bears aren't picky eaters, huh?" she asks with a quirk of her eyebrow.

I'm hit with a flash of insta-lust, my blood rushing south when I think about what I'd love to grab a taste of right now. My grin is purely predatory now, and the friend notices. From my side, I hear a responding challenge under Ash's breath that's too quiet for Evie to hear.

She's ours. My bear pushes the thought in my head, making my grin spread. This gorgeous, black hair beauty has her sights on me, not the friend she came with. My bear prances at her curiosity, loving that she's not scared to talk about bears.

Feeling encouraged, I bound up beside Evie on the rock, my legs having no trouble with the steep incline. The quick motion startles a squeak from those sexy lips, making me smile harder.

"No ma'am," I drawl, realizing I hadn't answered her question yet. "Black bears have huge appetites, but once a bear finds what he wants, he never gives up."

I want her.

"That sounds… dangerous," she says, sounding anything but put-off.

"Eve," her friend hisses from below, making my bear laugh at our win.

I ignore the friend, loving this new fire in Evie's eyes. "A bear is persistent. He's intelligent." Evie's head cocks meeting my hidden challenge.

"About food?" She's picked up on my divergent train of thought. *Smart girl.*

With a smirk, I meet her friend's eyes, wanting to celebrate my win. But part of me feels sorry for him. Even standing as tall as he can, his fingers gripping the rock edge we're standing on, it's not a fair fight. The smaller human is no match for my height and width, but he's bracing for a fight.

Bring it little man. My bear threatens to surface, his senses full of the beauty beside us. *My mate!*

Wh—what the hell?

Straightening my spine, I try to pull myself together and not focus on the grenade my bear just tossed in my life.

"Umm... yeah. Food," I stammer, turning my attention back to the group. Those two younger girls scowl, having noticed my fixation on the vision beside me, even in her yoga pants and baseball cap. It's not my fault I don't find clawing perfume and caked on makeup attractive, but I can't have them leaving a negative review because hormones have taken over my brain function.

At least, the other couple on this tour are so distracted by each other, they haven't noticed my lack of attention. Those two cast adoring looks at each other while dipping their fingers in the crystal-clear basin of water at the bottom of the fall. For a brief moment, I'm jealous.

Take the girl home. She's ours.

Dammit! My bear's getting ridiculous! I usually have better control of him, but maybe it's been too long since I let him out to run off his energy. I'm going to fix that today, even if it's just to save my sanity, but *especially* if he's going to spend an entire tour salivating over a woman. That's not professional.

Pushing off our rock, I clap my hands again to gather my hikers. I have to finish this tour of torture... quick. "Alright y'all, let's continue on up. And if you haven't done it yet, don't forget to hydrate," I remind the group, taking a swig of my own water before squirting some of it over my sweaty head. I need to cool the hell down. Right now!

Behind me, Ash grumbles under his breath, while Evie hisses something under hers. The roar of the waterfall muffles the conversation —even with shifter hearing—but their body language speaks volumes. She's pissed and it gives me a small thrill and enough energy to get the gang moving again.

Gradually, as we walk, Evie separates herself from the annoying friend. Their conversation is either non-existent or stilted. Whatever he said on that rock works to my benefit, because she obviously isn't keen on chatting him up now. Plus, she's slowly worked her way through the group until she's by my side.

Now, *I'm* the lucky one helping her over more difficult passes on our nature trail. Evie even asks me questions about things we see along the hike and my favorite places to visit on the mountain. It feels so natural.

When we pass another 'NO HUNTING' sign, Evie stops to check it out. "Are all these signs really necessary along the trail?"

I glance her way, curious why that would be a question. "Yeah, I think they are. We have too many accidents when hunters venture to these populated areas."

"But responsible hunters wouldn't do that," she says, her tiny fists planted on hips I've fantasized about all morning. The other hikers pass us by, something I shouldn't allow, but the challenge in Evie's eye irks me.

"What about irresponsible hunting? Poachers?"

"I don't mean useless killings. But some hunters are controlled, hunting for survival, for food... like my people." Her eyes soften and I'm torn between wanting to argue and wanting to hug her. My bear's even quiet inside, stunned.

Evie quirks her head, looking up at me. "Are you a vegetarian?" Those smug eyes drop to my leather belt, knowing the answer already.

"No—I'm not."

We kill when we hunt for food, my unhelpful bear reminds me.

"My goal with the signs is to protect as many animals as I can. Organized bear hunts killed eight thousand bears in the last four years! In our state alone!" I bite the back of my tongue to keep my voice from rising because I *feel* her heart despite my anger.

We turn to catch up with the group, but I need her to understand this, understand me. "I want education to take the place of fear. I want our animals to be safe to grow. I don't see how an animal being hunted is a good thing," I say, turning to look at the woman who has my mind all twisted around.

I can't formulate my thoughts clearly and it's pissing me off. An hour ago, I loved how she made my blood boil, though it was for a drastic different reason. But now, I feel flipped on my head.

Evie holds her hands up in surrender, like she's backing off, though her eyes say otherwise. "Look. I'm not saying hunting is OK, necessarily..."

"Necessarily!" I bark, heat burning behind my eyes that she could ever defend useless hunts.

Evie quickly darts her soothing hand to my arm before my anger unleashes. The cool touch stops my argument mid-sentence, giving her space to clarify. "All I'm saying, is, there are levels of hunting. I'm a veterinarian and I love animals, but I don't believe all hunters are evil."

My mouth hangs open, left in shock while my long-legged beauty jogs away, rejoining her friend for the rest of the tour. The separation annoys me, and I'm annoyed that I'm annoyed. It sinks my mood the more Evie's scent fades away.

And now, I'm left trailing the group for the last waterfall, when I should be at the head. *Dammit. Get it together!*

By the time we finish—an hour and a half later—I'm thoroughly confused, pissed off, and incredibly turned on. None of which I'm happy about.

My goodbyes come off a little rushed, but I need to be my truck before I do something stupid. Because, I'm not sure if I want to argue with Evie, or bend her over my hood and seal her mouth shut with a kiss. *She wouldn't be able to argue then.*

Why did you leave her?

My bear isn't happy that I rushed the goodbye with her at all. He's wreaking havoc in my mind as I crank my engine, but tough shit! I'm stubborn too.

The smartest thing I can do is drive out of this parking lot, ignoring my bear *and* the pesky hard-on that's bothered me all day.

Chapter 5

♥

Evie

"What's with that guy?" Ash grumbles, tumbling into my passenger seat.

"Hmm?" I can't listen to another rant. My phone is bad enough, pinging notification after notification in my pocket.

The whole trail, I had zero bars. It felt great to ignoring technology—and the world—for a few hours. But of course, the second we cleared those thick trees, a Price is Right showdown started dinging in my pocket.

Ash is full on bitching in my passenger seat, his voice carrying over the irritation of my phone. *Forgive me Ash for ignoring your grumbles. There's worse stuff happening right now.*

I press my phone to my ear, not even pretending to pay attention to Ash but a few seconds into the first voice mail, I make sure Ash can't hear the other side of this call.

Dr. Michaels' shrill voice hurts my ears. *Call me, Dr. Amos. I desperately need you to come back to the office.*

Thankfully, when I glance over, Ash is so buried in social media, he's oblivious. If he'd only stop griping about our tour guide, I might be able to concentrate on the other irritation in my life.

Sighing, I crank the car and hit next for the third voice mail. One where Dr. Michaels sounds much pushier. His dark threats mix with abject desperation, reigniting the twisting anxiety I spent all day getting rid of.

Normally, I'd never ignore my boss and part of me feels awful. This is all so out of character. But every time I question my decision to leave, I think about Michaels' lies, how it cost me my future. The carefully planned out, ten year map that I busted my ass for... it pisses me off.

Screw him! Michaels is the whole reason I need this break. I'm not going to feel bad for it.

After the voice mails, I've had enough. The texts are going to remain unopened. I don't care.

Pocketing my phone, I back out, my eyes pulling automatically to the rear view mirror. Just one last look at the hunk of a tour guide. Good Lord! His thighs could cut granite! They almost bust the seams of those worn jeans every time he bends to pack away his gear.

That mountain man is magma hot!

It doesn't matter though. I don't have time for a man who makes my mouth water like he's an oasis in the desert! Even if I haven't found one of those the entire time I was gainfully employed in Tennessee.

Of course not! He had to be in my tiny hometown, when my career is on the skids, and my life is in the air. That's exactly the best time to throw a prime rib level man in front of me. One I can't have. Never mind that he's the first guy ever who's made me wet with just the heat in his eyes. *Sure, happens every day...*

Peering over at Ash, I wonder if this was a bad idea. Is it possible to drop myself into life at home and like the old Evie?

Today proves, coming home won't be a simple escape, and I don't have the brainpower for more stress. Stress and tears are like a needle and thread for me. Worse if I feel like I've done something wrong, or if someone's mad at me. I hate it!

Right now, there's a two-ton elephant's sitting on my chest because no one knows why I'm really here, or why I can't go back. Ash is acting all crazy. Ama would rather I stay gone all together.

Actually, the more I think about it, the harder it is to breathe. Getting out of this Knoxville situation isn't going to be as easy as running away for a few days. At some point, I'm going to need to tell my family and that's going to be harder than trying to wrestle a Great Dane into the bathtub.

I just wanted a safe place to think, to figure out a new plan, a way to go to the cops without getting myself killed.

The sudden slapping of Ash's phone against his thigh makes me jump, the sound breaking me from my reverie.

"What. Was. With. That. Guy," Ash repeats, his voice heated in a way I've never heard before. He's noticed I'm not paying attention to his ten minute drone. And I would if he's stop acting like a crazy person.

"Alright, cranky pants. You seriously weren't in the mood to be around people today." That's stating the obvious but honestly, I could have stayed home strategizing—or moping—instead of dealing with this machismo routine. It's so unlike my normally gentle friend. I don't like it.

"I'm not cranky," he huffs. "That guy was all over you today. We barely got time together."

"Huh?" I can't hide my confusion at this point. I'm exhausted, sweaty, and super annoyed. If Ash keeps whining about a guy I have no chance with anyway, I may just scream.

Earlier in our hike, I laughed his rudeness off guy weirdness, but after I chatted with Wyatt at the waterfall, I got a sinking feeling that Ash was jealous. Except that's never been our relationship.

I waved it off and paid more attention to my friend, instead of the walking sex god, and boom... Ash's mood improved.

Sure, I may have some nasty looks at the little bimbos throwing themselves at our guide all day. But I'm claiming that as feminine indignity over those outfits. No way was I jealous of the booty-short wearing college girls. Not even when they were hanging off Wyatt's biceps or bending over with half of their ass cheeks hanging out. *Not jealous at all.*

Gah! Aren't those girls afraid of mosquito bites… or poison ivy? And nope, I did not wish that manner of torture on them. *Not even admitting that in my head.*

I stopped paying any attention to Wyatt after he got all righteous toward hunters and Ash got that obnoxious grin on his face. Both guys were on my shit-list, and now with Ash repeating that same stupid question about Wyatt, his shit-score is growing.

Inhaling, I hold my breath and count backwards from ten. I need to calm my annoyance enough that I can placate Ash and not rip his head off.

Going for broke, I aim a smile at my life-long buddy. "I had fun today, Ash. Didn't you? We saw some beautiful waterfalls we didn't know about." Maybe good old-fashioned guilt will smooth his feathers.

His snorted response is a very unsexy sound, and the last words I catch before he turns to the window is a muffled comment about me wanting to show Wyatt my fun places.

"Excuse me?" *Did he just say that?* My temper flares, roaring blood though my ears like the waterfall we just left. "Do you wanna say that again?" *Is he that stupid?*

I know my distance strained our friendship, but this bitchiness is not how we handle things. Ash seems pissed I would flirt with a guy. Who cares? Nothing happened. Wyatt and I ended our day on such a sour note. And the worst part is how much that bothers me.

The sexy galoot didn't have to bend me over for a public kiss, but the way he looked at me all day... I thought he'd ask for my number at least. He came on so strong until Ash got possessive. Maybe our disagreement over hunters irked him into losing interest.

"Look, E. I'm not trying to be a dick, but that dude was all over you. He practically stalked behind you, acting like you couldn't step over a rock by yourself." *Ugh!* Ash sounds like a whiny child—like someone stole his toy. "I'd chop his hands off if he grabbed you one more time."

"Ashwin Hicks! What the hell?" My head jerks to the passenger seat, my car following the quick motion before I can correct both.

Damn it, Eveline, look with your head, not the wheel. I'm pissed, but I won't let Ash's ridiculousness skid us off the mountain.

"Hey!" Ash's voice squeaks, his arm bracing between the dash and the door.

"What?" I shrug, using mock innocence as payback for Ash being an asshole.

His wide brown eyes stare at me in shock, but I keep my expression neutral. The next time I look Ash's way, he's fighting a grin.

"Holy cow, E! It's like riding with you in Driver's Ed," he teases, his laughter warm and familiar, settling my frazzled nerves. "You haven't gotten any better? Do you stick to pedals and buses in Knoxville?"

"Har. Har." I smack Ash's shoulder with the back of my hand, venting my lingering annoyance. The light hit only amplifies Ash's laughter, and I return my hands primly to ten-and-two, trying to settle my heart rate.

After a few minutes of silence, he leans against the headrest, his voice somber. "Look, I'm sorry about earlier. I was being an ass." I don't correct him—he was an ass—but I don't make him feel worse for it. When he sees that, Ash turns his gaze out the window. "I just miss you, Evie." He pauses, frustration vibrating his voice. "I looked forward to today... maybe a little too much. And it just felt like... like that muscle head was getting in the way. He took away my time and I acted out. I'm sorry."

"I'm sorry too. For not paying more attention. And for getting distracted, today and the last years. I'm really sorry!"

My hand rests on Ash's forearm—pleading for his understanding—but when I glance his way I'm met with a blank stare. After a second of confusion, Ash raises one eyebrow and I get it.

"*Ugh!* Come on." My hand moves back to position on the wheel.

With a laugh, Ash claps his hands. "Alright!" His arms stretch in front of him, making a dramatic show of rolling up his flannel sleeves. The goofiness reminds me of the kid that was my best friend. "I vote redo. We shake off today and plan tonight."

I smile, but worry a bit about the sneaky way Ash rubs his hands together. Pointing an accusing finger to my passenger seat, I warn, "you have the same face you had when you tried to convince me to sneak out of the house as a kid."

"Tried, my ass. I got you to skip chores every time." I scoff, but it's true. At least Ash would help me catch up after our adventures were done though. "You remember when we'd hide from Ama and Kayah in the cornfields?"

"Yeah, but they'd pelt us with mud-pies every time they found us. And mama'd get all mad that she had more laundry," I remember, laughing.

Eventually, Ash and I brought them into our adventures, and we became the four musketeers. Our personalities are as different as vanilla and rocky road, but we took care of each other... always.

"So, what are you thinking for tonight?" I ask, catching that look from Ash. He knows I'm over-thinking, but in my defense, we were lucky to make it out of our early twenties. We took my sisters to the shabbiest bars before they could legally drink. The ones that don't check IDs.

"I propose we get your sisters and shoot some pool, sing karaoke, or shake it on the dance floor." He winks and I'm already having a hard time saying no. Our nights out are some of my favorite memories, but it seems like so long ago.

"I don't know. I just got home." I should probably put in some face time with my family. And work on a solution to my current stress load.

"Come on.... you can't bail." Ash cocks his head to the side like I just grew a third head.

It's not bailing if we never made plans, but OK. I shrug, enjoying the silliness. I needed to see this side of Ash after today. This is the version of my friend I missed so much.

When we pull up in front of his house, Ash turns to me with that boyish grin, but his face is determined. "Look... today was a bust. Largely my fault—ish—but I propose tonight be a do-over." Ash lifts a three-fingered boy scout solute. "Let's get your sisters, dress in our best honky-tonk wear, and go out for some lagers and line dancing."

The genuine hope in his eyes is enough to convince me. *What the hell? I could use a little fun.*

·♥·♥·♥·♥·♥·

A few hours later, I've collected Kayah and we're pulling into the Grizzly Growler's parking lot that's overflowing onto the grassy area.

"Ash didn't tell me this place would be so crowded." My nerves are getting the best of me.

"It's the hottest bar in town!" Kayah excitement doesn't help.

Groups of all ages spill across the property, milling in circles for smoke breaks, making out against trucks. The nip in the night air isn't enough to stop people from being outside and enjoying one heck of a mountain view.

Kayah and I luck into a parking spot before my brain can formulate an excuse to go home. After today's emotional roller coaster, I was hoping for a calm night out with my old crew, not joining half of Cherokee County in their Friday night party scene.

A vibration from my pocket tenses my shoulders as I'm climb out of the car. I am not looking at text tonight. No way.

Good Lord! The air out here has a nasty stench rolling through it. Holding my breath doesn't help, but Kayah links my arm and drags me fast enough toward the frosted iron doors in front of the building that my nose doesn't suffer too long.

"Come on," Kayah urges. "There's something nasty in the air sending everyone inside. We need to get a seat before they do."

"No shit!"

We jog to the entrance and the moment we're inside, the thumping sound of bar chaos engulfs us. I'd turn on a dime if my sister didn't have a death grip on my arm.

"Um, Ky, it's a little crowded," I yell over the noise. "Why don't we just go home and try again another night?"

"Don't look so nervous." She smiles, nudging my shoulder while we scan the packed tables for Ash.

"There are like fifty eyes on us right now," I hiss. *I hate being the center of attention.*

"That's because you look hot!"

Ugh! At least Kayah convinced me to make a little effort tonight. We got ready in our old bedroom, blaring some late 2000s clubbing music, like old times. I'm thanking my lucky stars right now to feel semi-put-together, even if I complained a few hours ago about Kayah dolling me up.

I may not be looking for a man, but I can look good for my own confidence.

Kayah seems to find what she's looking for pretty fast. She tugs my arm through the cocktail area that's packed with just as many cowboy hats and baseball caps as work slacks and date skirts. My dark wash wranglers fit right in with this eclectic countrified scene. This place is like a meat market inside a sample bag of jellybeans.

One particular creeper at the end of the bar screams warning bells. He's fully salivating over this meat market, his thin lips curled in a sneer that no woman would find attractive. That doesn't stop him from eye-humping every one of them that passes though. Like he's hunting his next prey. *Does that guy honestly think women go for the ax-murderer vibe?*

I'm thirty seconds from grabbing my gorgeous sister and running out of here, but we pass his bar stool unscathed and I release a breath I didn't realize I was holding. I use my body to shield my sister's petite frame from that weirdo, until we reach one of the open high-tops in the middle of the room.

Gah! There's nothing more out of the way? I look around but nope, there's not a one left. People spill from every booth and bar top in the place. Self-consciously, I tug on my curls but slide into one of the chairs.

"Looks like Ash isn't here yet," Kayah says, sitting next to me and adjusting the soft pleated skirt I picked out from her closet. The chiffon hid behind all those teacher appropriate outfits and college t-shirts, but it swishes at the perfect spot on her thigh when she crosses her legs. We paired it with a sleeveless button up so Kayah would be comfortable. One that shows off her toned arms and skims her waist at the perfect spot, giving my little sister more curves than she possesses.

"You look gorgeous tonight," I compliment and she looks down, almost surprised.

"You sure the boots aren't too much?" She eyes the Justin boots I gave her last Christmas with skepticism and I scoff.

"Those boots scream honky-tonk, Ky." I wave my a finger up and down her outfit. "You are the perfect mix of sexy without the slutty. And the boots are just icing on a stunning cake."

Kayah giggles, turning a soft shade of pink, but I speak the truth. We did a fantastic job of fancying up my baby sister, of getting her out of her comfort zone for our night out.

Immediately, Kayah's shoulders straighten, seeming to gather strength from my assessment. "Ok, well… I think since we both look like tasty cakes tonight; we should focus on roping you up a man to sample your icing ."

"Hnh," I cough, my eyes going wide as I choke on my tongue. "Why are you thinking about getting me a man? I don't even live here," I squeak. And when did my sister start talking like that? It's weird.

When we left the house, I had to almost tie the girl down to show a little skin; now suddenly, she's a dating bulldog.

Kayah cracks up. I give her my meanest glare and tug at the neck of my shirt, waiting for my sister to gather herself.

Finally, when her laughter dies down, Kayah slaps my hand away from my top and pulls it off the shoulder again. "It's supposed to be like that… stop it!"

I sigh, drawing my shirt back up so it at least shows less skin than Kayah exposed.

"Evelyn Amos, stop fidgeting. That shirt is damn sexy. Every man in here's trying to get a peak tonight. Watch." I don't appreciate her smug look when she elbows me in the ribs with a little nod of her head to our right. My spine jerks straight. *Oh my God!* The guy at the next table is totally trying to catch a wardrobe malfunction in our clothing battle.

"Kayah," I hiss, feeling my cheeks go beet red. Silently, I pray for the waitress to find us or either the earth to swallow me whole. I'll take either one.

"What?" Kayah shrugs, like she didn't just embarrass the crap out of me. "I see you getting all self-conscious and I won't let you. You look hot."

"You say that like I want every man looking down my shirt." My eyes drop to read the Friday drink specials so I have something to look at other than perv-o at the next table.

"Why wouldn't you? At least you got the rack to show off," she pouts, evil-eying her trim figure before she snatches the drink menu from my hand.

I'm having trouble blending this sassy mouth woman with the baby sister I left for college. I mean, by day, she's chinos and soft sweaters. She spends hours reading to children at the library and teaching classes on our dwindling Cherokee language. But tonight, she's the leader, the brave words of wisdom and confidence. She's everything I thought I was until I got tossed on my ass two days ago.

Laying my head on Kayah's shoulder, I realize how much I've missed her. Also, how much I'm being 'out-lifed' by my sister. "I miss this, Ky."

"Me too." Her head tilts on top of mine. "It's been a long time since I've gone out."

"Really?"

"Yeah. I'm busy with last semester stuff, and getting my teaching hours in before graduation. It's a lot."

She sounds exhausted. My hand squeezes hers, understanding that last push of college stress.

"Plus, there's no one left to have fun with. You're gone, Ama works the hours we go out, and Ash... I barely see him anymore. I'm a lowly teaching student and he's department head" A shadow falls across her face, but the server shows up before I can ask about it.

Kayah orders a glass of Pinot, but I try to embrace a little more fun tonight with the mountain margarita, a Grizzly Growler specialty.

Especially since I feel bad about leaving Kayah here all by herself, basically.

"I do wish we could do this more often," I admit, and Kayah looks down at her menu, tucking a lock of black hair behind her ear. She's fighting what she wants to say. I see that.

"Have you thought about moving back?" There it is. The question that hits a bullseye on my conscience. My intuitive sister, who inherited Gran's gift of sight, sees right through my secretive trip home.

"I have thought about it... lately." My eyes fall to the stage where a rockabilly punk band set up instruments. "Are they old enough to drink?" I point to the youngest, clean cut kid with the sharp jaw and spiked hair on stage, praying for a distraction since about all I can offer my sister is 'I've thought about it.'

"Probably not... but neither was I when you took me out."

She has a point. I laugh, but my heart squeezes thinking about how much I missed this. "A lot has changed."

"You got that right," Kayah says, lifting the glass our waitress delivered. "I can drink now."

My laughter joins Kayah's, our rowdiness drawing a few eyes from neighboring tables, but I don't care. With two fists, I tap my giant schooner against Kayah's wine glass before taking that first sip.

"Holy cow! That's a bad-ass margarita!"

"Yes, it is." Kayah beams, scanning the menu Brie dropped off. She flops the menu down and scans the packed bar.

"This place is a lot more top shelf than we're used to," I comment, taking in the polished wood floor and comfy booths. "There's no ripped vinyl or wobbly tables." I feign annoyance, loving that Kayah plays along.

"Yeah, and where are the peanut shells? My shoes are a walking risk without that crunch to give me traction." Kayah flutters her face dramatically, and the band picks that moment to launch into a warm-up. Kayah throws her hands in the air. "Oh, come on. The speakers don't even pop!"

Our faux outrage crumbles into full giggles. Both of us lean in, trying to catch our breath, when Ash bounds into the chair at my side. His clamor of commotion startles screams from me and Kayah until we see who it is.

"Ash! You scared the bejesus out of me!" My hand flies to my chest, pressing the frantic rhythm there.

"Bejesus? Really?" Ash cocks his head, comically scrunching his eyebrows. "Are you eighty?"

I back-slap his arm, trying to calm my pounding heart. From the look on Kayah's face, she's not fairing much better. "Shut it, ass. You scared the crap out of me, okay?" His masculine shoulders shake with laughter I can barely hear over the toddlers warming up on stage.

"There's a visual for the books, Eve."

"Be nice!" I shove his body, annoyed by the heat crawling up my neck. Kayah's head ping-pongs between the two of us. She's watched our antics for twenty years, but Ash and I are off balance right now, his snark a little too sharp, my defense a little too heated. Joking with him doesn't feel as natural as it normally does.

"Ladies, I apologize for scaring you." Ash tilts his invisible hat like an old cowboy, but spends too much time giving our outfits a once over.

"Don't be weird," I warn when his face twists unnaturally.

"I'm not weird. You're weird." Ash sticks his tongue out, going old school childish, and waves a pointy finger between me and Kayah. "I'm just wondering where the yoga pants and khakis went," Ash says, laughing like he's the funniest clown at the circus. "I'm not used to you girls getting all dolled up and pretty."

Offended, I hit Ash's chest hard this time, not keeping it gentle or friendly at all. His yelp of pain gives me slight vindication, but it doesn't fix the pain in Kayah's eyes. Just one comment from Ash, and Kayah's cheeks glow beet red. I hate seeing her head duck behind a curtain of hair like a shy teenager, while pretending to focus on the menu. It's a total retreat into her shell.

"Aww, come on," Ash chides. "I was joking. You ladies clean up nice."

"Shut up, Ash the Ass," Kayah hisses from behind her menu, rolling her eyes when Ash winks. I've never seen Kayah's anger flash quite so strong. "You know, Ash the Ass... if this is your game with the ladies, it's no wonder you haven't had a girlfriend in years."

My sister's slam hits the mark, judging by Ash's stricken look. Now, it's my turn to ping-pong between those two. Ash's tomato red face matches Kayah's from a few minutes ago, but he submits, holding his hands up in defeat.

The strain from earlier today settles across our table, dropping us into uncomfortable silence that's deafening under the bar noise.

"Is Ama coming tonight?" I ask, venturing for a distraction.

"Not that I know of," Ash sighs, his voice subdued. "I texted her. Just figured she had to work tonight."

"She's off on Fridays," Kayah corrects, her eyes cutting to me. "The new boss gives her more flexibility, but she didn't respond to my text either." A pitying look passes between my tablemates, making me feel like the odd woman out.

"Hey! What's that about?" I ask, pointing between the two of them. "What did you guys just not say?"

"Not a thing. I promise." Ash shakes his head, suddenly engrossed in his menu. "Why don't we order food?"

"Yes," Kayah exclaims quickly. "If Ama comes, she comes, but let's enjoy the night either way."

Neither Ash nor Kayah will meet my eye. "Is she not coming because of me?" My voice is louder than needed, but I can't help it. "That is complete bullshit! We used to hang out every Friday night. She put up with me fine then."

That Ama would avoid a night out because I'm here hurts. I wish I hadn't come out at all. Nothing about tonight feels like old times. I'm thinking the idea of rekindling those feelings was just a fairy tale.

"I'm sure it's not you, Evie." Kayah places a hand on mine, but I don't feel comfort. The cold pity in Ash's eyes reflect the truth. He agrees with Ama, and the vindication he's trying to hide shows that.

I shouldn't have come home.

The depressing thought that I don't belong here anymore has been bugging me since my talk with Gran. I just wanted a safe place to rest— to plan—but everyone's moved on with their life. They're either annoyed with me or by me.

At least I'm trying! What's Ama doing?

The more I think about it, the angrier I get. "Do either of you know what the hell her problem is?"

I'm putting them in a hard place, but my blood has hit its boiling point. All the rudeness, the bitterness these last few years… it pisses me off. My stomach's flipping over itself, a nasty side effect when I'm under too much stress. Even my margarita tastes sour. *Ugh!*

"Nothing? No answers?" I eye each of them suspiciously, just wanting some flipping answers for once. Their heads shake solemnly, that secret look passing between them again. "Enough!" My palm slams the table, frustrated.

"If you guys are going to have this covert little eyeball conversation, you can do it without me." I right my shirt on my shoulders just to annoy

Kayah and hop out of my chair with about as much grace as a puppy coming off anesthesia. "I'm going to the bathroom." Yes, I sound like a pouting child, stomp off like one too, but my inadequacies are making me want to run and hide. I don't care if it's immature.

Kayah's voice follows me, but I need a minute to myself. Their judgment stings, causing hot humiliation to burn behind my eyes. I nudge people left and right, feeling the entire bar stare as I clear a path. I mumble apologies when I tousle a few beers, but at least I reach the restroom without tears or further embarrassment.

Of course, the reverberation of the bathroom door bouncing off the wall makes me wince, but after a quick check of the stalls, I realize no one's here to witness my outburst. Thank God!

Exhaling, I lean over the counter and take in my red cheeks and frazzled expression in the mirror. Other than the perma-frown plastered to my face, I look the same as I did a week ago. Before my life went sideways. The thought dulls my anger. Tonight is nothing compared to everything else that's going on.

And how can I get mad over Ash and Kayah having secrets, when I have a Titanic-sized one of my own?

The problem is, I didn't realize how much I missed my family until I came home. I also didn't know how hard it would be to fit back in. *This sucks!*

Turning around, I rest my butt against the sink and press my fingers against my temples, wishing I could massage away this awful guilt. I don't like this out of control chaos in my head.

Opening my eyes, I push off the counter to pace the tiled floor. At least my hidey-hole's clean. This is no grungy bar bathroom. There're no dead bugs, no graffiti, no broken doors on the stalls. *Gah! How disgusting were the places we hung out if no bugs on the floor impress me.*

Sadly, I can't stay in the bathroom forever, though. I have to face the music... with my current situation and fixing the rift in my family.

First step is apologizing to Kayah and Ash. Then, I'll come clean about my ignorance these past few years... later... to Mom and Dad. Maybe they can help me figure out a way to tell the cops without painting a giant target on my back.

Determined to get the first annoyance over with, I pull the bathroom handle and exit before I lose my nerve. Unfortunately, I'm only two steps out the door when my face connects with a brick wall. At least, I think it's a wall—one with a hint of lemony cedar.

My eyes squeeze shut and I brace a hand, and my throbbing head, against the hardness. I just need a minute to steady myself.

A low rumbling chuckle pries my eyes open before they're ready and I groan. OK, not a wall... I slammed my face into the six and a half feet of mountain muscle that drove me crazy on the trail today.

Ugh! It takes every ounce of my willpower not to squeeze and test the hardness under my heated hands.

"Hey, darlin'. Where's the fire?" Wyatt's deep drawl vibrates through my core, tingling across my skin.

"I-I'm sorry," I stutter, wondering if I'm apologizing for hitting him or that I haven't pulled my hand away from his tempting muscle yet. In all fairness, Wyatt's firm grip on my biceps seem like he thinks I'll fall over without his touch. *Frankly, with that cologne making me lightheaded, I just might.*

"Not a problem. It's always a pleasure to rescue a lady." Wyatt smiles, but his eyes scrutinize every inch of my face. The thin golden ring around his pupils are fascinating. They make his eyes glow under these neon lights, flickering back and forth between excitement and concern.

When a dimple pops on Wyatt's cheek, I'm done for. He's full, swoon-worthy southern charm. Somehow a gentleman with his words, but igniting a fire with the challenge in his eye. My neck almost hurts to look up at that gorgeous face and it dawns on me... someone this handsome is probably laughing at the ridiculous girl falling all over him —literally.

Sobering, I press back a little for some breathing space, and so I don't give in and climb his body like a mountain trail. Wyatt's hands don't let me go far and I can't help the skeptical bluntness that sneaks into my brain.

"Thanks for catching me, but I honestly can't tell if you're messing with me with half of what you say." My honesty doesn't seem to offend him just by the answering laugh that echoes the back hallway.

"Evie, how on Earth would I be messing with you?"

He remembered my name!

And, his question sounds sincere, that happy smile working my heartstrings like a pro. That optimistic excitement running through my head confuses everything further. I don't know what to feel when I look at him, but he sure makes it hard to stay jaded.

Especially because Wyatt doesn't rush my answer. He simply waits, gazing into my eyes with an openness while his hands hold tight. Considering I'm practically a melted puddle at his feet, I appreciate that. Especially tonight, when my emotions are all over the place.

What the hell is wrong with me?

Realizing I'll never be able to answer his question without looking like a self-conscious idiot, I gather what dignity I have and back up, letting his hands to fall from my arms. Immediately, I feel the loss of his touch. *Wow!*

Apparently, just being near Wyatt turns my brain to hormonal girly mush. I can't have that—no matter how gorgeous he is.

"Well, uh—it was great running into you." I laugh at my corniness and rub my palms against the material of my jeans. I move to step around Wyatt's large presence in the hallway, refusing to admit how clammy my hands are.

But instead of going on his way, Wyatt turns with me, his hand falling to rest on my lower back—just above the curve of my ass—like he belongs there. I scoff, but his velvety voice speaking too close to my ear, smooths my ruffled feathers at being handled.

"I saw your friend in the bar." Wyatt nods toward our table, his golden eyes flashing under the bar lights. "I assume that's your table." It's not exactly a question, and before I can straighten my brain cells out enough to answer, he's guiding us back to my crew with the slightest pressure against my back.

"Uh, yeah. It is." My cheeks heat, embarrassed over the temper tantrum I left my table with. "We're having a night out with my sister."

"Date night?"

The question throws me. So do the sparks flying while Wyatt waits for my answer. There's a current of electricity in the air and I can't help laugh. I squash it fast though when Wyatt doesn't smile.

"Do people often bring sisters on date nights in your world?" I ask incredulously, aiming for levity but basically floored at the sudden temperature drop in the room.

Wyatt's stern expression stops me in my tracks, and I stumble over my feet again in a five-minute period. Thankfully, his fingers keep me upright for the second time tonight.

"Are you always a body hazard or is this new tonight?" he asks, turning my body to face him like I'm a doll to be handled.

I'm suddenly hyper-aware of our closeness in the center of the billiards room. The hairs on my arms standing on edge, but everyone around us is just going about their fun, not paying any attention to the random couple gawking at each other between the pool tables.

A cue sticks flies a little too close to my head but I find that hazard safer than staring at Wyatt.

"Don't worry, I won't let them hit you," Wyatt promises, his dark voice a stark contrast with his fingertips softly stroking the line of my arm. Goosebumps follow the trail of his finger, short circuiting my brain again. All I can manage is a grunt of acknowledgment, so in a trance that I barely hear him over the clank of balls and the party raging behind us.

"Is this a date?" Wyatt repeats a little louder.

My mouth falls open, but the pull of his eyes is too much and I have to look down. That's barely better. The cobalt blue fabric that stretches across the hills and valleys of Wyatt's chest, hardly settles my thoughts.

Still, I answer speaking to his chest, my voice barely audible over the rush of blood in my ears. "What would it matter if it were?"

"It matters," he answers stoically, tilting my chin with his finger until I meet those Goldenrod eyes. When I do, his gaze ignites. "I need to know."

Chapter 6

♥

Wyatt

An unsettled feeling bothered me all afternoon, making me restless. I came a hair's edge from canceling on Caleb tonight. Eying him to my side... I really wish I had.

I'm used to my brother rambling every Friday night, but he's been at it for two hours straight. It's grating on my last nerve. He does this every week... guilts me into going out, then spends most of the night complaining about his life, or women.

"Wy, look around this place, man. Our well is dry." His grumpy voice interrupts my mental bitch-fest, and I gape at him, wondering where this random train is going. "There's no new meat," he sighs. "The pickins have been picked."

"Caleb! Don't be a dick." I smack the back of his floppy hair, flashing a warning with my eyes to watch his mouth. "There are plenty of women on this mountain. Just because you're the man whore who slept with most of them, isn't their fault. It says nothing except they have poor taste." I laugh to soften the brotherly insult, but Caleb knows I hate when he's obnoxious toward women.

"Ow, man. Cut it out," he whines, rubbing the back of his head but then that arrogant grin spreads wide. "A player's gotta play, Bro." Caleb laughs at my scowl.

"Just because you're not interested in a mate, doesn't mean you have to parade around like a frat boy," I say, chastising, but Caleb just snorts.

The problem with him is, those McAllister good looks make women flock to him with very little effort on his part. He never has to earn their attention. It bores him... and his bear. Men like us need the thrill of the hunt, but for all these years, Caleb's sole focus has been scratching that itch. Short term.

Shaking my head, I turn away and take another large gulp of lager. It's my first of the night and I'm already twitching to leave.

Caleb's games have agitated me more and more this past year. The more I isolate myself, the more focus I put on the business, the worse it gets. Maybe neglecting my own needs hasn't been the smartest decision.

We met a woman today, my bear taunts, waiting me to brag to my brother.

We met a beautiful princess today, I correct my bear.

He chuffs, annoyed, and starts pacing through my head until it's extremely difficult to stay planted on this stool. I haven't had a second of peace since the hike today and it's driving me batty.

Caleb, however, couldn't care less if I want to be here. Or that I'm extra prickly and less tolerant of him griping in my ear about someone he dated making eyes at him across the bar.

Caleb avoids repeats… his words, not mine.

Without warning, Caleb's voice fully drowns to the background, an intoxicating scent taking over all my senses—honey and vanilla. A thrill ripples up my spine and suddenly, I'm sniffing like a madman.

My bear smells it too… *our mate.*

The blood that had been coursing south freezes and my back shoots ramrod straight, warning bells ringing in my head. Unfortunately, I can't focus with my bear chuffing excitedly. He's itching to make himself known and that would be a disaster.

I turn my bar stool as smooth as I can, feigning nonchalance so Caleb won't catch me scanning the crowd for the one face I want to see. And there she is. As gorgeous as I remember, even under fluorescent bar lights.

When that beaming smile aims at the younger girl on her arm, I'm filled with a frantic hunger. An urge to walk up and claim that smile in a kiss. It battles against my common sense. This girl would not appreciate a practical stranger intruding on her night out, especially in the 'sling her over my shoulder' way I want to.

She's our mate! My bear roars, frustrated.

I marshal every ounce of willpower I have to turn this chair back to the bar and ignore the curious look from Caleb. Apparently, I missed a question he asked, because my brain is locked on keeping my ass in my seat.

Thankfully, Jackson brings a new round of drinks for the perfect distraction, though I didn't realize I had downed the last one.

Jax has been my best friend since we went through our first shifts together and I shortened his nickname. He knows me like one of my blood brothers and judging by the cocked eyebrows he and Caleb have aimed at me right now, they both know I'm off tonight.

"You alright, man?" Jax squares his hands on the bar in front of me, his eyes questioning. Their shifter abilities make it hard to hide the tension rolling through my body, but I nod and thankfully, the guys let me slide on my questionable state of mind.

Both shift focus to the big screen behind the bar. Caleb and Jax pick up their typical argument over college loyalties and football standings after last weekend. The conversation is the same after every game, but their macho nonsense is better than them digging into my rattled emotions.

Only problem is, my bear won't drop his feelings so easily. He's circling. Digging into my muscles, trying to force my hand with his overbearing antics. He wants us to claim our female, and I'm determined to resist, keep my inner spirit at bay. We're at a battle of wills.

The struggle continues for the next half hour. And when the sound of Evie's laugh tickles my ears, despite the bar noise, it kicks into high gear.

I'm tuned to her; my eyes pulling like a compass, pointing me due north. That dark hair curls in fanciful ringlets tonight, resting against the female she's with, so at odds with the trail-ready woman I met today. My only issue is the somberness of her face. Whatever's troubling those soulful eyes extinguishes light there.

Let's make her feel better, my bear pushes, making me sigh.

From the corner of my eye I watch Evie quietly, playing a spy game into her world while Caleb fixates on the game and Jax handles patrons down the bar. It's not until the annoying guy from our tour today joins their table that I fight to hold in a growl. It helps that both women look thoroughly pissed at the little human.

Hah! I chuckle under my breath, pleased to see the guy striking out.

"What's so funny, bro?" Caleb asks, lifting his glass to signal another refill.

"Nothin', man. Just saw something funny."

I have no intention of telling Caleb about my suspicions yet. I don't even know if he believes in mates, but a flash of Evie jumping from their table yanks my attention her way. I don't like the deep furrow in her forehead, nor her feet stomping through the billiards room toward the back of the restaurant.

Our mate's upset. My bear's growl rises to obscene levels, forcing my feet into motion without my brain thinking.

"Nature calling," I mumble, leaving Caleb with my beer. Fewer questions this way.

In the backroom, I scan the neatly organized tables, but don't see her. That sweet vanilla warmth lingers though, guiding my nose where it's strongest by the bathrooms. And I wait, pacing the hall with Evie's agitation calling to me through the door. Her jumbled emotions summon my bear to soothe her distress. She can't know she's doing it but he's scratching for escape, his growl ricocheting like thunder in my head.

Calm down, I command the beast. *We don't want to upset Evie by tackling her the moment she leaves the bathroom.* The beast whimpers, successfully chastised.

Mercifully, my pep talk worked in time for the women's door to fly open. A whirlwind darts out. Our princess is on a mission.

Unfortunately, without using shifter speed, I can't react fast enough to move out of her war path and my chest takes the sharp hit of her body. Though I don't feel any pain, I can tell the impact stunned Evie.

He doesn't want her hurt, but my bear does purr when I grab our little vixen to keep her upright. My biceps twitch, yearning to wrap all the way around Evie's soft flesh, not just hold her arms. That would overstep liberties I haven't earned yet, though. Especially when she's this disoriented, her heart stuttering on hyper speed.

I'm about to ask if she wants to sit down, to calm her shallow breathing, when she rights herself. She goes to pull her soothing heat from my grasp, but I don't want to let go.

"Hey, darlin'. Where's the fire?" I smile to cover my disappointment, but it's harder to hide the hard-on standing up to say hi. I pull back enough so she won't feel the impact she has on me—yet.

Too soon, Evie moves to step around me, with little concern that she slammed face-first into my chest. Let alone that having her in my space has my hormones boiling for release.

Am I the only one feeling this?

That harsh thought stabs me. I know she's human, but the draw of fated mates is unbearable—from the first meeting. She should feel it too, but so far... nothing.

Not willing to let go so easily, I slide into step beside Evie, gravity pulling my hand to her lower back. I'm desperate to preserve contact somehow.

"I saw your friend at the bar," I admit, inhaling that sweet smell close to her ear. "That's your table, right?" I'm trying to be a gentleman for her sake, because nothing inside me wants to walk Evie to that table. I'd prefer to throw over across my shoulder and carry her home—away from any other man. Especially Evie's friend, Ash. The idea of him sitting beside my mate riles me up. To seriously unhealthy levels, but I force my fists to remain lose, despite the load of energy surging my muscles.

He's not a threat. I repeat that in my head a few times after Evie assures me this is not a date.

The mantra works until we're within eye-shot of the table. A girl, who I assume is her sister judging by the resemblance, pops her eyes wide when she sees Evie has company. Her shocked awe makes me chuckle, but I'm used to looks from women when they see a pair of muscles. A bear shifter's body is tall and wide, our strength unparalleled. It happens to attract the opposite sex, but that means nothing anymore.

No one but Evie, my bear argues, making me frown.

I know that. My face struggles to remain neutral, to not advertise my internal war.

"Your sister looks like she swallowed a frog," I whisper, hoping to ease the jitters coming off of Evie. Her body shakes under my hand with suppressed laughter, and the beaming smile she aims my way has my chest puffing with pride.

It's a tremendous victory to make my mate happy. Except, I have no plan to look like a total moron, so I reign in my ego and watch Evie take a seat beside her sister. Unfortunately, that leaves the only open chair across the table… not happening. Her friend, Ash, would have the prime position next to Evie.

I don't think so!

"Sorry you guys," she apologizes, and I tense, wondering if she's apologizing for my presence.

I remain standing, and place myself securely between Evie and Ash with my hand locked to the back of her chair. Ash notices… I'm staking claim. His eyes drip venom, but I ignore his useless glare to smile at the rest of the table.

"Want to join us?" Evie asks, signaling the open chair. She peeks up at where my height towers over her seated position, a blush creeping across her cheeks that makes me grin.

I like this feeling of surrounding her, of being able to touch those soft tendrils flowing down her back. Not a chance in hell I want to sit across the table. But, being a smart man, I know I'm the intruder here, so I play nice and keep my smile light. "I'm good with standing."

My ears pick up on Evie's quick heart rate. The steady thump of blood along her neck calls to me. *Is she excited or nervous?*

From the corner of my eye, her sister's mischievous smirk catches my attention, though she tries to hide behind a sip of wine. She's eating this up.

My bear needs to do something to calm his mate's racing heart… and for the first time tonight, I agree with him. My thumb reaches to caress the soft skin on the back of Evie's neck, humming at the tiny squeak Evie can't hide.

Her sister chuckles outright, but Evie is stock still, except for the hand that darts for her margarita. Gradually, I increase the pressure of my thumb, massaging away the rigidity in her shoulders stroke by stroke.

With Evie cocooned in my warmth, I extend a handshake to the sister. "I'm Wyatt. I took these two on the trails today." Evie's eyes bore into the side of my head, while her look-alike accepts my hand, smiling a sweet smile of admiration my way.

"I'm Kayah, the nice sister," she says, her quip earning a giggle from Evie. The sister's smile only dims when her eyes flick in Ash's direction. "Guess you had to put up with this one all day, so you already know him." The joke earns a scowl from Ash until I let a growl slip and his eyes jerk to me, surprised.

I don't like his look toward the little one.

Kayah's eyes light with curiosity... and vindication. She flips back and forth from me to Evie before Evie speaks up, seeing the irritation taking over Ash's dark scowl.

"Ash was actually the one who picked the tour today," she offers, her eyes darting to Kayah in some silent code.

Ash grumbles under his breath, swirling his empty beer bottle between tense fingers. "You guys need another round?" I offer, hoping the olive branch will lighten the strain a smidge... and possibly, thank Ash for bringing Evie into my life. "My man Jax owns the bar, he'll get me in and out before the server makes it through the crowd."

Sure. Sure. No thanks. All three answer over each other, making me laugh. Two sets of eyes glower at Ash. Want to guess where the "no thanks" came from?

"It's alright man, I gotcha." I rap a knuckle on the table before turning to leave. It doesn't take a psychic to feel the eyes boring into my back. Ash is probably catching a load of crap from the girls. Nobody denies a woman her free margarita, Ash. Live and learn, man.

At the bar, I slide back in beside Caleb who stares into his beer like it holds the secrets of life. Jackson's stuck pulling beers, so it'll take a minute for him to head my way. His new bartender is popping bottles and running the well, but he'd never fully trust anyone with a slammed bar. Jax is slow to trust. He'll take care of the more difficult drinks himself.

Caleb raises his head, finally noticing I'm back. "Who's the chick you're hanging on over there?" He nods in Evie's direction, but I'm not ready to admit what I suspect about Evie to my brother yet.

"Someone I met today."

Caleb rolls his eyes, spinning his stool to face the dance floor. Couples parade the wood surface, two-steppin' around clusters of ladies who dance in circles the way girls do.

The kids on stage begin their rendition of a popular country song—one of my favorites—and the crowd shouts the song's chorus in unison, like one loud, drunken patron.

Caleb's sharp elbow jabs my ribs. My brother, who typically bucks country music, practically falls in my lap gawking at the girls gyrating on the dance floor. But, my attention's on Evie's table, hidden behind a crowd of people.

Her head bops to the tune, dancing in the chair, one of her exposed shoulders wiggling against her sister's so she'll join in the silliness. Both girls crack up, bringing a smile to my own face.

"Check those asses, man." I sigh at Caleb's thick tongued slur. He's past the point of inebriation, another annoyance to deal with later. "You should get out there, Wy. We could work that like old times." Ok, he's a lot past inebriated.

"Caleb, how much did you drink while I was away?" He waves off my question, slapping my shoulder like he's oblivious. This is not the first time my brother has heard my annoyance with his drunken routine.

"You gotta get laid, man." His head shifts to Evie, concern etched in his brow.

I wonder how many shots he managed in the twenty minutes I was away. When Jax finally checks in, he glances at Caleb with a silent apology my way. I shake my head and place the order for Evie's table. Once I have drinks in hand, I nod toward my brother. *Slow him down.*

Jax's head dips in understanding, a solemn look passing between us before I walk away with my boozy cargo.

Caleb's comments roll through my brain, slowing my steps. I've been on that dance floor picking up women with my brother many times. Brotherly wingmen every weekend. So, why does that idea leave an empty feeling in my gut after meeting Evie? Not a single woman has ever compared to Evie's curves... her sweet face. *Why would I want another woman?*

Smell her. My bear chimes in with his two cents, making me laugh under my breath.

Yeah, I got it.

As if sensing my thoughts, Evie's eyes find me through the crowd. Her molten chocolate eyes electrify the space between us, tracking me all the way to her table.

With our eyes locked, I place two margaritas in front of the girls and slide craft brews for me and the prick. Kayah's cheeks are on fire, clearly reading the way I want to devour her sister. And I don't even pretend to care about the sour patch spread across Ash's face.

"Thank you," the girls offer awkwardly before silence blankets the table. I frown, feeling like the odd man out—not something I'd expect after a free round of drinks.

Taking a deep pull from my beer, I rest my hand on Evie's shoulder, the small contact going far to bring my bear peace. Her touch calms his earlier agitation.

God, what would it feel like to have her fully in my arms? Getting to hold her... stroke those lush hips.

"Would you like to dance?" I blurt, rubbing the tips of her curls between my fingers absentmindedly.

"Oh... uh." Evie's eyes dart around the table, obviously uncomfortable to answer in front of her friends.

The ass at my elbow pipes up, disrupting my fixation on the curve of Evie's high cheekbones. "Look, man. Thanks for the beer and all. But we were in the middle of a friendly night out, not a date night." The rude challenge makes my bear stand up and stomp his paws.

Let me out to play with this little shit.

"Is that right?" I press, turning in the space where I tower over the little prick. "So, you're saying if I want to spend time with Evie, I should ask her out on a proper date, then. Is that it?" I pivot back to Evie, who's mouth hangs open in surprise.

"No... dammit!" Ash's beer slams the table. He shoves his chair back, aiming a sour frown at the girls. "Eve, come get me when the air clears in here." Ash stalks off to an empty pool table in the back room, leaving his barely touched beer behind.

The urge to fist-bump the air is hard to resist, but I manage... barely.

The problem is, neither girl seems to share my amusement. Kayah's eyes bore holes into her napkin, her fingers shredding the corners awkwardly. Evie, on the other hand, gawks at me with a beet-red face, causing my stomach to tilt. I'm too afraid to ask if she's red with embarrassment or anger. Neither way is good.

Our natural pull toward each other isn't helping. My brain is all but useless, not able to formulate a good defense with Evie's mouth tipped down. All my focus is preoccupied with the urge to taste those pretty lips.

"Listen, I'm sorry if I overstepped." I squeeze Evie's hand, praying she doesn't pull away. When she doesn't respond, I assume I've completely struck out for the night. "I'll just go. Let you ladies get back to your night." *Please say no.*

The split second of silence drags for eternity, solidifying the dread in my stomach with every tick of the clock. Resigned, I give Evie's hand a little pat.

I overstepped too fast.

In less than a day, I've gone from lonely and wishing I had a mate to share my day with, to finding her and pissing her off multiple times in just a few encounters. I should have gone slower, but knowing deep down that Evie's my mate, feeling the tornado of hormones raking my body just by breathing her scent, makes me want to skip every frivolous step in the human dating process.

It gets harder to resist the longer I'm in her presence. It's not just my emotions, but my body's natural response to my mate. I'm desperate to soothe her stress, to ease her anger… and worst of all, satisfy the arousal wafting to me from under the scent of vanilla and margarita.

"You ladies have a good night." With beer in hand, I back away, feeling more dejected than I've felt since striking out for the first time as a teenager.

Chapter 7

♥

Wyatt

Go back! My bear demands, stomping his paws in resentment. I'm a few steps away, not fully into the darkness, when a tiny hand wraps my wrist.

Evie's big, brown eyes plead up at me. "Look… I don't know what's wrong with Ash. He's been off all day." Confusion storms behind her eyes. "I don't know why, but you just… set him off."

I'm not confused. Ash wants her.

She's mine.

I know, I know. Calm down.

"It's OK, darlin'," I say, turning our hands so my callused fingers can rub along her silken ones. I glance down, where her shoulders slump below me. "What is it you want, Evie?"

The edge of that tempting shirt falls to reveal more golden brown skin I'd love to mark. That place where shoulder dips to collarbone, where it tilts up along her neck waiting for my bite.

Quickly, I reel in those thoughts, banishing my needs to the back burner. My unsettled mate is the top priority. I'll do anything to ease the stress radiating off her, even if it means my time waits for another day.

Evie's gaze drops to our joined hands. "I want a fun night with my friends." My stomach sinks. "I want my life to feel like it used to-." She pauses, her teary eyes meeting mine. "I—I want to get to know you too, though. As crazy as that is." Her lip quivers on that last admission, the most adorable blush coloring the length of her neck. It makes me wonder exactly how innocent she is. If just admitting interest turns her pink... this will be fun.

Would she blush the first time I expose her gorgeous skin? The first time I sip from her sweetness.

A big ole grin covers my face, but I force it down. Obstacles are still in my way. Restraint is the only way I'll have a chance with Evie. The desire to do exactly that burns like hot coals in my blood, but if I go Alpha on her idiot friend, I'll look bad, not him.

I tilt her chin up so I can admire those chocolate eyes with their whirlwind of emotion drawing me in. "That's exactly what I want too." Evie's eyes widen, like she's surprised I feel the same way. Or that I admit it... I don't know.

"How about this? Can I join you and your sister for some pool with the weirdo?" My joke does its job of making Evie giggle. She slaps my chest playfully and I know I at least lightened her mood.

"Don't call him that," she chastises under breath, but I smell a victory when Evie glances at Kayah for confirmation. She's watching our interaction with a tilted head, while not so smoothly eavesdropping on our conversation. When she jerks back to sip on the margarita I delivered, trying to hide her curiosity, we both crack up.

"OK. How about if we play pool with the not-weirdo?" She offers, grabbing her purse so we can free up the table.

"Sounds good. I'm up for anything that gets me more time with you," I answer honestly.

"Damn." Kayah's impressed hiss makes my smile grow. I help the girls' gather their drinks before we move to greet a sullen Ash at the pool tables.

For the next two hours, I watch Evie dominate us all. We take turns playing the winner, but Ash is the only one remotely holding his own with her.

Pool is so not my game. I flex my oversized fist around the neck of my beer bottle and chuckle in my head. These hands were not built for a skinny stick. But it's my turn, and while I love watching Evie in her zone, the sweet curve of her ass makes it impossible to concentrate on my own game.

Like now... Evie waits for my shot with her hip leaned against the table. That tease of temptation has made me miss more pockets than not and the challenge in her eye says she knows it. Our soon to be victor holds my gaze while I line my chalked stick to sink one the the four stripes I have left on the table. Surprise... I miss.

I smirk and keep her eyes locked for a whole different challenge. I'll accept my defeat like a man, but I'll win the woman. Evie's grin warms the air around me and I stay close, watching my beauty bend over and sink the eight ball.

I chuckle at her triumphant whoop, trying my best not to gloat when she bounces into my arms for a celebratory hug. My arms scoop her waist and lift in a swirl that has her giggling in my arms.

"Congratulations, baby," I whisper, watching her swallow thickly and turn an adorable shade of pink.

"Another," Ash barks from the end of the table, holding his glass to a passing waitress—not our waitress.

He's the only one who shifted to stronger drinks when our game started. I nurse my third beer and Evie and Kayah still sip off their—now watered down—margaritas. Unfortunately, with every refill, Ash ups his obnoxious quota, his game suffers, and his comments drop deeper in the gutter.

Reluctantly, I let go of Evie and discreetly adjust my misbehaving erection before moving to sit at the table with her sister. When Evie starts her game with Ash, I pretend not to notice the stink eye he sends me while she preps to break. Those back pockets have drawn both of our eyes where she bends over the table. A growl rumbles in my head, but I squeeze my beer bottle just short of breaking the glass to keep it down.

Evie's cue snaps my brain out of murder mode. She nails a solid hit, spreading the balls and landing a solid in the corner pocket.

Kayah cheers, laughing when Evie winks in our direction. She's getting braver, our connection pulling her out of her shell as the night roles on. Every smile and tease between us grows our heat, building a comfort together that only mates have.

When Evie flubs her next shot, too distracted by Kayah and myself, Ash snickers. "Aww, Eve-alyn. Tough break." His goad sounds slightly slurred, but he walks straight to line up his next shot. "Let the master clear the board, baby girl." Ash's body passes a little too tight by Evie in the open space, pulling an awkward laugh from my girl who's still trying to pretend her friend isn't a pervert.

Kayah's back jerks straight, noticing the same uncomfortable rub I did. The agitation rolls off her in waves. All night, she's tried to hide the longing glances in Ash's direction, having bowed out of playing pool an hour ago. Poor kid's pining away, waiting for Ash to notice the beauty right in front of him and he's too oblivious... vying for Evie's attention and making a total ass out of himself instead. The signs are there, as glaringly obvious as daylight, and it's testing every ounce of self-control I have.

Beating up her friend will not win you points! I repeat that every time Ash rubs a little too close.

After two shots, he scratches the third and stumbles back to the high top we're perched at with squinted eyes. *His arrogance is heavily influence powered by the drink... remember that.*

Being a nice guy, and hoping it wins me points, I let that smirk on his face slide. "Having a good game there?" The question is neutral, but my eyebrow lifts, inviting him to come at me with whatever attitude he'd like. If this is gonna happen, it's starting on his side.

Behind our stand off of male egos and tightly wound pressure, Evie runs the table on Ash, taking the game down to a single ball. *Holy hell!* That barely took five minutes.

The last shot is difficult and Evie walks the table, bending at different angles to find the best position. It distracts me from the growing tension at our table. I've never wanted to write poetry but I could produce fifty limericks, sonnets, and haiku's to Wrangler watching Evie play a game of pool.

Unfortunately, Ash also notices. Hell, every man in the room turns to ogle what's mine. It ignites something in my blood, sparking my senses to high alert.

She's my mate.

Frustrated, I tap a rapid rhythm on the table, wrestling for control in a room full of men eying Evie's sensuous curves.

Ash's scowl transforms with a mixture of humor, jealousy, and rage. The kid sees an opportunity to poke the bear. He just has no idea how real his danger is there.

He steps up to where Evie has lined up her winning shot, his clouded features now smooth and friendly. She looks baffled to why he's standing so close, but Ash pretends not to notice. That charming smile might work if his blood shot eyes weren't learning as he goes to leans over my woman.

"Need help nailing the shot?" he asks, one hand covering hers on the pool stick, the other grabbing one side of her hip and lining himself over her body.

A snarl pushes me out of my chair, hands shaking. My body's primed to rip Ash limb from limb when Evie's gasp keeps me at bay. Waiting.

"Ash! What the hell are you doing?" Her eyes pop wide at the same time her tense shoulders jerk against his hold. Unconcerned by her response, he takes liberties to whisper in her ear. The embrace sends a signal to the room that they're way more than friends. *I don't think so!*

When Evie jerks upright, her cue stick scrapes Jackson's brand-new maroon felt, but at least she knocks Ash back a few feet. From the side, I see Kayah escape to the restroom, hurt turning her eyes glassy.

I've had enough.

Evie may not want me to pulverize her friend, but her anger has magnified my own. It's spiked above the jealousy of someone touching our mate. Evie's face is a jumble of emotions and considering this little pip of a guy is supposed to be her friend, he doesn't seem at all concerned that he upset her.

If she wants this dumb ass that'd be a different fight, one of trying to win my mate. But Evie's stiffness says otherwise. She's as close to steam exploding from her ears as I've seen outside of Saturday morning cartoons.

Her rage has me by her side in less than a second, shifter speed be damned. The idiot casts a cocky look at me over Evie's shoulder, not understanding my real threat even when he grabs her pool stick and sinks the eight ball.

Ash's lack of awareness rings loud and clear when he fist pumps the ceiling with a celebratory shout.

Evie's panic is visceral when she turns in my arms, her hands pressed against my stomach to hold me at bay—a near useless effort with my rocketing temper. "Calm down. Please," she begs, those dark eyes pleading with me to not kill her friend.

Pulling her body close, I drag her scent into my lungs to calm my raging need. "Are you OK?"

My hands massage her tense shoulders, but once Evie sees I've backed off my immediate threat, she pulls away, frustrating me again. Her eyes look torn, sliding back and forth between me and Ash like she doesn't know what to say to either of us. Anxiety ripples off her... I feel that, but her mind is too jumbled for me to get a good read. She looks torn between wanting to deescalate the situation and being ticked off enough to amp it up herself.

Resolve hardens her features when Ash takes a shot glass from a passing tray, victory in his eyes. He thinks Evie's going to stick up for him since she told me to calm down. She's our buffer and he knows it. Too bad the alcohol that made Ash brave, also made him stupid. He thinks he won.

I want to knock that mocking grin right off his face, especially when he takes another step closer. I match it, pressing closer to Evie. "You wanna chest pound, buddy?"

"Wyatt!" Evie hisses, stepping a few feet away. My body immediately feels the loss.

"Oh, come on, big guy. I was just playing around," he whines. "My Eve knows that."

A snarl grinds itself out… *my Evie.*

Ash saunters closer, flopping his heavy arm around Evie's shoulders. His mistake is not looking the least bit afraid when I step close again.

"We've been besties since we were in diapers," he challenges smugly. "Isn't that right, bestie?" Sarcasm laces his voice even as he lays a wet kiss to her temple.

"What the hell, Ash?" Evie jerks her head away, pushing his arm roughly off her shoulders. Cold distaste radiates off Evie, her nose scrunching as she wipes Ash's slobber off her face. His shoulders crumble at her rejection, but he doesn't acknowledge the strain he's caused with an apology or backtrack in the least.

And unfortunately for her, Kayah picks that supremely awkward moment to walk up. "Is World War III breaking out?" she asks carefully.

Ash turns his glazed eyes back to me, not ready to give up his drunken rant yet. He still thinks he's proving a point despite the hiccups undermining his words. "Eve, tell 'em. Our mothers are gonna get us married one day."

I choke on a cough, my bear pressing to the surface with outrage. It requires every ounce of my concentration to keep the pins and needles at bay and not spontaneously shift.

Evie pales. "Ash!" He winces at her volume, finally recognizing she's not happy with him.

"What," he pouts. "They are." Soon to be broken fingers stroke the length of her hair with a look of adoration.

My fists tighten. I'm about to show this guy exactly who's the alpha in this bar. "You need to watch your mouth, you little shit. She's mine." I realize the mistake in my warning the moment it's out of my mouth.

"Woah!" Evie's head jerks back in shock, her hand flying up like she can hold our idiocy at bay with just those five fingers. My sentence hangs in the air, all of us quiet, until Evie shakes her head and reaches for her sister, tugging so fast, the poor girl nearly topples off balance.

"I can't take it. Both of you... I'm done." Evie's anger grinds through clenched teeth, her seething breaths upping my guilt at having caused more stress.

Ash and I follow her frazzled movements, stunned temporarily out of battle. She gathers her purse and coat, tossing a few bills on the table for the server. I step forward, opening my mouth to object, but the venom in her eyes stops me.

She's running. My bear feels his connection to Evie's psyche fraying.

She walks back to where we stand gawking at her and jabs a pointy finger in Ash's chest. "If you ever want to be my bestie again… you will not do this," she cautions, waving her hand between me and him and the pool table. "I know I've been gone, and I miss you. But this... this is not OK."

Kayah stands behind her sister, backing her up, while a very pissed off Evie stares down the two of us men posturing for alpha.

My heart stops when Evie turns those sad brown eyes on me, resigned. I start to apologize, but she shakes her head, turning away to grasp her sister's hand and walking out the door.

She's got no words for me. *No reprimand? Nothing?*

My bear curls up in a ball, mourning Evie's separation. The physical pain nearly to drops me to my knees. I have to get out of here before I lose it in front of all these people.

Sending one last '*don't fuck with me*' look to Ash, I walk to the bar to cash out. Jax takes my card with a frown, but I can't let him start asking questions or I'll never hold it together.

"Can you get that kid over there a ride?" I ask, pointing where I left Ash sulking. "He's in no condition." I frown at my brother, who's practically drooling on the countertop. "Him too. If you don't mind."

"Sure thing, brother." Jax nods solemnly and runs my card before going back to pouring rounds.

I pat my brother's back. "See you tomorrow, Cale." He 's coherent enough to give me a two-finger solute and I don't wait for more. *I need to get out of here.*

My bear's pain is hard to control. He's more volatile than I've felt since losing our parents in middle school. My cabin would never hold us like this. His pent up anger burns the back of my throat, ready to bubble up and cause a scene.

I need to run.

Problem is, we're too close to town to be safe. I circle behind the bar where there's no sign of people—no couples steaming up cars or making out in the shadows.

Exhaling, my feet pound the ground, beelining for the seclusion of the woods. Impatience makes my hands clumsy, fumbling to strip off my outer clothes the moment I'm hidden in shadow.

Growling, I work my laces, tossing my heavy boots at the base of a thick pine. The dead silence of the forest is ominous tonight, matching my mood. It heightens every sound in the air, even the cicadas are silent tonight. The only breaks in the stillness are my panting breaths and the pop of shirt buttons when I rip through them in a hurry.

My mind is too agitated to slow down. The more I think about that idiot ruining my progress with Evie, the more...

He can't have our woman!

Goddammit! My bear rages from my mind, shredding my pants before I have a chance to loosen my belt. My bones crack and pop into their elongated shape, already launching into a run before I land on four paws, fully transformed. A thick, black fur spreads across my body, warming my naked skin. I shake my body violently in the air, letting the last tattered shreds of clothing fly.

My bear has control... no sign of man left.

His sharp claws scrape the dirt underfoot, slashing at the ground with a fury that has me darting through trees faster and faster. The lower limbs batter my face, but I barely feel it. His pent up aggression numbs everything except the anger. Leaves pelt my face, whipping my ears as I pass deeper into backwoods. None of it matters. This ursine body will protect us from the elements, it's the fractures inside that feel like they're killing me.

A shifter can survive most things, including being alone—prior to meeting their mate. Tonight, I felt that connection to Evie and when she walked away... she ripped the air from my lungs. Now, my body craves her.

When we reach the edge of a drop off, I skid to a stop, scaring a nest of mocking jays. The birds take flight and my gravely howl follows them to the sky. The sound rips from my chest as my bear's desperation takes over. He's screaming for release—to hunt.

If I can't have my female, I will have blood.

Chapter 8

Evie

In the distance, a continuous jingle breaks through my dream. I'd call it rude, waking me up faster than I'd like, except the side of my head getting bombarded by a jackhammer is happy to get rid of the nightmare that chased me all the night.

When I manage to pry my eyelashes apart, the sun's already pouring through the bedroom curtains, making the room too damn bright... too cheery.

Headache and exhaustion argue with the eight-a.m. glowing from my old Minnie Mouse alarm clock. They'd prefer I roll over and sleep long enough to forget my own name. Too bad my phone has other plans. The jingling stopped, but a new voicemail alerts right after it.

Not answering that!

Honestly, I don't want to talk to whoever's calling this early in the morning. I'm pretty sure a bus ran over me, backed up, and did it again. How is that possible? I only had two margaritas before the macho egos unleashed.

Squeezing my eyes shut, I realize I haven't had an actual hangover since my twenty-first birthday. That's sad! Especially since the headache I'm currently trying to push out of my temples seems more stress related, and a desperation for sleep since I tossed and turned all night.

Around four-a.m., I woke up from a dream and couldn't get back to sleep. Even now, with a fuzzy head, the details are way too vivid. I was chatting with a black bear on top of a mountain like we were best friends. I wasn't afraid of the bear, but I was afraid of being stranded. Every choice in the dream took me farther down a twisted path. I would lose sight of my bear friend and then find him around another corner.

The worst part was being naked. The woods scratched and cut me until I couldn't walk at all. I sat down and cried in a pile of leaves, calling for the bear to save me, when I woke up.

Oh my God! I just remembered, the bear was wearing a ranger hat!

What the hell kind of dream is that?

The hilarity of it would make me laugh if not for the symphony playing behind my eyeballs.

Dragging my head to the side, I spot Kayah tucked under her covers. She didn't go to her apartment after we got home last night. She was more than a little irritable and it seemed to be about more than the pissing match at the pool table.

I tried to get her to vent, but when she wouldn't, I ended up complaining until well after midnight myself. About Wyatt... about Ash. Their annoyances, the chest-pounding ego trip... my confusion.

She finally told me to shut up around two in the morning, claiming she'd had enough and wanted to go to bed. Sadly, I'm no less confused this morning, just more drained.

Why was Ash such an ass?

Responsible Evie would have stayed at the bar and made sure Ash got a ride home. The man was blatantly drunk. But drunk Ash used to be fun. I don't know the guy from last night. He was weird. Even if we've been friends for damn near twenty-five years, my tolerance for people running over me lately has hit the crashing point.

Ugh... frustrated, I grab my phone from the nightstand. I'll never be able to focus until I make sure Ash got home. Thankfully, the lock screen shows two texts waiting from him. Ash must have sent them before going to sleep, like we used to do in high school.

Ash: Eve, I'm sorry for my behavior tonight. I'm sorry about today all together.

Ash: Please speak to me tomorrow and I'll make it up to you.

OK, that at least makes me feel better.

Me: I assume you got home OK?

To my surprise, he texts back immediately.

Ash: Yes, and again, I'm so sorry. No excuses, but I want to talk to you today. I need to explain.

Weird little butterflies dance in my stomach. I just can't deal with any more stress... it's throwing me on my butt.

Me: Sure… text later. No plans so far.

OK, one ridiculous man down, one kissable one to go. But, not this early. Not without coffee.

I slide out of bed, taking extra care not to wake Kayah. The first thing I smell is Mom's cooking wafting down the hall. It tortures my empty stomach. Though, it's hard to brush your teeth when you're drooling over salty bacon.

My only hope is that I don't have another dreaded run in with Ama, this morning. Especially after she couldn't put up with me long enough to have a drink last night. We may be on a merry-go-round of bitchy, but I still have to figure out how to function in this family again. I've let too much slide. Right now, I fit in to this family as well as a one-horned Billy goat at a county fair.

Squaring my shoulders, I give myself a tiny pep talk in the bathroom mirror. *Just don't get defensive, Eveline. Rise above. You got this!*

Sighing, I gather enough nerve to walk toward the clang of dishes in the kitchen. Another text notification vibrates my hand. It's probably another from Ash. He never was good with me being mad at him.

I'm starting to have second thoughts about getting out of bed. When I look down at my phone, the feelings confirmed. It's not Ash; it's another text from Dr. Michaels.

Michaels: *Call me. You had two days off. I expect you back here Monday! Important meeting!*

My stomach clenches, the nausea I thought I was free of threatening to make a grand appearance. At this rate, I'll have an ulcer before I straighten out the mess in my life. I close the text window and plaster a smile on my face as I walk in the kitchen.

The view here never changes. Gran's at the table, like always. Mom's stirring some batter in her oversized plastic bowl.

"Aren't you tired of cooking, ma?" I know the answer—my mom loves taking care of her family. Her 'get real' glare makes me smile. "I know. I know," I say, dropping a kiss on her cheek.

"Guess you don't want any of my blueberry waffles then, huh?"

"I would never say that, Ma." I feign offense, pouring myself a cup of coffee—that delicious nectar of the Gods.

"You should be happy to have my cookin', girlie. You're wasting away in Tennessee."

I snort, loving how my mom thinks losing ten pounds of baby fat is wasting away. My chubby cheeks have just moved to more appreciated areas. *Hallelujah!*

"How was last night, Bug?" Gran asks, patting my arm when I slide in the chair beside her, careful of my pounding head. "Looks like you're sweating a little bit this morning." She laughs, lightening her critique and a sliver of my morning funk.

"It was fine," I hedge, not willing to share the details of last night's drama. Or that I met a man yesterday who's embedded himself in my head after only twelve hours.

"Didn't you go out with Ash?" Mom scoops the first finished waffle on a plate, looking eager to hear more scintillating details than what I'm giving.

"How d'you know that Ma?"

Gran rolls her eyes and I have to hide a laugh behind my coffee cup. Mom bungles her mixing bowl, trying to play it cool.

"Oh, you know... small town," she says but Gran's smirk says it all.

"How would our small town know that Ma?" I ask, already knowing the answer.

She swats my question from the air like an annoying fly. "I saw the boy at the grocer yesterday, Evelyn. That's all I meant."

"Well, we went to that new Growler place with Kayah." I glance at Gran. "Ama couldn't make it... apparently."

"She'll be by later," Mom offers, misunderstanding my complaint. "I'm helping her make a new robe for next week."

Of course, Queen Ama wants a new outfit. The girl acts like she's fifteen, not twenty-five, always needing something... a new outfit, her lunch made, her apartment cleaned. But our mom's wrapped around her manicured pinkie.

"What are you wearing to the festival, Bug?" Gran asks, nonchalantly steering my mind from the rabbit hole it was sliding down.

"Oh, uh... I thought I'd just wear jeans and a top this year." I don't miss the disappointed look between Mom and Gran. It tightens my throat when I meet Gran's eyes again.

This is the second year I haven't taken an active role in a single Cherokee ceremony. After growing up doing all seven of them, every single year, I've enjoyed the break. It's hard to dedicate time to the prep work, the dances, all the committees, when you're building a career in another city. But this year's New Moon Ceremony is taking on a life of its own since it's the whole pretext for my trip home.

I just never expected coming home to be such a damn shock to the system.

Annoyed, I try calling a little balance to their perception. "Guys, there are other people who don't dress up for this thing, you know." I hate disappointing my family, which is why it's hard to get the words out.

"Yes, my dear, but as a representative family, we lead by example." That's always been Mom's stance. My dad serves on our tribal council, so these traditions are very close to their hearts. Every argument with my mom, I end up feeling like I'm failing my Cherokee heritage if I don't enthusiastically don robes and feathers for every ceremony. *It sucks!*

Thank God, Dad picks that moment to walk in, interrupting Mom's grilling of my personal life with the loud stomping of his field boots on the doormat. Mom's pet peeve.

"Kota!" she shrieks, eyeballing my dad's dirty boots.

"Sorry, Ma. How are my beautiful ladies this morning?" Dad's big smile creases his tanned face, charming my mom out of a potential bicker. The man's boisterous mood is a staple in this house, no matter how early he's up in the morning. Unfortunately, none of his daughters inherited that trait from Dad.

I cringe when he ruffles my head, wishing I had already taken some pain relievers for my headache. "How're the goats, Dad?"

He beams. We all know Dad enjoys those early mornings with his goats more than any other part of the day. He feeds and walks the herd before most of us wake up, coming in for mama's breakfast, before heading back out to tend the crops or visit the tribe's residents.

"Perfect group of kids, baby girl, just like my own." Dad's joke makes me laugh. We all know what kind of estrogen hell he's surrounded with having five women in his household. "What's goin' on with you today, Punkin'?"

"Not much." I shrug. It's the truth. For the first time since graduating, I have no plans. "I have to see Ash at some point, but I'm gonna hang around here a bit, maybe drive into town."

"We could use your help to get set for the New Moon," Mom suggests, her pointed look hitting its target.

"Oh-"

"That's a great idea, Ma! There's a ton you can do," Dad says, interrupting my attempt to backtrack. "We already chose the seven women for food prep and dancing, but we're behind in making the Black Tea. You can help with that, can't ya, Punkin'?"

"What's she helping with, Dad?" Ama asks, strutting into the kitchen, her hips sashaying like its a runway. Only the scowl marring her pretty face gives any clue to her true feelings about my presence.

"You're up early," Dad remarks without answering her question. His cheek angles at the head of the table, waiting for the expected kiss she gives him. "Grab some breakfast, Nugget."

"Dad, stop calling me that. And I'm always up this early." Her huff of annoyance almost makes me smile. She hates that childhood nickname, earned because two-year-old Ama refused to eat anything except chicken nuggets for a year. "Just because I manage a casino doesn't mean I can't function like the rest of you."

Dad pats her hand, his voice placating. "Of course, baby. We were just talking about the festival next week." His proud smile hits me square in the chest. "Evie's gonna help with Black Tea preparations since we're short on time."

"Oh, is she?" Ama glowers at me from under her eyelashes while Mom sets the table with plates of scrambled eggs and waffles.

How long can my sister give me the cold shoulder? I can't help that my schedule's been packed the last few years. I'm building a career, for God's sake.

"She is," my mom answers for me, setting empty plates in front of all of us. Crap. I just sat here and let Mom serve us food without helping. *Worst daughter ever award!*

"Mom, I'll clean up after breakfast, OK."

"Suck up!" Ama coughs into her fist making my mom groan.

I can't do it. My eyes bore into my scrambled eggs, avoiding Ama's nasty scowl all together. The whole table settles into an all-around uncomfortable silence. It's only interrupted when our baby sister walks in, sleep rumpled and grabbing the chair beside me.

Sometimes, Kayah still seems like a little girl to me, with her fuzzy pig slippers and baby face. Her head rests on my shoulder, eyes wary of Ama. "What's got her face all scrunched up?"

My shoulder's shake with suppressed laughter. Dad too, except he hides it better, clearing his throat while he cuts little squares in his waffles and swamps them in syrup.

"I heard that," Ama grumbles, launching into another tirade. "Daddy! These two are always ganging up on me." She jabs a finger in our direction, which makes me grin, despite her annoyance and my headache. The scene has an inkling of old times—of tattle-telling little girls with sticky faces and fingers.

Now we sit here with cold shoulders and coffee while we devour our breakfast. "Ma, I've got dance practice after lunch. If you don't need Evie, I thought I'd take her into town and show her the new shops."

"You better not work her in the dance," Ama warns, her pinched face enough that Kayah holds up her hands in mock innocence. "She shows up last minute and gets to jump right in with no effort at all." Ama shakes her head, her complaints falling on deaf ears for the rest of the family.

I'm a week early! So, hah!

"She's not gonna dance, Ama. She's coming to keeping me company." Kayah's eyes flash with exasperation. "What's your problem with Evie helping next week, anyway?"

"She doesn't live here!" Ama's anger flashes. *Is she this territorial over ceremonial jobs? Really?*

"It's tradition," Gran presses, interrupting our bitch-fest. "Everyone's included."

Ama's lips snap shut, knowing better that to argue with Gran's tone. She quietly gathers her plate—even though she's only half done—and carries it to the sink. The dish drops with a louder clank than necessary, making Gran's eyebrow raise.

"How long you home?" Ama asks, addressing me with her arms crossed, her butt leaned against the sink, as if this conversation isn't worth her effort.

"Dunno." My attempt at a light-hearted response is overshadow by my roiling stomach. I had hoped the family would stays away from questions I couldn't answer. "I thought I'd stay for the ceremony and then figure it out."

"What do you mean… figure it out?" Dad asks, his fork stopping mid-bite. "I assumed you were using vacation time."

"Well… I just..." I cut eyes at Ama, who's grinning like a Cheshire cat. "I sort of took a leave of absence."

"What?" both Mom and Dad yell in unison.

Gulping, I try to think of something believable to tell my parents that's not a lie but not admitting the mess I'm in. "Look. I don't know my plan yet. There're some things up in the air at work." I meet the table's concerned gazes. Dad's eyes are dark with worry. But Mom looks positively… giddy?

"Do you think you'll move home?" she asks, voicing the suspicion I dreaded. Mom's getting her hopes up when, honestly, I have no plans to move. I just need a new job. Preferably with a non-criminal this time.

Kayah catches my eye, munching bites of waffle while mom hits me with the dreaded expectations. Ama, however, looks like she swallowed a pickle down the wrong pipe.

"What happened, Evie? Couldn't hack it in the big city?" Ama asks, her nasty grin knocking me for a loop.

"Ama!" Dad warns, his deep voice resounding through the kitchen. "Be nice," he barks, taking my hand. His big comforting warmth prevents my temper from blowing a gasket. "If our Evie needs to come home and stay for a while, that's great. Maybe she'll find her place was here all along."

The hope in my dad's eye guts me. I clear the thickness from my throat, hoping to avoid tears this early in the morning.

"Dad, my plan is to help out this week and catch up with everyone before heading back to figure out my next steps." His weathered brown eyes flicker with sadness, knowing his little girl is likely to leave again. But Dad pulls it together like he always does, giving us a foundation of support, even when he hates it.

"Welp." He claps his hands, ready to change the subject. "There's plenty to do." Sharp eyes moves around the table, to the generations of women in his life. He starts suddenly, slapping the table like the most brilliant idea popped into his head. "You know, Punkin', I got a call from Hank this morning. He heard you were in town and needs some help with Billie Buff. He wouldn't give me details over the phone, but do you think we could stop by his ranch tomorrow?"

I nod, happy for the distraction. "Sure, Dad. Tell Uncle Hank we'll be by in the morning."

"Awesome. If you check out Billie, maybe Hank'll calm his paranoid papa routine." Dad laughs lovingly at his brother, his pride obvious. "It certainly helps to have a veterinarian in the family."

"Ack! It's getting stuffy in here. I'm out." Ama pushes off the sink, stomping her heeled booties toward the door.

"Where you going, young lady? We need to work on your dress," Mom calls after Ama's retreating back.

"I've got stuff to do before work. Unless our magical Evie can snap her fingers and fold my laundry with her epic magnificence," Ama says, pretending to wave sparkles in the air with her fingers. That snideness wipes away any goodwill I felt after our dad's praise. "I'll drop by later, Ma."

And, just like that, Ama's out the door without a second glance to me.

"What's her problem? " I can't control the whine in my voice, not caring one bit if I sound like a misbehaving six-year-old. The noose around my neck keeps tightening and pretty soon, something's gonna crack. I take my last bite of blueberry waffle, but it hits my stomach like a rock.

Mom pats my hand, trying to make me feel better. "Honey, don't worry about her. She's tired from those crazy work hours. And her boss is a nightmare." She cuts her eyes at my dad, waiting for him to pipe in.

He takes the baton for Mom. "You know your sister, Evie. She acts tough on the outside, but inside, she's all gooey center."

I snort. "She just keeps that part hidden, right?"

"Yeah, like a rotten Cadbury Egg," Kayah scoffs, her grin lightening the comment.

I send my sister a thankful smile and gather up an armload of empty dishes that I drop into Mom's sudsy basin. My hands dip in the stupid hot water while my family's chairs scrape the floor behind me. Everyone brings me their breakfast plates, so I can wash and they can start their morning.

Dad squeezes my shoulder on his way out. "Have a good day, Punkin'."

"Love you, Dad," I call, my voice wobbling.

Kayah's right behind him, she hip checks me after putting her plate in the bubbles, but her warm smile goes a long way to smooth over my agitation. "I'm gonna go shower before we get started, OK?"

"Yeah, no prob," I say, mustering a half-hearted smile before doubling down on the stack of dirty dishes.

Mom finishes clearing the table and walk over to give me a hug before she heads off to her converted sewing room. "Thanks for the help, baby girl." Mom will probably have Ama's dress done before she gets back this afternoon but that's our mom. Always taking care of her girls.

Gran's the last one out, but even she has better things to do today—something about book club and errands. And then I'm alone... nothing but me and my thoughts.

My hands work through the dishes robotically. Ama aside, this morning still would've felt about as strange as a tap dancing chihuahua. Last night was completely out of character for me and that doesn't sit right.

Hell, maybe I had a legit mental break that night at the office, like blowing a fuse or something. That would be a good reason why my mind has suddenly been taken over my a new person. It's something to think about.

If the trauma broke my common sense, my self-control, that would explain why my inhibitions took the night off around that pool table last night. I practically waved my ass at a near stranger and actually enjoyed the fact that I could torture him. How is that any better than those co-ed floozies from our tour?

Ugh! Just remembering how I acted is enough to make me want to bury my head in the bubbles. *Eveline Amos does not act like that. Never has.* If I had my right mind, I'd never let a strange man hypnotize me, no matter how well he wore the smoldering, mountain man look.

I just have to remember that next time. If there is a next time.

Mom's last pan takes a beating under my scrubber while my brain processes excuses. I know what did me in... that damn soft heart. It was Wyatt's warmth, his passion when he talked about saving the forest animals. I made a simple mistake, gave him too much credit. It blinded me to the other shoe... that Neanderthal-ass part of his personality. It wasn't until his pissing contest with Ash in a public bar that I got to see that glory up close and personal.

What I can't figure out is why it was so hard to walk away. Every step made me nauseous. My body screamed at me to turn around and work it out. Wyatt's gravitational pull makes trudging through a wind tunnel with a parachute seem like a walk in the park.

If I had his number, I could text that muscly brute this morning and figure out if my response to him yesterday was a fluke. But no... egos went berserk and I'm stuck driving myself crazy with what-ifs. Though he may not want to hear from me after the way I left last night.

That's OK. *Sure it is.*

It's not I have room for any extra problems right now anyway. I keep thinking that just because my life plan blew up in my face, doesn't mean I should give up the way I've handled everything else in my twenties.

Set a goal, make a plan, fight like hell for it.

That's just going to be what I have to do. Keep my head down and fix one problem at a time, starting with the shit-storm I rolled into town on.

Chapter 9

♥

Wyatt

Mondays suck!

The rain pelting my windshield on the drive to Uncle Mac's cabin ratchets that hate up about fifty degrees. Maybe I can use that heat to warm the cold fingers squeezing my heart. It's not like Mother Nature's helping. Her gloom matches my mood in every way now after temperatures dropped this weekend.

OK, winter sucks too!

It may only be fall, and not an acceptable opinion for a warm-blooded bear, but this dreary, wet mess seeps energy from my bones. At least for my human side. My bear loves this weather. His instincts signal for famine, to prep for the bitter cold.

I'm already craving spring, for the fresh. That first scent of mowed grass in the air and flowers budding on the trees. It's as if the earth warms to new life every year.

But not today. This isn't fresh or new. It's a lousy forecast that blows the hell out of my day. All my tours canceled. Canceled tours mean canceled money, canceled opportunities... a basic shit on the entire day.

After my day got trampled, I figured my mood would lift if I accomplished something big on my down time. So, I called my uncle for our monthly roll-call meeting for the Building Our Future program.

The clan requires accountability and regular updates from the bears who sign up. We get a loan to build businesses in the human world and the clan takes a share of profits as both repayment and for clan upkeep. It's a very forward thinking program to help young cubs succeed.

The problem is, by taking the loan, clan elders become highly involved in your business. Half your time is spent arguing with stodgy old men with outdated thinking. God forbid you control growing the business you've dreamed of for years! *That part sucks!*

And the majority of them can't make up their minds. If I hear one more time... *blend with humans. Use them, but never trust them. Don't be stupid, we need humans... humans aren't good enough.* Back and forth... I may just scream in one of their faces if they catch me in the wrong mood one day.

Like today. I'm starting to second guess dealing with clan business when I'm already ready to bash heads. I just thought I could get it over with, but that thirty-minute drive up a rainy, twisted mountain road has jacked up my stress level and given me way too much time to think.

My mood sinks with every mile passed.

Groaning, I scrape tense fingers through my too-long hair. I needed that haircut I skipped this weekend, but after Friday night, I didn't trust myself around anyone I wanted to keep a relationship with. My temper is on a hair trigger that even the slightest issue... like my shower taking longer to heat, set me off.

So, to be safe, I canceled everything.

It just sucks that going recluse didn't help me. Regret and yearning have warred with each other all weekend, constantly second guessing my actions on Friday. The mess of feelings kept my bear riled through Saturday tours, through poker with the guys, through the research—I won't admit to doing—on Evie's life. I only gathered bits of information, because she's not big on social media, but the bare bones gave me a modicum of distraction. Enough to hold my desperation at bay.

When I woke up Sunday still reeling, still about to crawl out of my skin, I gave into at least part of what my bear craves—a paw numbing, exhaustive run through our secret falls. We haven't made amends with his mate yet, but we did land a large buck that filled our belly for dinner *and* gave me plenty of meat for the deep freeze.

Even after all that though, he still tossed and turned all night. My head bounced across panicked dreams until I woke up growling this morning. The sleepless night left me tired and pissed off... with a slamming headache to boot.

So basically, I've decided... *my bear is a bitch!*

He just has to calm down long enough to finish my meeting with Uncle Mac and then I'll take him home to roll in the mud if I have too. Anything to stop this insanity. Mac is a man who lost what small amount of frivolity he had in my early years. Since taking over as Alpha of the Big Paw Clan—a roll that will be mine in the future—every conversation is all business and politely rigid expectations.

I mean... Uncle was never warm and fuzzy, but he did raise three boys in the prime of bachelorhood, so I know he has a heart. It's just hidden under the stern alpha role he took over for my father. However, I suspect a lot of his blustering is from never finding a woman of his own to help with the chaos in his life. Not that any of us would ever say that to his face.

Lucky for me, I know how to work Uncle Mac's favor. I brought his favorite burger from Jackson's bar. In fact, it's my favorite too, which is probably why my mouth is watering from the smell of bacon and barbecue sauce in my truck. I'm honestly not sure it's anticipation for lunch or dread for our meeting that has my stomach rumbling. But at least there's a good chance the Triple B burger will lighten his mood.

Who doesn't love bacon, burger, and barbecue sauce?

The muscles in my hands clench when I turn down the long driveway leading to the clan lands. Tall pine trees shade the remote cabins, protecting them from prying eyes or stragglers from the road.

Our clan lives excluded from main civilization so they can shift and run their beast freely, but they also understand the importance of assimilation. Members infiltrate the human world, build highly skilled shifters that come home to manage our land, our community, and run the infrastructure like a well-oiled machine.

Hell, there's not a rut or mud pit in sight on our gravel roads or meeting grounds. The clan is very proud of their progressiveness on certain things.

As I approach Unc's cabin, my brain strains to shape an argument he'll accept for failing on last month's goals. Hopefully, streamlining my schedule and increasing the numbers of tours will be impressive enough that he'll forget his not-so-subtle pressure to drop the Wild Things protection program.

Sometimes these clan elders are just too short-sighted for their own good. They've ignored how my program will benefit our shifter species because it detracts from the bottom line. But how I spend my profit from the business shouldn't matter as long as I'm making payments on the loan. I'm determined to increase conservation across animal-kind, so they can forget about that money funneling back into the clan.

What I'm doing is just as important, dammit! I'm planning our future here.

And it doesn't distract from the business, no matter what Unc says. My adventure tours are unique. They fit tourists and adrenaline junkies, alike. Our excursions fully immerse hikers into the native mountain. We teach about the life there, animals, safety… every gorgeous marvel of our mountain.

Hell, we're so inclusive, that a good portion of the afternoon tours end up at Jackson's brewery, which benefits his business as well, which was also started with clan funds.

But that premium treatment is why Smokey Mountain Rugged Tours has a high rate of repeat bookings. If only I can convince Uncle Mac of that fact. That quantity doesn't measure our success, but overall experience and benefit to the community.

By the time I cut my engine, irritation over every imagined argument has coiled around me like a tight ball of barbed wire. My hands cramp from wringing the life from my steering wheel on the drive up here. I pull cleansing air into my lungs and stretch my fingers, prepping myself for the show. If I'm red faced when I greet my uncle, those knicks to my psyche won't be my largest problem. As future Alpha, I can't appear to crumble under pressure so easily or the weakness would be a huge liability.

I open my door when I catch sight of Uncle Mac walking from his workshop. His toothy grin triggers fond memories from childhood, back before propriety strained our relationship. When me and my brothers would follow our Alpha to his shop and watch him use the impressive tools there. We fetched supplies, while he constructed custom furniture to sell in the local shops.

Glorified shop monkeys, but we learned *how to build things like men.* My uncle's favorite saying.

Now, the enormous man, who's been my steadfast mentor, greets me with the same enthusiasm he did ages ago, wiping those calloused hands on the shop towel hanging from his belt before swamping me in a hug.

A hint of sawdust and rich leather follows my uncle, now. It's only muted by a fresh rain dampening the air. The nostalgia washes away some of the anxiety I drove in with.

I have to remember, Mac has been my compass since taking in me and my brothers after our parents' unexpected deaths. I was only twelve when we bombarded his life, but we never heard a single complaint. He left bachelorhood and became solely responsible for raising his three grieving nephews.

"Unc!" I return his bear hug—literally—welcoming that thumping back-slap that follows my uncle's laughter every time.

"Wyatt, my boy!" Unc's booming voice falls into a devilish chuckle, his nose sniffing as he tries to peak over my shoulder for his treats. "You got me the good stuff, didn't ya?"

I laugh and grab the two white bags emblazoned with Grizzly Growler's logo. I send a quick mental thanks to my best friend for packing the best of the best for my lunch meeting with our clan Alpha. Jax knows—like I do—that the best way to grease Uncle Mac's palm is literally to grease Uncle Mac's palms.

"I never come empty-handed, Unc." I hold the bag out with a grin. "Triple B burgers and those curly fries you love."

"Nice! That's why you're my favorite." He winks, slapping my shoulder again with a hard love pat. Mac may be a little brutish, but it's nothing I can't handle.

Mac may be in his late fifties, but he exercises everyday... his bear and human forms. He claims it makes up for his hair leaving the party too early. This is the part of my uncle I miss. And it lasts all the way through unpacking our food on his outside table and Unc running inside to grab us beer.

I wait outside—semi-patiently—until he comes back out with napkins and two bottles of water to go with the beer. My stomach greets his return with a grumble.

"Somebody needs to feed his bear," Mac jokes. He has a talent for making me feel like a child, but the deliciousness of bacon and barbecue tempers my annoyance. I learned early on that it's easier to talk business with a full belly. Less hangry bears for everyone to deal with.

The table falls into companionable silence when we dig into our foil wrappers. Only hums of appreciation fill the crisp air under the pines. When Unc glances up from his half-eaten burger, he grins, not caring one bit that a drip slides down his chin around a mouthful of burger.

"I assume today was a bust for tours." It's not a question. Unc takes in the fat drizzle trickling through the pine trees and I feel the weight of his statement like a rock in the stomach.

"It was," I hedge, swallowing my last bite and bracing for his next question. I see it brewing.

"What do you do for business on rainy days?"

"Oh… we-" My brain stumbles as Uncle Mac moves past pleasantries with the grace of a Mack truck. It's a swift reminder of why I'm here.

"Let me stop you." He holds a hand up, sensing my mounting tension. Those stern lines on my uncle's brow soften. "I'm not starting our meeting on a negative. I'm wondering what you do with a *down* day."

"On down days, I take care of internal stuff: office work, marketing, computer crap… all the goodies that keep me inside when I want to be in the wild." I tick off the items on my fingers, enunciating my annoyance with the kindergarten level of micro-management.

Unc nods, listening like he isn't judging every word out of my mouth.

"A few weeks ago, I invested in a scheduling tool that's a complete life saver!" I'm proud of my initiative. To the point that I'm struggling not to dust the proverbial dirt off my shoulders. "Since then, the number of tours given in a week has tripled."

"Why's that?"

"No missed calls. No office assistant. The program feeds from the website straight to my calendar so there's less to manage."

"Sounds good," he concedes. "Anything that makes life easier is a win."

"Agree!" I slap a palm on the patio table, ecstatic with my apparent win. "I have more time for all the other stuff. Right now, I'm prepping for a meeting with the Dean of Animal Sciences. It's a huge win for *Wild Things*, in the middle of all the other progress, too."

"What type of meeting?"

"We talked about it last month, Unc."

"Yes. And if I remember correctly, I instructed you to focus on this tourism business before the other distractions."

"Unc."

"No, Wyatt. *You* applied for the clan's enrichment program for starting capital. That means you listen to our advice." Unc's coffee-colored eyes flash, intimidating me as if I'm still a young cub. But the adult in me doesn't require someone else's approval on my life... or my business.

As a shifter, he can hear my increased heart rate. He knows my temper is barely held in check, but Uncle Mac squeezes my forearm to ease the bite in his words. "Look. You're accountable to the clan until you pay off their investment. It's just how it is, son." A tired sigh follows the same argument we have every month. "This program sustains a future for Big Paw, but only if the next generation props it up... succeeds. I can't give you special lee-way, Wy."

"I know that, Unc." Resigned, I force patience to my voice. "All my actions benefit the business. Believe me. Rugged Tours is growing. We add new tours every month, like Caleb's fly-fishing tour. We just cram a ton of animal knowledge down their throats, as well. That way people learn how to avoid wild run-ins and keep everyone safe."

"How's your brother handling his new expectations?"

"It's Caleb... so yeah." I scramble for a way to not throw Caleb under the bus. "When he's not booked, he pulls office duty to stay out of trouble. We can't hire extra people yet... except an accountant. Oh. My. God! I need an accountant!"

Uncle Mac cracks up, his booming laugh turning his stubbled cheeks rosy. "Don't like numbers, huh?"

"Hell no! I get by," I admit. "But, mainly by running a tight ship money-wise. I'd rather get someone in who'd budget us for growth, and make sure I didn't have to do it."

"That's good, son."

My eyes lock on him across the table. "But Unc... you know my protection program is important, too." I search Uncle Mac for the slightest understanding. "Shifter numbers are dwindling. A lot of hunting accidents happen when we're mistaken for mountain bears. If I can make a small dent in unnecessary deaths, why not try?"

"I get it, Wy. As future Alpha, it's important you focus on the health of our species. Focusing only on money would lead to the clan's eventual downfall." Deep lines crease Mac's forehead, aging him before my eyes from the responsibility. "But it's a balance, son." The stressed pinch to his nose builds my dread for what's next from his mouth.

"On that matter, how's your dating life? You boys are older now—men—and not a one of you have found a mate, yet."

Yes, we have! My bear threatens to lash out against our elder's judgment. He's more than willing to claim our baffling mate.

"I'm barely thirty, Unc. I have time. Why are we talking about this, anyway?"

"Every month, our meeting sets a goal. Maybe this month should be about choices." I search his stormy eyes, sensing a hidden meaning I doubt I'll like. "Just remember Wyatt, when you choose a mate, choose right, my boy." He stands with a patronizing pat to my hand and disappears in his house.

What the hell does that mean?

My feet spring to motion before I can stop them, molten lava burns my blood, overpowering common sense. *Does the clan think they get a say in my mate now?*

In Uncle Mac's kitchen's doorway, I let my fingers dig grooves in the frame until the pain can dent my anger. He won't meet my eyes. Instead, an awkward silence suffocates the air between us.

Really?

When I can't take anymore, my impatience erupts. "What does that mean, Mac?" His lips pinch shut, but that side eye raises my hackles. It's what he's not saying that worries me. "Uncle, my mate is my mate. Fate, and no one else, has a say in that."

A red haze clouds my brain, but Uncle Mac rolls his eyes, immune to my anger. "Does it seriously need clarifying?" His voice pitches, waiting for my stiff nod. "You want to grow our shifter numbers?"

"Yes."

"Then, you choose a proper mate. A Black bear mate," he clarifies in case I lost brain function in the last hour. That chastising tone hits its target... I feel like a child.

"Unc... come on. Fate hasn't even sent you a mate. Why are you pushing to find mine?"

"Fate?" Laughter booms off the kitchen walls, breaking through the buzz in my ears. Uncle Mac bends at the waist, one hand braced on the stone countertop like I just said the most hilarious thing ever. "That's child's play, boy. This is leadership. Sacrifice."

"Fate or sacrifice... doesn't matter. In what world would anyone else get a say in my mate?"

"A mate is a choice, kid. In all these years, I've never come across a woman who made my bear's knees weak. That's just plain stupid! As future Alpha, I expect you to make this decision with your head, not by some misguided fairy tale."

Fairy Tale? I haven't seen many fated matches in my time… except for my parents. They were the gold standard, though; fated in life and death. Nothing less than that is good enough. I won't miss that kind of love because of some misguided sense of duty.

I know my mate!

My bear seethes just below the surface, his growl rolls to the surface, ricocheting through my head and off the walls of my uncle's cabin before I can stop it. Unc's laughter stops as he catches sight of my fingers splintering his door frame beneath them.

"Look! Wyatt. You're not a cub anymore." His threatening bark turns on me, anger distorting his features that mirrors my own. Our glowers lock—stubborn bear to stubborn bear.

Unc sighs. "Wyatt, producing young cubs is just as important as saving older ones. Focus on building your business, son. Solidify your place in the human world, for your family."

"I handle my business, Mac. The clan is taken care of and so is our future. As for my mate, who and when are solely my decision. Nothing's gonna change that!"

"Keep thinkin' that. You boys can sow your oats with the humans all you want, but before you take Alpha, an approved mate will be in place." His dark laughter drips with sarcasm, irking my nerves.

"What the fuck does that mean?"

"What do you think? Humans are dangerous when it comes to our secret. Your chosen mate better damn sure be Black bear if you want to protect this clan."

We can defeat him! My bear's temper flares. I drop my head, dragging in ragged breaths to shove my bear down so he doesn't try to jump our Alpha.

"What century are you living in?" I ask, my voice hoarse from trying to control the growl there. "Shifters have blended into the human world for ages. It's never threatened our protection before. What's the sudden issue with dating humans?"

"Wyatt! Less and less cubs are being born. Those humans dilute our blood pool, kid. We get weaker... we end up birthing fewer shifter cubs! Don't you get it?" Unc turns his back, walking to sit at his kitchen table like this conversation exhausts him. "Besides, you haven't found your mate yet. What do you care if I find one for you?"

We have! My bear stomps his feet, not liking this train of thought at all.

"My mate is my mate. No one's picking her but me!" I bellow, pissed at my uncle's calm facade in the face of his life-wrecking decree. My spiking anger worsens the headache I started this morning with.

At least my growl finally got a response from our Alpha. His back has jerked ramrod straight, finally recognizing the headstrong tendencies of my younger bear.

Uncle's eyes glow in warning. "Wyatt... son. Calm yourself. And your bear." He leans back precariously in his chair, not stopping the old-fashioned garbage spewing from his mouth. "I'm just looking out for your future... your position as Alpha. You create some half-breed or come home with a wolf—or God forbid, a cat—you'll be the disgrace of Big Paw Mountain."

My mouth gapes, shock distorting my vision as I lower myself in the chair beside him. "Unc, that is utter nonsense."

"Is it? Clan leadership's under scrutiny. The central committee has threatened to take over for years. They want to transition Alpha's out and rule by bear council. Dammit! I'm not gonna give them a reason to push that along." His voice lowers, checking his window like he expects to catch a peeping Tom.

After a few watchful minutes, Unc's eyes drift back to me, his calmness sending chills through the air. The only sign of Unc's internal stress is a bead of sweat rolling from his vanishing hairline.

"Uncle, I'm aware of the threats."

He mumbles something under his breath that even my shifter ears can't hear. It seems to have solidified a decision in him because a blink later and he's out of his chair, pacing.

An anxious tension circles the room, colored with a hint of sweat that finally shuts up my bear's incessant grumbling. I don't want to cause my uncle to have a heart attack and that redness under his beard worries me. He's been hell bent on training me as his successor these last few years, the natural order. But it's always been a one-day thing. Seeing Unc's stress painted like a Times Square billboard makes me wonder.

This meeting has gotten way off track.

Unc stops and turns to face me, arms crossed over his large bulk. A hulking stance to full height as he waves a hand in the air, our entire lunch boiling down to his next declaration. "As of now, passion projects are on hold, Wyatt." He cringes, like he dreads his next words. "And our mates... need to be Black bear proud, approved by leadership."

My bear rears to his hind legs, fury altering the priorities of man and beast. He's prepared to claw to the death. It forces me to stand, needing to move quick, to leash my bear before he loses control and embarrasses us both.

"Listen, Unc. I've always respected you as my Alpha. And I am beyond thankful to the clan for lending me starting capital on my business." I pause, knowing I damn well don't plan to follow that last decree. "Rugged Tours is my dream, but so are my conservation efforts. I'm happy to pay the clan it's ten percent for their management fund…"

"The cost is worth it, Wyatt. It's how we take care of our people."

"It is. But… I have limits, Uncle. I'm a man, not a puppet and there are freedoms in my life, you don't get to control."

"Those freedoms are not unlimited, my boy. We're responsible to our people. Accountable to our people, too."

"Yeah, I got it… future Alpha. I'm happy to contribute to our success. Our financial success." I shake my head, trying to find the right, appreciative words that will also help him understand.

"Great!" Unc claps his hands, cutting off my attempt to say more. He's on me in a second, ushering me out the front door with a firm hand, like our business is done for the day.

I huff, knowing there's no point in arguing more, but at least Mac stops on the porch, leaving me to sulk to my truck in dejected peace.

My confidence has been drop kicked to the gutter, but I'm fighting like hell to hold my head high which is hard when I accomplished absolutely nothing this morning. And when my lungs are smothered under grand expectations I have no plans to follow.

Even parked a distance away, Mac's level voice still follows me as I climb in the driver's seat. "Let's stay focused, my boy. We'll meet again next month and see how growth's coming... in all areas of your life."

I look to where he's standing, shadowed under the tall pines, his tell-tale frown pulling those partially graying eyebrows tight. Off to the side, the triplets watch our interaction, ever vigilant in their security patrol since returning from deployment. They must have hear our raised voices and prepared for backup.

While I'm happy my clan is hyper-vigilant with safety, I don't appreciate the extra eyes watching my every interaction. *I'm future Alpha dammit!*

Knowing when to call it quits, I wave a hand good-bye and back down his driveway. I'm eager to get off clan lands before my bear decides to make an appearance. His choices have been challenged and neither of us are happy about it. There's just nothing I can do about it... yet.

Chapter 10

♥

Wyatt

I'm still bristling a day later when I walk in my conservation meeting. But, I don't want my funk affecting BPAC—otherwise known as the Big Paw Active Conservation—so I deliberately shake my head, trying my best to clear the cobwebs leftover by my uncle. The cafeteria that doubles as an auditorium for our meetings isn't large enough for that much drama.

So far, the room's only about a third full. Distinguished members of our community squishing their butts in these tiny kid chairs. And no one complains because we use the town's elementary school for free.

A benefit I will adamantly deny earning by sweet talking the elderly secretary with donuts once a week.

Speaking of desserts... my nose picks up a sweet vanilla scent wafting from the snack table in the back. That's my first stop. I need coffee—and a treat—before the meeting starts. Especially a treat from Little Lucy's Pastry Shoppe.

Lucy donates refreshments to BPAC every month. She gets publicity for her bakery, and willing guinea pigs for new recipes. And we conserve overhead and focus donations where it counts... helping the animals. A win-win all around.

My stomach growls on the way to that back table, following my nose like a beacon.

Unfortunately, there're too many regulars here tonight stopping me from my favorite fringe benefit. Men from the neighborhood stop me for handshakes and trite weather conversation. My eyes dart to the back table. People are munching through that diminishing cookie tray while my brain struggles for an excuse to politely break away and get my own.

"Guys, I see someone I need to speak with. I'll catch y'all after the meeting."

Tossing a wave over my shoulder, I step away before they can answer and almost collide with a group of women I knew from high school—one of whom I dated. *No, thank you.* I plaster on a polite smile and a nod, but steer around the invitations to chat.

The problem is, the closer I get to the back and the cookies, the weaker that tantalizing vanilla scent is. I frown. There's only lemon cookies and mini chocolate tarts. So, where is the sweet vanilla that's drawing my nose?

Confused, I pour a cup of coffee and load it with cream and sugar until the muddied water is drinkable. Getting some passable coffee donated just moved itself up on my to-do list. I feel too guilty to ask Lucy so she doesn't have more coming from her bottom line, but this school provided crap has to go.

With pseudo coffee in hand, I scan the crowded rows of elementary school chairs until my eyes land on the last person I expected to see tonight. It can't be. In the third row, two dark-haired females, with olive skin, and matching almond-shaped eyes whisper over their own paper cups of coffee. And the vanilla puzzle locks in place.

Yes. My bear purrs immediately, lifting the haze blanketing my mood. *Our mate.*

For the first time in my thirty years, I don't know what to do. This beautiful female fries my brain cells. But I can't deny the inner pull of this woman—this human. And, after yesterday's meeting, I know our match is going to cause trouble.

Too bad my unruly cock couldn't care less about my issues. Or my twisting nerves. Not a single thing is convenient about claiming Evie, but my bear's ready for his mate.

And when Evie tosses her head back laughing, the entire room shifts on a tilt-a-whirl. It quiets every argument in my head, human versus shifter, clan responsibility... all of it.

Evie's beauty is the sun warming my body, brightening this drab room until I'm blinded to everything but my mate.

The searing flush that creeps up my neck creates a man on a mission. I grab two extra cookies on a napkin, honoring the lesson my dad taught me as a child. *Never show up empty-handed to woo a lady.* It puts a lot of pressure on a cookie... charm the lady who turns my system upside down. No big deal.

With cookies in hand, and about half my wits, I stalk up the aisle, eyes locked on that chair beside my lovely, tanned goddess. When I reach her row, Evie's honeyed vanilla scent whacks me in the face, and I don't know how I missed it.

"Hi, ladies," I call, trying my best to look smooth while lowering my too-large body in the tiny, plastic chair.

"Wyatt!" Evie's mouth gapes open in shock, giving me the slightest peek of a pink tongue I desperately want to taste.

"Cookie?" I smile, holding out my offerings between the two ladies. Evie's wide eyes lock on mine, drowning me in their chocolate depths, but she doesn't reach for the cookie.

Thankfully, Kayah saves me from awkward rejection and reaches around her sister to grab both cookies. Humor dances in her eyes when she wraps Evie's fingers around one like she's a toddler and needs guidance to eat. Despite the little one's laugh at our expense, I'm thankful for my surprising ally. She could have been just as pissed at me after Friday night. And I'm gonna need all the help I can get, here.

Evie's brows furrow but she still doesn't acknowledge the cookie in her hand. "Wyatt?" Her stunned voice makes me twist uncomfortably in my chair.

"Yes, ma'am." I grin, hoping my trusty dimple will entices my little vixen to call a truce after the mess I made with her at the bar. "I didn't expect to see you here tonight."

"I came with my sister," she challenges. "What are you doing here?"

"This is my group." I pause, wondering if there's a way for my next question not to piss her off. "I just thought you were pro-hunting. Why would you come to an animal protection meeting?"

"I can be pro-responsibility and pro-survival at the same time," she huffs, grinding out each word. Evie's voice is a touch defensive, but also... hurt. "I'm a vet. I'm not pro-poaching, for God's sakes."

Evie's miffed.

Her shoulders straighten, ears turning a bright shade of pink that, for some reason, I find incredibly exciting. Naturally, my eyes fall to her chest, fascinated by how it heaves under the struggle to calm her panting breaths.

Damn, my mate is sexy as hell with ruffled feathers.

My bear doesn't find it so cute. He roars for me to shut-the-hell-up.

You're upsetting our female.

Fine. As much as I enjoy watching Evie get all heated up, it's not the best method to earn her good graces.

Shifting tactics, I nod to the cookie in her hand. "It won't bite." I nudge the bottom of her hand, loving the sparks igniting where my finger grazes her smooth skin. "In fact, it works best when you take a bite and chew."

Evie buries her chuckle under a cough, but I count the win when she takes a bite, her lips twitching with a smile that she hides behind the cookie. And, then my pants become unholy torture when Evie moans.

"Oh my God! These are amazing!"

Yep, I'm erecting a statue for Lucy the baker in appreciation for Evie's face tasting the lemony goodness.

The sexiness of that throaty sound is thin ice for my sanity... and for my jeans tightening to an embarrassing level. Not a brilliant strategy for projecting responsible business owner to our community.

"Yeah... good." I swallow around the dryness in my throat, stretching both of my legs so I can discreetly shift the fabric at my groin, desperate for breathing room.

Even my palms have a thin coating of sweat watching Evie's pleasure. I rub them down my pant leg, hoping she won't notice, but those observant eyes track my movements. *Did she lick her lips? Was that because of the cookie or me?*

My voice catches on the hope, coming out throatier than I intend. "I didn't want you ladies to miss the best damn cookies in Talon."

Evie's responding smile chips away at the boulder that's hung around my neck all weekend. I have to grip one thigh to resist grabbing my mate. When Evie's eyes slide leisurely up my jeans in a trance, the relief is palpable. Does my presence affect her, like she affects me?

"I'm glad you did. We assumed they were stale lunchroom cookies." She shivers her shoulders comically, taking another bite. "It's our first meeting."

"Gotta appreciate a personal delivery, though," Kayah says, toasting her cookie in my direction.

My bear chuffs at the women's praise, but before we can elevate our little flirt-fest with Evie, the committee president taps his gavel against the podium on stage.

With the meeting brought to order, our gray-haired leader reads the minutes from last month and thanks our sponsors for the night. He announces tonight's agenda, with my name as speaker, and I hear Evie gasp beside me.

It takes an act of congress not to sweat again, but I can't stop myself from fidgeting in the chair. I've spoken at plenty of these things. I should not be nervous.

Sadly, my mental pep talk doesn't help when Evie's gaze is on the side of my face. She's too potent. My brain's stuck wondering what she's thinking. Does she like what she sees? Do I have cookie on my face? Right now, I'd trade some shifter speed for telepathy in a heartbeat.

As if by magnetic force, my eyes pull toward my mate, ignoring the president droning on from the stage. Evie's cheeks pink when she's caught staring, but it comforts my restlessness.

"You're speaking tonight?" She whispers, as the first guest takes the podium.

"I am. I'm presenting a proposal to the preservation board."

She smirks. "That's a lot of Ps." Her comment makes is hard to hide my laugh, but thankfully no one notices me being rude.

"If the board approves my trail and park suggestions, they'll budget the improvements for next year." Evie's head cocks to the side, but she's listening so I explain more in a whisper. "Basically, getting worked into the budget will drastically help my protection plan financially and make executing all the safety changes I want a hell of a lot easier."

She nods, and I can tell she wants to ask more, but we're distracted by a call to vote. I raise my hand for the aye's before turning back to Evie.

"I need to impress that guy over there, tonight." I point to the tweed blazer in the front row. "He's a dean at the university, and basically, the last sign off to get my program for conservation and safety accredited." Even I can't believe I'm this close to the finish line after so many years.

"Wow!" Evie's voice is low, but her eyes shine in awe. "That's amazing."

"Yeah?" A satisfied grin spreads my face, and I'm not gonna lie... my chest may puff a little bit with pride at her approval.

Before I can say more, Kayah clears her throat and I hear my name called from the stage. *Show time!*

"Wish me luck." I smile, honestly needing luck because butterflies have taken root in my stomach.

The burden of responsibility weighs heavy with this speech. My dreams are so close, but the anxiety of it all clouds my brain. The inevitable disappointment from Uncle Mac when he finds out I'm not giving up my 'passion-project' as he calls it. I'll catch a full reign of hell if he saw the many ways I'm ignoring his wishes tonight.

I have to put that all out of my head at the moment to be able to function. My legs are already numb climbing to the stage, but I draw strength from knowing I'm the responsible one, the mature one. I'm destined to be Alpha, but the world won't end if I take a moment to live for me too.

Sucking in a deep breath, I shake the president's hand and take his place at the podium. Curious eyes reflect from the audience, including the professor in the front row. There's a few bored faces, a few hyper-interested ones, but my eyes naturally seek Evie's. Her barely disguised lust rushes my blood south so fast I'm left dizzy.

With forced effort, I grip the wood podium for balance. and rip my eyes away to focus on my goal. *Knock this one out, then you can move to the next.*

"Ladies and gentlemen..." I pause, laying my most charming smile on the crowd. "I'd like to thank everyone here for your continued support for animal rights, protection, and education. I always like to start my time with a joke, so…" I rub my hands together for effect. "What's a grizzly bear's favorite sandwich?"

Murmurs work through the audience, a few younger kids calling guesses, but after a few beats I help them out. "Growled cheese sandwiches." I grin at the obligatory laughter and the few shaking heads that roll through the audience. "OK, OK. Sorry for the 'cheesy' joke." I can't help but laugh at that one myself, immediately feeling a release of stress.

"For those of you who don't know me, I run Smoky Mountain Rugged Tours. We provide fun, exciting excursions on the mountain, but my goal is not to become another tourist attraction. We educate our guests, make them knowledgeable about safety precautions, wildlife protection… avoidance. The importance of every creature in the life cycle of our mountain. I believe it's the best way we can protect our native animals and their dwindling numbers."

I can count on these people to feel me here. Throwing some of the shocking number of useless bear deaths at them, in our state alone, has a murmur working through the crowd.

My eyes fall to the dean and find him jotting in a notepad. I hope he understands the staggering amount of progress still needed and why approving the college course is important.

But people are getting fidgety from sitting so long. It's a win just to have the information out there. I smile, risking a glance at Evie. Her contemplative expression makes me uneasy. I look away, already uncharacteristically nervous in front of this beautiful woman.

Ms. Beachum, our town busybody, sends me a wink from the front row. Her gaudy costume jewelry pokes from under her massive, beehive hairdo. My face fights to hide the smile at seeing her here. That one targeted invite will spread the word on my program before her next beauty shop appointment.

Those well-meaning grandmas, with their old lady hairdos and nosy tendencies, are part of why I love this town; it's a tight-knit, smothering web of support.

With a wave to my support system, I thank the audience and work my way off stage to polite applause. *Hey, at least I didn't put anyone to sleep.* Win number one.

Now with my eyes on Evie, I'm imagining win number two before the night's up. Her eyes sparkle with pride. "Great job," she whispers, and I exhale, feeling the first glimpse of hope I've had in days.

Mentally, I pray the other speakers to hurry along. There's a vote on a budget change for the next quarter, and then, *Hallelujah*, the meeting is over.

Gradually, the applause dies down, and the girls stand, waiting for the clumps of people who crowd toward the exit. A few members stay behind, straightening the lunch tables and chairs, a task we rotate, and I have never thanked the stars more that tonight's not my night.

"I'll walk you out," I offer, enjoying the secretive elbow from Kayah that Evie tries to slap away.

I steer them clear of distracting conversations, not wanting to get pulled from my second goal tonight. It's not the smartest business strategy, but my bear doesn't care. His instincts are happy to walk the girls through the dark parking lot at this hour.

We need to protect our mate.

When we walk through the double metal doors that exit the school, I'm happy we did. Evie tilts the phone by her side, glancing nonchalantly toward her hand. For some reason, the aloofness feels false, but the frown that strains the corner of her pretty eyes doesn't. I hope she's not looking at the time to run off fast.

"Everything OK?"

"Sure." Her answer's distracted, but I can't call that out right now. "We're this way," she says, noticing her sister's already ahead of us in the parking lot.

I need to thank Little One for noticing I wanted a minute alone with her sister. When the girl does peek over her shoulder to check on our progress, I shoot her a thankful grin. This almost feels like having a chaperon as a love-sick teenager, but I'm not even embarrassed by that if it gets me closer to my mate.

"So, listen... about the other night..." We both laugh when we talk over each other.

"I'm sorry," I start again, desperate for her to understand. "I was an ass to your friend, and I interrupted your fun night by antagonizing him." I reach for Evie's hand, praying she doesn't pull away. "I'm just sorry for how it all ended. It's not an excuse, but I can't explain what comes over me when you're around." I growl, stepping closer. "You... affect me."

She doesn't look angry, and she doesn't back up, so I bend a bit to get a better look at those shadowed eyes.

My cock throbs from being this close to the vanilla scent my bear craves. I'd love nothing more than to lift those muscled thighs and wrap her fully around me, but I'll take what I can for now. With another step, I'm invading her space, thankful she doesn't push me away. I hear her heartbeat rush the closer I get. The throb of it matches the pulse in my shaft. It's hard to ignore. Especially when the pressure of my zipper is the only thing preventing me from losing control.

Go slow, man. Don't scare her.

Evie's eyes fall to our connected hands where I squeeze, wanting to give her comfort. "You do something to me too," she admits, that husky voice striking me low in the stomach.

In the darkness, I see her sister's already climbed in their car. She's giving us a moment alone, and though I barely know her, she's my best friend in this very moment.

Gently, I lift her chin with one finger, yearning for those chocolate pools to be on me. I don't shy away from her need, from our connection. She's mine... even if she doesn't know it yet.

"Could I have your number tonight? That way, if I need to apologize, I don't have to wait through a weekend of torture before I get to do it?"

She chuckles, a hint of seduction mixing with the mischief in her eyes. "Maybe, don't be an ass and you won't have to apologize." Her tone has gained that spitfire quality that challenged me on the trail.

"Touché," I laugh, handing over my phone before she can talk herself out of giving me those ten little digits. She eyes my grin with narrowed eyes.

"You think you won, don't you, big guy?" I say nothing. I know I won.

After she types her number, I pocket the thing, preferring to give Evie my full attention. "I'll text you when I get home, so you'll have mine, and hopefully our next meeting won't be by chance?"

I hate how my voice rises at the end of that sentence, and I force a masculine cough to clear it up. Still, my heart's lighter as we continue the short walk to her car.

Evie's all smiles too, though she startles when I open her passenger door and we find Kayah leaning across the console. She beams sweetly at the two of us, like she hasn't been waiting five minutes for us to finish our talk.

Evie giggles, but rolls her eyes as she slides into the low bucket seat. My cock stirs when her skirt rides up those shapely legs and gives me one hell of a view of under the moonlight.

A strangled sound leaves my throat, but I squeeze the cold metal roof to relieve the arousal flooding my system. Especially since my groin is eye-level with Evie's face... another thought I absolutely cannot process. *Baseball, baseball, men in speedos, gangrene toenails.*

Ugh! It's straight torture controlling myself. My Black bear's barking uncontrollably behind my eyes. He want to lay claim. And, that right there means I need to get out of here.

Backing my lower half behind the door, I use it to hide while Evie buckles her seatbelt.

"You ladies have plans Thursday night?" *I need a redo of last weekend.*

Evie glances at her sister questioningly. "I don't think so-."

"Would y'all like to join me and the guys for trivia night Thursday? Same bar; different crowd. The Growler a lot less 'party' on Thursdays." I air quote, feeling like a dumb ass, and wait through that silent eyeball argument sisters do. My patience frays the longer they make twisted faces at each other. And, I'll only admit it's slightly adorable if they return a favorable verdict.

"Sure, sounds like fun," Kayah agrees over Evie.

Evie nods my way, but flattens me with warning eyes. "As long as everyone's good with any friends that decide to join. You know... since it's a group thing."

"Point taken." I hold my left hand up and cross my heart with the other like we're kids. "Best behavior. I promise." I need to capture the heat that flared between us a few moments ago, the momentum, but it's not progress I can make tonight. I have representatives from the university waiting to talk business with me. I can't let that slide, no matter how much I wish I could right now.

"Evie, I will text you tonight. Drive safe," I call just before closing her door. I watch the ladies drive away, wondering if they'll talk about me on the way home. The thrill of Evie going to bed with me on her mind hits me deep, but for now, I have to push those thoughts aside and go present my animals.

Chapter 11

♥

Evie

By Thursday afternoon, I've riled myself into a ball of nerves over trivia night.

One minute, I'm thinking about Wyatt's dimples, his love of animals... that sexy swoop of hair that curls a little wildly over his ears. A second later, I'm remembering his caveman act on Friday night.

"I don't think we should go," I repeat for the third time. Kayah doesn't understand how nervous Wyatt makes me. She thinks my flustered state is cute. I don't.

Something odd comes over me around Wyatt. I lose control... like an invisible force takes over my body. It fuzzes up my brain, and all common sense flies out the window. It's not normal. Ama's the boy-crazed sister, not me.

"Oh, we're going," Kayah says adamantly. "Other people will be there... like me." She grins from the door of our closet before going back to rifling through hangers. "Besides, it's a public place. You'll have a buffer so you won't cave and rip Wyatt's butt-hugging jeans off to see what's underneath."

I ignore my sister's laughter, and her all-to-accurate prediction of my worries, in favor of applying a topcoat to my pedicure. She's singing 'K-I-S-S-I-N-G' from the closet, all off-key falsetto, when my phone dings with a text. I've hated that notification this week.

When I didn't show up for work on Monday, the texts and voicemails increased. It's been hard burying my head in the sand, but I'm enjoying the little bubble I've created to ignore it all. If Michaels won't listen to my request for time off, when I have so much built up anyway, then he deserves exactly what he gave me the last few years… darkness.

Another ding. What if it's Wyatt checking on tonight?

Gah! There's a seesaw of excitement and dread churning my stomach. It's so unlike me. This whole week I've felt like a wishy-washy, overly emotional mess.

"So, do you want to invite Ash and Ama?" Kayah's voice breaks through my mental whining. I haven't exactly been paying attention to my little sister rambling like an excited pre-teen getting ready for a first date.

Kayah's off on a tangent, describing the difference in the wine sipper crowd at the Growler and the beer guzzlers on Friday nights. I don't care about the other people, I just need something to wear that'll fit in beside the sexiest man on the mountain. Last week, Wyatt's button up shirt made my mouth water. The way it hugged those solid biceps, and cupped the lines of his chest...

"Evelyn Amos! Are you listening to me?" *Snap!* I wasn't. I'm too busy wondering if it takes two hands to wrap Wyatt's bicep.

"I'm sorry, Ky. I'm a little distracted," I say, cringing. I desperately hope my face isn't beet red, but I keep my eyes focused on painting my last toe just in case.

Kayah sighs as I cap my dark purple polish. I don't want to accidentally spill it on the quilt Gran made me for my tenth birthday. It's a prized possession; one I hated leaving behind after college, but I thought my move would seem too final if I took it to Knoxville.

"Yeah, serious, E. You're no help tonight." Kayah's eyes roll dramatically, one hand cocked on her hip, but the girl can't hold a scowl long. Her face cracks into a goofy smile, and with a whip of her ponytail, she's back to rifling through my clothes. "What are you going to wear?"

Ugh! I flop backwards on the bed. "Clothes are Ama's world, Ky, not mine. You should go raid her closet... and bring something back for me."

"Hey! I'm no slouch."

I laugh at her protest, cutting my eyes in a 'get real' look where her face pokes from the closet. "Of course not, but you have... teacher style."

"What!" She screeches. "Take that back. It's rude."

I flinch, but before I can stop her, my little sister has tackled me to the bed, pinning my arms under her knees. The jolt knocks a bark of laughter from me that grows the harder Kayah bounces on my chest.

"Gah! Woman!" *Gasp.* "What. Is. Wrong. With you." Kayah bounces me after every word, giggles shaking her tiny frame until we both have tears rolling down our faces—or for me, rolling into my hair. "You're going to ruin my nails, you pip squeak!" My insult doesn't have much impact with my arms pinned. She's obviously strong enough that I can't toss her off. *When did that happen?*

For extra torture, Kayah leans over my head, digging those bony little fingers into my ribcage. "Take it back or I won't stop." *Tickle.* "Take it back." *Bounce.* "Take it back or I'm sitting on you for a week," she insists, squeezes her knees tighter as she bounces harder.

We crack up harder, her squeals and my screams batting for dominance. Eventually, Kayah's laughing so hard that a rope of her drool drips on my forehead and I screech, bucking until I make some wiggle room to slide out.

"*Ah!* Oh my God. I take it back! Seriously!" I gasp for oxygen under the tiny mercenary on my bed. "Truce, you pint-sized ninja."

Kayah shoots me an evil eye but hops off my chest to sit cross-legged on the bed. She dusts fake dirt crumbs off her shoulders with a satisfied grin on her face.

I'm free to wipe the tears and my sister's saliva from my face. I probably shouldn't target the fact that Kayah hates when we pick on her nun-like style, but this is the most I've laughed in years. Even though I'm breathing like a pneumonia patient running a marathon.

Finally, when I'm able to breathe again, I right myself on the bed. "Look, fashion aside, I'm not sure tonight's a good idea."

"Of course, it is. You're going!" Kayah crosses her arms stubbornly just as the bedroom door flies open.

"What the hell's going on in here?" Ama glares at us, her face pinched in a grumpy picture of annoyance. "We could hear your craziness all the way in the kitchen."

Resentful eyes dart between Kayah and I sitting on my bed, taking in our red faces and tear-stained cheeks. *Is Ama miffed we're having a good time?*

"What are you doing here?" I glance at my bedside clock. "Shouldn't you be getting ready for work?" I don't care if I sound rude at this point. My sister's constant combativeness is getting on my nerves. Why can't she just come in and join the fun instead of ruining it?

"Well... in case you don't remember, the festival's tomorrow."

Like I'd forget something this important to our family.

She crosses her arms, leaning against my door frame. Her body looks relaxed, but it hasn't shared the message with her face. "I was here for my last fitting with Ma. And I don't have to be at work for another hour, thank you very much."

Ama's snide voice and mocking twist of her face make her seem ten years younger than Kayah, even though she's three years older.

Sometimes, I'd love to tell her that I'd show more interest in her life if every conversation wasn't a battle. Even when she shows actual pride for the New Moon Ceremony, it's laced with disdain for me. That sad thought breaks my already stressed-out heart. I feel bad for thinking so negatively about Ama sometimes, until her bragging starts again. Then I'm back to square one.

"You know, our dance is going to be the best this year! Last year was great and all, but all the practice we put in, the months of work... this New Moon is going to be the best one yet."

There it is. She has to drop that snarky comment, how they practiced for *'months'*, just to point out how much she's doing, and how little I am.

"That's great," I say, keeping my voice even. "I can't wait to see it."
See, Mama, I can be peaceful with Ama.

It feels like a tiny win for adulting on my part. Even more seeing Ama's blank look. Her gloating pauses, confusion swirling those smoky eyes. The slight cock of her head looks like she's waiting for a punch line. There isn't one.

With a sigh, she takes the olive branch for what it is, inviting herself in to sit on our old homework desk. "So, what had you guys acting like idiots in here?"

Kayah and I share a look, but being the nicer sister, Kayah answers anyway. "I was harassing Evie for trying to back out of her date tonight." I pop Kayah's crossed legs for giving Ama ammo.

"Date!" Ama shrieks, the high pitch ringing my ears.

"Not a date." I shake my head. "We're going to trivia night as a group thing, and I'm having second thoughts." I shrug like the whole night's no big deal, hoping Ama drops the conversation.

"No..." Kayah cuts in. "She's chickening out from seeing the hottie that's all over her, and I won't let her do it." Kayah's eyes are victorious.

She thinks Ama's going to help her side of the argument. "It's about time you went on a date instead of working all the time."

"Like you're one to talk. When was the last date you went on?" My voice is sharper than I intend, but dammit, I'm annoyed she's airing my business in front of Ama.

Kayah shrugs. "I get out."

Ama and I both look at our baby sister like she's grown dragon scales, and laughter cracks both of our shocked faces before we realize what we're doing. Ama grabs her stomach, letting the humor carry her away, even after I freeze mid-laugh. Seeing the hurt on Kayah's face, and knowing her social life lacks as much substance as mine does, stops me. I can't upset the *one sister* I get along with.

"What?" Kayah grumbles, her shoulders tightened defensively. "Y'all don't know what I do." She points accusingly at Ama. "You're always busy." She shifts that pointy finger to me. "And you... you're not here."

We both gawk at Kayah, feeling the sledgehammer of her accusations. She's the baby by eight years, and we've picked right back up on this trip like we always do, but I have a feeling Kayah feels my absence more than she lets on.

"Well, we're here now," Ama points out, glancing at me from the corner of her eye. She sucks in a breath like the next sentence is painful. "Tell me about the date."

"Not a date," I groan, slapping my knee for emphasis. "A guy asked *us both* to come to trivia night. That's it. Nothing special." Kayah chuckles under her breath.

"Yeah, nothing special at all," she mocks is a hyper-sarcastic voice. "Only possibly *the* sexiest man on the mountain who looks at Evie like he wants to eat her for dessert... but, nope... nothing special."

I feel my face redden and go to bop Kayah again, but she hops out of my reach too fast, giggling.

"Why would some hot dude want the brainiac?" Ama asks, seeming honestly confused, which is insulting.

I stop our playful battle. The cold pit in my stomach sucking all the joy out of our earlier truce. I won't admit out loud that those exact thoughts are a major reason I want to cancel.

Sure, I'm affected by Wyatt—the man is gorgeous—but where can it lead? He either wants a booty call, which is not exactly my thing, or he's going to realize I'm a brainy dork and I'll bore him to death. *Great!*

Even if, by some miracle, the super hottie was legitimately interested in me and we hit it off, then what? I don't live here. I'm hiding out... temporarily. Before my life blew up, I had zero plans to live on this mountain full time. I don't fit here anymore.

Do I?

"Ama," I grind out, shoving her comments to the back of my mind. "Just because you've been under every single man on this mountain— and probably some married ones too—doesn't mean there's not a man left who wants quality." I despise nastiness, but it's the only card that'll get to her.

And I'm tired of pretty girls looking down on me for being smart. That shouldn't pass outside of teenage hormones!

She snorts. "So, you and 'hot guy' are going to nerd night at a bar? Fun..." she drawls sarcastically, hopping off my desk and walking to the door. I guess sibling pleasantries are over.

"You know, I may not spend hours on my appearance, Ama, but I'm not a troll, for God's sake!"

Ama's eyes roll to the ceiling when she pauses, her hand gripping the door. She looks to be waging an internal war with herself. After a few seconds, she turns, her expression guarded. She's holding back.

Before whatever venom she's holding lets lose, I offer a false smile and a light-hearted finger wave. I don't want Ama seeing how much her comments sour my mood.

The chime of my cell phone on the bedside table distracts us both. I lean over and unplug the thing from its charger, using the excuse to end our unpleasant conversation. When I see Dr. Michael's number flashing, I debate which evil is easier to deal with... for a brief second.

I need everyone out.

Fixing Ama with my best 'I don't have time for this' look, I do my best to get her out of the room. "Look, if you can get over your jealousy by tonight, feel free to join us at the Growler. Wyatt's friends will be there. Maybe one of them can show you how to have fun while vertical."

Oh, if eyes could kill, I'd be dead right now.

"I can have vertical fun, big sis... vertical, horizontal, and sometimes upside down," she snarls, her eyes forming glaciers with every syllable.

My phone rings again, but I discreetly push ignore, still trying to get Ama out of the room. I can only deal with one drama at a time. With Michaels calling repeatedly, I know he sees through my ruse of a family emergency. I know, he knows, I know.

Crap! My brain's running in circles, now.

Ama needs to leave before I break down in tears from too much stress. The sting already burns my eyes, so I keep my head down, hoping she'll take the clue. When a text chimes in my hand, then another, and again, I bend my knees up and rest my forehead against them. My fingers fly, pretending to answer the texts that won't go away, but the tears get harder to fight. If Ama doesn't walk out of here this minute, she's going to get a show and I may blow what little sanity I have left.

"Ugh, fine! If you're going to ignore me, I'm out!" Ama stomps her foot in full tantrum-mode. I glance up briefly, shocked that a twenty-five-year-old woman stands in front of me with her hands on her hips like a pouty kid. Seems our middle sis has a sensitive spot. Jan Brady

suddenly pops into my head and I wish I had the ovaries to call out...
Marsha, Marsha, Marsha.

Instead of humor, I go for bitchy, knowing it'll work better. "What are you four, Ama?" My voice's thick with unshed tears, but Ama doesn't notice. Does she honestly think I'm going to be warm and fuzzy after that nastiness she was just spewing?

"Really?" A scowl creases Ama's otherwise pretty face.

"I'm out too," Kayah interrupts, grabbing her robe from behind the door. Crap, I forgot she was here. "I need to shower, and yes," she points my way. "We are going tonight, so after I shower, you're hopping your nervous little tush in, too."

Kayah's carefree nature distracts me enough to give her a smile and a salute. "Yes, ma'am." I'd agree to anything right now to get my sisters out of the room, but I am honestly thankful to have Kayah's good heart in my life.

When she walks out, Ama's glare is the only obstacle left. "What?" I throw my hands in the air, hoping she takes the hint.

"Nothing." Ama's face drops, dejected. I almost feel bad for lashing out until she opens her mouth again. "You know, Evie. I'm not sure why you came home if all you're gonna do is to sit on your phone all day."

My mouth drops, but before I can respond, she's gone. Probably off to complain to mama. She always claimed that Kayah and I were mean to her in high school. We weren't.

How long can I even stay in this house? I can't ignore the family drama. Not to mention the fact I'm sleeping in the same twin bed I've had my whole life, in the same bedroom, with the same purple lace curtains, the same pictures hanging on the wall.

It's too much.

I stare at my phone, wondering how the thing became my enemy. How its chime became a Pavlov tick that makes me want to tuck tail and hide. *Come on, Eveline. You're an adult. Deal with your life already!*

Hitting the voicemail icon takes more courage than ever before, but ignoring the doc hasn't made him, or his poor decisions, go away. And, just because I'm still not sure what to do, or how to go to the cops, doesn't mean life isn't still rolling along.

My biggest issue is reconciling the man who gave me my first real job, the one who said he had faith in me, that he'd support me owning my own clinic one day, with one who would willingly work with criminals. My brain knows I shouldn't feel guilty about turning Michaels in, but it's eating me alive. I guess that's why I've waited so long.

Maybe that betrayal's why this all hurts so much.

The more I think about it, the more validated I feel taking this time off. It's the first break I've had in ten years. Who cares if I don't work for Dr. Michaels anymore? I still have my license. I can still help animals. It's not a complete loss. There's a new clinic close to my apartment in Knoxville. I can apply there.

For once in my adult life, I have no idea what tomorrow holds and it's terrifying... in such an exhilarating way. That optimism lasts the whole thirty seconds it takes for my phone to load the first missed call.

Doctor Amos... Eveline. Call me immediately.

A loud thud through the phone spooks me and I jump, even though I'm at home, safely sitting on my childhood bed. The sound flashes me back to the bones crunching in Dr. Michaels office a week ago. My hands shake, but I hit save on that one in case I need it for evidence. I'm not sure Michaels deserves whatever punishment he's getting, but neither do I, and with every call I feel dragged in deeper.

Eveline! The panicked way Doctor Michaels shrieks my name bolts me upright. My back's rigid as I hug the phone to my ear, rocking through the doctor's ragged breathing. When he comes back on the line his normally nasal slang is scratchy, roughened with pain. *I need you in the office. We have to talk. There... there are things to deal with.* Slam. The line goes dead.

Every logical part of my brain screams to run away, to ignore his calls, go to the cops... disappear. Honestly, my resignation should already be on his desk, but I'm hitting a brick wall, trying to calculate the safest exit strategy.

How involved was Michaels with these people? And exactly how dangerous are they? The guy who watched me drive away knew I heard something... that much was obvious. But how hard would it be for them to find me? My apartment address is on file, but did I put a next of kin? My last known address?

Shit! I did. Why wouldn't I?

The thought pours concrete inside my veins, tension strangling my muscles as I click voicemail after voicemail, each one more desperate than the last. Eventually, all I hear is my own blood pounding through my temples. A seizing panic takes over, rocketing me off the bed to pace. I need action.

Listening to a week's worth of voicemails in one sitting may have been too much. Each message escalated from the one before. What started with professional coercion, shifted to threats on my job, and flat out bribery for my return. But the last few pitchy, panicked ones scare the hell out of me.

Have I brought danger to my family?

Kayah rushes through the door after her shower, startling a scream from my lungs. She pauses when she registers the angst on my face, but at least she interrupted those chilling thoughts. Her motions slow down from the hyper speed she entered with, that sweet smile going a long way to soothe my frantic pacing.

"So... I don't see a pile of hair extensions and fake nails on the floor. Did Ama leave peacefully?" Her joke muffles under the drumbeat in my head, but I smile anyway, hoping it doesn't look as painful as it feels. "Don't scrunch your eyebrows so much, E. I'll find you something hot to wear without Ama."

Kayah prances off to our closet with a wink, thinking I'm stressed over some irrelevant bitching from our middle sister.

Gah! If I don't do something with this Olympic-sized pool of guilt, I'll never survive tonight. My fingers have gone numb from squeezing the phone. I toss the time-bomb on my bed, knowing what I need to do.

Tonight, I suck it up and go through the motions for my sister. Tomorrow, I'll get to work fixing this fuck up I brought to my family's doorstep.

I swear it!

Chapter 12

Wyatt

Waiting in a bar has never been such an exercise in torture.

We're waiting for our mate.

If she shows up. I remind my bear.

Caleb and I snagged a table for six near the large picture window. The sun may have set hours ago, but with no clouds in the sky you're able to see every star off the edge of the mountain. It creates a spectacular illusion of flying through the heavens from this height.

I fixate on Ursa Major, remember how my brothers and I would fight over who got to be major and who had to be minor when we'd traipse the woods and play pretend as cubs at night.

The thought has me chuckling when I turn back to Caleb and Jax. They're griping about the recent influx of drugs on the outskirts of town. Seems their meeting with my uncle this afternoon got interrupted by our security team after they had a public run in with a meth head in town. Worry has sent both of my boys spiraling.

Crime problems in the poorer sections of small towns are typical, but we try to keep that kind of riff-raff out of our area. Except, I can't find a single brain cell that cares at the moment. The bar entrance is my sole focus. Every time it opens, I hope it's the one long haired beauty I'm waiting for.

I swear tonight will be different.

"Dude, chill!" My brother grumbles when I swivel my chair again.

It drags my gaze back to the table, and I meet Caleb's lifted eyebrow with one of my own. He laughs, circling a finger in the air to signal the server for another round. I've obviously been distracted. My half-full beer has condensation spreading underneath it from the ale warming to room temperature.

"What?" I bark, irritated by the mocking smirk on my brother's face.

"You sippin' tea, tonight?"

"I have a date coming." My defensive answer hangs their mouths open like I'm being ridiculous. Granted… we don't bring dates around the group. Women have been too temporary to make the effort, but it's happening tonight. Sue me.

"Yeah, well… good for you, but chill out, man." Jax knocks his bulky shoulder into mine, easing some of the stress sitting there.

Wincing, I confess, "sorry, I'm a little excited, J. It's making me twitchy."

Evie and I texted a few times this week, nothing earth shattering, and she was always slow to respond, but I loved having a little piece of her when we were apart.

"You're wiggling again," Caleb points out. "It looks like you got a rash or something, bro. Stop it."

"I am not wiggling."

"You are," he says with a scowl. "You look desperate."

"Don't be an ass," I warn, my ears cringing when someone taps the mic on stage. *Shit! She's not here.*

I didn't confirm with Evie today, but yesterday everything was fine. She wouldn't change her mind in one day, would she?

"Ladies and gentlemen… I'm Sir Tricks-a-lot. Here to get the party started, questions rolling, and beer flowing. Y'all ready for another round of Growler Games?" A rowdy cheer booms from the crowd, encouraging the corny MC's Price is Right style voice. "First up, let's go over the prizes for our lucky winners..." Our potbellied entertainment reads the list of donated prizes, thanking each sponsor with a pun or dirty joke.

Tonight's entry fee benefits the Boys and Girls Club, which is great and all, but a little out of place with the naughty-limerick guy prancing across the stage. At least his corniness is distracting against the well of disappointment in my chest.

Just as the guy gets to the rules of the game—no cell phones, no peeking, no mid-question trips to the restroom—a soft hand lands on my shoulder. It practically rockets my ass off the seat and the hand jerks back quickly, as if burned.

My bear growls his annoyance, but I'm not sure if it's from being startled or that I'm acting like a fifteen-year-old virgin.

"I'm so sorry." That angelic voice sooths my ruffled fur and I turn in my chair to find Evie's doe eyes staring at me with timid humor. She's trying very hard not to laugh.

But she's here. My bear circles, prancing in my mind's eyes for a piece of her attention.

"I'm sorry." I start, feeling myself blush under the dark-lit bar lights, which I hope hides any evidence. "I was looking for you the other way." I realize how dorky that sounds, but I can't seem to care.

"Yeah, we uh... we came through the back entrance. That front lot is packed," she chuckles nervously and looks around the room. "Is trivia night always so crowded?" Her sister ignores our awkwardness and slides in the chair across from me, laying a beaming smile on my brother and Jax.

The tiny one introduce herself, holding her hand out for a polite shake. Excitement flares in Jax's eyes, but Caleb... Caleb looks absolutely gobsmacked. I watch fascinated while pulling out Evie's chair beside me. The shy smile on her face triggers my protective instincts, overwhelming any common sense left in my head with an overwhelming urge to hover.

"Dude… introduce us," Jax prods, extending a hand toward Evie. I growl a warning in his direction that catching Evie's attention. She stares flabbergasted, and I realize I hadn't confined the sound to my head.

Clearing my throat, I try to cool my embarrassment—and my head—while introducing my mate to what amounts to half of my family.

Caleb being Caleb, wiggles his brows obscenely, making me slide closer and rest my hand on the lower curve of Evie's back. She's mine and I've got no time for his games. Yes, he's my brother, but I'll battle anyone in this room to show who has claim here. And annoying little shit that he is, my brother gets what I'm dishing out, and laughs at me for it.

Behave. My bear growls at him through our subconscious link. This time Caleb physically laughs out loud and I narrow my eyes in warning.

"Nice to meet you ladies," my brother says instead with a nod of his non-existent cowboy hat. His grin is still mischievous, even if he's outwardly polite.

When Caleb's like this, his grin is hard to resist, but I still wish he weren't across the table so I could pop him upside that mop top of a head. But if I did that, I'd look like the bad guy—a giant no-no after last week's fiasco. *Do not be a douche. Do not be a douche.*

My bear doesn't care if my brother's pulling my chain though. He can't resist tucking Evie into the crook of my arm, preferring her body close to us and protected. Hell… our mate's sweet honeyed-vanilla beats the stench of beer any day.

I glance at Evie, who's turned into a glorious, ripened strawberry. But she doesn't protest my high-handed move, only averts her eyes to the rest of the table trying to hide her darkened cheeks. The corner of her lips quirk when she sees that Jax, my very handsome best friend, is laying on a pretty thick charm for her sister, making Kayah to cover in a pretty blush as well.

Caleb notices too and frowns, shifting focus to Evie's little sister, as well. Either he's growing bored with torturing me, or he dislikes the interest Kayah's showing to Jax.

Neither of those two notice our attention. They've slipped into their own world, ignoring all of us, including Caleb, who's shooting daggers at Jax every time he smiles at Kayah. Both men are eying the prim little female like she's wearing stripper glitter underneath that sleeveless turtleneck.

"OK, folks. Let the games begin!" Shit! We're way behind on our setup.

Brielle, one of the newer waitresses, drops off a score card for our team's name and another stack of square papers where we'll write our answers. That gets everyone's attention and now names are being thrown rapid-fire across the table. With Evie distracted by my idiot friends and their silly name suggestions, I have free access to study her beauty.

My eyes immediately fall to the curve of hip wrapped in a snug blue-jean skirt. It stops just above her knee, exposing a sensuous line of calf where her legs cross. The tight fabric calls to my hand, a siren of temptation only controlled because I can't help notice how Evie's foot bounces anxiously in those sexy little bootie things under the table.

"Thumb wrestle?" Kayah's voice breaks into my over-stimulated fixation on Evie's lower half.

I look up confused to find Evie shucking her outer corduroy jacket like a prized-fighter entering the ring. Her fingers link with Kayah's, ready for battle, but Evie's face flushes with an adorable bashfulness when she looks my way. I grin when the giggles take over, lighting up her face, and she shrugs.

"Winner gets to write the answer," Kayah states for my benefit. I guess she noticed I hadn't been paying attention after all. I smile at my mate, but now with her feminine perfection laid out in front of me, I'm even more distracted.

The way Evie's long hair curls around her shoulders in thick, black waves. The way it kisses the tanned skin peaking from that tank top. It all tempts my bear, who wants to nuzzle the soft lines of her shoulder and lose himself in her scent. With every turn of Evie's head, a waft of her delicious shampoo hits my nose, making my cock stand up and take notice.

God... what would she look like waking up in the morning, her scent all over my bed? Her hair would be wild from my hands, rumpled from a night of rolling around on my pillow. She'd be wearing my shirt, but it'd fall around those sexy thighs on her much smaller frame. There's something about a woman wearing her man's shirt, covered in his smell. It makes us primal. So primal that the blood flow to my cock is about to betray my train of thought.

Mmm, I could devour this woman. My bear is so riled. He sounds hungry, not horny.

Down, boy!

All the blood has left my brain and headed south which makes it hard to control my inner beast. The only thing helping is the fact that my dark-wash jeans are strangling my cock. I dressed to look good for Evie tonight, but this constricting material is not my favorite.

Compression underwear might be a good investment around this woman. At least those would be soft. I don't have any because I've never had such a problem controlling myself or my bear before. This is all so new.

It's imperative he doesn't gain too much control here or his aggressiveness could scare Evie off. She's human. She doesn't know of fated mates or how hard it is to deny my need for her. By the time she sits back, having decided on our name and responsibilities, I'm panting.

I go to tuck my arm back around her, when Evie's body jerks, waving her hand high to get someone's attention at the door. My back stiffens involuntarily when I see who that someone is.

"Be nice," she murmurs under her breath, landing a slap of warning against my stomach.

I cough in surprise, though her tiny hand does little more than tickle. But when I peer into those deep, beguiling eyes that I would do anything for, my smile is for Evie alone. Like we're the only two people in the room. Still... part of me wishes to God that we had a four-top.

As it is, there's plenty of room for Ash to join us, which I knew was a possibility after Evie's comment on Tuesday. But I secretly hoped he'd still be too pissed to come.

While Evie introduces Ash to the table, Kayah runs our name-card for The Grizzly Gang to the judges. I extend my hand to Ash, hoping to look like the bigger man... a peace offering. It works in my favor when the kid looks at it with a mix of disdain and disbelief playing off his features. His surly eyes lift to mine, crinkling with a smirk. He knows what I'm doing, but when his eyes dart to Evie, he must read something that keeps him in line, because the fight on his face fades like it was never there.

"Wyatt." Ash dips his head, his voice low and grumpy, but to his credit, he swallows his pride enough to shake my hand. I even refrain from laughing when he squeezes with more force than what's polite, or crushing him the way my shifter strength could. At least he looks chagrined when I don't flinch, and backs off. The hint of resignation on Ash's face is more victory than I expect. So is Evie's hand squeezing my upper thigh in reward for making nice with her friend.

"Ash, good to have ya, man." The kid's eye twitches at my unexpected welcome, but I have to prove I'm a civilized partner to Evie. It'll help to do it, before she finds out I'm so much more.

Thankfully, swallowing the 'be nice to Ash' pill is easier with the warmth of Evie's hand still resting on my thigh. Except, Ash seems to notice her snuggled position against me and sidles up to her other side for a hug. I growl when the motion pulls her from my grasp and I lose the comfort of her heat.

"Hey man, open chair... join the fun," Jax offers sensing the tension. He jerks his thumb to the chair conveniently across from Evie and beside Kayah, knowing Ash needs to be outside of my arm span in case I decide to swat the little gnat.

I gotcha, Wy. Jax passes the silent communication, along with a beer from the bucket, and we settle in to start the game.

After a few rounds, we've worked into a solid groove, taking lead over the other teams. Between the six of us, our knowledge covers a wide range of subjects. Evie nailed a hard science question, Kayah and Jax battled out two history questions, and Ash got the British Lit one.

My biggest surprise this evening is how bent out of shape Caleb gets when Kayah bickers over an answer with Jax. She leans close so the other tables don't overhear, but I think it's how quickly their banter shifts to laughter that has him bristling. Every time she slaps Jax's arm or giggles in his direction, Caleb growls. I raise my eyebrows at him, trying to get his attention to calm himself. His ears have turned an alarming shade of red against his tan skin, and so far no one has noticed except me, but that doesn't mean they won't.

I know how you feel, man. Caleb's eyes jerk to me and he takes a large swig of his beer, tearing his body away from Kayah.

He grabs a passing server. "Another bucket, man," he grumbles rudely, earning a pointed look from both Jax and Kayah.

During the break, when teams refill drinks and empty bladders, Evie's other sister joins us, taking the seat between Jax and Caleb on the end of our high top. She looks to be here under duress, no smiles... nothing. I don't know her, but I don't exactly get the warm and fuzzies either.

"Hi, Ama." Evie's voice is strained toward our new arrival and she only receives a small wave in turn, the other girl's face remaining glacial.

Picking up on the drop in temperature at our table, Kayah lifts her hand and orders the girls a round of margaritas. That lifts the edges of Ama's mouth slightly, though she keeps her chatter aimed at the rest of the table. It's an odd dynamic for sure between the sisters, but the worst part is the tension rolling off Evie. I keep steady pressure with my thumb rubbing along Evie's shoulder blade, just trying to help her relax as much as I can.

Under her stiffness, I catch a few secretive glances Ama sends Jax and wonder if they know each other already. It's a small town, so that's very possible. But why wouldn't they want the rest of us to know?

I'm stopped from asking by a new round starting. Evie and Ama basically ignore each other, but by the time she reaches the bottom of that margarita, Evie has definitely loosened up in my direction. It's hard to have an actual conversation in a group setting, but her touches have gotten freer. The way she squeezes my arm... my thigh, rubs my back. That sneaky way she checks me out when she thinks I'm not looking has me itching to get her out of here and somewhere I can explore her more freely.

Especially because those little touches and glances stop when Ash is watching. Evie must know he wants her and she's nice enough not to rub anything in his face. Too bad I don't have the same qualm. Evie's mine.

It may take time to convince her, to make myself irresistible, but I will. I'll make it so when I finally drop the big bomb of who we really are to each other, it won't matter. That thought makes it bearable to go slow for her… it's why I suggested trivia tonight. And despite the extra eyes on our private moments, I still relish the fracture of time when I have that window to her mind, when those long eyelashes flutter and let me in.

In turn, my own touches have taken on a life of their own. They've gotten… freer. My hand may have started on the back of her chair, slowly rubbing whatever skin was within my reach. But now, after every conference with the table, Evie's body has slowly inched it's way closer.

A simple side hug on a victory got her tucked perfectly into the crook of my arms. It's easier to stroke her back in between answers, easier to give a little squeeze or to play with the tips of her curls. I take a gulp of my freshened beer, needing something to cool my thoughts of Evie's smooth skin before I self-combust.

I'm not paying attention to the game anymore. Let the rest of them win. This is the first shot I've had to free play with my mate, and though I'm holding myself in check, I'm too fascinated by the way her soft tendrils twist around my finger. Using my free hand, I slide the thickness to the side so my thumb has access to the back curve of Evie's neck. The tingle of electricity from stroking my mate and hearing her soft sighs of pleasure has made my fingers oddly numb.

Evie casts eyes over her shoulder that swirl emotions like a pinwheel: humor, lust, excitement, nervousness. They all play across her face as our table gets called out for being the leaders of the night heading into the last round. Neither of us notice.

I do notice the way her heat sears straight through my jeans where our thighs rest against each other. It ramps up my anticipation, urging me to strip us down skin to skin.

Inside, my bear rumbles his agreement as I attempt to shift discreetly in my chair. If she glanced down and saw my erection straining her way, it wouldn't prove I'm a calm, respectable mate. It's just near impossible to control myself when I'm dying to tangle my hand in those curls and bring her in for what I expect would be the best kiss of my life. Audience be damned.

The steady rotation of alcohol doesn't help our heightened chemistry. With every fresh glass that arrives, my ability to control myself lessens. I'm at the point now where I'm worried the pressure in my cock may just volcanically explode. *OK, I'm shifting to decaf.* By the time we leave I need to be able to control my hands around this woman and not sling her over my shoulder and carry her home. That's gonna require a fully functioning brain.

"Alright, ladies and gentlemen, we have two teams duking it out for the lead… The Grizzly Gang and Team Taco Cat."

Our team hoots, slapping the table to create a deafening drum over the rest of the crowd. Even with our impressive score, we're still only one question ahead.

"But y'all, it's getting past my bedtime, so this will be the last question for the night." Sir Tricks-a-lot fake yawns, patting his mouth comically to a few boos around the room. "After this one, we go to bonus round, where all points are on the table, bet big, bet small, bet it all."

Another round of cheers fills the bar and Evie leans in, her breath whispering against my ear. "I've had a great time tonight."

I smile, enjoying the color tinting her cheeks. Turning, I nuzzle my nose along her temple, giving my lips perfect access to her ear. "Me too, baby," I whisper, loving the shiver that runs through her body.

A mug slamming snatches my attention from the beautiful eyes shining up at me. If looks could kill, Ash would have turned me into his namesake already. His face's as red as Caleb's truck—before it rusted.

She's ours. My bear taunts and it's hard not to repeat the words out loud. *Ignore the loser or take him down.*

Choosing the former, I tighten my arm around Evie and turn back to the stage for the last question of the night. "Who won the Cy Young award the most times during their pitching career?" Satisfaction spreads a grin on my face... I know this.

"Roger Clemens," I whisper to the group, making sure the other tables can't hear.

"No!" I hear a another slam across the table before I feel the vibration under my hand. Curious heads turn as one from the rest of the group.

"What do you mean, no?" I ask, surprised by the vehemence in Ash's voice.

"It's not Clemens. It's Roger Johnson." The stubborn set of his jaw begs for my knuckles. That cocky shit thinks he's right.

Our team swivels between me and Ash, like we're playing tennis, not planning the other's gruesome death in our heads. Evie's look of desperation is the only thing holding me back from turning on this kid. She wants me to play nice with her friend and holy shit... I'm trying.

"Don't think so, man. I've got every baseball card printed since the late 50s. It's Clemens. One hundred percent." My grin may lean slightly menacing, instead of confidently friendly, but it is what it is.

"It's Clemens, dude," Caleb offers, backing me up with a conciliatory look for Ash. "Quick! Write it down before time's out." He taps the paper in Kayah's hand while the rest of the table stares, waiting for the explosion of tempers.

"You're wrong," Ash puffs, frustrated.

"Ash, come on," Evie pleads. "He sounds confident in the answer. Let's take the chance."

His eyes glower at my mate but hurt registers underneath. I'm torn. My temper pops that this boy is challenging me... it's ramped more by the look he's giving my woman. But the tiniest part of me feels pity toward Ash at having to swallow his man-balls tonight. He's losing this argument for one, but he's also not winning the girl he's dying for either.

After a few strained seconds, Kayah squeezes Ash's shoulder and whispers something in his ear. She rushes our response to the judge just as the buzzer sounds. The rest of us sit in awkward silence.

We're waiting for the verdict when Evie's body startles. Her shoulders tense under my hand and she slides her phone from the back pocket of that sexy as hell skirt. *How is there room for anything in that pocket back there?*

I try my damnedest not to snoop, which is hard given how close we are, but she keeps the phone under the table to read the screen. A frown mars her pretty face, making my gut churn, but before I can ask if everything's OK, we're interrupted.

"Teams, only one of you got the last question correct." The announcer shakes his head, faux disappointment aimed across the bar. "The answer to who won the most Cy Young awards in his career is…" His mouth blubbers a cheesy drumroll to the audience. "Roger Clemens! And Team Grizzly Gang was the only group who knew their sports in this bar. Shame, shame, shame." He hangs his head, laughing as grumbles rise around the crowd from his antics.

Evie hides her phone in her purse this time, her head down for longer than needed to secure the thing inside a zipper. From the side, it looks like her eyes shimmer more than they did, but her gaze quickly shifts to the stage as they get ready for the bonus. Ash hops down from his chair, muttering something about getting another beer. He won't meet any of our eyes as he walks away.

The bonus round begins, and we place our bets, playing it safe by only betting half our points. Most of the table is out of their chairs, leaning over the paper in the middle.

"Name as many of Garth Brooks' Billboard hits from the nineties as you can. The most correct songs win."

Yes! I have country down! But the entire bar should, too. This is a town full of southerners who sing Dolly Parton going into work, Kenny Chesney on the weekend, and Garth at every karaoke.

After our last scribble, Evie runs the paper to the stage and returns to my side, looking brighter than she had a few minutes before. She beams, distracted with excitement when Ash walks up, setting his fresh beer on the table with a look of resignation and a small smile on his face for Evie.

We all turn and wait for the judges—or bar employees—to tally the points.

"Alright, songs have been sung, points have been tallied... and the winner... of the monthly Grizzly Growler Trivia Games, is..."

Chapter 13

♥

Evie

"The winner of the monthly Grizzly Growler Trivia Games, is…"

I look up at Wyatt and smile; the anticipation of the game takes away my stress momentarily. *We got this.*

"The Grizzly Gang!" The dorky MC shouts our name, and the entire table jumps up cheering, hugging, high fiving. Even Ash, who's been noticeably pouty since he lost the baseball question to Wyatt, smiles.

Kayah grabs him around the neck, forcibly dragging his body sideways into her hug, and getting the first genuine laugh I've seen out of him tonight. Caleb grows larger beside Kayah, firing torpedoes at the two of them from his eyes.

God, men's egos!

At least everyone's getting along now. Victory lightens the mood at the table, the boys bumping fists, Kayah and Ama slapping high five. As I lean over to join my sisters celebrating, Wyatt grabs me around the waist and hauls me back to him, squeezing me in his own celebration.

Good Lord! The big brute's so strong, he nearly picks me up with one arm.

At almost five-eight, I am not a tiny girl, especially when I wear boots or heels, and a surprised giggle slips out from being manhandled. I glance over my shoulder, expecting to laugh at his silliness, but see instead that Wyatt's face is only inches away. There's a smoldering heat behind those dark coffee eyes that sends shivers down my spine and my smile fades. It feels out of place with the intensity zinging between us. *Panties melt, now.*

"Come on up, ladies and gents, claim your prizes." The MC's call breaks our spell.

Wyatt's smile turns warm now, less suffocating under those chiseled good looks. His breath is heavy, but slowly, he releases his grip on my middle. In my position, tucked just below his chin, I feel the planes of his chest firm on my back, the swell of those biceps where they've draped my shoulders now. And best of all... the hard length of him pressed into the curve of my behind.

Wyatt's cheeks color with the most adorable blush, so I'm pretty sure he wasn't intentionally rubbing his erection against me. Especially because he backs away as soon as it becomes noticeable. I open my mouth to break the awkwardness, but Kayah grabs me and Ama by the hand, dragging us to the stage with the men following in our wake.

A gorgeously quirky woman with dark-rimmed almond eyes under reddish cat-eye glasses stands to the side. She takes the photo of us accepting our gift certificate for a free dinner tied to a bottle of wine. Her shoulder-length blond spirals bounce back and forth as she moves across the stage, snapping us at difference angles.

Most of the teams have disbursed, not caring to watch another team's celebration, but Kayah stands front row center—the belle of the ball—at for this photo. Everyone smiles and I grab Ash, tugging him close for the group photo. I just want him to feel better tonight, not out of place or not welcomed.

Wyatt squeezes my shoulder but says nothing about our friendly intruder. As a thank you, I lean my head back on his chest briefly, hoping he understands the thanks for what it is. Wyatt hums behind me and a warm sense of acceptance flows through my heart.

Ash smiles politely for the camera lady and waits until after we return to the table to bow out of our group. "See you tomorrow, Ash," I call hopefully. He nods, and though his face smiles, his eyes look conflicted as he walks away to join a table of teachers he knows. The progress in how Ash handled the night gives me hope that if I end up home for a few weeks, we'll be able to fix our stilted relationship.

Jax is next to leave. His new bartender needs backup now that trivia's over, but I catch his eyes lingering on Kayah for a second, then Ama, like he wants to say something to both but changes his mind. "I'll send over a pitcher of margaritas to celebrate our win, guys." And with that promise, he makes his way through the crowded bar, greeting most people by name before washing his hands and getting down to business.

It doesn't escape my notice how crestfallen Ama looks when he's gone. Her eyes track his muscular back the whole way to the bar before she sighs. "I'm gonna head out too. This was about as lame as I thought it'd be," she quips, making my fists tighten under the table. "At least I got some alcohol out of the deal." She holds up her winnings with a shrug, making Wyatt's brother bark a laugh from the end of the table. I hate that she ends our night with a bitchy comment. *Why can't Ama just admit we all had a great time and leave it alone?*

At least, I had a good night... mostly. Kayah did, too.

If I go by Wyatt's roaming hands, he has thoroughly enjoyed himself tonight.

Even now, his eyes burn holes into the side of my head. The intense scrutiny rushing heat to my face from such a beautiful man watching my every move, hanging on my every word. It's a struggle not to wiggle in my chair. I've spent most of the night with moist panties, but now that our game is done and the possibilities are endless, my hormones have turned me into a furnace of burning, backed-up need.

The brush of Wyatt's thumb on my neck, the way he sifts my hair through his fingers, playing me like a piece of putty. I've never been so turned on in my life... especially fully clothed.

Oh my God. I wish I had thought to pack more carefully before I left my apartment a week ago. I could seriously use some B.O.B. action when I get home tonight.

Kayah fixes me with a curious stare. I'm worried she and Caleb can see how hot and bothered I am, that they can read my face. Wyatt seems oblivious to my distress, judging by the hand he keeps rested on my thigh. He never moves more than a stroke of his thumb along the denim. But the more our conversation at the table relaxes, the higher his hand roams until I can barely keep my legs crossed in the seat. My thighs have a mind of their own. They're imagining opposing magnets as inspiration, and may have no choice but to fly open, to give in. Otherwise I might just pass out if Wyatt's pinkie slides any closer to where I so desperately want it.

Don't lie, you love it.

Why am I letting a guy I've known less than a week get so handsy up in my business? Is Wyatt that damn sexy that he gets a pass? *Yes! He's the sexiest man I've seen outside of movies... inside, too.*

Those roughened hands have lit me on fire all night, with every graze. But, it's not only physical attraction. Something else pulls me to Wyatt. Like he's home, not a complete stranger. But even that thought scares the crap out of me. I haven't thought of Talon as home in ten years, but with Wyatt, there's a connection.

Even now, while he chats with his brother, his eyes flash passion like there's no need to curb his feelings. He doesn't protect his emotions or play the 'game'. He's safe... honest. Wyatt has a gentleness I want to protect, even though his fist could pound a person as easily as a hammer could shatter a shell.

The question is, does he feel this link too? He could be a typical douche trying to get in my pants, but I don't get that vibe from Wyatt.

Don't date douches—Gran's idea for a class for teenage girls pops into my head. If I could have a civil conversation with Ama, I'd pick her brain to see if I'm being played. She has more experience with men than I do. It'd be nice to know, so I'm not waiting for that other shoe to drop.

I mean, his chest-pounding macho vibe from last week is polar-opposite from tonight's careful, attentive side. Granted, both sides are hot as hell but tonight was less about male posturing tempers. Wyatt stayed calm with Ash—which I know was for my benefit—even when Ash threw his man-trum. That means a lot.

As if he can tell what I'm thinking, Wyatt turns my way, a sinful dimple denting his cheek that increases my mortification at being caught staring for the third time. Caleb chuckles across the table when Kayah nudges him in the ribs, and I wish I could smack that knowing grin off both their faces.

The Elmo song blaring from Kayah's purse interrupts my plans for violence. It's the ring tone she programmed for her freshman roommate —now best friend. They met and bonded over cheesy kid shows, but I still have no idea how grown women don't mind kid songs following them around public places.

"Hey, Kaylee," Kayah answers quickly, holding a finger to her ear to block the bar sounds.

Before she utters another word, she's out of the chair so fast she nearly falls trying to get her feet under her. Something's wrong.

"What's up, Ky?" I ask, jumping up and rounding the table to help my sister. She's trying to gather her things, but her hands are too frantic. They shake trying to pull cash from her wallet for the bill. "Kayah, stop." I cover her hand and squeeze. "I've got the bill. What's wrong?"

"Don't worry about it," Wyatt soothes right behind me, concern crinkling the corner of his eyes.

Kayah glances up at us both, her face a mix of gratitude and worry. With a nod, she jerks my shoulders into a quick hug. "I gotta go," she says quickly, stepping back like she's going to scoot out without an explanation.

I grab Kayah's arm, holding her still. "What's going on, Ky?"

"I'm OK. Really." The sincerity in her eyes is real but I don't like that tremble in her voice. She darts a questioning glance at Wyatt who's close behind me. "I have to go, though. I'm so sorry." She shoulders her purse, and leans her head close, like the two men aren't hovering less than a foot away. "Are you OK calling a car? I hate leaving you here."

My sister is suddenly more agitated scanning our surroundings, the bar full of people versus the two big brothers towering over us. I think she's anxious about their size, and our girl code of 'no woman left behind', but I feel perfectly safe here, as weird as that is. Yes, the brothers are intimidating, but not for the reason she's imagining.

"I'm OK, Ky." I give her words back to her. "Go. Do you need anything?"

"No." She takes a deep breath, lowering her voice to a conspiratorial whisper. "It's Kaylee."

I nod, but guilt pierces my heart when I realize I'm clueless. *What she's talking about?* My lack of involvement in my sister's life is coming home to roost apparently. I know her best friend, Kaylee, but not much else. They've been friends since freshman year, have similar names, and share an off-campus apartment… but, nothing about what's currently going on in their lives.

"Let me come with you. We'll call a car." My sister shouldn't drive with her hands trembling like they are. It makes me nervous. I glance back at Wyatt with regret. His face registers that our night just came to an abrupt halt.

"No!" She barks before calming herself. "You can't." Kayah's shaking her head while she digs for the keys in that massive purse she carries. I'm relieved when she finds them, and even more when Caleb reaches over and takes them from her shaky fingers.

"I got her," he says firmly, taking out his phone and opening the ride-share app. Kayah's dazed, letting him take her hand and tug toward the door, but her worried eyes stay on me. "I'll text ya later, bro." Caleb waves two fingers at us, steadily moving for the exit with Kayah guarded in his wake.

She turns back and calls over the crowd, "text me when you get home, E. I need to know you're OK." She smacks the shoulder that has her hand locked, but Caleb doesn't flinch and Kayah allows the tank that is Wyatt's brother to keep dragging her safely behind him.

"Don't worry about me. Let me know if you need anything." She nods quickly before ducking out the door. My shoulders sag but my mind's rolling scenarios like a tilt-a-whirl, tying my stomach up in knots after that odd spectacle.

Wyatt and I are both subdued when we climb back in our chairs. "Do you want to go?" he asks when I glance up. There's a flash of regret in Wyatt's eyes and he looks like he dreads my answer. "I'll take you home if you like."

Should I go home?

I feel out of sorts after that interruption, but I don't want to be alone either. There's a half-full margarita here. At home, I only have the dumpster fire that is my life to think about. I'd rather let Wyatt distract me from the text in my pocket and whatever stole my sister out of here so fast.

With a smile, I take a lick of my salted glass and cross my fingers that Wyatt isn't just trying to get rid of me.

"I'd like to stay, actually. If I go home now, my brain will run out of control and I'll never get to sleep." I laugh, but it sticks in my throat and sounds like a cough instead.

Taking a larger swig of margarita, I try to pull my eyes away from the door. "Is she safe with your brother?" I ask, hoping Wyatt doesn't take offense. I trusted my gut with them, but that didn't work out so well for me before. And honestly, I barely know these guys. Only that they are insanely hot, outdoorsy, and seem extra loaded in the testosterone department.

Wyatt cocks his head with an understanding smile. "Caleb may be a bit wild, but he's a solid guy. He'll take care of her. I give you my word," he promises, his eyes darkening into rich pools of moody chocolate. "If he doesn't... he knows he'll have to deal with me. Trust me. He'd rather save the battle." That deep growl in his voice stuns a laugh out of me.

That may seriously be the sexiest sound I've ever heard! Thankfully, I stop short of fanning myself.

"Look. We're here. Why don't we use this time?" He suggests, piquing my curiosity with the nervous tick of his jaw.

"What do you have in mind?"

Wyatt nods at the dance floor, where couples move in a circle to the soft, two-steppin' music while the trivia team cleans up. "We could dance," he offers, reaching for the hand not holding my margarita. His focus drops to the space between my knuckles where his thumb strokes in a steady rhythm.

I shrug. I'm not exactly in a dancing mood, but silently I kick myself for not being one of those girls who can flip a switch from testy or scared to flirty and desirable.

"Any other time, I'd love to, but I feel like we just got off an emotional roller coaster." I shake my head, knowing I sound like the wet blanket Ama accuses me of being. "Can we just hang for a bit... get to know each other? I've only been back in town a week and I've already run into you three times."

"Small town?" Wyatt shrugs like I did a few seconds ago and we share a laugh over fate throwing two practical strangers together repeatedly.

He taps his empty pint glass against the table like he's thinking, but then slides the thing away and turns that sculpted body in my direction. The determination on his face makes me smile, though I'm startled when he swings my barstool—and my knees—until we're facing each other.

My margarita stays on the table so it doesn't spill, because I don't imagine my hands are going to work that well with Wyatt's eyes suddenly taking up all my brain space. Well his eyes, and the fact that he's got my knees squarely trapped between those muscled thighs. Wyatt's hands squeeze the top of my knees, setting off a chain reaction of heat and hormones that liquefy my insides so fast, I nearly swallow my tongue. The man just grins, leaning his body closer until my field of vision is just... Wyatt.

"So, what would you like to know? Go..." His palm motions to me, welcoming any question while he studies my face with rapt attention.

I giggle when he tries to school his features into faux severity, his grimace mocking that he expects the third degree. The funny thing is though, I suspect he'd honestly answer those questions if I did start laying into him.

"How about two truths and a lie," I suggest, trying to hide my sneaky smile because I love this playfulness with him.

"Is that a get-to-know-you game, or an excuse to see how well I lie?" His cool smirk tells me he knows the answer already.

I squint my eyes, teasing him with a glare that I know what he's doing, but really I love how easily Wyatt distracts me from real life. "I'll go first if it helps." My voice sounds innocent enough but I'm pretty sure I'll be able to stump Wyatt easily.

"Number one, I had a pet goat growing up. Number two, I was valedictorian in high school. And three… I have a tattoo."

Wyatt's eyebrows shoot to his hairline; his eyes darting all over my body like he has x-ray vision. The way he scours my body could make me believe it. I already feel myself blushing, but I lift my chin and level him with a challenging eyebrow instead.

"Oh my God, I need to know if the tattoo thing is true," he moans. The desperation in his voice verges on a whine, but Wyatt quickly clears his throat and turns to grab Jax's half-empty bottle of beer. His Adam's apple works as he chugs, like he's desperate for the cool liquid. I can't hide my laugh at watching a grown man twisting in his chair like a feisty toddler.

One thing is definite, being around Wyatt makes me feel alive again. I have laughed more today than I have on any day since college. He has a way of making me feel desirable, not swamped by responsibilities and expectations.

"Your turn." I wave my hand in his direction, but he's shaking his head.

Huh?

"Nope. I need to know the answer. I'm guessing the lie is the valedictorian thing… not that you aren't brilliant. But that's… wow level!" He shakes his head back and forth, those sultry eyes still squinting at the parts of me hidden under clothes. "Plus, now I'm visualizing a little butterfly tattooed on your ass, and I can't unsee that."

I choke on a sip of margarita and smack my hand against the hard ridges of his stomach. *Crap, are there bricks under there?* The motion is more punishment to my hand than his mockery, but once I can breathe again, I put Wyatt out of his misery.

"Nope. No tattoo," I shake my head and we grin like fools over the top of our drinks, his eyes crinkling at the corners with his big smile. *How is his face so beautiful?* I can't think. And I can't stop smiling, either. "Plus, if I did get a tattoo… it wouldn't be of a little butterfly, though. I'd want something cool like a dragon. Something mythical, magical."

Wyatt's eyes fly open, taken aback. "You believe in magic?"

My face goes white-hot. "Not *believe* in magic, just fascinated by it…" I stumble, trying to find the right words to defend my sanity. Any second I'll hear the wind whistle when Wyatt flies out of here like his tail's on fire. "Wouldn't it be cool to live in a world with magical creatures and all their beauty? It would feel like anything's possible… you know."

OMG, I sound like a five-year-old in fantasy land.

At his shocked expression, I shift tactics, now simply needing this conversation to end so I can get out of here. "Look, I'm not crazy. I just like these stories that my Gran used to tell, of beings, or protectors, on our mountain. She made them sound so sweet and… honorable. With their otherworldly abilities that could hurt us, but never would. It made me dream of worlds like that as a kid. I guess-"

I stop rambling when I notice Wyatt's ashen face, his mouth slack as he gapes at me. "I'm sorry. I didn't mean to freak you out," I backtrack, trying to remove the foot from my mouth. "You obviously think I'm insane. I'm not. It's just a fable I liked as a kid." My back straightens and I turn, finishing the last of my margarita so I can get out of here faster.

Setting the empty glass back, I go to stand up, not willing to look at the ridicule on Wyatt's face any longer. "I'm gonna get going," I say, shouldering my purse. "I'll call a driver." The awkward ride home after mortifying myself in front of Mr. Walking Orgasm would be too much to handle.

Tears burn my eyes, but I duck my head down, hiding them under the guise of finding my phone in my purse. I'm still trapped between the table and Wyatt's massive body and I seriously hope he takes the hint without me having to look up. At least face recognition gives me another reason to keep my head down. It takes a little more effort to locate the right app since the little icons are swimming across the screen, but I use the distraction to nudge against Wyatt's spread thighs, waiting for him to release me like the polite gentleman he's been all night.

Wyatt doesn't move his leg though. Instead, his hand covers the one trying to call a car for pick up. His warm breath leans into my space, that deep voice whispering against my ear like a secret confession, "Evie, I don't think you're insane. I think it's… wow!"

Wow?

I truly loved those fables growing up. What kid doesn't get lost in fairy tales and magic worlds? But, when a man looks at you like you grew a third eyeball, the fables don't seem so cool, anymore. I swallow the lump in my throat, just trying to keep it together until I get home and can suffocate myself under the pillow.

Wyatt slides his callused finger under my chin, turning my face to his for study. I fight his pull, not wanting to see the judgment for my wishful fantasies or for Wyatt to see the tears I'm barely holding back. But he doesn't let me off that easily. Wyatt grips my chin, forcing my eyes to meet his. There's a ring of gold shining around his dark irises I've never noticed before. It distracts me from completely freaking out.

What I don't see is the judgment I expect or laughter.

"Listen, gorgeous. Those stories are beautiful. I was just… shocked. I never imagined you'd wish for a magical world, or special beings." I jerk my face out of his hand, successfully this time. Humiliation flames up my neck and I bump my chair to move it, not wanting to hear the 'but' after that sentence. It doesn't earn me much room, but the quick movement stalls the gentle let down I know was coming.

I turn back to face Wyatt, needing to preserve a tiny amount of my dignity. "Seriously! I don't believe the things are *real*. I'm not crazy." My voice heats and Wyatt opens his mouth to interrupt, but I forge ahead, knowing tears are coming fast. I have to get out of here. I look for an opening to wiggle between the chairs but realize just how much his giant body has man-spread around me. Now, I'm stuck between his massive thighs—which I hate myself for noticing—without an escape route. I meet my captor's eyes, tired of this game and ready to go home.

"They're just stories, Wyatt," I say sadly. "Old family stories."

Wyatt stands suddenly—with much more grace that I managed—and seizes my hand securely in his while he drops a few bills on the table for our tab. Despite my fight-or-flight urge, I don't want to cause a scene by screaming or trying to wrestle free, so I wait, locked in his vice-grip.

When Wyatt turns around, my heart's hammering out of my chest. He's all seriousness... no smile, no dimple. Time stills as those dark gold eyes bore down on me. The world crawls in slow motion as Wyatt leans in, resting his free hand on my hip and pulling my body square to his. I suck in a sharp breath, tensing when those soft lips graze the outer shell of my ear.

"I believe, Evie," he growls, his voice dropped to that sexy, low register, like he's confiding a deep dark secret.

He can't. My brain stutters, questioning every word out of his mouth until Wyatt rests those sensuous lips beside my temple and breathes.

My body trembles under his hands. Its confined energy begging for release as Wyatt overpowers my senses. He's taken over every thought until I can only focus on that wide chest towering over me. It's too much and not enough at the same time.

I've lost the urge to run. I don't know if it was his breath whispering across my face, or that masculine cedar scent saturating the air, filling my lungs. Either way, my feet are firmly planted, unable to turn away from the fire in those eyes.

Carefully, Wyatt tucks a stray hair behind my ear, his roughened fingertips lingering on my earlobe, rubbing it softly. Each movement is slow, at odds with my increased heart rate. A soft whine escapes as my mouth falls open, stuck in Wyatt's trance, surrounded by his warmth, and desperate for something I can't put a name on.

The sound wakes me from my hormone-induced stupor and I snap my mouth shut, firming my resolve. "Are you being honest with me or making fun of me?"

I'm not sure which answer would sit better. Honestly, I don't believe Gran's fables are real, but I won't let a man mock me either, no matter how much I want to climb his body like a tree.

"Oh, I believe there is magic in the world, hidden or otherwise. And I would never make fun of you, Evie. Never." Wyatt's vow is haunted. The depths of his eyes conflicting with his hopeful smile. He doesn't wait for my response. Since he's still holding my hand, he turns, leading us through the crowd and out into the chilly September air.

I blink, needing to shake off the daze of the last five minutes so I can keep up with Wyatt's determined gait. His long legs are difficult to keep up with and quite honestly, I'm a little miffed from feeling like a naughty toddler being dragged out of a party by its pissed off parent.

I'm winding up to tug my hand free and set my own—less marathon —pace when my clutch vibrates on my shoulder and the rock I had momentarily forgotten settles back in my stomach. My body covers with goosebumps again that this time are not from the cool mountain air, nor the electricity this man fills me with.

The worst part is I can't avoid the phone tonight. Not when Kayah rushed out of here like her ass was on fire. I tug, but Wyatt's grip on my hand stays firm. Bouncing a little, I try to wiggle my phone out with the one hand, my heart sinking when the screen lights up.

You must call me tomorrow! Imperative. Not playing Dr. Amos.

The nausea hits hard, and I know I can't hide from my problems much longer… unless I want an ulcer by my twenty-ninth birthday. Thankfully we've reached Wyatt's lifted—already cranked and running—truck. The errant thought of how Wyatt's truck gleams under the streetlight makes me wonder if he gave it a fresh wash before our group date.

Ever the gentleman, Wyatt opens the passenger door and I find him staring. The darkness is gone from his face, now replaced by concern that melts my heart. "Is it your sister? Is she OK?"

Shit! Great poker face, Evelyn.

I toss the phone I've grown to hate inside my bag. "She's fine. I'll give her a call at home."

Wyatt watches me, looking like he wants to say more, and I fidget. His ferocity hitting me with guilt for lying . I shouldn't care. My problems are none of his business, but it feels weird. And it feels weird that it's weird.

He must decide to let it drop because that dimpled smile is back when he holds a hand to boost me in the truck. I'm glad for the help because this tight skirt is not going to work with that monster.

When I'm settled on the plush leather, I turn to thank Wyatt but find his eyes plastered to my ass. The ass he obviously got an eyeful of when I climbed up. My giggle breaks the spell, but instead of looking embarrassed, his gaze heats, slowly dragging up my body to my own reddened face.

"A picture will last longer," I say with a smirk and that boyish grin grows.

"You promise?" Wyatt wiggles his eyebrows, not bothered at all that he got caught ogling.

"Hey," I squeak, feigning offense when the insinuation of what I just offered sinks in. I push against that massive chest to shove Wyatt out of the doorway. He actually stumbles backward, his laughter booming in the night air. I giggle harder at his silliness. *Sure, like I could move that colossal body.*

"Can you blame me?" He shrugs one beefy shoulder, the mischievous glint in his eye making the question adorable, instead of cocky.

Wyatt slams my door and stalks to the driver's side, keeping his eyes on me in the beam of headlights. They emphasize his predatory frame of stacked muscles, the way his shirt caresses the line of his shoulders, the muscular curve of ass being cupped by those sexy, dark wash jeans.

I hurry to wipe my sweaty palms before Wyatt climbs up. And thank God I did, because the first thing Wyatt does after buckling his seat belt is grab my hand back in his. He sucks a deep breath in, his eyes flashing when he pulls that hand to rest on his thigh. I flush, but leave my hand perfectly still, letting his heat sear me.

Wyatt smirks, like he can read every dirty thought rolling through my mind. And I pray with everything inside of me that that's not true, but I have obviously not been great so far with controlling my expressions around this guy.

Wyatt puts his hands on the wheel and waits expectantly. I'm confused, until it dawns on me what he's waiting for. *Idiot!*

I gesture in the direction of my house, but Wyatt hits a button on his wheel and I call out my home address for the navigation system. It takes some of the stress off our drive through town. I turn toward the window, taking in the changes to my home town in companionable silence.

"So, is it my turn?" Wyatt asks, drawing my eyes to his profile.

"What do you mean?"

"Our little game," he reminds me with a lifted eyebrow.

"Oh. Yes... your turn."

Wyatt hums like he's thinking hard before answering. "I... am a champion marksman." He quirks an eyebrow in my direction. "Zucchini is my favorite vegetable and... Lady and the Tramp is my favorite kid movie."

I can't help but chuckle at the randomness, enjoying at least another few minutes of relaxed feeling of fun with Wyatt. "Those are good! The marksman thing I can totally see," I admit, using the game as an excuse to study Wyatt's face in the darkness. I love getting unfettered access while he drives. "I'm torn. The Lady and the Tramp movie *is* stinking adorable, although most guys wouldn't admit that, even if it were their favorite movie. But zucchini? Zucchini is nasty and mushy and... gross." I stick my tongue out to emphasize the nastiness.

"So?" I watch Wyatt's smile dance under the light of the street lamps.

"Zucchini for the lie," I shout, noticing Wyatt pulling onto my street. "That one." I'm disappointed when he parks in front of my parents' house. That drive went by way too fast.

Surprise lights his face. "How did you guess?" With the truck in part, he twists in the seat to face me.

"Your lie?"

"Yeah, I mean... I assumed you'd guess the movie since it's an odd favorite for a guy." His ears pink at the admission and my insides melt a little more.

"I thought the movie was too adorable to be a lie. What guy would make that up?" I squeeze his hand, letting him know I'm teasing. "Plus, zucchini is awful!" I fake gag, loving that Wyatt's laughter fills the cab of his truck. Because of me.

I adore making this guy laugh. I've never been considered funny. But when Wyatt's toothpaste smile beams at me, my worries slip away. That this gorgeous man might enjoy my company, the *brain* of the group—a term I've never used, but Ama pigeonholed me there in high school.

I never got away from that nerdiness, even in a new city. It's always been stuck in my brain, until a week ago, when the mountain man beside me took notice. All of a sudden, I feel like a whole new person. Not the boring, safe Evie who had a bug collection at eight and cared more about playing with animals than putting on makeup. No, when Wyatt looks at me, I feel seen... sometimes too much.

Wyatt hops out and comes around to open my door like the proper gentleman. When I take the hand he offers, I realize we've held hands most of the way home like teenagers on a first date. It felt nice.

If someone would have said a week ago, that the scariest night of my life would lead to this, I'd have thought they were high. My opinions changed in such a short amount of time... about so many things: my job, my hometown, my family, and partially about what I needed to make me happy. All in one week.

In only a few days, Wyatt has turned from a hottie who I wanted to strangle for his high-handedness, into someone I feel safe enough to be myself with. Like a long-lost friend I never knew existed.

Wyatt's footsteps slow when we're close to the front door. "I'm glad you came tonight," he says, stroking his thumb along my hand, lost in some other world.

We're both delaying our inevitable separation which feels even more like a surreal first date. Although, my first actual date had braces, a squeaky voice, and chicken legs. He certainly didn't set my heart—or my hormones—on fire like Wyatt does.

I glance up, reading the genuine concern reflected in Wyatt's eyes. "Will you text me later? Let me know everything's OK with your sister."

"I will," I promise. "Thank you for... caring. And for the ride home." I fumble with my house keys, my mind wrestles with how to be proactive for a goodnight kiss. That's not usually my style, but even with our a large group, this felt like a date in every way.

Leaning in for a kiss wouldn't be so horribly out of the blue, right?

Plus, it's been so long since I've gotten this far with a guy, I don't want to miss an opportunity to taste a man like Wyatt. Even with my lack of experience, I know that kiss would burn any memories that came before him. Hell, probably after him too.

Should I go for it? I'd have to stand on my tip toes because the guy's a freaking giant. My head rolls through the best ways to look receptive while unlocking the door.

I'm still debating the options when I turn around, secretly hoping Wyatt will put me out of my misery and make the first move. But he doesn't look on the verge of a first kiss, he looks torn. The extreme range of emotions flickering through those soulful eyes stops my over-active brain.

"Are you OK?" I ask, waiting for some sign of what to do. The question seems to snap Wyatt out of his fog and that finely-crafted body moves in, crowding me on my parents' small front porch. Enough that I feel the millimeter of heat trapped between our bodies, but not a single part is touching.

"When can I see you again?" he asks in that low, sexy rumble.

He wants another date!

Those golden-brown eyes fall to my lips, and instinctively my tongue darts out to wet them. It's like the man has control over my thoughts, or maybe he can just read them. I don't know. But the lure of Wyatt is too damn hard to resist.

"We have a festival tomorrow night... the New Moon Ceremony for our tribe. There's dancing and food... although you'll have to put up with my whole family being there. Like, the *whole* family." I'm babbling, but snap my mouth shut when Wyatt lays a finger against my lips.

"I'd love to go," he says, a bright smile warming those eyes I want to drown in. I swear I hear a chorus of cicadas singing us a song on the breeze.

He lowers his finger, but the tingle from his touch lingers. I press them together and watch Wyatt. A teasing glint sparkles like the sweetest victory as he shifts from sweet to seductive so fast it throws me off balance.

"So, you wanna show me off to the family already, huh?" Wyatt's grin pops his deep, unfair dimples into those tan cheeks, making it hard not to swoon like a dork.

"You wish." I laugh, shoving at that hard chest and yes... secretly sneaking another feel of muscle under the well-filled fabric. I'm sure my hand isn't much punishment—his body doesn't even budge—but Wyatt traps it flat against his heat before I can pull back, beaming down in victory.

"I do wish," he says in a gravely voice. "As a matter of fact, I think we should up the ante... I'll come here tomorrow night, blend with the festivities, and you can introduce me to the family." He winks, tangling our fingers together and curling them into his chest.

Wyatt's feet move closer, his thumbs stroking slow, sensual lines along my hands. The anticipation of what I hope comes next spikes fresh hormones through my body. "After... Saturday... you're mine. I'll cook for us, no zucchini," he adds, his eyes dancing with temptation under the porch light.

I can only manage a nod since my mouth is the Sahara, my brain short circuited by lust. I swallow around the dryness in my throat, but with Wyatt's body pressing into mine, that mountain, woodsy scent drowning me, I'm left dizzy.

Losing all smoothness, I close my eyes and breathe in Wyatt's masculinity, waiting for the inevitable kiss. When it finally happens, instead of my mouth, Wyatt's soft lips brush my temple, breathing in along the skin there.

My eyes dart open. The vision of Wyatt's sexy stubble is so close, I want to lick it, but Wyatt straightens to look in my eyes before I can. He moves one hand to hold my chin in place, dropping a soft kiss along my cheekbone. The gentleness is shocking. My mouth falls open, my tongue itching to find his, to lay claim, but Wyatt's moving at his own pace, controlling our passions. The sensuousness of it drives me crazy.

My fingers grab the hem of his shirt, twisting to balance myself against the sudden wobbliness in my knees. If only I weren't dying for this man on my parents' front porch, about to sleep in my childhood bedroom. Not that I'd bring him inside otherwise, would I?

With Wyatt this close, I can't think. I don't care about decorum or fighting the chemistry between us. What's wrong with enjoying a little vacation fling on the mountain?

Except, instead of going for the kiss or asking me to his place, Wyatt sighs, laying his forehead against mine and effectively dumping a bucket of ice water on my libido. I assumed he was right there with me on the sexual tension, but obviously not.

I'm feeling all loopy from Wyatt's testosterone. And from being on the verge of begging a guy I've known less than a week to kiss me, then only getting a peck on the cheek. I can't help it... I feel denied.

Thank God the porch is private so no one else saw me panting all over Wyatt and getting shot down. Ama's comments from earlier haunt the recesses of my mind... why would a hottie want the brainiac? It makes more sense this way—I'm friend-zoned.

Great. What was with all the hand holding then?

Straightening my back, I yank my hand from under his and turn the handle behind my back. "I-uh... I guess I'll see you tomorrow. Although... if you have something else to do, no worries." I offer the out, turning before Wyatt can see my eyes well up.

How embarrassing that I already invited him to the ceremony! Ugh! If he does come, tomorrow will suck worse than I already expected.

I wish I could text Kayah right now. Ask her advice on how to fix my pride.

Risking the humiliation, I glance over my shoulder and give Wyatt a small wave. My smile is strained but I fake composure so he doesn't see how completely lost I am. Wyatt's mouth hangs open, his brows furrowed with confusion.

You're not the only one, big boy.

Sighing, I shut the front door and flip the lock. My forehead rests against the hard would, listening for the sound of Wyatt's retreating footsteps. He waits for a few minutes to leave, but when I hear the telltale slam of a truck door, I head to the bedroom I'm sharing— temporarily—with my sister, refusing to think about anything other than putting this night to bed.

Chapter 14

♥

Wyatt

I'm not sure what I expected, but after the weird goodbye last night, it wasn't to be sitting at a Cherokee ceremony with Evie's family and actually enjoying myself. The laughter, the food, the music… it's really just a gigantic party with a fire blazing in a center circle of stones. *Who wouldn't love that?*

Tables surround a large dirt clearing where men, dressed in traditional robes and feathers, performed earlier. It's a sight to see, especially when I see the same people in town wearing jeans and farm-wear like the rest of us. They have no problem putting themselves on show to honor their ancestors. It's pretty incredible.

Even the kids sat through story time with tribe elders. Now, with cookie in hand—a reward for their patience—those kids run the field playing games, both staged and pulled free of their imagination.

Almost everyone in sight is having a good time, except the woman beside me. Kayah looks grumpier than last night, but when I tried to bring it up in front of her family, she jerked her head quickly, letting me know to drop it fast. *I can take a hint.* And I'm happy to keep my mouth shut as long as she's safe.

I'm more concerned with the fact that I can't make Evie smile. I've tried all evening but it seems the only thing I'm good at around here is sticking my foot in my mouth. I don't like it.

Fix it! My bear roars, pissed that I messed things up again.

I would if I could. I have no idea what I did. Most of last night we laughed and held hands. Evie seemed open to my advances. I loved it! Especially because I need the woman to trust me before I reveal myself, and I must do that before we can fully mate. Mandatory.

Although, when she mentioned her Gran's mythical stories and her love of the magic worlds, my hope for our future erupted like Mount Vesuvius. The situation just requires finesse. I have to keep a slow and steady course for as long as my bear can hold out.

Uncle Mac's voice echoes in my head. *Be careful, son. Humans can't be trusted.*

Glancing up from the plate that I've nearly licked clean, I see the wise woman herself eying me from across the table, smack between Evie's dad and baby sister. The hair on my arms stand up under the scrutiny of those perceptive eyes, but I'm grateful the woman seems to approve. Evie's grandmother can clearly aware of how smitten I am with her granddaughter. The corner of her eyes crinkle every time she looks at me, that secretive smile—like right now—causing an embarrassing heat to crawl up my neck in front of my mate's family.

Unfortunately, my beautiful Evie has barely spoken a full sentence to me since we got to the ceremony grounds. I've tried everything! I carted over heavier pots for set up. I laughed every time her Gran made a good-natured remark about Evie catching a man with muscles. I kept hoping she'd agree, maybe cop a feel, but every comment gets a cold shoulder. If I could just make her smile like last night, me and my bear would both be able to relax.

Now, Evie's sitting beside me, miserably picking at her food more than enjoying it. Ash sits on her other side, clearly annoyed that I'm here, but I've yet to be around the man when he wasn't cranky over something. Hell, even the overcast sky matches the atmosphere on our side of the table.

"Can I get you a refill?" I offer, just to get a sliver of contact with my mate.

"No. Thanks."

Two. Words. I sigh.

The rest of our table is lively, either ignoring, or trying to make up for, the tension firing off Evie.

From the head of the table, Evie's dad tries to pull us back into the ceremony, casting me a sympathetic smile I wouldn't expect from a father meeting the man who wants to court his daughter.

"So, Wyatt, is this the first time you've been to a Cherokee ceremony?"

"Yes, sir. It is. Thank y'all for letting me come."

"Yeah, Evie gets to have a date while the rest of us honor heritage," Ama quips, the grumble hitting its mark by making Evie flinch, those dark lashes dropping to hide the sadness in her eyes.

She is no more pleasant than she was last night, and though there's not a single thing I can do about it, Ama going after my mate rankles my temper. Instinctively, my hand moves to her lower back, offering support, while Evie's mom glares daggers at her middle daughter.

Gran chuckles loudly. "It's no wonder, Ama... have you seen him?"

Both Evie and I blush, though part of me can't help but up sit taller, fighting the urge to preen at her praise. My bear is more than happy, but I cut my eyes to Evie, hoping Gran's comment didn't piss her off. Thankfully, a small smile teases the corner of her mouth. She meets my eyes and catches the blush still burning my cheeks. That quirk of her lips turns into a bright grin, making suffering even a grain of embarrassment more than OK.

I catch a glare from Ash over Evie's shoulder. He's clearly not appreciating the attention I'm getting from our table. A fight with him will not help my situation right now so I smile the secret smile of a guy in over his head with a woman. He blinks, scanning the people around our table. Evie's mom gives him an apologetic smile that he returns with a nod. I hope he can finally see that I'm not going to one up him here. I'm just trying to keep my head above water with a girl I like.

"Gran, you need to behave yourself," Evie admonishes with no actual heat behind her words.

"Never!" Gran counters, wiggling her barely there eyebrows. Ama rolls her eyes, but a laugh bubbles from Evie that she coughs to hide. Her grandmother's spunkiness seems to lighten the load that's been weighing down my mate this whole meal.

I like this family.

Kayah slaps Ama on the back, seeming to understand the need to remove the girl's straining presence from our conversation. "Time to go dance, Sis."

Both girls toss their plates and join five other women already lined up and waiting to perform by the fire. I turn in my chair to face the dancers, fascinated by the rhythm of shakers and drums that fill the open air. Their movements are an art form. The way the girls move and shake, twisting their arms and stomping their feet in a beautiful rhythm.

"Do you know how to do that?" I ask, leaning down to Evie's ear. I hope to engage her in some sort of conversation. Maybe win a few points for showing interest in her family's ceremony.

"Do what?" she answers curtly. *OK, that's not what I was hoping for.*

"That dance." I smile, needing desperately to smooth whatever ruffled her feathers with me. "You'd look sexy up there twisting to the music." Disappointment flashes behind her eyes. I thought she'd take that as a compliment. Instead, Evie collects the empty plates from our table and carries them off to the trash.

Gran shoots me a sympathetic look. "You have an uphill battle with that one."

My chest tightens and I glance to Evie who's by the table of food, chatting with a man who looks like a younger version of her father. Even with the frown on her face, I can't help admiring Evie's natural beauty.

Leathers weave through her braid, matching the native jewelry wrapping her forearms below the soft brown shirt that felt like suede under my fingertips. Evie's makeup is heavier than I've seen her wear, but only her eyes. The mascara and liner smoke the rims of her lashes to sultry perfection. Those eyes have tortured my straining cock all night. Same with the tight jeans squeezing her back end.

But even with the extra paint and sexiness, Evie still exudes a freshness that draws me in. She doesn't try too hard and that realness is one of her biggest draws. Especially to a future Alpha who needs an intelligent mate with a good head on her shoulders.

The sisters finish their dance by the time Evie finally returns to our table. Everyone stands, walking over to a platform where her father climbs up and addresses his community. He starts with a few words on the bounty of the year's crops, but his speech turns personal quick, honoring his own spiritual growth with his family.

"All our blessings on this Earth deserve thanks but remember, some blessings can't be counted with our hands. They're blessings on our hearts." The sturdy man has everyone's rapt attention. He places a hand on his heart, as if holding his blessings inside, while he gazes adoringly at his family.

"In this new year, take forth lessons learned. Accept changes and growth with an open heart and mind." Mr. Amos pins his eyes to Evie, who stiffens beside me. Her eyes sparkle as she presses her lips together, but she can't quite prevent their tremor.

"Our people have always fought hard and fought smart." He enunciates his powerful words with a wave of his fist. "We survive. We work together, stronger as a whole than we are as one. And just like this crop, the happiness and reward on the other side of a struggle, are well worth the wait."

Instinctively, my hand reaches for Evie's back, rubbing circles while the gathered families clap and cheer, inspired by the respected man. Evie's clap is weaker, her face a mixture of awe, fear, and hope as she watches her dad shake hands with people in front of the makeshift stage.

"You OK?" I ask, tugging her elbow to move her away from the celebrating crowd.

"Yeah." She clears her throat. "I'm good." Nice words, but her face is still pale.

Taking a bottle of water from a nearby cooler, I guide Evie to an empty chair out of the way. When she obliges my manipulations of her body and sits without argument, I know something's really wrong.

I unscrew the cap for her and squat in front her knees, gripping them more to calm myself than Evie. She sips slowly, eying me over the bottle. She's antsy with me in her space, but I'm not moving. Once she's had enough, I sit the bottle on the ground so I can keep hold of her knees. I'd prefer her hand, but I don't think Evie would be receptive yet.

My eyes draw to the renewed wetness on those luscious lips, but I squeeze them shut, determined to get Evie to open up before pushing her again. I don't like this closed off version of the girl I had so much fun with yesterday.

"Want to talk about why you looked like a ghost a minute ago?" I lock on her eyes, hoping to read even a hint of a secret under her words. Evie doesn't seem the type to be upfront and honest about what bothers her.

"Not really," she snaps, her knee bouncing with nerves under my hands. *Yep, she's the trudge through the trenches type.*

"Was it your dad's speech? He was incredibly inspiring." I slide my hands a little higher, rubbing the toned muscle of Evie's thigh to calm her anxiety. A satisfying hitch of her breath hits my ears as the knee jerks to a stop. Confusion swirls through those dark eyes when they meet mine, but Evie's lips stay tight.

"How about walking the games? We can watch the kids play stick-ball." Hopefully a distraction will soften Evie's guard so she'll finally talk to me.

Her head does fall to the side, eyes squinting at me like the most confusing crossword puzzle. The puff of air that blows my hair shows the force of her frustration. "Why are you doing this, Wyatt?" Evie's question is both defensive and vulnerable, but I don't know what the hell she's talking about. Does she mean taking care of her? I want to do more than take care of her.

"What am I doing?"

"Pretending you want to be here. You don't have to make conversation with my family or pretend to be interested just because we hung out a few times."

I feel like I've been slapped. That's the most shocking thing I've heard from those sexy lips since I met this infuriating female.

Straightening to full height, I cross my arms against my chest to keep from hauling her gorgeous ass away from this crowd so I can prove how interested I am. Biting my tongue, I ask, "why the hell else would I be here?"

"I don't know!" she huffs, throwing her hands wide as she jumps from the chair. It startles a few passersby, reminding me to be careful with what I say at a family celebration.

My feet move forward on their own, needing to soothe the irritation vibrating off my mate. Reaching out, I cuff her elbows, just so Evie has to stay long enough to hear me out. "Baby, I like your family. They're nice. And mostly accepted my intrusion on their evening." I keep my voice low, cocking an eyebrow that dares her to challenge how pleasant our evening has gone, if she'd just open her eyes. "The ceremony is fascinating, as are your people and their beliefs. My people aren't that different in celebrating the Earth, we just show it differently."

I wonder what my uncle would think of Evie's tribe, if the two families could eventually accept each other. Around us, happy families eat and drink, laughing at the squeal of kids bouncing across the open field. It paints a wholesome vision of our future, one that trips a staccato rhythm to my usual steady heartbeat.

I reach for Evie's hand, pressing forward even with it limp in mine. "Evie, we all have a duty to those who brought us into this world. You guys embrace that, the family values, traditions. All things I believe in, by the way, so why wouldn't I want to be here tonight?"

"So, you came because you were curious about our ceremony?"

It's my turn to cock my head at her. *Did she not hear what I just said?*

"You think that's all this is? Curiosity?"

Instead of answering, Evie flips her braid over her shoulder and stomps off toward the open field. "Evie!" I call, stepping faster. "Evie." The growl in my voice is unmistakable this time and I grit my teeth, grabbing at my own control at the same time I grab Evie's arm to stop her retreat.

Though my hand is loose, people in a mix of traditional and modern clothing watch our interaction. Their guards are up as they cut us a careful side eye. If Evie would just look around her, I think she'd see more love and protection than she realizes she has.

"What?" Evie snorts, jerking her arm from my grasp. Her eyes flash dangerously, but I'm not one to back down.

"I didn't come here out of curiosity, Evie. I came to spend time with you. To get to know you, like we *started* last night."

"OK, sure," she drolls, rolling her eyes with a smirk that's pissing me the hell off.

For the first time tonight, Evie steps toward me instead of closing off. Her words come out with frustrated heat, her finger jabbing my chest. "But why? That's what I don't get. I don't need a friend Wyatt; I don't even live here."

Huh?

Sensing my confusion, she continues, "this is an extended vacation for me. I don't know where I'll be in a week, or hell… if I have a job in a week. I thought that… maybe we had some chemistry." She looks down, her cheeks burning red at the admission. "But that was obviously one-sided, so…"

What the hell!

Grabbing her face, I dive in, putting an end to the nonsense spewing from Evie's very pretty, very soft lips. *One-sided, my ass!*

I see now why she's been pushing me away; why she ran away last night. Capturing her mouth, my kiss is hard at first—not how I wanted our first kiss to be—but I'm not giving her a chance to push me away. Evie's surprised gasp gives me extra access to her sweetness, and I take full advantage, testing her allowance with a swipe of my tongue.

A low rumble vibrates my chest and I pull her tight, forgetting where we are for a minute and locking one arm in the dip of her waist. Her soft curves snuggle perfectly against me, turning our heat up to scalding. I have just enough awareness to keep my hand in safe territory as I nibble the softness of that plump lower lip.

Lightning flashes behind my eyes, straining every muscle I have to not devour the frustrating woman who's tangled me up inside. That struggle grows with the tilt of Evie's head, the more access I'm given to dive into our kiss. The dance of our tongues earn a little moan from my vixen, and her body melts deeper.

Evie's arms slide around my neck, testing my self-control. The evidence of my need is painfully obvious against her curves and I'm pretty sure she feels it. Her smile against my lips is the first clue, so is that little hip wiggle when her fingers twist in the lower length of my hair. Her nails scratching my scalp fire electricity through my body, straight to my groin. Groaning, I jerk back from our kiss before I grind against her like a horny teenager.

To my relief, Evie looks as dazed as I am, a satisfied smile lifting the corner of her mouth even as the pink hue creeps into her cheeks. We have a few watchers.

A soft hand lays itself on my bicep, drawing my eyes to the grinning face of Evie's grandmother. "Now, in my day, we kept this sort of heat behind closed doors, you two." She gives me a once over with a wiggle of her eyebrows that burn the tips of my ears. Evie squeaks and jumps as far as my arms will release her—it's not far.

"Not that I blame you, Bug, but why don't you take this big ole hunk back home where you guys can continue your date."

"Gra-an!" Evie drags her grandmother's name into three syllables. I'd bet my left leg her tomato face matches mine.

Ama saunters up, laughter dancing in her eyes when she catches us at the height of our embarrassment. She seems friendly enough, even slings her arm over Evie's shoulders, but the moment she opens her mouth, it's a different story. "Yeah, big boy. Might as well get, while the gettin's good. Who knows how long my sister's gonna grace us with her presence?"

Inside, my bear roars at the insinuation: the diss, the idea to use Evie for sex, but worse... the idea of our mate leaving us.

Evie twists out of her sister's grasp, turning for a battle, but Gran beats her to it. The elderly woman is a lot faster than I'd expect. Her bony hand pops the back of Ama's head with a smack that makes *me* flinch. "Don't make me put you in time out, girlie."

Gran grasps a surprised Ama by the shoulders and and turns her away. She winks. "You kids get back to your evening. And Bug..." Evie looks at her Gran shell-shocked. "You only have one life, make it count."

"Did your grandmother just quote Jimmy Carter?"

"Umm, sort of." Evie glances up at where I stand over her shoulder, and I take the opportunity to wrap her in a hug from behind. Our connection is back. I watch those sultry eyes brighten subtly. If her brain's anything like mine, she's thinking about our earlier kiss and wanting a repeat.

"How about I take you home and we make use of those comfy looking rockers on your front porch?"

She pauses for a second and I hold my breath, waiting for fate to answer me. "Sounds good. But do not pay any attention to my grandmother." I'm leveled with twin beams of warning and try my best to hold the laughter when I get her meaning.

"So, you're saying, don't get any ideas?"

Evie's pink cheeks deepen to a bright red sunset as she tries to avoid my eyes. I love that she's non-stop innocence one second and steaming passion the next. Evie ducks her head and takes off toward her car, but I catch up quick. My longer legs give me the advantage to recapture her hand as we walk.

Mr. Amos waves from where he sits snuggled with Evie's mom like honeymooners. *Relationship goals for sure.*

Since Evie drove to the grounds, I jog ahead to open the driver door. If she thought my intentions earlier were unclear, I'll be more obvious this time. Except, in the thirty seconds it takes for me to walk around to the passenger seat, she's back to pensive.

My hand automatically goes to rest on her thigh as she drives down the dirt road toward her home. All I want to do is alleviate the stress lines scrunched on my mate's forehead.

Tonight, I've managed to fill in the blanks enough to know Evie's uncomfortable being back in her parents' home. She's a jumbled knot of raw nerves, stuffed under a blanket, hidden by the Berlin Wall of defenses, but if she'd just look around, I think the girl would see most of her family radiates their love for her. Ama obviously has an unspoken— or spoken—complaint with Evie, and the fact that Evie hasn't strangled her yet shows my mate's immense restraint.

"Did you have a good time?" I ask, wanting to kick my own ass with that lame question. I can't think of another way to break the ice though. Our car is dead silent, not even background music to soften then tension.

"I did. You?" Evie's hands never leave ten and two, but they twist the wheel slightly, like she's grinding someone's neck.

"It was great. Your family is awesome, Evie."

Her head angles my way momentarily, checking my sincerity, I guess. "Ama was in full form tonight," she hedges, her voice stilted... testing.

Should I come down hard on Ama? I wish I knew if the beef between the sisters before I entered war territory. Any path other than agreeing with the woman you're trying to woo is rocky.

I grunt an acknowledgment and hope she accepts it as agreement with her opinion either way. "So, what did she mean about you sticking around?" I study Evie's exquisite profile, deciphering each little quirk in her features before she schools them back to neutral.

"She means, I don't live here, like I said. And she's made it clear, she doesn't want me here many, many times." The air freezes in my lungs at the cold finality in her voice. We never talked about her living situation, but I assumed she was local, even if her parents' home was temporary.

She can't leave. She's our mate.

"How long are you staying?" My voice lodges in my throat, but I need to know what I'm working with, how much time I have to win her.

"I don't know. It's an extended vacation right now." She glances at me, those dark eyes radiating sadness and uncertainty and… fear. It mutes her normal sweet vanilla and agitates my bear... my need to protect.

She needs our help.

Unfortunately, we're already pulling up to Evie's house and she's out of the car before I can open her door. *Not so fast!* I'm hot on her tail, jogging to reclaim the hand that's mine. "Talk to me, Evie." I have to stop her from putting distance between us—physically *and* emotionally.

She's pulling away. A mournful howl bounces through my mind, giving me a headache.

Evie obviously thinks this is temporary. I'm gonna have to prove her wrong or deal with my bear's anguish.

She turns before we get to her porch, plastering a fake smile on her face like I won't see the torment storming her eyes. "Listen, I know we planned to sit for a while, but I'm beat," Evie lies. "But, uh… thank you for the coming. And for putting up with my family." The end of her sentence is rushed, her body angling for the house before the last word is spoken.

I grab Evie's elbow, making sure I have her full attention. "You don't have to thank me, love. It was my pleasure to be with you tonight. I feel something here…" I pause, battling over the best way to handle this. The easiest way for her to understand. "You feel this, Evie. I know you do. Whatever's bothering you, whatever's going on... you can talk to me."

She shakes her head, those sad brown eyes fixated on my feet.

"You know, I do have brains under all this beauty," I joke, lightening my voice. My attempt at humor wins a reluctant chuckle from Evie that feels like a reward, even if she hides it just as fast.

I sigh. We're less than a foot apart, but it feels like miles.

"Wyatt, you are sweet." She pauses, shaking her head like she doesn't believe what she's saying. "So much that I... I don't actually believe you're real. But there's no point in all this. My sister was right. I'm temporary!" The anger in her voice rises with every step to the door. "I never planned to move back to home. I have a life in Tennessee, an apartment, a... job." Evie's voice trails off, her shoulders drooping as the argument drains out of her.

A powerful sadness slams me square in the chest. I stoop lower, my hands on Evie's hips, urging her to meet my eye. She turns away in the circle of my arms, her breathing shallow. One hand swipes at her cheek once, keeping her head down to slide her key in the lock.

My mind throbs with a frantic roar. My bear's pushing to get out. He needs to comfort our mate, but that would be the worst possible outcome.

Down boy! With a snort of aggravation, he eases the pressure so I can focus on Evie before she runs again.

"Evie, what about tomorrow night? I'll cook, you tell me about your plans, or your life in Tennessee... whatever you want to talk about. We'll just hang out and have some time together." Desperation raises my volume, but I don't hide it this time.

How am I supposed to tell a human about myself, that we're mates, if I can't get the girl to trust me?

Reluctantly, Evie turns to face me, placing a shaky hand on my arm. It gives me hope. The breath I didn't realize I was holding releases as Evie presses to her toes. Her body trembles against mine for the sweetest kiss she plants on my cheek.

In my gut, I feel it when she backs away. The finality.

"I'm sorry, Wyatt. It's better if we don't." If Evie would meet my eye, she'd see every word is a punch to the gut. "It's been nice getting to know you."

With that cracked platitude, she's gone, and I'm left staring at the scarred wood door that just slammed my heart in two.

Chapter 15

♥

Evie

A thunderstorm hangs over my mopey head while I eat my cereal... alone... in my parents' kitchen. It's eight a.m. on a Saturday morning. Where the hell is everyone? They obviously have places to be.

Not me. I'm not a part of their daily life anymore... although that's my fault, too.

Maybe they're fed up with cranky Evie.

It's not my fault I'm on an emotional roller coaster though... right?

Dad preaches about keeping our brains active. That's what this is. I'm addicted to the work, and someone else's choices threw me into no-man's-land. No path, no plan. My entire life has been working toward something, and now, I'm useless... sleeping late, bitching at everyone around me, including the sexy man with no business being as sweet as he is.

I tanked that too. *Perfect.*

Ugh! Now, my cereal tastes like mushy sawdust. Another point added in the 'this morning sucks' category. I dump the bowl in the sink and lean against the counter, debating on the best way to fix the day. Everything starts with a day, right?

First annoyance... my phone mocking me from across the table. It's silent, which means Wyatt took my send off at its word last night. It's stupid to be sad about a quiet phone. I asked for it. But when the thing has been a nuisance all week, the silence is a giant arrow pointing at the void of my morning.

Frustrated, I snatch the phone up and open the notifications… twenty-three missed texts and eight voicemails. How is that even possible?

Dr. Amos, call me back.

Dr. Amos, it's important that I speak with you.

Dr. Amos, this vacation was not pre-approved. I need you back in the office.

Dr. Amos, come back to work tomorrow or your pay will be docked.

The messages continued, so did their escalating threat. The last voicemail is downright desperate excuses. The man has the nerve to reference that terrifying night, insinuating I overheard a conversation I may have misunderstood.

My ass!

The only thing I misunderstood was thinking Dr. Michaels was a good man. Now, my iffy thoughts about his abilities as a doctor seem justified, considering I gave more attention to his clients than he did. But I was always grateful he hired me. Never in my wildest dreams would I think our office hid criminal activity, though. I wouldn't have worked there. I can't live every day in fear.

Sighing, I refill my coffee and take my phone to the wood rocker on our front porch. Fresh air should make breathing through this conversation easier. I let the bite of chilled wood ground me before I hit send on Dr. Michaels' number. One ring. Two.

"Hello! Hello. Dr. Amos?" The doctor's rushed voice answers the phone sending a shudder of dread down my spine.

"H-Hi. Yes, it's me, Dr. Michaels." My hands shake holding the phone, pissing me off more. I focus on our goats climbing over each other in their pen, playfully oblivious to stresses in the world. It's the perfect distraction and allows me to take a fortifying breath, so I can remember that a phone call can't hurt me. And I need to get it over with, anyway, so this dark cloud stops hanging over my head. "Listen, I wanted to touch base with you after my sudden-."

"Yes, Evelyn. About that. I need you back here ASAP," Michaels interrupts. His voice is firm, not used to me not jumping to his wishes. "Your sudden absence is unacceptable. I've left you many messages."

"Yes, I know, Doct-."

"No, I don't think you know," he snaps, his twang getting thicker as his temper spikes. "You don't understand the pressure I'm under. We have responsibilities, Dr. Amos. You left me high and dry." He pauses and I'm frozen, dumbfounded over his audacity. My mouth opens a few times, struggling for the right words. I have never purposefully disrespected an elder or a boss... never. "Dr. Amos... are you listening to me? We have clients you're responsible for."

That's it!

"You mean, I have clients." The nerve of this little man! He's not admitting why I left. He knows I know. And, he couldn't care less about our clients, so that excuse is complete bull! "I'll call them, Doctor, don't worry. I'll let them know that, due to circumstances beyond my control, I'll be taking a leave of absence."

"Don't you dare," he threatens. "I need you here on Monday. I do not approve your leave, Eveline."

"Yeah, well... I can't work for you, Doctor." Sarcasm drips uncontrollably, but I can't fight it. Every word out of his mouth is infuriating.

"Young lady, if you don't get your pretty little ass back here on Monday..." A slam of a door behind him halts his argument. Good thing, because I'm torn between throwing up in my mouth and reaching through the phone to strangle him. The line crackles, sounding like Dr.

Michaels muffled the phone with his hand. It doesn't block the agitated voices in the background, though.

"Doc... Doctor!" I'm shouting into the phone, impatient to get this call over.

"Yes, Eveline." He clears his throat, the noise behind him going quiet. "I expect you'll be in the office Monday morning. We have some issues here that..." He pauses. "That can't be left... up in the air."

A sinister chuckle muffles in the background, chilling me to the bone. Arguing with the doc is pointless and possibly dangerous. My brain screams for me to get off the phone. Plus, Ama's car just parked in the driveway, so I have about two minutes before her catty self can eavesdrop on my conversation.

Stealing my voice, I fake enough confidence to ignore my churning gut. "Doctor... I am sorry I left on such short notice. I'm sorry I didn't get to transition my clients." He hums, assuming I'm conceding to his wishes. Goody-two-shoes Evie, bending over backwards to please everyone. It's the confirmation I need... this change is mandatory.

"Look, Doc. I think we both know I won't be there on Monday. It sucks, but considering recent events... you're going to have to get your own balls out of the air." I hang up before he spews some excuse, or threat, that'll eat me alive with guilt. My stomach turns anytime someone's upset with me, but I can't think of it that way. This is all on the doctor.

Rampant questions toss through my head as I pocket my phone. I have no idea what would happen if I did go back to my job. Would there be blackmail? Would I have to stay quiet or get involved?

Ama ambles up the steps, her leisurely pace at odds with the frantic nature of my thoughts. My sister definitely looks fresher than she has a right to after such a late night. Her mini skirt highlights the miles of toned leg that I bet she takes time to moisturize. Her shiny hair's styled and blown to perfection. I, on the other hand, woke up and slid on a slouchy pair of joggers from high school, and only had enough energy to brush my teeth and wash my face.

There's no lying... me and my sister are opposite sides of a magnet, in every way it seems. No wonder we push each other apart so hard. For that reason, I purposefully ignore Ama's curious stare as she watches me rock in my chair. She doesn't move from her spot against the banister. If she were our mother, I'd have withered already, spilled all my secrets. But with Ama, it's just irritating.

"What?" I bark, figuring she'll walk away and tell mama I'm being a bitch.

"Geez." Ama's voice hides laughter, her raised eyebrow waiting me out. Is she waiting for a fight or shocked by my outburst?

Cautiously, she pushes off the railing and comes to sit in the chair beside me. Her movements look like she's trying not to frighten a wild cat. I keep my mouth shut, not having the energy to engage this morning.

When I glance over though, I see a smile threatening the corners of her mouth that I desperately want to slap right off her face. *Bad Evie!* I hold back... barely. But it's not Ama's fault my life is upside down.

"You look like crap," she states matter-of-factly.

"Thanks." My sigh earns a chuckle that I ignore. I squeeze my eyes closed and lean my head against the chair, so she won't see the wetness blurring my vision.

"You know what I mean, E. I thought you'd be walking on clouds today after that NC-17 kiss with the man candy last night." Her snicker widens the crack in my heart. I squashed any chance I had with Wyatt last night... out of fear.

"No clouds. I ended things when we left." I'm unable to say more without my voice cracking.

Ama jerks forward, her chair squeaking against the old rockers beneath. "Why? That is one hunk-of-a-man." Every word is a right hook to my stomach, or my heart... I'm not sure which one. When my head angles her way against the head rest, she must see my sadness, because immediately, she backs off the teasing. "What happened?" she asks, her voice uncharacteristically sincere.

Just thinking about how much loss is stacking up lately makes it hard to talk, so I turn back to the safer view of our family land. Taking solace in the animals and the history, the giant pecan tree I fell out of, the barn we played hide-n-seek in, the trail that leads to the back pond where we caught fish too small for dinner.

"E—" she presses.

"Nothing happened, honestly. It can't go anywhere, like you said, so there's no point." Except the moment I closed the door on Wyatt, I felt like there was a vacuum inside my chest. I refuse to say those words out loud, though. Not to my sister. And not when I've only seen the guy a handful of times. It's ridiculous!!

"Hah!" Ama's laugh turns my head. When I see her finely arched brows halfway to her hairline, I nearly laugh too. "The *point*, as you so calmly put it, is to get laid, Evie. Have some fun. Relax a little."

I pause at her matter-of-fact tone. "It's not that simple."

"Of course not. Nothing is simple, but not everything has to be complicated, either." I groan. Jealous that Ama's view on life is a much happier way to live.

I'm not willing to use the words *'you're right'* with my sister… yet. I just wish I could take back the last twenty-four hours and have a do over. Everything except that kiss. That, I could never forget.

"What are you going to do?" For once, Ama sounds curious, not critical. This is the longest conversation we've had without fighting in years.

"I don't know." What can I do?

My apartment lease is on a month-to-month. I've been working too much to go into the main office and sign the year renewal. Maybe I should take it as a positive... a sign. I hadn't realized how much I missed my family until I got home. My everyday rolled along in one big, status quo. I guess I could look at everything as fluid right now. I don't *have* to stick to a timeline or a location. I'm at the point where my world's an open book, no matter how odd that is, I'm going to have to adjust.

Ama's subdued voice cuts through my tornado of thoughts. "Let me ask you this... how long are you staying?" The question doesn't rankle me like it usually does.

"I don't know that either."

She laughs, but there's no malice this time. "What's up with you, E? You're the planner. You never fly by your pants."

I bury my face in my hands, fighting off the rising panic. "I don't *like* flying without a plan, Ama. Everything's all crazy right now." I chance a look at Ama and see only sincerity, so I risk getting this giant elephant off my chest. "I can't go back to the clinic."

"Did you get fired?" She looks worried. Her eyes squint as she waves that pointy, red fingernail in my direction. "I knew something was up with you. You show up with no explanation, no talk about work or Tennessee. It's not like you."

I shrug, not willing to explain the idiocy at the clinic. A little afraid to, as well.

"Talk to me. What's going on?" Ama's head cocks to the side, her own curiosity waiting me out.

"I'm taking a leave of absence until I figure out what I'm gonna do."

"But something happened. You wouldn't just 'take a leave.' You've wanted to get out of Talon for as long as I can remember."

"I haven't," I huff, not liking that mirror turned on myself.

This time her smirk makes me chuckle, too. We both know I wanted to get out of our small town, away from people who know every embarrassment you've had since the day you were born.

"Did your boss hit on you?"

"Ack! No." I cringe, visualizing old man Michaels getting frisky. "I found out he was doing some shady stuff. And I don't know how to handle it or what I should to do about it. But I can't work at a clinic like that, so I left."

Ama's gaze shifts, worry clouding her dark brown eyes. "It must be big for you to say that."

"Yeah, I'm working on figuring everything out." I sigh, going back to rocking this nervous energy away. "My apartment isn't a problem. I could move. A new job is mandatory, I just need to work on my resume."

"Well, I'm glad you got away from whatever Mr. Creepy was doing." Ama squeezes my arm and I actually feel solid support from my sister for once. She smiles mischievously. "You know… you could stay here. Small towns need veterinarians too. And Talon may have a few other finely sculpted benefits walking around it as well."

I nail my frisky little sister with a don't go there look… I hope. "Finely sculpted has nothing to do with this," I warn.

"What the hell's wrong with you?" Her laughter is becoming obnoxious, echoing off the front porch until I'm afraid she's going to attract attention from wherever Dad's hiding on the farm.

I bite my tongue, trying not to glare and ruin our progress at moving away from bitchy. "I told you what's wrong with me, Ama."

"No, I mean you have a sexy man wanting you, with nothing holding you back from pursuing it—even for temporary fun—and you're still not acting on it." She looks at me like I'm beamed down from space. Like she can't imagine why I wouldn't change my entire life because a gorgeous guy shows some *temporary* interest.

I roll my eyes. Technically, I said I was thinking of moving, but I never thought about moving home. Not really.

"Ama, you would hate it if I moved home." I'm dead certain of that fact.

At my comment, Ama jolts from her chair, her shoulders held stiff as she walks to the steps. "Evie, I don't hate it when you're home... I hate that you left."

My eyes follow Ama to her car, feeling unsettled by the guilt swirling in my head.

There's too much to get done to worry about Ama right now, though. And none of it will get done with me sitting on the porch all day. I called Michaels, however unproductive that was. It's still a check off on my list, and after that enlightening conversation with my sister, there seems to be more possibilities in the air than when I woke up.

Looking out at the sun shimmering off the wild grass in our pasture, I take a deep breath and let it brighten my outlook on the day.

Chapter 16

♥

Wyatt

This morning, Evie's parting words have acted as a soul-crushing *Groundhog's Day,* repeating in my head on an endless loop. *It's been nice getting to know you.*

Bullshit!

I've spent four hours chopping a winter's worth of wood and the words still prickle. Sweat soaked through my shirt before I removed it, but I kept chopping. Now, the wetness is slicking my hands, adding difficulty—and an extra level of pain—to slinging the ax. Even for a shifter, there's only so much my body can handle. Taking a large gulp of water from my thermos, I curse the sun beating down my back. It mocks the shadows hanging over my mood.

Evie shut down all the progress we had made this week. She shut down my future. Now, I want to wallow in peace without Mother Nature insulting me.

If I had never met my mate, there would have always been a part of me missing, never whole. But at least I could have gone on living my life. Now that I know she exists, I can't rest. And my bear will never accept another, so I'll be stuck in this inevitable despair.

Only her. Give me my mate.

I growl at the fresh log in my hand, the irritation of constantly fighting my instinct wearing me down. I keep reminding myself that Evie's human. Her behaviors toward our relationship are especially human. But the glimpses of our mating bond are within her. I see it when she lets go and just feels... or when I get my hands get on her. That's my favorite way to spark the lightning between us.

Shit!

Blood floods south remembering Evie's soft curves pressed against me during our kiss last night. The way her nails scratched while I devoured her flavor. A fresh tidal wave of hormones rushes my body as the ax flies downward and just like that, all the headway I made toward suffocating my need for Evie—my need to claim—just washed away.

I realign the half log and lever the ax, ready to strike.

"Bro!" Caleb shouts, breaking through the clouds in my head. His voice sends my ax dangerously close to missing its target and I jerk around, annoyed by the interruption and for nearly chopping off my foot.

"What the hell, Cale!" My brother ignores my glare, handing me one of the iced beers in his hand before dropping his pajama-clad ass on the picnic table we chop beside.

I guess I could use a break.

Using my earlier soaked shirt, I wipe the streaks of dirt from my face, even if it's useless to dry the sweat. "Dude, not a good idea to surprise a man with an ax!" His smile drops at my tone, but I'm too irked to care.

"What's eating your berries?" "Got too much shit to do," I lie, not wanting to admit my inability to woo my mate.

"I see that."

"You still have the tour, later, right?"

"Yeah, man. Though, dude... when you named it exotic fly-fishing, I had a whole other picture in mind." His joke does it's job of softening my anger, as Caleb takes stock of my haphazard stack of logs spread across the grass. "Apparently, you decided to cut enough wood for the whole winter."

"I got enough for you, too."

"Sweet!" He grins with that boyish charm that wins him the ladies. "Any particular reason?"

"Gotta do something." My muscles bunch, finally straining after hours of work. I take the bench opposite my brother, noticing something looks off in his eyes. They're unusually dim. Dark circles pillow underneath, showing at least a few sleepless nights. "You alright, man?" I ask, inspecting my brother.

He shrugs. "I'm always good, Wy." But, Caleb stands to grab my dropped ax without meeting my eye.

"Then why's your face pinched like that?" I tease, waving a finger around his puckered expression. That's not the face of my normal, happy-go-lucky brother. Caleb lifts a choice finger, flicking off my laughter. Busting his balls feels good, despite my sour mood this morning. "Is it Kayah? Did something happen with you two?"

A provoked growl flies from Caleb at the same time the ax does. His brawny muscle cracks the log violently, sending an array of wood splinters flying from the power behind it.

"Not at all, Wy. Not. A. Single. Damn. Thing." Caleb bends over collecting shattered log pieces like they personally insulted him before tossing them on my stack. Caleb grabs a new victim.

Line, grunt... crack!

I chuckle as another shattered log hits the ground. I don't want his camaraderie over shared misfortune, but it seems my baby brother is just as enamored with an Amos sister as I am.

"Join the club, brother." I shake my head, but that has his attention.

Caleb's eyes widen. "But you and Evie were so close the other night. I assumed mating was imminent." I scoff, dragging a hand through my hair and squeezing past the pain in my head. "What happened?"

"Same as you," I growl. "Nothing. She's hot and cold, Cale, but... I swear she's hiding something." I guzzle the rest of my beer and jump up, the urge to pace making my skin crawl.

"So are you, brother."

Pointing out the obvious is not helpful, but his comment does bring me to a stop. I turn to face my brother, my teeth grinding in frustration. "She's my mate, Caleb. My fucking fated mate, and I can't get close enough to win her trust. Let alone tell her the big one."

Caleb wedges the ax in our stump and walks to my side. "You better tell her fast, Wy. I don't know a lot about fated mates, but your bear won't be denied for long." He pats my shoulder sympathetically, leaving me dumbfounded as he grabs our empty bottles and takes off to the sanctuary of his cabin.

How does my younger brother have a better grip on my life than I do?

Needing to normalize us again, I call out. "Caleb!" When he turns back, I flick him off with a grin. His laughter fades into the wind as he heads inside and leaves me to think over all the business tasks I've neglected in my past few days of distraction.

·❤·❤·❤·❤·❤·

By afternoon, I've knocked out so much work that I've barely thought about a certain Cherokee goddess. I'm pretty sure Evie would hate being called that, which reminds me of the few times she's gotten in my face and yelled her annoyance. The fire that flies from her angry eyes tempts me to call her the new moniker, just to get a rise. Too bad I have no idea when I'll get the chance.

My heart constricts.

No, I'm stuck flipping through my Rugged Tours binder, wishing I weren't too chicken to call my mate. She'd be perfect to help with my current dilemma. Sure, I can cart random strangers across the mountain and white-water raft through the forest, but when it comes to calling a woman I like… nope, making excuses.

Win her back.

Yeah, yeah.

My obnoxious bear was more than vocal during my tour this afternoon. Thankfully, it was a bunch of college guys who didn't mind a growly guide on their beginner rock climb, so it worked out. But now that I'm back in the office, trying to write a grant proposal, my brain is on a merry-go-round of Evie.

Ugh! Stop it!

Frustrated, I slam the binder closed on my laptop, taking joy in the snick of hard plastic against metal. My stomach rumbles, reminding me that I haven't eaten since breakfast. With a hazy pink glow taking over the sky, I know I'm well beyond my need for food.

We should be feeding Evie. My bear's plaintive groan annoys me.

You don't think I know that!

I've worked my ass off today trying to forget. I could have been shopping, prepping. Getting ready to show my woman I could provide a good meal and take care of her. Instead, the sinking disappointment hollows out my chest. I drag my feet to the fridge and riffle through the few Tupperware boxes that are well past their use date. The only edible items are a half empty juice container, some water bottles, and one beer. *One beer!*

With all my meat in the deep freezer, I've got no choice but to suck it up and drive to town. It's nights like tonight that I curse my remote cabin, and a shifter's need for privacy. I usually love it, but on these exhausted days, I envy people who live close enough for pizza delivery.

Twenty minutes later, I'm parked in front of Zeet's Grocery & Gas. It's large enough to get supplies for dinner—including beer—but small enough that I'm still supporting local business.

Zeet, himself, is an old wolf shifter who's lived on this mountain as long as I can remember. He stays in the quiet apartment over his store, never mingling much with the townspeople. Still, between wolves and bears, we have a 'you mind your business, we mind our business' type of respect.

Even Zeet's store has an element of privacy built into it. The frosted windows prevent it from resembling every other convenience store in small town America, but they also add an element of mystery to what's inside. No one sees the stacked rows of traditional store shelves, the two walls of freezers, and micro-organic section of produce.

That mystery is fate's best-friend tonight, because they obviously share a twisted sense of humor. I think both are responsible for the surprise I'm hit with when those oddly frosted automatic doors slide open. She's a vision.

Evie walks toward me, blinded by the armload of paper bags, and I smell her coming long before I catch sight of her tattered sweatpants and fitted tee. Those pants have had the life wrung out of them by a washing machine, but that shirt shows every dip and valley from her breasts to her waistline.

Finally, the woman who has occupied my thoughts all day—no matter how much I deny it—stops short. For a minute, I forget she put me out to pasture last night and step forward to relieve the bags from her hands.

"Evie." I smile. "You're looking beautiful today."

Startled, she glances down at herself and goes bright red when she realizes what she's wearing. "I uh, I borrowed leftovers from Ama's closet."

I smile at her nervous squeak, and say my first prayer of thanks to Ama. That shirt is heaven, stopping half an inch from her rolled up sweatpants, and making my thumbs itch to rub the smooth tease of skin it shows there.

Evie catches me staring and clears her throat. The haughty way she crosses her arms, should put me off, but it only draws my eyes to her pert chest, even though I'm trying my damnedest to behave.

She's got me too twisted... on edge. Finally, I give in and let go, my eyes caressing the soft curve of her breasts the way I wish my hands could. My cock throbs, completely unashamed of how this woman affects me. Still, I thank the stars when Evie laughs at the grin I give her, instead of slapping me like I know she could.

With her groceries in my hands, we turn toward her little red Jeep, as natural as if we're on a couple's shopping trip. The idea sounds like heaven to my bear, but as Evie opens her trunk, I notice that she keeps some distance between our bodies.

After sliding the bags inside, my arms are cleared and I realize I'm going to have to push Evie out of her comfort zone—at least a bit. It's the only way I'll break down whatever wall she's put up with me. I watch her fiddling with her keys, keeping that distance between us while she tugs the band of that mini-shirt lower.

"Are you afraid to get to close to me?"

"What?" Those nervous eyes jerk to me, shocked that I'd call her out. It only makes her more enticing and the victory's going to be even sweeter when I win my mate.

Stepping closer, I dare her with my eyes to disagree, laughing when she presses the trunk button and moves to the driver side. I'm right behind her, my lungs drowning in the sweet aroma of my mate's arousal. She's not unaffected. I want her to admit she wants me... to be honest with herself.

"Where you running to, Evie?"

Her choked laughter verges on hysterical, our bond must be torturing her with my close proximity. She doesn't know what to do with it. It's to my benefit that she's too stubborn to back down or I think my mate would be a blur of tailpipe right now.

My bear howls when we're interrupted by a chime in her pocket, just as I was about to move in and remind her of why we're good together. The alert causes the same v to crease her forehead as last night, diminishing the scent of her arousal almost immediately.

"Is it your sister?" My question distracts her for a minute, but when she looks at the phone, the stress is back. Her eyes scan the parking lot with... fear.

Now, it's my turn to freak out. *What is she afraid of?*

When the wind shifts, I'm hit with a bigger surprise... shifter. Whatever was there is gone now, but the scent lingers in the air. I breathe in, trying to place the awful stench. It's not bear... or wolf. I know other shifters live on the mountain, but as far as I can tell, this scent is unique—foreign.

Does the weird shifter have something to do with Evie? Does she know it's a shifter or is something else threatening her?

In my distracted state, Evie pockets her phone and slides inside the car. Only my mate's accelerated heart rate advertises trouble, the rest of her does its best to hide whatever stress is out there.

Bending down, I put myself in her doorway, blocking her view from the outside, or whatever's out there view of her. "Evie... Evie." I snap my fingers, waiting until she breaks the trance and meets my eye. "You can tell me anything," I promise, hating how she's white knuckling the steering wheel.

Doubt swims behind Evie's eyes and I reach out, cupping her chin until she has no choice but to listen. The confusion on her face breaks my heart. I need her to talk to me.

"You barely know me, Wyatt." Her voice is choked, her fingers digging into the hand that holds her still.

Before I can argue our deeper connection, her features harden. Determination firms everything from the line of her lips to the rigidity in her shoulders, the straight line of her back. The tiniest puff of air blows across my skin and I let her remove my hand from her chin. I'd never truly hold her against her will.

Evie squeezes my hand, almost conciliatory with her strained smile as she cranks the car. "I have to go, but… we'll chat later."

Reluctantly, I straighten and let her door close. After she drives away, I scan the parking lot, wishing like hell I knew what was bothering my mate so I could fix it. There's barely a trace of the odd stink in the air. I contemplate shifting so I could track it in bear form easier, but I'd have little luck after waiting this long. I need to accomplish step one first, finish my shopping. The rest of my plan is completely up in the air, but whatever it is, it will involve winning my mate.

And she will be mine. Because I know damn well, if Evie is my mate, under my protection, she won't have to worry about something looming over her in the night air. Nothing will come close to hurting her again.

Chapter 17

♥

Evie

By Wednesday morning, I can't take it anymore. I've rolled over my interaction with Wyatt on Saturday and my conversation with Ama a million times. It's a well-shined piece of coal at this point, but I still have a disgruntled feeling that something's missing.

The only solution I see is to make amends—or at least get on civil terms—with Wyatt. We're adults. There's absolutely no reason to avoid the guy because I've embarrassed myself one or two—or twenty—times.

His expression was so earnest on Saturday, offering an ear for me to unload my problems. Offering his support, if I'd only trust him. While I can't do that, I owe it to myself to explore the other side of our relationship. Even for the sole reason that the only time I've felt whole since leaving Tennessee is when I'm close to Wyatt. I was so close to giving in when that unknown text hit my phone and scared the crap out of me.

Don't think your new boyfriend will protect you, Doctor.

It was a stake through the heart. As enticing as Wyatt's is, and no matter how much I regret not snuggling up with him after that kiss on Friday, I could *not* shake the feeling he was in danger by being with me. My brain couldn't think past the overwhelming need to protect him—by removing myself—so I ran. Well... drove away.

Unfortunately, the rest of the night, like the last four days, replayed the lust in Wyatt's eyes in all its Technicolor, 4K glory. No man has ever looked at me that way, so sometimes it's hard to get out of my own way and believe someone who looks like Wyatt isn't playing some cruel joke. But I don't want to constantly wait for the rug to rip out from under me.

My heart says give in... trust. Only, it's been years since I've dated anyone. It took three whole days, but by last night, I realized I needed to explore a relationship—even a physical one—for as long as that look lasts. And to stop with the guilt.

You are not a slut if you explore a purely physical relationship at least once before you're thirty.

Ama would agree. Especially if I told her I couldn't remember the last time I had a relationship that led to the bedroom. So, sue me if my backed-up hormones have brought me to Wyatt's office cabin at a stupidly early hour with two cups of coffee, a bag of donuts, and a branch I cut from an overgrown tree in my yard.

Smokey Mountain Rugged Tours is hand carved on a wood sign over the cabin door. The rustic building nestles under tall pine trees, perfectly fitting in its surroundings, like not a piece of nature was disturbed when they built the place.

Arming myself for a solid apology, I walk between the neatly trimmed honeysuckle vines and holly bushes that line the front walk, not even realizing I'm holding my breath until my lungs start to burn. Exhaling, I lift my arm to knock, but the door flies away from my fist before I make contact. I startle, my other hand—the one holding the stick—darting out to defend myself and nearly whacking Wyatt in the face. *Smooth.*

"Olive branch," I yelp, thrusting the branch into his chest before I lose my nerve. "It's a peace offering." I hold up his rewards, the non-plant variety, and smile when he grabs the coffee first.

Wyatt's deep, masculine chuckle relieves my lingering stress, but I still feel like a dork. My face is probably flaming. I know I deserve it though, after the roller coaster I've made the man ride this week.

"No offering needed, but I'll never turn away coffee and sweets. Come on in," he offers, his dimpled smile denting the five o'clock shadow he hasn't taken the time to shave this morning. It's masculine kryptonite and completely impossible not to smile back.

He leads me into his cozy office, which is a small minefield of notebooks and binders, papers spread all over sections of the floor and a second-hand coffee table. He looks nervous trying to clear the thing off, like he's embarrassed for me to see his mess. It's a rare switch of our roles, since I'm usually the one tripping over myself around Wyatt's intimidating personality.

I'm loving the slight reprieve. From the chaos in my head, as well as, the chilly September air, so I give him some time to collect himself and toss my coat on the back of the chair by the door.

Finally, I follow Wyatt with my own coffee to the plaid couch he has set up for clients, trying my best to keep my eyes from dropping to the vision that is his backside. Big surprise, I fail, and Wyatt turns before I'm able to pop my damn eyes back up from those distressed jeans that cup his very fine set of muscles. He smirks, but lets me off without calling me out.

"Did I interrupt?" I ask, watching Wyatt stack his paperwork. He's obviously been up and working well before my seven-thirty intrusion.

"Nah, there are no tours today, so I was getting some office work done." His smooth calm soothes my worries that he'd reject my peace offering after Friday night... and Saturday night.

He looks at his papers, and then back at me, like he's torn. It's not my place to read over his shoulder, so I lean back and take a sip of coffee. "If you're busy, I can just come back another time," I offer, already hating the idea.

"No!" He places a hand on my knee, almost like he wants to hold me in place, so I take him at his word and relax into some small talk before the awkward apology I came here for.

"What're you working on?"

"A grant proposal," he sighs, his voice wary... tired. Wyatt lets the papers fall to his lap as he flops back against the couch with me.

Those massive hands dive into thick strands of hair, scratching his scalp in a rough massage. The flipped ends stand on edge by the time his fingers finish the trek, and it looks like he's been tugging for hours already. *A nervous tick?*

Wyatt's turns to me with a small smile, his red-rimmed eyes showing exactly how little sleep he's gotten since the last time I saw him. I feel awful, hoping I didn't add to his stress level.

He takes a sip of coffee and moans, those sinful eyes rolling back comically while I mentally thank the bakery in town for putting that look on Wyatt's face. Looking renewed, he grabs a page of rough draft notes from his binder and passes it to me.

"My problem is... I know bears, but I'm still learning how to present their preservation in a way a school will accept." He looks at the page in my hand, self-consciousness radiating off him in waves. "College homework isn't my area of expertise," he admits, that usual spark of excitement I associate with Wyatt gone. I want to give it back, to put that light back in his eyes that give them that golden glow.

"Anything I can do to help? I excel at being a dork." My offer earns a grin from Wyatt that turns his handsomeness up to an unhealthy level. *Seriously, I've never gotten that look from offering to do someone's homework.*

He practically shoves the rest of the papers and the binder he's been studying in my hand. "This is what I have so far."

Those caramel eyes are hopeful and maybe slightly relieved. Plus, the binder isn't the mess of work I expected. There are line graphs and pie charts, statistics of animal deaths, protection numbers, and rescue strategies. It's organized, structured... my nerdy girl word porn.

"Holy cow, Wyatt! This is incredible!"

He must have a lot of stress riding on this presentation because even that small approval deflates his lungs, the exhale of air physically dropping his shoulders. Even though Wyatt and I went head-to-head over his hunting stereotype, this information is well put together, more of an educational strategy than any prejudice.

"You're off to an impressive start." I swipe through pages of research, the integration of local ordinances, short-comings, and future educational pathways. "Could you show me? The areas you plan to protect." I glance up, nervous to invite myself into his day. "It would bode well for your project if a veterinarian signed off on the strategy."

Wyatt stops, his laser focus freezing me on the spot. "You would do that?"

I nod, feeling myself go warm, like when I asked out my first date to the school dance. I hate putting myself out there, but judging by Wyatt's face, he's not minding a little feminine forwardness. Especially if it helps his passion project. Suddenly, that smile is back and I feel ten-feet tall for putting it there.

And then, Wyatt's in motion, pulling me up so quickly, I nearly drop my paper coffee cup. One hand tangles with mine, tossing a grin over his shoulder that nearly melts my panties. The other lifts the massive pack sitting by the front door like it's nothing, and then we're out.

I'm surprised when we skip the truck and head behind his office to a crude nature trail. It's barely more than a narrow dirt path rutted into nature, one that, judging from the signs, he deems too dangerous for tourists.

Wyatt still has my hand. As we walk, he fills me in on his progress so far, some of which I see in the warning signs and citation postings.

There're strategic map postings guiding tourists to safer travel routes where they'll encounter less dangerous wildlife.

"Did you know a bear with access to human food halves its life expectancy?" I turn, surprised to find Wyatt's handsome face shadowed, the anger emanating from his eyes raising the hair on the back of my neck.

"I didn't know that."

"The number of preventable species deaths along the east coast is staggering," he vents passionately. "I want to teach these kids, starting with the littlest, elementary ones on those field trips, that Black bears are nothing to be afraid of. If they know how to avoid them, a lot fewer accidental run-ins would end in human injury, which usually leads to increased bear hunting." He looks nervously over his shoulder. "Bears only lash out if they're hunting food or protecting their cubs."

I chuckle, thinking about every animals' basic instinct for self-preservation.

"What's the end goal? Won't people still run into bears? It's the forest, they should know that going in."

"The goal is decreasing the number of useless deaths. If a bear attacks a camp for food because trashcans don't have a simple, lockable lid, or people didn't do their research and stay on a state-approved trail, that bear should not have a death sentence. If bears get used to human foods, they'll search that out instead of salmon or small game. Or, if people are swimming in the feeding rivers because there were no posted signs, guess what they're gonna find?"

I sarcastically cut my eyes at him. "Bears?"

"Yep! And guess who gets the bad rap after a human attack, even though that human is in their habitat? Or if they stroll where a mama bear is protecting her cub?"

"The bear."

"Yep! Do you know how many idiots come to this forest with zero knowledge of survival techniques?"

I chuckle, even though Wyatt's face does not find the topic funny. "Hundreds?"

"Thousands." His somber tone stops my laughter immediately, the weight of our conversation thickens the air between us. He cares about these animals.

"So, your plan is to get humans to stop being idiots?"

"I hope to train the future generation." He taps the binder I'm hugging to my chest. "This part will decrease the number of idiots. My survival tours will help the current idiots." Wyatt turns up the hill again, pulling my hand behind him like it's the most natural thing in the world.

Our trek is tough, but Wyatt stops a few times to let me catch my breath without making a big deal of it. The efforts Wyatt has made so far are visible along the hike.

A posted sign illustrates survival techniques for each breed of bear. "This sign is awesome," I admit, studying one chart. "I didn't know *not* to play dead with every bear." I almost don't hear his chuckle, but I definitely feel the squeeze of his arm around my shoulders. It relieves some of the sting from Wyatt laughing at me.

"That's why we need these signs," he says, watching my reaction. "I want to teach people avoidance tips, then the techniques they need—like this—because it's inevitable that hikers and campers are going to run across wildlife. That's part of communing with nature."

Wyatt fills in more facts about bear habits and feeding grounds as we continue up the mountain. Eventually, we cross a riverbed known for salmon fishing and I tense up, searching for bears.

"We offer a fly-fishing tour, so we can steer people away from here. This area is common for bears preparing for hibernation. If people invade it, there could be dangerous repercussions… for both sides." His warning draws my eyes to the forest, scouring for wildlife.

Eventually, I fall behind Wyatt's steady gait, practicing more careful observation, but also enjoying the view of Wyatt's cargo pants climbing the steep incline in front of me.

I have no idea how far we've walked, but in front of us, the forest thins, opening to a wide clearing. Mountain laurel lines the edges of a wild grass bed, cooling under the canopy shade while bluets bask the same sun that warms our faces. The perimeter fades into a jagged rock wall that acts as a natural barrier from falling off the mountain.

A trance-like state washes over me, the mountain's serene beauty drawing me closer to the edge. My soul is drawn to the nature around us, the energy that buzzes like a hive of angry bees being called home. I gape, standing at the mouth of a rock bridge that forms a connection between two sections of our mountain. It's majestic. The earth molded by God and the environment, into the structure it needs.

"Eveline," Wyatt whispers hoarsely, stalking closer with smooth, panther-like steps.

I've never heard my full name on his lips—didn't know he knew it. But the vibration of Wyatt's voice hits me low in the stomach. An overwhelming sense of need tightening my chest, surrounding me with everything Wyatt: his shining eyes, that sharp jawline roughened with stubble. The longer I watch him stride closer, the larger his presence is, the stronger his pull.

A whoosh of wind whistles across the cliff, stirring the leaves under our feet. The longer grasses tickle my ankles as we gaze out on the dizzying height. "It's beautiful," I comment, needing a distraction from the chaos churning through me.

"Yes, it is." Wyatt nudges my chin to face him, his eyes piercing and holding me in place. There's no doubt, he's not talking about the view.

The implication heats my cheeks, but Wyatt's thumb slowly tracing its way along the blush distracts me. "Exquisite," he breathes, closing the last bit of space between us.

The wind from the valley below lifts my hair, swirling it around us in a wild party, but all I feel are Wyatt's strong hands cupping my face. That briefest touch of Wyatt's lips melts my insides, erasing everything: the chill against my skin, the blinding glare of the sun, the exhilaration of standing on the edge of danger. None of it compares to the heaven of Wyatt's kiss.

His lips part mine, delving in for a deeper taste that steals my air. Our scents mingle in this cocoon of passion, Wyatt's rough woodsy to my softer honey. The mixture reminds me of home, of roasting s'mores by a campfire. I'm drowning in it and for once, not embarrassed or feeling out of place.

A puzzle piece locks in place. I would have missed so much if I had pushed Wyatt, or he would have let me.

When Wyatt pulls back, my lungs are on fire, but I'm desperate for more. I don't want to let go, so I don't. My fingers tighten around Wyatt's biceps, keeping him close. At least I'm comforted that Wyatt's ragged breaths mirror my own. With our foreheads pressed together, every exhale pants against my lips and I revel in it.

"Wyatt…" His name is a sigh tickling my lips. I don't want to break this spell, but that beaming smile eases my worry.

"Let's go." Wyatt's hand on my neck slides lower, guiding me away from the rock face even though the crisp wind has died away. Wyatt protects me from the rough terrain as we walk unified down the mountain.

A full ten minutes pass with my mind reliving that kiss in vivid detail, but Wyatt is chatty. Our conversation is full of sexy innuendos, but it's flirty... fun. More natural than any date I've had, and this didn't even start as a date.

I learn about Wyatt's life on the mountain, his struggles of starting the business and dealing with pressures from his family. I fill in details of my life he doesn't know, which is a lot. Though Wyatt got a magnified Polaroid of my family on Friday, I give a backdrop into each persona, my relationships.

"So, what's better? Your family being all in your business here, or your coworkers ignoring you in Knoxville?" he asks after I tell him how the office staff—especially the females—ignored me at the clinic.

"I used to think nosiness was the worst thing ever! When I couldn't sneak to a party without a neighbor reporting my car or hold hands in a theater without my dad giving the third degree about the boy." He laughs, easing my tension at sharing such personal thoughts. "It's not until you're older that you see that meddling as effort from people who love you. Hell, maybe I wouldn't have seen it without my coworkers ignoring me. I don't know." I've only recently discovered how powerful my loneliness in Tennessee had been.

So far, Wyatt has said all the right things along our walk. It feels so easy now. I share as many details as I feel safe doing about the convoluted office I just left, which I haven't fully cut all ties to yet... but soon. He's a peacemaker, even-keeled, logical without being heartless.

I am so happy I brought him coffee this morning.

We're halfway down the mountain, when Wyatt stops short, the hard-line of his body cocked tight like the band of a slingshot. His uneasiness makes the hair on the back of my neck stand up. I scour the landscape looking for whatever spooked Wyatt. *Did he see a bear?*

Before I can ask, Wyatt sprints away from me, his body darting around trees with an athletic nimbleness I've never seen before. I follow as close as I can, partially amazed by the bunched muscles powering

Wyatt's legs, and partially pissed off that he left me behind with whatever scared him. It's apparent he panicked, because I can't come close to catching up, no matter how fast I run.

What the hell happened?

"Wyatt," I yell, watching him disappear around a curve. I swear I'll kill him if I get lost in these woods. I'm already considering it just from the burn in my legs. They're pumping hard to keep up with his massive stride.

A hot bead of sweat rolls down my spine, convincing my own worn out body to give up the chase just as I round the bend where I lost sight of Wyatt. Thankfully, Mr. Agility Pro is right there, kneeling over a whimpering bear that's sprawled on the ground.

A pained growl circles the clearing of an old campsite, but I can't tell if the sound is coming from the distressed bear or Wyatt. He shouldn't be that close to an upset bear.

Fear for his safety—and my own—freezes my feet in place.

"Wyatt," I whisper, willing him to back away from the dangerous animal. "Wy, you've got to back up." He ignores my urgent whisper, but I'm afraid to speak louder. Wyatt said you have to project calm around all bears in the wild, no matter their breed. But, while Wyatt isn't calm, he doesn't seem afraid in the least.

Is he crazy?

Slowly, I creep closer, my curiosity leading me to investigate. Or at minimum, pulling me within reach to get this crazy man away from danger if it comes to that. I know he loves these bears, but this is a little much. Wyatt should know better.

Injured animals are dangerous. Although, for some reason, this one allows Wyatt's hands to rub deep in his fur, groaning like he's basking in a human's comfort. Getting closer, I'm mesmerized. Wyatt's calming fingers massage the bear's thick black coat along his shoulder, shushing like it's the most natural thing in the world to be petting a bear.

A howl of pain echoes through the campsite, jerking me forward in case Wyatt needs my help. The animal's reaction when Wyatt stroked his shoulder means his injury is serious, and so is the danger.

As if in a trance, Wyatt backs his shaky hands out of the fur, finding .them coated in thick red liquid. Now I see why he's so upset. This incident is *exactly* what Wyatt fights to prevent, and judging by his stricken expression, he feels like he failed. From his perch beside the massive bear, Wyatt lets loose an inhuman roar, startling me back a few steps from man and bear.

"Wyatt," I hiss. "You're gonna scare the bear." This thing could attack any minute.

Although, from his prone spot on the ground, the bear doesn't look that frightening. In fact, it looks like his giant paw is resting on Wyatt's knee... without sinking his talons in. No aggression is coming off the bear at all, only that pitiful moaning sound.

Wyatt, on the other hand, is a turbulent mess. His anger is palpable through the air and I worry if I feel it, then this bear may feel it too. Wyatt is going to get himself killed at this rate.

That concern kicks me into action, doctor mode conquering my fear enough to nudge Wyatt's shoulder out of the way. I need to inspect the bear's wound and Wyatt needs to get us help.

"Walkie for help, Wyatt." Pain-filled eyes drag to mine, not comprehending my words. "Wyatt," I repeat louder. "We need to patch him up and I'm sorry, but we can't carry a few hundred pounds between the two of us."

Finally, Wyatt blinks, fighting his daze to stand and grab the walkie from his bag. His hands leave a red trail down the front of his pants where he wipes them, but I don't think he cares. He does look anxious to leave though, and I smile.

"I'll be fine." *Hopefully.* I'm not sure how, but I sense this bear understands we're here to help. He hasn't made a move to attack. Not even threatened to.

Tenderly, I press into the bear's fur, moving across his shoulder to inspect the wound Wyatt found. I try to be gentle, and hear no protest from my patient until his slight grumble bear when I find the exit wound under his back.

I shush the beast, hoping my voice sooths our injured friend. "I know that hurts, big boy. Shh… it sucks, but this is what we want. It means that nasty bullet's out of you." He purrs roughly, seeming to agree with with me, so I rub behind his ears. I hope he feels my intentions to comfort. Maybe it can sooth him through a pain I'm sure he doesn't understand. "That's right, tough guy. Shh… that big one over there's gonna call you some help. We'll fix you up soon."

From somewhere behind me, the sound of Wyatt's walkie buzzes, but I'm concentrating on the task in front of me. I trust Wyatt to get us out of here. I just have to figure out how to triage a bear in the middle of a forest.

Using the flashlight on my phone, I check the bear's pupils, trying not to disturb him or piss him off too much. They dilate properly and thankfully the large Black bear doesn't mind me leaning over his head, not that I want to test my luck too much.

My movements are slow, but I manage to lift the side of his massive jowl, trusting the bear won't suddenly decide to make my hand lunch. "Good boy," I praise when I see no signs of blood. The bullet must have struck muscle and stayed away from internal organs. The steady rise and fall of his chest show a healthy breathing pattern, despite the pain I suspect he's in. The bear will need x-rays and a proper flush of his wound, but I think this is one lucky bear, all things considered.

Having done what I can without proper tools, I tear a strip of fabric from my t-shirt and wad it into makeshift gauze. It works to press against the bear's wound and stem the blood, though I don't like the amount of blood covering my hands after such a brief exam.

When I turn to check on Wyatt and our status for a ride, he's only a few feet away from my crouched position. His face is a marvel of artwork no matter if he's looking at me with heat like earlier, or with shock... like right now.

"You aren't scared?" he asks, his voice awed.

Surprised, I glance at the bear, realizing how idiotic this looks. Except, I'm not feeling fear of the massive animal, only pity and worry. My heart gets why Wyatt devotes so much of his life to protecting these creatures. And, I think I'm ready to join his battle.

Chapter 18

♥

Wyatt

It takes every ounce of willpower in my body to step back from Jackson and let Evie take over. The only extra push I have is knowing she's a doctor and better able to care for my friend than I am.

The problem is, if I don't remove myself from this situation and get control, I'm going to announce our secret in a huge way. My bear's already frantically clawing from the inside. He's ready to hunt down whatever asshole shot Jax.

Groaning, I scratch my hands through my hair, relieving the tension headache building at the roots. My senses muted the second I saw Jackson lying on the ground. My vision tunneled, my awareness centered on my bleeding best friend and nothing else.

The shocking thing is, Evie *hasn't* panicked, and I don't smell fear. I kept an eye on her while I walked further into the campground, searching for even the smallest square inch that has cell service under these trees. *Nothing!*

Fuming, I drop my pack to the ground and unsnap my radio, pressing the button to alert Caleb in rapid succession. *He'd better have his radio on him.*

I buzz again impatiently, knowing my brother leaves his walkie in a variety of locations not actually on his body. The radio is dead silent. I press again and finally, on the fourth chirp, Caleb's voice breaks through the static.

"Yo, bro. Standby." He clicks off before I can utter a word. My hand grips the radio, squeezing until I hear a crack in the hard shell. Immediately, I let go. *You need a functioning radio to help Jax, dumb ass.*

"Fuck standby, Caleb. We've got a gunshot wound. I need the truck, *now!*" I grind my commands through clenched teeth, wondering how I'm going to get a clue to Caleb that this is Jax without alerting Evie.

"Go again." Caleb's concerned voice pipes through the radio, no longer flippant.

"Gunshot. Bear. Need the truck. Over." I'm pacing, watching Evie's face for signs of panic.

"Local? Over." It's a smooth way for Caleb to ask if this is shifter emergency over an open line.

"Affirmative. 9-1-1, over." Dread chokes my voice as Evie works on my best friend. Jax can't die. He just can't. *Goddamn hunters!*

"What's your twenty?"

Caleb's breath puffs through the radio, so I know he's already running to the truck and on the way. Relieved, I let the smallest exhale escape and radio our location, confident Caleb will be here soon.

With my heart lodged in my throat, I walk back to Evie who's leaning over one of the most important people in my life... and she has no idea. Guilt washes over me. All the secrets I'm hiding... how do I even start that conversation. My brother's words flash through my mind... *better tell her yourself, before she finds out on her own.*

Witnessing Jax allow Evie to care for him while he's in so much pain shows how much he trusts her. Yet, I'm not doing the same. He must sense her tie to me, our fated bond.

We tell her when we get off this mountain. My bear pushes the thought into my mind, solidifying my resolve.

Evie continues working diligently while I stare. I'm completely useless... in awe. Until she tears the bottom of her shirt to use as gauze. That snaps out of my stupor. Finally, pushing me to kneel and help.

"How's he doing?" I ask, rubbing the tense muscles along Jackson's neck. I have no idea if it's comforting Jax or myself, but either way I stroke his ears, letting Evie finish her crude bandage.

From my hip, Caleb's voice chirps through the radio. "Bro, can you get 'em down the mountain to the lot?" A weak growl vibrates in Jax's chest, making Evie's hands jerk back from his wound, fear clouding her eyes briefly.

Realizing what Caleb said, she stares at me in confusion. "Does he think you can carry a five-hundred-pound bear by yourself?" I try not to take offense, knowing human males would have no chance to carry such a load. She shakes her head in amusement, swinging my pack to her back for our hike down the mountain with Jax's extra load.

I radio my brother in front of Evie, letting him know I need help to get the injured bear down the mountain. His laughter rings back, but I pocket the radio before he can say anything else incriminating.

Part of me wants to confess now before my brother arrives and busts my balls for being chicken-shit. Especially because Jax needs medical attention. My nerves shouldn't come before that.

Evie's still chuckling under her breath when she walks back over. I'm still squatting over Jax, trying to visualize how to confess the truth to the woman I want to be my mate.

She will be our mate! She will accept us. I know she will.

"Look, I know you're big and all, but does your brother honestly think you'd be able to carry a full-grown Black bear down the mountain?"

My laugh is stilted, even to my own ears. "Well, there's uh... a lot about our family I haven't gotten to share with you yet." I chance a look at Evie but only see curiosity. She's waiting expectantly for me to continue. "We have certain strengths… abilities."

Her shocked giggle cuts me off. "Did you guys win a strong-man competition or something?"

She flusters my train of thought. How do you explain to a human that you're actually a beast with supernatural abilities? She'll think I'm crazy and run away. Or get scared and run away… she's alone in the woods with a man she barely knows—by human standards. If I tell her my secret now, there's no way this will work.

"Well, uh, this big guy here is actually our friend." I know it's the smallest bit of truth and the easiest to explain.

Evie's face softens and I fully expect 'aww' to come out of her mouth any minute. Or, if she were Ms. Beachum, my cheeks would be squished between her fingers right now. Self-loathing tries to take over, making it difficult to navigate the trickiest conversation of my adult life.

"You have a Yogi Bear friend?" she jokes, drawing a disgruntled noise from Jax. I open my mouth to clarify, but clam up, embarrassed that she assumes I'm just extra cuddly to this bear because of my protection program. "Do you have him tagged? How do you know who he is?"

How can I possibly explain our reality?

"Not exactly," I grumble, struggling to think straight with my friend bleeding on the ground.

"That's adorable!" Evie's sweet tone irritates my oversensitive bear, but thankfully, before his anger snaps, the rumble of a truck engine catches both our attentions.

My radio squawks. "Flying in, over." A relieved breath whooshes out hearing my brother's voice. Without Evie here, I wouldn't need Caleb's help. So, the faster he gets here, the less risk my lies put Jax in, and the less guilt I have to swallow later.

In half the time it would take a human, Caleb rushes into the clearing holding a thick blanket for us to carry Jax's body down. His feet quicken seeing Jax in bear form on the ground. In a few steps, he's at our side seething with judgment that could fill the Grand Canyon.

"You could have done this faster," Caleb growls under his breath.

Before I can defend myself—that I'm protecting our species with my caution to reveal our secret—Evie comes closer, hovering where Caleb and I work the large fabric under Jax's bulk. She bends, helping us lift one side of the injured bear, cooing to him as she does. Caleb's gaping shock doesn't escape my notice. We lock eyes. His *'told ya so'* painted in neon letters across his features.

She's stronger than you give her credit for, Caleb pushes into my head. Like I don't notice Evie's smooth handling of a normally feared beast.

When the three of us get Jax settled on the blanket, Evie scratches her fingers into the fur behind his ears, soothing our friend like the big-hearted animal lover she is.

"See, big guy. You're in excellent hands." She winks at me, and I try not to trip from the remorse roiling my gut. Evie's soothing voice speaks to Jax like a person, narrating our journey down the trail to keep him calm. "These guys are going to get you help, and I promise I'll check on you since you were so good and didn't bite me." Caleb snickers, but Evie ignores us both and keeps focus on her patient, petting him on our hike to the truck. "That's right, boy. Such a good Yogi for letting me treat your ouchie."

Caleb barks with laughter, never faltering in his steps, but Jax finds less humor in the situation. His bear-head tosses, dislodging Evie's hand, but his onyx eyes stay on me… chastising.

If either of you ever think of using that nickname, I will bury you under a pile of discarded whiskey bottles and burn you alive!

Nothing I can do to change that right now, so I focus on keeping the pace of a normal human. I still cringe when Evie huffs under the weight of my backpack.

Your lies have strained our mate. Even my bear tosses criticism, making Evie the only person in this forest who doesn't want to kick my ass.

Thank God the parking lot's only ten minutes from where Jax was shot. Caleb and I heft his body into the back of my brother's old truck as gently as we can. I jump to the ground with one last worried look for my friend. *He has to be OK!*

"I'll ride in the back with Mr. Bear here, so I can keep pressure on his wound," Evie offers, hoisting herself onto the tailgate.

"No way!" I grip her elbow, tugging until Evie's lithe body falls off balance and back in my arms. She squeaks in surprise, but I hold tight, unphased by the press of her hands against my chest. The annoyance eclipsing her smile is another story. I'm not loving so many people judging my actions. I'm Alpha, or I will be in the future.

"What the hell do you think you're doing?"

The wiggle of Evie's body to put space between us is doing delicious things—none of which she intends—to my cock. It hardens uncomfortably just from holding her body against mine. Right until her knee accidentally—*God, I hope it was accidentally*—connects with my groin.

"Ung," I moan painfully, releasing Evie to her feet. She crosses her arms, all traces of the sweet, bedside manner gone while she stares me down. Caleb snickers but slams the tailgate, effectively siding with me against Evie's dangerous ride down a mountain in the back of a truck.

I'm going to win this argument.

"You riding in the back would be ten levels of stupid," I snarl. "The safety alone is a no-go... plus, you'd be in a tight space with an injured bear you don't know."

Evie momentarily drops her arms to her side, her glare shifting to offended confusion. "Well, I'm sorry if I'm not on a first name basis with every bear in the forest. Should I take him out for coffee? Exchange screen names for a little cyber-stalking?"

A chuffing snort reaches us from the back of the truck, and I know Jax is loving every second of me getting schooled by a woman. If my friend wasn't in the middle of an emergency and I wasn't in a hurry to get his ass to Doc V, there'd be a load more ball-busting.

Evie casts an uneasy look at my friend, her expression softening for him—not for me—though I still have a hold of her arm. Mainly because I can't bring myself to let her go.

"I just want to help, Wyatt." Her eyes brim with pain and frustration. "I miss helping animals, doing good… I need to have a purpose." Her voice trails off as Caleb climbs in his truck, pretending he isn't eavesdropping into her private moment. I tip my head to confirm I'll handle Evie and watch him take off toward the shifter friendly vet in town.

Resigned, I reach behind Evie and transfer my bag she's carrying back to my shoulder. "You OK for a short walk?" I ask, not waiting to take her hand. She glances down, fixated on Jax's blood covering both our hands. "There's a stream about five minutes from here, close to my cabin. We aren't too far away."

She nods but stays silent as I guide her through the lower, beginner trail that leads to the Rugged Tours cabin.

Just like I promised, a bubbling stream breaks our path a few minutes away. I steer Evie to a flat boulder along the edge and sit her beside my bag. I don't like the silent treatment she's giving me, unless she's traumatized. That would be worse.

Evie's eyes follow my every movement as I grab the empty water bottle from my outside mesh and load it with stream water. Mechanically, she holds out her rust colored hands and arms, accepting the cool wash of water I pour over them. The spill of red against the dirt below burns the back of my eyes, but Evie remains stoic.

I have to reload the bottle twice to get all the blood from both our hands, but finally, when it's all gone, gratitude washes over me for my mate. Evie was here on the worst day in my adult life, and she didn't show a single hesitancy when she saved my friend.

Mine.

Looking down, I wrap her now clean hands in mine. "You were amazing out there," I whisper, my voice choking around the lump in my throat.

Her head dips under my praise, a sweet blush kissing the top of her cheeks, but at least the fog that was dimming her glow has lifted. Evie takes the towel I offer and dries her hands, focusing on the muddied dirt swimming with bear's blood instead of looking me in the eye.

Kneeling, I lift those sweet, chocolate eyes to mine, saddened by their glassy expression. "Thank you for saving Yogi." I smirk at her earlier joke, happy to swallow my pride if it'll restore my mate's smile.

"It's my job." She shrugs, her flush deepening. I smile at her shaking head. She doesn't get how amazing she was.

"It's not *just* your job," I insist, holding her face so she can't turn away. "It was your bravery, and your brain. The way you jumped in there when you saw an injured animal. It didn't matter that it wasn't a cute little puppy, or that you had no idea what danger he presented." I bring her forehead to mine, just to feel our connection tingling below her warmth, letting it light up my skin. "It. Was. Amazing."

Deep inside, the yearning for my mate's connection threatens to take over my common sense. Especially standing this close, after the emotions of the day. Breathing her air like it's my favorite source of oxygen.

It's very difficult to bury my baser instincts.

Before I can make a move, one way or the other, Evie surprises me by levering herself off the flat rock, using my shirt for grounding to bring her body tight against my front. Our eyes hold for a split second, the air steaming the cold air between us, and then my brain is wiped clean. Those pillowy lips press firm to mine, igniting the fire raging in my blood with her uncharacteristic forwardness.

My inner beast roars, feeling like a king being given a pot of gold. I take the opening, one hand tilting her face for better access while the other braces the slope of her waist, dragging her warmth against my raging hard-on. It has a life of its own around this woman.

Evie's arms reach up, her fingers scratching through the longer hair on the back of my head, sending chills across my body. Her touch makes me ache with a need to have her hands everywhere. A desperation teases through me until my bear takes over our kiss. His nose picked up the scent of Evie's arousal, gas-lighting my hormones.

My tongue licks across her lower lip, nibbling lightly before I press harder, urging her to give me access. White noise thrums through my head, blurring every sensation except the press of Evie's body, the stroke of her hands down my shoulders. A soft mewling noise hits my ears when she opens for us and my bear purrs. The deep sound vibrating from my own throat without my control.

Sliding both hands under the lush curve of Evie's ass, I stand, relishing the way her legs wrap my hips, squeezing me tight against her middle though I hold her weight easily in my hands. For a few minutes, we devour each other, our passions intensifying until need overcomes me and I walk forward, slamming Evie's back against the side of a tree.

Inwardly I cringe, worried I hurt my mate with my lack of control, my desperate need.

Shit! Just because there's a beast inside, doesn't mean I have to act like one.

Pulling back, I meet her eyes but there's no pain or regret. Only a sexy flush brightening her skin as her pants time with mine. Those blown pupils grow wider when she realizes the position we're in. That shy smile teasing her lips, playing tug-a-war with my mind. I'm torn between devouring my woman like the finest filet and wrapping her in bubble wrap, so she'll never be hurt.

It's... startling.

"Can you let me down?" She asks with a soft chuckle, wiggling against my iron grip on her hips.

Grinning, I let her weight slide down my body. My bear's eager to show Evie her effect on us. Normally, I'd have more control, but with my mate close, it's getting harder and harder to reign in my bear. The painfully hard erection pressing against her stomach wants nothing more than to bury itself in her soft wetness. Evie needs the truth soon so I can claim my mate and make this insanity streaming through my veins stop.

The only comfort I have is hearing the matching rhythm of Evie's heart. I stroke my thumb along the contour of her jaw, hating that our day is over, but knowing my responsibilities are calling.

"We better get out of here before I do something in public that could get us both arrested," I joke, startling a throaty laugh from the honeyed temptation in front of me.

Little does she know, I'm one hundred percent serious in that warning.

Chapter 19

♥

Evie

After Wyatt dropped me off yesterday, I spent the evening cooking out with my family, goofing like old times over burgers and grilled pineapple on an unseasonably warm evening. By the time the air chilled, we had coats and blankets, even a bag of marshmallows. We roasted those babies in the fire pit until they were black, honoring our family's long-time preference for saving dishes until the party's done.

Everyone shared stories about our day. Even Ama, who's been pulling the day shift since she took over as manager at the casino. The whole family had a collective conniption when I told them I saved a bear in the woods.

"Bullshit!" Ama cracked up, earning a back-handed love-tap from my Gran. She never truly minds our language, just puts on the show.

"Evelyn, was that smart?" My mom's eyes creased with worry every time I mentioned touching the gigantic beast. To her credit, she's kept her opinions of my risky behaviors to that one question.

"I was careful, Mom. And what was I gonna do, let the sweetheart die in the forest?"

"How do you know it was a sweetheart?" she asked, her voice pitching high.

"Because he didn't bite my hand off." I shrug like it's the most innocent thing in the world.

"Oh, Lord." Mom looked to the heavens for sanity, but I just smiled sweetly at her and enjoyed my sisters practically falling over each other in their camp chairs. They tried and failed to hide their giggles at my mother's grief for her most stubborn daughter.

The entire night healed something broken inside, producing the best sleep I've gotten in two weeks. I woke up revived, less stressed, and actually happy to help with the morning chores and errands for my dad.

However, by lunchtime, my stomach demands its well-earned sandwich, which is why I'm heading home. A place quickly feeling more natural than it did a week ago. And after the fattest sandwich Mom has ever made, I head out back to find Dad.

The yard's empty though, except for Dad's Snapper parked in front of the barn after his morning mow. And if that weren't enough of a clue, the bleating goats are a dead give-away he's paying them a mid-day visit. Those goats have a pampered-posh relationship with my dad that makes me laugh. I'll never grow tired of teasing him about that.

Walking to the back acre, I lean against a wood post on the goats' metal fence. My dad, a corn farmer for forty years and one of the most respected members of our tribe, is perched on a five-gallon bucket baby talking his goats. He looks as happy as can be, even when one kid sneaks behind Dad and nibbles his shirt. The baby is obviously not happy being pushed out of Dad's feeding radius by the larger goats. Dad's surprised laugh floats across the pen and mine follows.

"Can I interrupt?" I ask, grabbing the goat brush and the other bucket-seat on my way in. At lease I can help with his chores.

"Hey, Punkin.' How's your morning?"

"It's alright," I hedge, pressing my lips together to rein in the glee taking over my face. Dad smiles, watching me brush his favorite goat mama patiently. He knows I'll spill details faster if he waits me out instead of pressing.

"How was your date yesterday?" The question heats my cheeks, which I know are pink by the deep chuckle he hides under a cough.

"It wasn't exactly a date. More breakfast-time peace offering."

Dad's eyebrows draw in, probably wondering why the hell I needed to offer peace in the first place. But no matter how much I love my dad, I don't care to share the *tuck tail and run* approach I've had to dating.

He opens his mouth to respond, but I'm saved by his ringing phone. The sound surprises me, and I jump before remembering I left mine in the car. I couldn't take any more *Guess Who* game on my texts. Would it be a Wyatt text that gives me tummy bubbles? Or, my boss's, which pops those bubbles like a snap of ten cent gum.

The sad part is, I don't expect Michaels to give up so easily. I'm four days after my return deadline and two weeks since I didn't show up for work in the first place.

Dad watches me with a side eye while he answers, his voice shows none of the suspicion that colors his face. Lucky for me, the other voice on the line snaps his attention away from assessing my nerves. "OK. OK. I gotcha, Hank. Be there in a few."

"Is Uncle Hank alright?"

Dad examines me, his eyes serious like he's itching to say something, but afraid to do so. I guess he decides against whatever he it was, because his usually pleasant expression returns before he stands to pack away his supplies, a trail of goats following in his wake.

"I have to run by his ranch. We were supposed to stop by last week, but things got a little crazy. Now, Hank said Billie Buff isn't eating and you know your uncle... he worries over every little thing with that buffalo."

I smile at the image of my uncle with his prized buffalo, worried like a first-time parent. Not to mention, the irony that my dad doesn't see he's the exact same way with these goats.

"You wanna come with? If something's wrong, it'd be nice to have a doctor and not just two old farmers."

I scoff. Odds are, Dad is more qualified than I am with livestock, but I see what he's doing and I'm more than happy to help. "Sure, Dad. Let me get my bag."

Five minutes later, we've packed up his new off-roading buggy. It looks like a golf-cart mated with a four-wheeler and produced this fat-wheeled, sportier version of both. I didn't know he would ever enjoy something this fun, but that smile on his face as we jump the hills across the pasture toward Hank's house says otherwise.

My grin is every bit as large as Dad's, my hand grabbing the metal handle for safety after he bounces us over another large hump, whooping from the adrenaline as he does. "When did you get this thing?" I squeak, one rough landing jarring loose brain cells and turning me into the paranoid parent hanging on for dear life. It's an odd turn of tables.

"Just having a little fun, Evelyn. I needed something to get 'round on without driving the truck all over, so your Ma convinced me to spring for one of these buggies." Dad's grin takes ten years off his face, lighting him up like a little boy. "Ma and I take this thing on the back ten sometimes to watch the sunset." My eyebrows fly up at my dad's wink and I try to hide my cringe.

Avoid back pasture like the plague… noted.

In no time, we reach Hank's barn and find him rubbing down Billie's big belly while the massive animal rests in a pile of hay. Dad and I approach cautiously, knowing Hank is the only human that buffalo lets close… usually. When we get no resistance in the holding pen, I get worried.

Positioning myself out of harm's way, I break out my stethoscope and pen light and get to work. Hank continues to coo, his stroking keeping the big girl calm so I can check her vitals. By the time I've rubbed stomach to flank, I have a pretty good idea of Billie's issue. Especially when she kicked in defense of my hands pressing internally.

I remove my disposable gloves and look at two of the most solid men in my life, trying hard not to laugh at their matching worried expressions. Their faces are identical, separated by only a few years of brotherhood.

"Gentlemen." I hold out as long as I can, only because they make the funniest picture waiting for my conclusion like I'm shipping them off to war. My dad's hand comes to rest on his brother's shoulder, lending support though it's really not needed. "Our Billie Buff here... is about to be a mama."

I can't help but snicker when their mouths fall open. My dad cracks first, his grin turning on Hank whose face is white as a ghost, his eyes as big as saucers when they flop between me and Billie like I'm the culprit.

"Well, I didn't do it." I hold my hands up, laughing that I feel the need to prove my innocence. The buffalo actually picks her head off the hay, and I swear she gives Hank the animal version of *duh*.

"How did it happen?" He screeches, eyes blowing wide when Dad slaps him on the back. My dad is laughing so hard, he's bent at the waist, wiping tears from his weathered face while Hank backpedals as fast as he can.

"Oh come on, I *know* how it happened. I mean how did it happen?" My dad's laugh ricochets off the walls of Billie's covered shelter, and I try my best not to join in, aiming for cool doctor demeanor and not Hank's niece that used to chase around his chickens.

"Well, Uncle Hank, when two buffalo fall in love..." Dad's bark of laughter breaks me and I crack up too, patting Ms. Billie on her neck before standing up. She feels too grown up now to call her a Miss.

"You two are hilarious," Hank grumbles, following us to Dad's new buggy like a grump. "I have to get on my little lady. This must've happened while we were at the show last winter because I certainly didn't bring any bulls in."

Dad and I share a look at Hank's crossed arms and sour expression, loving his use of *little girl* for a three-hundred-pound buffalo.

"Uncle Hank, I'll run to town and grab supplies and supplements for Billie. She's close to calving, that's why the lack of appetite, but call me if you have any issues once labor starts." He nods stoically, the idea that a bull tainted his princess without permission making him cross. I know he'll be in that pasture the moment we're gone, taking care of his oversized baby.

Dad and I wave goodbye and ride home at a much slower pace, enjoying the comfortable silence of a rolling pasture. When he parks, I grab my bag, ready to drive into town for Hank's vitamins and just-in-case supplies since my uncle had no time to prep for a calf.

"Evie." Dad's voice interrupts my check list. "It was nice having you with me today." He reaches for my hands, blanketing them under his rougher calluses for a loving pat. "And, just in case it's ever an option, you're welcomed to bunk at home for as long as you need, Punkin'."

I lean in and kiss his cheek, so Dad doesn't see the tears about to overflow. He smiles mischievously. "I have a feeling that young man of yours wouldn't mind you staying at home, either." His quip pulls a watery laugh from of both of us.

Dammit, Dad.

·♥·♥·♥·♥·♥·

My plan for the afternoon is to knock out as many *'plan for the future'* items I can. A shower was mandatory after the morning of stinky farm animals and sweaty chores, considering I've run into Wyatt how many times without planning to. And if I do see the man, I don't want to smell like the backside of a buffalo.

At least when I stop by the vet's office for Bettie's vitamins, I can follow up on my wounded bear. Maybe the veterinarian in town would be willing to put out a few feelers for me, too. Dad's words rolled around my head while I shower, making me wonder about the potential jobs on our side of the mountain... even as a backup. *Could I honestly be ready to move home?*

No matter what, yesterday proved I can't stay in this limbo. I felt more alive working on that bear in the woods than I've felt in years. The energy of the situation fed my soul.

I never looked at becoming a large animal vet just because my goal was to get away from farm life, but maybe I was wrong to chase those flashy clinics all these years. I thought I wanted new equipment and shiny surfaces, a sterile white coat, and soft cuddly patients. I assumed *that* life would be better than coming home smelling of hay.

Turns out, a small animal clinic can have just as many asses in them as the barn does... you just don't know to watch out for their kick.

Would I have been happier working our community like my grandfather? I loved helping Uncle Hank this morning. Loved getting respect for my knowledge, and not only being Daddy's little girl who had more brains than common sense growing up.

After dressing in a pair of Kayah's Bermuda shorts and a bake-sale t-shirt, I check my phone, relieved to find no new messages from Dr. Michaels, and sad to find none from Wyatt.

I glance down at my poorly fitted clothes and wonder if they're any better than smelling like animal if I do run into Wyatt. I didn't pack to impress a hunky mountain man. And Kayah's clothes take up the lion's share of our old closet, but she's a lot tinier than I am. She hates her lack of curves, but she also doesn't have my extra padding. I usually steer clear of unflattering clothing like this.

Since Ama and I are functioning with a semblance of peace, maybe I'll raid her apartment for an outfit or two to hold me over.

If anything, my lack of clothes requires I get my butt in gear. If I'm staying in Talon, I need to clear out my apartment, or at least grab more clothes than I brought until I figure out my next move. There have been no other threatening texts since the night at the grocery store. And with Michaels dropping off in the last day or so, I wonder if it's safe to head back and straighten things out.

Loving the idea more and more, I head for the door, excited about my possibilities this afternoon.

Gran's on the porch relaxing in her favorite chair. I stop for a hug, not having seen her since I woke up. She's watching Dad and one of the older farm managers mending the goat pen.

"Hey, Gran. You need anything from town?"

"I'm good, Bug." She turns her perceptive eyes on me, a naughty smirk twisting her lips when she takes in my outfit. "You plan on seeing your young man today?"

"Not sure. No plans right now. I'm just running some errands." I smile, trying to hide my giddiness at *hoping* I may see Wyatt.

Man, what a difference a few toe-curling kisses and an emergency rescue have on a girl's outlook!

Gran harrumph's with a small chuckle. "May want to stop by the boutique in the square then, Bug. Get yourself something a little more... comfortable.

I glance down at my outfit and flush. "I know. Ky's clothes leave very little to the imagination." Gran rocks her chair, stifling her giggle so she doesn't hurt my feelings.

"I heard you gave Hank one heck of a surprise when you told him his beloved buffalo was pregnant."

"Yep." My grin spreads, visualizing all the time Hank dotes on that beloved buffalo and his stricken look when he heard the news. "You should have seen his face."

Gran snorts, my fanciful imitation of Uncle Hank spot on—all shocked hand to the chest, swooning like Hank was gonna pass out.

"Those men and their babies." Gran shakes her head, eying my dad in the yard. "And how did it feel working on the reserve, following in Gramp's footsteps?"

I perch against the porch railing and face Gran's soft brown eyes, so like mine. "It was different. But good." I know my grandmother would understand any feelings I share with her. She always has. I just don't know how to word what sort of chaos has taken over my life—and my mind—these last two weeks. "It sort of... changed my opinions about working at home." She smiles encouragingly.

"Growing up, it felt like the men ruled around here. And everyone knew everyone's business. It's why I wanted to strike out on my own... find my own path, you know."

Gran's lips tip at the corners. "And how do you feel now?"

I let out a gush of relief getting to talk to someone about this. "Honestly, I was a little surprised when Dad invited me to Uncle Hank's. He's always said he was proud, but since Gramps died, I haven't been included in the workings on the ranch. It was always a boys club and I was left babysitting."

Gran levels me with a no-nonsense look. "Gramps died when you were in college. How often have you been home since you graduated? How do you know you weren't included?"

Wincing, I nod agreement knowing she has a point. "I know, Gran."

"Do you?" The question isn't snarky like it would be from Ama, but it's still a sucker-punch to the gut. I never want Gran to be disappointed. When I don't respond, her voice softens. "All I mean, Bug, is have you taken a look at the men in your life since you became an adult?"

"I may, or may not, have let my younger stubbornness get into my head. I needed to prove myself," I defend, cutting eyes at Gran. My smirk hides behind a facade of annoyance, because I know Gran isn't judging, just sharing her thoughts.

My grandmother is a full-court, NBA level, ball buster. She'll have your back with her dying breath, but she is not shy about calling you out, either. The woman shakes her head, tsking with mock indignation.

"Hey! I got my stubbornness from you, Gran. You know it."

That snark earns a full guffaw from Gran, drawing my father's eyes. He grins at us both, waving from his squatted position where Mason nails the beam he's holding.

Gran's eyes go sharp, and I know to keep my mouth shut and let her say her piece. "Do you know many other heritages who allowed women to serve on councils through their history? Or who gathered materials to build homes or made weapons for their tribe?"

"Gran, I know we had more privileges than other tribes. I just didn't like being put in a box. I don't want to fill a role. I just wanted some freedom."

"And did anyone ever say you couldn't have that?"

"Well…" I glance over at Dad, who's supported all my dreams, even when it took me away from him. Then I look at Gran, who knows how devoted Gramps was to me, taking me under his wing and encouraging my love of animals.

"Exactly." She nods, the victorious glint in her eye annoying me. "We are traditional people, Evie, but we are strong women. And working for your home does not make you any less. Half the time, the women raising the families and building their future generation would kill for an hour lunch break or a chance to pee without an audience and fifty questions following you to the restroom." Gran pauses and I feel my cheeks heat. "Listen, you can be as modern as you want, and our tribe will embrace you. We applaud our strengths *because* we differ from men. But have you seen one of these men you judge not honor their women, not thank them, or look relieved when they come home after a tired day to a warm meal? Have you seen any of them not step up when their women need help?"

Dad always took care of bath times when we were little so Mom could rest after dinner. It was his thing, and I never thought about how special it was that he learned how to brush long hair and braid it for bed.

Sighing, I go to sit beside Gran and look out at my dad working the land that's been in Mom and Gran's family for generations. He's never showed an ounce of resentment over caring for someone else's history. I think I just assumed because male and female roles were divided in the past that they were uneven, but they really weren't. It's all a blend of what we can offer each other to survive. Celebrating our strengths.

Gently, Gran pats my hand, comforting the part of me that's regretting a lot of judgments. "You know, Bug, life gives us many paths, none of them are wrong as long as each teach you a little something." A smile warms her eyes. "Gramps taught me that. I was on a much different path when I met your grandfather." I've never heard this story. She turns her head, resting it on her chair to look at me. "It's not wrong to change what you want out of life, Bug. In fact, it could be the best thing to ever happen to you." She blushes and part of me wants to ask more but I understand she's lost in her memories of Gramps.

I cover Gran's hand, hating how thin the bones are against my arm, and decide to be honest. "Gran, I feel like I wasted so much time. I thought I was headed somewhere... building a future in Tennessee. I was on track to own my own clinic," I admit, focusing on Gran's soft hand, not able to meet her eye yet, when there are so many choices I wish I could change. I'd much rather hide than admit my failures out loud. "I was gonna be successful, Gran."

"Evelyn Amos, when have you ever given up?" Gran's chastising tone makes me chuckle, despite the regrets. "Listen, little one, don't confuse the path with the destination. Just because it's stormy, don't mean you ain't headed for sunshine."

"I get it, Gran. I do." I stand and shoulder my purse, ready for my overly strained emotions to take a break.

"You gonna go accidentally, on purpose, find Wyatt?" I blush, remembering Wyatt's muscular arms slamming me against the tree yesterday and giving me the best kiss of my life.

"I thought I'd see him… at some point… maybe."

"What's with the nerves, little one?"

"No nerves, Gran. I just have a lot of stuff to figure out." I shrug, pretending my feelings for Wyatt are no big deal. Gran nods, though I know she sees right through me.

"I get it. Just make sure you are following what's in your heart, not what's in your head, Bug."

I bend to kiss Gran before jogging to my Jeep, itching to figure out my next steps. "Love you, Gran," I call before climbing in. As I back down the driveway, Gran's eyes are on me. Her words circle in my head.

What is it my heart wants?

The entire drive to town, I waffle back and forth. Do I go back to Knoxville and find a job since Michaels let up? It should be safe, and that's where my apartment is.

But then I remember the loneliness. I spent all my time working. I had no friends, no nights out… no boyfriend. If I'm honest, the only thing I got out of Knoxville were stress knots, an empty social life, and a strained family.

I'm realizing now, how bad I want to fix that. Coming home to crash should have been temporary, but I've enjoyed reconnecting with my sisters and spending time with Mom and Dad.

By the time I pull in front of the old vet's office, I'm determined to not over think life like I usually do. I think baby steps are going to be the only way to not have a panic attack over all the things changing. Step one... I need clothes, my computer... basic necessities. I look down at the phone in my lap and text Wyatt.

Me: Would you be interested in a day trip? If you're not busy tomorrow?

Less than thirty seconds later...

Wyatt: Absolutely.

I laugh, climbing out of my SUV and head into the vet clinic.

Me: You don't want to know where?

Wyatt: Nope. I'm good. My day is clear. You drive or me?

Immediately my brain dips to the gutter, but I respond that I'll pick him up in the morning and to plan for a half day, at least.

Chapter 20

♥

Evie

The next morning, I show up at Wyatt's with muffins and coffee from the bakery. He runs out before I've got the car in park, despite our six-a.m. departure time. That boyish smile is a stark contrast to the overnight scruff he didn't take time to shave.

I hold out the oversized chocolate muffin I brought and the large cup of coffee. "I'm sorry. I guessed at which muffin you'd like. If you don't want choco-coco-chocolate, there's a few others in the box back there."

"I love that name!" Wyatt laughs, his eyes falling to my lips for a second before climbing in my passenger seat. "I'll ride anywhere with you, if you buy me treats," he jokes, reaching over to dust a crumb from my lower lip with his thumb. My face heats. I'd be embarrassed if seconds later Wyatt's lips didn't replace his thumb.

My eyes fall closed, enjoying the sensual taste of his morning coffee and the gentle sucks against my mouth. Despite the gentleness, I'm immediately wet, my yearning for Wyatt making me second-guess driving in jeans.

Thankfully, my brain takes over for my hormones, forcing me to pull back, though I still relish the time it takes for Wyatt to drag his eyes open. "Thank you for coming today," I whisper, not knowing what else to say after that kiss.

Wyatt's eyes brighten, matching the happy smile on his face. "Like I said, I'll go anywhere with you."

My heart melts, but I try to hide that fact as I put the car in gear and head for my old apartment. That old Barenaked Ladies song pops in my head and it's a good distraction, making my fingers tap out my internal beat on the steering wheel while I drive. I haven't been to my apartment in two weeks, but I'm not missing it. I just keep thinking how quiet the place was, how boring. Now, I'm crashing the two worlds together by bringing Wyatt.

We chat the first thirty minutes on the road, about our week in general. I fill him in on Bettie and Hank and my surprisingly pleasant conversation with Ama. Eventually, the mountain roads flatten and my stomach flips knowing we're halfway to Knoxville. I make an excuse and stop for gas so I can collect myself in the restroom. When I come out, Wyatt has an armful of snacks. He waits for me to pick what I want, then loads them all on the counter to pay.

"Wait! You don't need to get mine."

"Of course, I do. You're driving. You need road trip goodies." His playfulness pulls a smile, despite my anxiety over our destination. Suddenly, my mind flashes to the fun Wyatt and I would have on a real road trip, as a couple, or with a few kids.

I wonder where he'd want to go.

"Two scratchers, please, ma'am." Wyatt's sheepish grin warms my heart, and the check-out lady's too judging by the puppy love in her eyes. She snaps two off the roll and bags them with our treats.

When we're back outside, I see Wyatt has already filled my tank as well. The needle sits at F when I climb in to grab my discount card. *How long was I in the bathroom?*

"Wyatt, you shouldn't have filled me up. I didn't ask you along to buy stuff." He smirks.

"Can I at least get points for not commenting on filling you up?" That dimple pops out with the heat in Wyatt's eyes, and I laugh, shaking my head at his nonsense as I crank the car.

"You would, if you hadn't just mentioned it." He groans, snapping his fingers like he just missed his chance.

At least bantering with Wyatt distracts me while we pull out of the lot and point west. We pick back up on our twenty questions game, and now I know Wyatt has a scratch-off obsession, so I use that. Eventually, we work into some very odd 'would you rather' questions, laughing the entire trip.

Turns out Wyatt would rather eat a cookie from the dirt outside than off his bathroom floor. He does qualify that by asking the duration of time said cookie was in each location, and the length of time since the last male visited the facilities holding that cookie.

By the time Wyatt finished his qualifying rant, I had tears rolling down my face, and my sides were screaming with the need for air. I can't even drag in enough air to even tell him to shut up.

"Dude, I'm seriously questioning your cleaning habits, right now." Wyatt's laughter rings through the car and I grin again. Have I ever had so much fun laughing with a guy? Or actually felt funny? *Never!*

Before I know it, we're on the outskirts of the city, and I really wish we weren't.

Wyatt's thumb rubs absentminded circles on my inner knee, taking in the view of downtown through the passenger window. My skin is strung tight, my body on high alert. It vibrates with the rhythm of a tuning fork, nearly erasing the progress I made toward relaxing in the car.

The closer we get to my apartment, the faster my heart thrums a staccato in my chest. Wyatt's hand tightens on my knee, soothing my nerves without knowing it. I give myself permission to focus on that comfort, breathing through the nausea threatening to make itself known, when Wyatt groans from the passenger seat.

I look over and his face has crumbled. "You know… I just realized I didn't even offer my truck, Evie. I'm so sorry." His voice is thick with remorse, surprising me with the sudden sadness in a man who's had me in stitches this whole trip.

"It's OK. Seriously." I squeeze Wyatt's hand and take the exit for my apartment. "I don't have a lot of stuff to get today. I just need more clothes and toiletries."

"When are you coming back to clear out your apartment? We can use my truck for that, then." His offer is sweet, but I'm bombarded by memories of two weeks ago… the anxiety, the feeling of being watched. I can't focus on anything else right now, even Wyatt mumbling under his breath about failed duties, his forlorn gaze focused on my complex except for drastic different reasons. "You're nervous," he comments cryptically, his head cocked like one of my curious puppies at the clinic.

I try to swallow the feeling of doing something wrong and answer Wyatt honestly, at least about the move. "I'm not sure what my plans are yet," I admit, putting the car in park so I can face him for this conversation.

Wyatt removes his hand and I feel the immediate loss of heat, but since he stays quiet, I continue. "I love the city. Everything is bigger… faster. I like that no one knows my name, or that my shorts fell down on the monkey bars in third grade." That earns a small chuckle, but not much else.

I sigh, my ramble picking up speed when I see the distress on Wyatt's face. "Look, a lot of weirdness went on with my job. It's the reason I took that vacation at home. But, until about a week ago, that's what I expected it to be. A vacation. I never wanted to live on the reservation as an adult…" When I realize my voice is rising, I slow down, focusing on the windshield to find the best wording so Wyatt will understand. "So far… I've fought for my leave of absence and decided to hand in my resignation. That's the extent of my decisions so far."

"Got it."

"Wyatt, I'm working step by step," I huff. The headache in the back of my head is making me defensive, no matter how hard I fight it.

"I got it." Wyatt's face appears neutral, but I'm not buying it with that tone. He's upset, disappointment swings off him with the power of a wrecking ball. Though, when we get out of the car, he still takes my hand. His sweetness goes far to soothe the feeling I've done something wrong, when I'm really just struggling to find a new normal. Whatever that is.

Wyatt studies me while we walk toward my building. I feel his eyes on my face, but I can't focus on comforting him right now. The twitchiness I felt two weeks ago in this parking lot hits me hard, like I'm going back in time.

If I am, at least this time I have back up. With Wyatt here I don't feel like I'll be murdered and tossed in a ditch without anyone noticing. *That's something.* Plus, it's broad daylight. *There is absolutely no reason to be weirded out.*

Wyatt breaks our awkward silence when we turn down the breezeway instead of heading to the elevator or stairs. "You live on the bottom floor?" OK, that accusatory tone irks my nerves. That's something my dad would say, not a pseudo—or wanna-be—boyfriend.

"I do. It's in my price range." I'm struggling to breathe my temper into submission and not snap his head off because I'm already on edge.

"Is it safe?"

"Yeah… I know Knoxville's bigger than Talon, but I've lived here for years. It's been fine." Irritation slips into my voice from being talked to like a child. That's about to earn him a bus pass home! I don't care if he took time out of his day to keep me company.

Wyatt looks unconvinced, his scowl deepening with every corner we pass. "You walk this far all the time? At night?" His challenge piques my annoyance.

"Look!" I scoff, getting my keys ready so I can get inside, pack, and get back on the road as quick as I can. "I can—"

"What the hell!"

Before I get my key to the door, I fly backwards. *Agh!* The shriek leaves me before I realize it's Wyatt levering my body behind his, a rough snarl ripping from his throat that sounds both threatening and panty-melting sexy.

Bristling, I push Wyatt's shoulder, but the man doesn't budge. Even with all my weight pressing his arm, that iron grip is locked on my hip, rippling tingles across my skin from his show of strength.

"Stop being an ass, Wyatt." Grumbling, I slide the other way, ignoring my body's disappointment at the loss of his touch. However, the moment I reach for the lock, I stop. Deep divots surround the keyhole, tearing up the metal and wood like someone used a bowie knife to pick the thing.

"Someone took a crowbar to your door," Wyatt points out grimly. He leans over, inspecting the splinters at the seam, annoying me with the way his massive bulk curves over my body protectively.

"No shit, Sherlock." The butterflies in my stomach are trying to take flight.

No matter how much I'd love to elbow Wyatt in the ribs, I glance down the hallway and get the distinct feeling of someone watching. It ramps up my punchiness to an eleven, though Wyatt doesn't seem to notice. At least, he doesn't comment. He ignores my grumbling and tucks me safely behind his back... again. I'd be pissed at his high-handedness, except dread overshadows everything now.

Carefully, Wyatt nudges his foot against the door. It swings open too easily, obviously not latched after whoever went to town on my lock.

The two of us sneak into the entry, closing the door behind us as quietly as possible. There's not a pin-drop of noise anywhere. Our shallow breaths might as well be foghorns in the silent hallway.

Wyatt's fingers twitch against my hip when I go to walk forward, proving I'm not the only nervous one and I'm past the point of caring if he's overprotective. Right now, I'm extremely grateful to have that protection after living on my own for so long.

He presses a finger to his lips, silently communicating our need for quiet. *Like he really had to say that.* I behave though, letting Wyatt take the lead. My hands grip the firm muscles along his waist as I basically plaster myself to his back. Within a few feet, we're in my living room doorway.

"Shit!"

My back stiffens, and I peek around his bicep, wondering if someone's still in the apartment. "Shit," I gasp right behind him, running into the chaos that is my living room.

Wyatt tries to grab me again, but I'm too upset. Pillows are off the couch and shredded. My flimsy, discount store curtains hang by just a few hooks, no match for whoever ransacked my house. Shelves of books lay on the floor, pages torn, bindings ripped. Even my thick medical dictionary from college… who's even strong enough to do that.

In a trance, I turn a circle in my once pristine living space. The monsters even toppled my TV. *What kind of person punishes a TV?*

"Are you OK?" Wyatt whispers, his brows furrowed, watching me take in the ruins of my apartment… my life. I know who did this. I was fooling myself to think distance would make everything OK.

My zombie state leads me down the hall to my bedroom, finding more of the same. Ransacked drawers, shattered frames sprinkling glass across the carpet. My upended mattress sits catty-corner on the edge of the frame, not even giving me a place to rest while I freak the hell out.

I dart over when I see my underwear strewn across the ground, feeling violated. My hands shake at the mental image of that beefy thug going through my private things. I snatch them off the floor, struggling against the urge to crumble in the broken glass and mismatched underwear and just bawl like a baby.

It sucks that Wyatt's seeing my underwear like this the first time. Especially when the boring cotton drastically outnumbers the few silky pairs. I grab another dull bra and shove the armload back in the drawer, slamming it shut with rage burning through my system.

Guess you're learning Victoria doesn't have any secrets over here, buddy.

The room goes hazy for a second, making me jump when Wyatt's hands come up beside my arms, rubbing with a steady comfort I shouldn't take from someone I barely know.

"It's OK," his deep voice reassures, but I hang my head feeling my lip tremble and I'm powerless to stop it. "You're OK, Evie. Shh. We'll figure out who did this." *I know who did this.*

I feel myself turning, but I'm too numb to care that Wyatt walks me into his chest, pressing my forehead against his heart until I let the tears go.

Gently, he rocks my body, shushing quietly with his hands stroking my hair, pulling it away from my tear-stained face. He lets me blubber in the safely of his arms, pressing me tighter with every shudder I heave. *God! I hate this weakness!* But I can't complain about the hand stroking my back, slowly sliding up to tug my chin until my blurry eyes meet his angry ones.

"The important thing is you weren't here, Evie."

I nod, sniffling away the tears as I try to look down. My face must be a blotchy mess, and I'd someone this gorgeous not to see me at my snotty, sniffly worst. Unfortunately, my face gets redder when I see the giant wet spot on Wyatt's shirt, and I rub, willing the spot to dry even as another tear slips over my cheek.

Wyatt calmly removes my hand. "Don't worry about that," he soothes, but his brows furrow when he notices my shaky hands. He bends, pressing a sweet kiss to my temple that only clogs my throat more.

I swipe the wetness from my face, sucking in a deep breath and blowing it out.

"Do you need anything here we can't get at the store? It would be better not to touch things until the cops check it out."

I nod my head, emotions rendering my voice useless. Then what he said sinks in. "Cops?" My hands shake uncontrollably now, the worst images filling my head of the mob coming after my family at home, of Wyatt's protective nature getting him killed when he tries to hide me from the people who did this. Would the cops put me in witness protection? *I watch Law & Order... that doesn't always work.*

"Yes, cops, Evie. They need to fingerprint this place and I need to get you somewhere safe."

"You?"

"Yes me!" I stare up in his tormented brown eyes, thrown off by the heat mixing under the concern. Those stormy depths always have heat in them, even when he's angry or annoyed with me.

Finally, the reality of my torn-up apartment sinks in and I jump to action. Electric cables life in my sleeping motor. Wyatt stands back while I run to the closet, stepping over broken glass to rummage for one thing... the leather medicine bag my grandfather gave me before he passed. The bag I toted behind him when we'd visit the tribal herds. I keep my best memories in there: the arrowhead I found while hunting with Ash, my lucky amethyst from the cave near our house, plus some letters and trinkets I collected over the years. *My memories.*

Hugging the bag to my chest, I look around at the bedroom I've slept in for the last few years and feel nothing. There's only a collection of *stuff* here, no value. No nostalgia making me not want to leave. If ever there was a sign, this resolute feeling in my chest is it. *I'm done.*

Determined, I walk to Wyatt, grab his hand, and wash my mind of this room. I don't say a word as I pull Wyatt toward the kitchen. If I open my mouth, I run the risk of screaming bloody murder until we ring in the new year and I just want to get this over with and get out of here.

"Dammit," I hiss as we pass knocked over bar stools. "Looks like the kitchen matches the rest of the apartment." Every drawer hangs open, utensils spilling across the floor. *Damn!* These people go all out with their destruction. They even ripped the cabinet doors from their hinges. *Guess I can kiss my security deposit goodbye.*

Suddenly, the sight of the fridge stops my heart and I jerk my hand from Wyatt's, running to where my photos have been torn from their magnets. I pick up the crumpled pictures from the floor, straightening the edges before I gather the few left hanging.

"Are you OK?" Wyatt asks, watching me tuck the tattered pieces into Gramp's leather bag.

I nod until my eyes catch on the personalized stationery my mother bought for my birthday… the one with our home address stamped at the top. She wrote on that first page that I would always have a home with them. And though I never planned to return home, I was too sentimental to tear the page off. It's been hanging there for months. I just use the pages behind it.

My stomach plummets. "Get me out of here," I gasp. "We have to go now!"

Chapter 21

♥

Wyatt

Why aren't you doing anything?

Nothing I do will drown out my bear's screaming. Not even running him this afternoon when we got back from Knoxville. He's pissed someone threatened our mate. Not to mention that she isn't even our mate yet.

The longer I wait to claim Evie after realizing our connection, the crazier he gets. Eventually, he'll drive me mad. It's what happens when mating connections go unbound, or get rejected. I never thought I'd have that problem, but I also never expected my mate would be human, either.

Patience. I bark to my bear; the sound echoing across my front yard.

The problem is, mating requires a big conversation and honesty, but with our mate in danger, that larger problem needs handling first. I won't let anything hurt her… ever! But the dread in my gut tells me this won't be as easy as I wish.

On the drive back, Evie filled me in on the craziness that pushed her into this extended vacation, as she puts it. The sketchy veterinarian, the threatening muscle heads. Why did her apartment reek of burning ash? And that putrid undercurrent that's been all over town. My gut says I need to talk to Mac. This isn't going away. What worries me most is the use of the word 'boss' in the conversation she overheard. Every mile we drove lit a fire in my blood, scorching my temper into a barely held fuse.

My eyes fall to the dead buck lying beside the porch, his neck snapped by my seething bear. My spirit's yearning for blood was heavy. It didn't matter that I already stocked my freezer for winter, he needed the hunt, and his prize lays there waiting for future dinners.

You're doing nothing to help her and nothing to claim her.

I pace to the porch, anger spiking in my head. *She's human, dammit.*

My bear fights my actions as a man, trying to take over my thoughts, my movements. Growling, I bend and grip the stair railing, squeezing until the crack of wood jerks me out of my fog. Raising my head to the sky, I let out a throat raking, guttural roar that sends the birds that haven't left for winter scattering.

Caleb's voice breaks into my head, calling out as he walks over from his neighboring cabin. *Wy... calm, brother.*

When he gets close, Caleb returns to his human voice. "What's got you pacing out here like a maniac, man?" The question pokes at my already irritated nerves, but when I turn my glowing eyes on Caleb, he stops in his tracks. "Business or pleasure?" All jokes leave as his brotherly instincts pick up on my turmoil.

Slamming my palm into the rail, I turn to face my brother. "I'm in over my head," I seethe, pulling at the tips of my hair. The slight pain brings a little more of control to my senses. Enough to push my bear down where I need him. "My skin feels too tight."

"What do you need, brother?"

His calmness gives me pause. I've been thinking of Caleb as a walking train wreck recently, but when I truly take him in, there's no glazed eyes, no annoying smirk. He's a hell of a lot calmer than I am right now.

"I've got too much on my plate. I can't concentrate." It's a poor excuse for a half-confession and Caleb doesn't buy it. He follows me to my deer where I stalked to get away from him, even bending to help me cart the thing to the shed—though I don't need it—for dressing. Caleb's help does prevent my clothes from getting wrecked and hides the deer away so wildlife in the forest won't think I'm Snow White setting up a buffet outside my cabin.

Caleb is on my tail, but at least his snarkiness is on mute for once. I sigh and face him, hoping if I feed enough bullshit, he'll leave so I can think. "Look… there are curricula to plan, presentations for meetings in a world I only know through research." I sulk at the reminder of everything else on my place beyond today's problems. The frustration's real, just not relevant for my current train of thought.

"Is that seriously what's got you in a tizzy? Really?" He crosses his arms, his eyes doubtful before he slaps me on the back and bounds up my front stairs.

"It's part of it," I defend, watching Caleb strip off his boots and Carhartt with confusion. "The Dean of Animal Services agreed to visit us next month after I spoke with him at the meeting. He'll validate our business before I present to the board. It's a whole big thing." I wave a frustrated hand it the air, my resentment showing at Caleb's lack of involvement.

"Seriously, Wy?" Caleb's irritation means he reads my judgment, and I almost smile… almost. He glares down from my porch, his clothes tossed recklessly on the wooden swing.

As shifters, we're comfortable with nudity in front of each other, which is also why remote cabins are so important. Humans would not take so kindly to a grown man stripping to the buff, and we'd rip up a lot more clothes. "Wyatt, you've got this. How many years have you planned to get *Wild Things* off the ground, seriously?"

"A long time," I sigh. "I need a fucking distraction."

"No, you *need* action." My brother leaps off the porch, grazing me— on purpose—on the way down. *Grrr!* "Let's run."

Caleb hops away easily when I try to swipe his shoulder with an open-handed punch. By step three, Caleb's in bear form, his wide shoulders covered with smooth black fur, his face morphing into its animal shape with his caramel-colored snout, the only break in Caleb's ebony coat. Caleb turns, lifting and stomping his paws my way with a spray of dirt.

"I already ran," I complain, but Caleb isn't hearing it. He bounces on four paws, tossing his head back and forth with playful chuffs, urging me to shift. I snap my teeth at him, annoyed at the push to shift again so soon. Caleb pounces within a foot of me, snorting air that ruffles my shirt.

"Down, boy," I laugh, swatting at his face.

Caleb's bear teeth chop, grinning the best he can in bear form as he lifts to his hind quarters with a roar. Spit flies from his jowls in a shower that would terrify humans but only succeeds in making me laugh harder. I wipe the wetness from my face, feeling the ground shake under my feet when Caleb's immense size drops back to all fours.

Just when I think about giving in, my bear decides for me. My skin prickles, a warning that a shift is imminent, so I strip fast—thankfully before I rip another pair of jeans—and take off running past Caleb toward the backwoods. My bones ache from the speedy shift, but I push through—deserving the punishment—as mortification washes over me.

How the hell can I be Alpha if I can't control my bear?

My brain feels like that egg that got sizzled in the frying pan commercial. *Don't do drugs. Don't let an animal spirit take over your life.*

Caleb's hot on my tail. *What the hell was that?*

Nothing, I growl, running faster.

My claws tear tracks through the thick pine needles coating the forest floor as we dart past thick trunks with shifter agility. Caleb stays by my side but doesn't push to talk anymore. He lets me run. My muscles bound up the mountain along the familiar paths, the ones we know like the back of our hand, away from public access.

In bear form, I'm free from pressure. Completely able to enjoy the brisk wind whipping my fur, the owl hooting in the distance. This is my best form. It heightens my senses. My speed and my strength are unmatched. As a bear, I would always be able to protect my mate. One swipe of the paw and they're out.

Suddenly, I'm jarred from my thoughts by a heavy weight slamming me off balance. My own force carries me over into the soft dirt. The force of the ground knocks a grunt from my lungs, and I frantically roll my bulk to glare at the offending force. My brother's stocky build hunches over me with annoyance turning his ears.

I hear you thinking. He punches a paw against my shoulder. *Chill out, brother.* Even the air around you is tense.

Chuffing, I shove his weight back, getting four paws back under me. *I was relaxing,* I roar, throwing the weight of my bear into Caleb and sending *him* to the ground, this time. His chuckle reverberates in my head, pissing me off enough to not pull back on my next pounce. I'd never hurt my brother, but my bear desperately needs this release.

Unfortunately, Caleb braces for the impact, pressing his massive paws to my chest and letting the momentum—and my own anger—carry me straight over his head. Painfully, I land on my back, getting the wind knocked out of me in a huff. I groan at the root that had the misfortune of being under my spine.

Had enough? he teases, hopping back and forth like a playful cub a quarter his size. Caleb did the same thing when we were teens. We'd go to the woods when we needed to wrestle our aggressions away. Pretty much the moment we lost our parents, and those pent-up emotions took a more volatile swing. As the middle brother, Caleb has always taken pride that he could beat me and Seth in a tussle. We swore him to secrecy the first time it happened, Seth threatening to coat his bed in honey and let ants loose if he ever told anyone.

He's still watching me with that same energy, amped off the energy of battle.

I chomp my teeth at Caleb, but he knows I'm playing. I could only fight someone with his stocky frame and tolerance for pain if I were willing to hurt them and I'm not willing to hurt my brother. Our youngest brother, Seth, was always the strategist at games of war, and I'm the logical head. But Caleb... Caleb is our brute strength and I've never seen him shy from that.

I appreciate what Caleb's trying to do with this run, and I knock his neck with mine, giving him my brotherly truce which he returns with a bark. With a stomping chuff, I turn my rear on him and fling a mass of wet leaves in his face, laughing in my head when he pulls back and swipes his head with his paws to remove the clumps from his fur. My bear bounces around, just out of his Caleb's reach when he tries the same maneuver back at me.

We gallop farther up the mountain, messing up the earth in our playful fight. When my legs start to tire, I nudge my head toward the river, signaling Caleb to follow before trotting off to our favorite waterfall, the one we played in as cubs. Sadly, the fresh water is only a few miles from where Evie and I found Jackson bleeding. That thought sobers the playful vibe Caleb and I slipped into.

In the clearing, we rest on our haunches in silence, watching the wild water rush off the cliff and slam the rocks with a hypnotizing violence. *How is that possible?*

After a few minutes, Caleb and I shift back to human form, enjoying the quiet serenity. Course pine needles make for a scratchy chair without the protection of clothing, but I'm content to sit here and watch the sun lower in the sky. Feeling Caleb's support without a word spoken.

"Thank you, brother." I lean in and bounce his shoulder with mine.

"Anytime, Wy. You feel like telling me what had you so upset?" He looks over, the downward turn of his mouth etched with worry. "And don't say work. You've always had a hundred things on your plate at any given time. It never bothers you."

Chuckling, I know he's right. I'm feeling the pressure loom as future Alpha, but it's more than that. I've been in knots since realizing Evie was my mate... my fated mate. So many conversations hang in the balance... with her, with my uncle.

"Honestly, I probably do need more help with the business. It's swamping me to juggle everything with the protection program. At least in the beginning."

"Done."

I look over, surprised with Caleb's easy submission. He grins, his face the picture of happiness, sitting there naked as the day he was born.

Testing, I ask, "how 'bout women? Got any advice there?"

His laughter rings across the clearing. "You know I'm single, right?"

Chuckling, I follow Caleb to stand, wiping earth from my backside before shifting for easier travel down the mountain. This outing was exactly what I needed, centering my mind to focus where I need it. For the first time in a while, I feel like I can trust Caleb to back me up. That I don't have to be alone in handling it all.

Great! Now figure out how we help our mate.

Chapter 22

♥

Evie

When I walked in my front door this afternoon, my brain crossed that final bridge to accept my new life in Talon, North Carolina. I can't live somewhere I'm not safe.

So… there's no more life for me in Tennessee. No job, no apartment, no relationships… truly nothing. *Who cares?*

Wyatt and I called the cops on the way out of the complex, parked in front of the office with the manager, a cruiser, and any bystander that happened by and saw gossipy activity. I left a copy of my key, thankful the manager agreed to close everything down after the police finished their inspection.

To say Wyatt was a huge comfort is an understatement. He held my hand during the whole initial report, adding in what details he observed inside. The young lieutenant seemed to understand I wanted to be nowhere near that apartment, so he let us leave with a promise to follow up for a more in-depth statement soon. I think he could see I was at the end of my rope and took pity.

Now, I'm pacing my house after unpacking the handful of bags I got from the box store on the way home. Wyatt drove since I didn't trust my hands, nor my brain, to safely get us here. But I drew the line at him buying the clothes that would hold me over until my apartment gets sorted. That was a five minute argument, and then when I put my foot down, he pouted about for the next five.

By the time Wyatt dropped me off and I had to endure another argument that I would not stay in his cabin under lock and key, I was ready to be done. He called his brother to come pick him up because he didn't want to leave me without a car, and I promised to call him after talking with my family.

If only they would get home before I grow gray hair, we could sit down and get it over with. Dad's gonna be pissed I hid this so long, especially if I brought danger to their house without warning him. Stupidly, I had this delusion that since I wasn't actively a part of my boss's awful decisions, I could just hide away until those dreadful people forgot about me or moved on to something else.

Not surprisingly, it took a massive effort to convince Wyatt to leave me here in the empty house. I swear, arguing with that man is like swimming upstream in a waterfall. Too bad for him, my stubbornness is as strong as his obstinance. When I dig in my heels, he'd have better luck convincing a fish he could fly than winning an argument. Wyatt was out of his mind if he thought I'd hide away at his place. I have things to take care of, my own family to protect.

I would never admit to another living soul that I actually love that growly voice when Wyatt gets all bossy. I swear, that man could give a nun wet dreams and God would forgive her.

Unfortunately, pacing around my parents' house is starting to hurt my feet. I grab my laptop and settle on the couch to work on my resume just to be productive. Considering I've only had one job since graduating veterinary school, it goes fast and I'm hitting print when the front door bursts open. After the day I've had, the boom startles me into nearly dropping my computer, until I see my mom's face in the doorway.

Relief follows the blast of chilled air that enters with my parents, and right behind it, the delicious aroma of Tommy's pizza. My mouth waters at the hint of sausage and pepperoni. *Good Lord, have I not eaten all day?*

Mom sees me sitting on the couch and smiles. "Hey, baby girl. We brought leftovers. You hungry?"

She and my dad walk to the kitchen with the pizza, still holding hands and laughing over whatever tickled them on their date. The sight brings tears to my eyes. *I want what they have.*

Dread turns my feet to lead, but I still follow them, taking the plate Mom hands me from the cabinet. She and Dad chat and joke about some newly learned town gossip, until they ask about my day. I freeze, terrified to sit down and start this conversation. Mom shoots Dad a worried look, both sobering when they read the room.

"Sit down, Punkin'. You're white as a sheet."

In a daze, I follow his orders, focusing on my hands so I don't have to see my parents' worried faces. "I need to tell you something, but I don't know how, and you're not gonna like it."

Mom reaches over to squeeze Dad's hand.

"Are you pregnant?" His tone is soft, no judgment in the words, but it takes me by surprise. My head pops up, my eyes as wide as their dinner plates. It very possible that my cheeks match my Jeep in the driveway.

"Not pregnant." I drag a fortifying breath in to slow my racing heart. "It's about why I came home. There's a little more to it than an extended vacation."

"You get fired?"

Mom slaps the side of Dad's shoulder with a put-out look. "Stop interrupting, Kota. Let the girl talk."

Her annoyance helps ground me enough to explain the troubling scene I came across the night I left Tennessee. I have to stop a few times to calm myself, feeling the same level of panic wash through me as I relay the details to my family.

My foot trots a mile a minute under the table, matching the rhythm I drum on top. Dad is stoic, Mom gripping his arm for strength, digging in when she gasps at the scarier parts.

"You could have been seriously hurt, Evelyn… or worse." Mom's eyes well up and I'm right there with her by the end. Especially when I try to explain the creepy feeling of being watched that night, and after it a few times.

"I was scared, Ma. I ran. And when I got here, it was all too scary to think about, or say out loud. So, basically, I just hid and prayed it would all go away."

"It didn't," Dad states simply.

"No, it didn't. Dr. Michaels sent me texts and called non-stop for the first two weeks. I haven't heard from him in a few days though so I think he got the picture." Dad looks skeptical. "The thing is… this morning, Wyatt and I drove to my apartment so I could get more clothes and stuff, but… when we got there someone had broken in." The composure I was trying to hold onto cracks, releasing weeks worth of anxiety in a sob.

"Evie!" Mom gasps, covering her mouth with a shaking hand. Her own tears spill over, none of us able to hold our resolve to keep the conversation calm.

"I know, Mom. We called the cops and they're looking over the apartment. The manager knows. I doubt I'll get my deposit back after seeing that place but-."

"That. Does not. Matter." Mom very rarely raises her voice, but she's fuming like a warring mama bear right now, and if the situation wasn't absolutely horrible, I might laugh. "You are not going back there. That's all there is to it."

Dad pats her hand, but Mom's not having his effort to calm her. She jumps up and grabs her sponge from the sink, attacking invisible crumbs she sees on the counter. Mom's always felt calmer after cleaning. I'm sure scrubbing down an already clean kitchen is her way to process.

"I agree, Mom. I'm not going back." My easy give-in must surprise them because both my parents turn to me with mouths open. "I just need to figure out a way out of this mess. As long as you guys don't mind me staying here…" I trail off, feeling out of sorts asking my parents for shelter.

"Of course. This is your home, Punkin'."

"Thanks, Dad. But I can't bring whoever broke into my apartment here either."

"We're fine here, Evie. I'll alert the tribe and the town. They'll keep an eye out for anyone suspicious."

"Thanks Dad." For the first time in weeks, I breathe a small sigh of relief. I've got people in my corner.

"That's what family's for, baby girl."

The next hour, we work through the details of what needs to get done. How to get me out of my apartment and deal with the cops. I give Dad a description of the guy from Michaels' office while choking down a slice of pizza. Anytime I think of that night, I lose my appetite, it's seared into the recesses of my mind, but with Mom close, there's a vibe of my early years… my parent support, Mom taking care of my needs, urging me to keep eating while Dad takes notes.

When we're done, Dad's sharp eyes nail me with an expression I've only seen a few times in my life. "OK, so I'm gonna go call Hank and the sheriff, but I *do not* want you going anywhere by yourself. You hear me, Eveline." I swallow at Dad's use of my given name instead of his little nicknames.

"Yes, sir." Having my parents' support makes it hard to argue against any rule they want to throw down.

When he walks out, Mom squeezes my hand across the table. "I'm so glad you're here, Evie."

"Me too, Ma. Me too." We share a watery smile while she collects my plate for the wash. I'd argue, but I think my mom needs to take care of me tonight, and I'm inclined to enjoy the comfort of it.

It feels like a drastic weight has been lifted from my shoulders as I collect my laptop and phone to go work in my bedroom. Kayah said she was hanging with Kaylee tonight, so I have the place to myself. But first, I fire a text to Wyatt like I promised.

Me: I talked to my parents.

A few seconds later...

Wyatt: How'd it go?

Me: Dad's calling in support.

Me: I hate burdening them with this, but it feels nice not to do it alone.

Wyatt: You're definitely not alone, baby. When can I see you?

Me: I have to go to town tomorrow. Wanna meet for breakfast?

Wyatt: I'll pick you up.

I grin at his pushiness, seeing right through that over-protective text and remembering my dad's words about not traveling alone. The thought of there being real danger out there sobers me. I hit the little thumbs up on his last message and open my contacts, dialing Dr. Michaels for what I pray is the last time.

His voicemail picks up, but since I never want to see this number again, I leave the most detailed message I'm willing to give.

"Dr. Michaels, I wanted to let you know I was unable to deliver my formal resignation today. I drove back to hand it in, but found my apartment broken into and ransacked." Heaving a sigh, I expect the doctor already knows my breaking news report. "Anyway, this isn't how I'd want to do this, but here's my official, *'I'm not coming back to work'* notice. I'm sorry everything worked out the way it did. Good luck in the future, Doc."

When I hang up, I feel slightly calmer. The doctor probably won't check his messages until after five without me there to do his work for him, but I feel better closing that door officially. Speaking of which... I grab my laptop and resume my job search.

Chapter 23

♥

Wyatt

From the moment Evie got in my truck this morning, she looked nervous. I thought she'd be calmer after talking with her parents but there's dark rings under her eyes telling me she had very little sleep.

When I got home yesterday, I called Uncle Mac, needing answers for this ominous nastiness hanging over the mountain. He didn't have a lot of detail, only hints and clues picked up by the triplets—our clan security team… ex-military bad-asses that no one wants to trifle with.

The mystery behind the new invasion didn't ease my nerves though. All we have is that they're an *ancient breed*, which means advantage for us that shifting comes with more pain and difficulty. It's hard for prehistoric breeds to transform their bodies into original forms because the transformation has so far to go. But the fact that they still exist shows the species' survival strength. The odd beings that are spreading into our area are old yes, but ruthless and tough… nothing to be trifled with. We just don't know what they are yet.

The whole clan is worried about these beings, though. Their morals seem as loose as a moor tied in a hurricane, but so far, it seems this species sticks to their own. Not a one has made a direct challenge on clans because of their difficulty challenging in a fight. That part is the only respite for the anxiety crawling inside my bear, because my uncle's one decree is, if they are allowed to get a jump on their opponent, they will be detrimental.

Reaching over, I squeeze Evie's hand, stopping her from picking her nails. I want my mate to find comfort in me, but honestly, I just need to touch her. My bear demands it, and he's not being quiet, either.

"How are you doing after yesterday?"

Evie shrugs, a sad smile lifting the corners of her rose-colored lips. "I'm OK," she says, earning my best mock-glare. At least, she responds with a laugh. "Alright, I'm working on being OK, which is a lot of what today's about."

"How do you mean?"

"Well, I'm not going back to Knoxville... obviously. But I'm not going to hide out in my parents' house either, so I need to figure out my next step."

"What about the people who broke into your place? You're not hiding out. You're staying safe."

From the corner of my eye, I see Evie turn to look out the window, frustration creasing her brows. I can hear her heartbeat hammering harder at the reminder of the break in. It makes my bear chuff in my head, annoyed that I upset our mate. *What a dumbass thing to say.*

Lacing our fingers over the center console, I apologize, rubbing Evie's knuckles to ease both our anxieties.

By the time we park at *The Hungry Diner* in the center of town, our conversation has loosened up. "The diner has the best omelets in town," I offer, hoping a good breakfast will ease that tired look in my mate's eye.

"I'm more of a pancakes and bacon kind of girl, but I'll think about it." Finally, she gives me a genuine smile, but still, she's out of the truck before I can open her door.

Shit!

I jog around, taking Evie's hand before she goes too far, but a foreign scent triggers my nose. Quickly, I jerk Evie to a stop a little too hard, but play it off by tugging her into a my arms for a make-shift hug. I sniff over the sweet scent of her shampoo, noticing something off that I've smelled before… ash and sulfur with something… unknown. *I don't like it.*

"What is it?" she asks, noticing the stiffness of my body surrounding her.

Everything inside me screams to protect Evie, to hold her in my arms so whatever nastiness is in the air doesn't touch her.

"I wanted a hug. Is that a crime?" My joke sounds stilted—even to my own ears—but I don't want Evie to worry.

"O-K." She drags out the word but wraps her arms around my waist anyway, and lets me enjoy her warmth. Evie's scent covers the obnoxious swill the air, and while I'd prefer to bask in her sweetness, I can't shake the crawling worms on the back of my neck that says we're being watched.

With these threats looming, it may not be the smartest move to keep suspicions to myself, but I use my current advantage to scan the parked cars over Evie's head, looking for anything out of place.

I'm still rolling the idea over in my head when we walk into the rustic diner owned by a pack of wolves in the area. They settled in Talon around the same time as my clan, and from the looks of the diner, haven't updated the place since.

"Wow, this place looks the exact same as it did in high school!" I laugh as Evie scans the red vinyl booths with the same laminate tabletops that decorated the space in the sixties.

"You know, I don't think this place has changed since my *granddad* was in high school!" The dining room looks like it always does, packed with tourists and locals alike. The sounds of clattering forks and laughing chatter buzz in the air as tables finish their breakfasts. Sipping their coffees before going about their busy Saturday.

"It never used to be this crowded," Evie whispers, sneakily checking the crowd around us as well.

A young waitress with straw-colored hair and a big smile strolls up to drop us menus. The fact that I haven't seen her before is rare in our small town. She smells of wolf, which isn't a surprise at this restaurant, but that twitch at the corner of her nose tells me she smells bear, too.

"Hi, there. I'm Belle. Can I get ya'll some coffee? Water?" She takes one of the pencils from her messy knot to write our drink order—she must be brand new if she needs to write down two coffees.

"Coffee's perfect," Evie says, smiling as the girl begrudgingly slides her glasses from the perch on her head to write.

"Make it two," I confirm, watching Evie's eyes follow the waitress before turning back to the menu. I get the same 'Roaring Breakfast' every time I'm here, so I don't touch the one in front of me, but Evie looks lost in thought, a subdued quiet falling over the table as she scours the menu.

After Belle drops our coffees on the table and takes our order, I decide to take the offense instead of waiting for Evie to open up at her snail's pace. The girl's got so much on her mind, I'm surprised her shoulders can hold the weight.

"Penny for your thoughts." I can't stop myself from reaching for the hand not stirring her coffee, needing some sort of physical contact. She smirks, and with some difficulty, adds a good pour of creamer to the cup as well.

"Just thinking about my parents. It feels like they're taking care of a school bully for me." Evie sighs and I hate that tremor in her voice. "It just feels odd."

My thumb strokes circles on her knuckles, hoping it helps. Even if Evie doesn't know we're mates, our connection should calm her on an instinctual level.

"So, my mom and dad know I'm not going back to Knoxville, and Dad's talking to the tribe about upping protection in the area, but I still have to figure out what the heck I'm going to do in Talon." Evie blows a puff of frustrated air. "I never thought I'd live at home again, so I didn't exactly work this as a backup plan."

She's staying! My bear focuses on the part of the conversation that means the most.

Evie stops talking when our meal arrives long enough to dig into her bacon, egg, and cheese sandwich. I force myself to eat slow with the tidal wave of energy surging through, wanting to fix things.

We could keep her safe, my bear growls, pointing out the obvious.

"Do you trust me?" A plan's forming in my head, but for a second, Evie just stares, brown eyes assessing me. I'm nervous she'll say no, so I do what I do best... feign confidence. Lifting one eyebrow, I lay a cheesy grin across the table that gets her to laugh at least. It relieves some of the tension settling in.

"I trust you... I think."

My heart stops, but that bright smile softens her words, the tinkling sound of her laughter digging itself deeper into my heart. Being with Evie is so easy, even when there's a dark cloud hanging over us. All the heavy stuff I still have to tell her.

Glancing down at my nearly clean plate, I shake off the melancholy and the guilt tightening my chest. "Well, I was thinking I could introduce you to a friend of mine. He's the vet in town." Evie's head cocks to the side, waiting for me to elaborate. "He's a great guy, and he's wanted to retire for years now. He just can't find anyone who's a good fit *and* willing to stay in Talon."

"Doc V?"

"Yeah? You know him?"

"My Gramps knew him. I haven't seen him since I was a teenager."

"It's a small practice, but you'd have the market cornered if you were interested. He's the only vet within thirty minutes of town." I drop a few more facts about how nice the people are at the office but close my mouth when Evie grins. I'm rambling. *Yes, I'm desperate to keep you close, woman. Sue me.*

She chews for a minute, her smile fighting for freedom, but I think she's trying to not bust my ego over that bumbling delivery. *I can take it, darlin'.*

"I'd like to talk to the doctor. I stopped by the other day, but he was out on call." Evie's excitement builds, her movements animated with an energy I haven't seen. My pride swells at brightening her mood. "Is that where your brother took our injured bear?" My coffee nearly splatters the menu. "I wanted to check on Yogi today, anyway. We can knock both out."

The beaming light in Evie's eyes is the final nail in my coffin and I look away, flagging down the waitress for our check. Details are coming up too fast. My dodging is crossing from a lies of omission territory into just straight lies.

I have to tell her... soon.

Who am I kidding? That conversation's gonna suck!

I nod, but my brain is spinning to figure out a way around this. I wanted to take Evie to meet Doc, but I never thought Evie would wonder about the bear she saved. Drastic oversight on my part! Of course, she'd want to follow up. She's obviously a good doctor. I saw that watching her with Jax.

I slide my card to Belle before Evie can unzip her purse. It buys me time to think of an explanation for why a wounded bear isn't recovering at the clinic only a few days after he was shot, even if it was a clean exit wound. Honestly, Jax was lucky we were hiking that morning. He had lost a lot of blood before Evie stopped him up.

Caleb took Jax to his cabin for a few days so we can force him to sit on his ass and heal. Sometimes, a shifter's healing abilities and stupid pride aren't a good recipe for a restful, happy patient. Jax was up and walking the next day, thinking he needed go to work. *No chance, buddy.* We made him call in, but other than being a grumpy ass, he didn't seem too worse for the wear.

Think. Think. Think.

"Let's go see the doc." I hold my hand out, swallowing the worry churning the large breakfast I wolfed down and so I can focus on Evie's smile.

Doc will help us, right?

·♥·♥· ♥ ·♥·♥·

Our walk to the clinic takes all of four minutes. The diner and the vet are on opposite ends of our little mid-town square.

Temps have dropped this week, but since I run hot, I barely notice. Evie shivers though, sticking her hands in the sweatshirt we bought at the store. I take off my coat and wrap her shoulders, loving the bashful smile that doesn't slow her excited chatter.

I try to listen, but I'm distracted by checking over our shoulders the entire way. The last few days have rattled us both, and I need to keep my eyes out for that putrid stench that followed us to the diner. I thought about bringing it up to Evie, but I couldn't figure out how to ask if she knew about shifters without admitting how I knew about shifters.

Our mating conversation grows in importance every time that wretchedness hits the town. It worries me that I can't place it. If Evie is in some sort of trouble with shifters, even if she doesn't know who they are, I need all the information I can get.

You should have been honest with Caleb so our brother could be back up when we get these assholes.

"Oh my God!" Evie's shriek shakes me out of my mental rabbit hole. She points at the ice cream shop across the street. "Ash and I got busted for going there in high school for our lunch break instead of eating in the cafeteria."

I laugh when she slips into stories of all the mischief she used to sneak in this town. Apparently, Ms. Beachum had a big hand in getting the girls in trouble. She tattled on Ama to their parents for making out with a boy in the library. Evie tried to cover the scandal for her, but her parents didn't believe Evie had kissed a boy—which she took a large offense to—so she went out and grabbed Jacob Nixon from the trumpet line and laid a kiss on him. Her hilarious shiver when she describes how his braces cut her lip has me doubled over in the middle of the street.

My only problem with our fun little walk is the time flew. Now we're at the clinic, and I haven't figured out how to tell Doc to play along. We don't have a family connection—only a clan one—so it's more difficult to communicate telepathically.

Too quickly, I open the frosted clinic doors with Dr. Viktor Bishop, D.V.M., emblazoned on the front and usher Evie inside. We're greeted by the sound of barking dogs and animal chaos, and I hear Evie sigh under her breath.

Inside the building, Evie passes me back my heavy coat, leaving my scent lingering on her skin. She looks adorably nervous, but straightens herself as best she can for a good impression. Instinctively, my hand falls to her lower back, curling her closer when Doc V. approaches.

"Mornin', Wy. What do I owe the pleasure, son?"

I feel myself break into a sweat, the heat under Evie's clothes searing my hand like a judgment from Hades. Over her head, my eyes bore into the Doc's, hoping he catches the hint to play along. Somehow I manage to keep my tone light. "Doc, Sir. This is my m-friend, Evie." Her courteous smile greets his handshake. "She's been practicing in Knoxville, but recently moved home. She's a talented lady," I say, bragging. Evie's appreciative eyes dart to me and I feel ten feet tall, but it's the old vet who brightens the most.

"Is that right?" Doc's eyes study Evie, seeing an opportunity for retirement knocking.

"Yes, Sir, Dr. Bishop. I doubt you remember me, but I used to tag along with my granddad when he'd visit the herds for their checkups."

"Oh yea! I remember a tiny little thing carrying Crayton's bag, despite it being half her size. You're all grown up!" His joke receives a laugh from Evie and her cheeks pink. "God, I feel old," he says, chuckling. "And call me, Doc V. Everyone else does."

Our conversation is interrupted by a little girl tugging at the doc's trouser pants. "Dockee, my mom says Maisy swallowed some Lego's. She needs you to help her tummy." The little girl rubs the pit bull, who's almost her height, while her baby blues swim behind a wall of tears. The girl's lip trembles with the broken heart of a scared child and she tucks one of her red ringlets into her mouth, obviously a chastised habit because she looks at her mom when she spits it back out and plows on. "I didn't mean to leave 'em out, Doc. I had to go potty and got a snack… then I got discracted." That pitiful whine breaks the hearts of every adult in the waiting room.

I catch Evie's squeaked 'aww' as her eyes watch their interaction with fascination. The doc lowers himself to the girl's height, his voice comforting while he pats his patient on the head.

"Does Maisy have a tummy ache?"

The little girl nods, her curls bouncing around that angelic face. "S-she gonna be OK?" she hiccups. Doc reaches to his front counter and grabs a sucker from his treat bowl, glancing at the mom for confirmation before holding it out to the girl.

"You did a terrific job bringing her to me, Lizzy. Why don't you take this and sit with your mom while my new friend and I check over Maisy, OK?" Evie startles briefly when Doc mentions her, but at his convincing wink she steps right into his game.

She slips out from under my arm and takes Maisy's leash when the little girl deems her trustworthy. "I promise we'll take good care of her," Evie says with a smile.

A nurse guides Evie through the back door with the dog and Doc nudges his head that way so I'll follow my girl. *As if I need to the told.*

In the back, I find Evie in the same room Seth used a few years ago for stitches when he got too ambitious with the chainsaw, and where Caleb had his eye bandaged when his bear got too curious with a skunk. Evie's beaming, chatting with the sweet pup while she takes her vitals, completely in her element.

I flashback to the Doc stitching up my chin, after a particularly rowdy fight in fifth grade. I sat on the examining table in this sterile office while Caleb and Seth defended my actions with the school bully to our dad... back when he was alive. Dad's scowl is etched in my memory, as clear as if his ghost were standing here beside me.

A throat clearing snaps me out of my memory. I turn to Doc rolling a mobile x-ray machine in front of him toward the wiggly pup who's enjoying some behind the ear scratches.

I watch in awe while Evie rattles off observations from her prep-exam. Doc nods, murmuring affirmations while his hands rub Maisy's lower tummy, checking for internal issues. Medical jargon flies between them that gives me a whole new level of respect watching their interaction.

Doc nods for me to help hold Maisy's lower half still so he can steady the sonogram wand for a good view. With a flick of the switch, Doc projects the dog's inner workings on the flat wall behind us. Evie's chuckle matches mine when we all see the tiny Lego piece sitting in Maisy's belly.

"Guess you realized hard Legos aren't as good as sneaking a slice of turkey. Didn't ya, Maisy girl?" I tease the little dog, wondering what sort of attraction she found in a cold piece of plastic.

"Yeah, it's not as bad with one little piece in there," Doc says, doing a thorough lap across her stomach. "It doesn't look like any more are hiding lower. If it's just this small two-prong, she should be able to pass that without surgery."

"Whew!" I exhale a breath I didn't realize I was holding. *That little girl's going to be so happy!*

After Doc cleans the wand and stores it, he turns to me and picks up our earlier conversation while Evie wipes the pit's tummy. "So, panicked six-year-old handled, let's talk about what brings you by today." Doc folds his arms, leaning against the white cabinets that hold the pet supplies.

Evie speaks up before I can, having gotten her foothold with the doctor now. "Well one, I wanted to check on the bear that Caleb brought in this weekend," Evie says, pausing when the doc's eyes fly to mine. Deep wrinkles cut into his forehead, his confusion is obvious. Thankfully, Doc recovers quick enough, reading my blatant stare correctly, but Evie noticed something's off.

"Oh-oh yeah... the bear. He was well enough that we sent him on his way after some monitoring." Doc turns his back to gather the paperwork for Maisy's owner and Evie looks at me incredulously.

"After a gunshot wound!?" she asks skeptically, her eyes turning into saucers. Evie's hands stay steady, guarding the fidgety dog from jumping off the table and injuring herself while she thinks. "I mean, it was clean exit, and we slowed blood loss on the trail..." I have a touch of panic because I don't want her to think Doc is irresponsible and not want to work here either.

Doc's recriminating glare when he realizes Evie has no idea of shifters or our healing powers reminds me of Uncle Mac and I just *can't wait* for this visit to work its way back to the clan. Yes, I roped him into my story without notice, but managing these old bears takes balance, and I'm already too tied in knots for my conscience to add one more thing.

"Caleb said he was a quick heal after some fluids and stitching. Right, Doc?" The man's eyes flash exasperation.

"Yeah... yeah." He nods, pulling himself together for my benefit. "Few days and big boy was energized and wanting out of the hospital." The smile he lays on Evie is sympathetic, nothing like the one he gave me.

"Was he really OK?" she asks, her head flipping between the two of us like she's watching a game of ping pong. "How-?"

Doc interrupts, "Well, you guys did excellent critical care. I just had to clean 'em up, couple stitches and bam... good to go." He shrugs his bony shoulder before steering the conversation back to a safe topic. "So, tell me about you, Evie, now that you're not a wee thing following around your gramps. Are you in town for good? Looking part-time? Full-time? Gimme the goods." Doc V wiggles his fingers in a 'give me' motion, his smile distracting.

Evie looks amused. "Well... I'm *considering* staying in Talon. But it only became a reality this week, so I've got nothing at all figured out. Except, I updated my resume, so I can send you that." She sucks in a breath while Doc studies her, quiet and calm. His pause spikes Evie's heart rate. I hear it, which means the doc can hear it too. "The truth is, I recently left a clinic in Knoxville where I interned and worked two years after. Most days, I handled the patients, while the owner, Dr. Michaels, ran the business side."

"You're so young. How have you been working two years already?"

She shrugs. "I took a lot of AP classes in high school, and summer school in college. I knocked undergrad out in three years and went on from there."

Our mate's strong, my bear tuts proudly.

Doc V. is officially impressed. "OK, so you got your granddad's work ethic. That's good." His chuckle fills the tiny room as he walks over to attach Maisy's leash for transport to her tiny owner. "Do you mind doing these emergency walk-ins on a Saturday morning?"

"Not at all. But I have to tell you, sir… my boss and I didn't part in the best of circumstances. We had a… a difference in moral philosophies." Evie grimaces. "They won't be a very reliable reference for my work, if you give me an interview."

Doc reaches for the door and waves us in front of him. Evie slumps, assuming she's being dismissed after that revelation, but Doc soothes her quickly. "See, young lady, I'm not a person who relies on other people's opinions very often. I judge what I see and feel from people myself." Evie brightens at his comforting grandfather voice.

Doc lays a wrinkled hand on her shoulder, giving it a squeeze. "As long as your credentials check out, I'd love if you'd come work a few days a week to start. We can get used to each other and see if you can tolerate being home in our crazy little town."

"Sounds great!" I can hear Evie's exhale from a few feet behind her, lowering her heart rate at the same time the smile lights her face. She turns her head, shooting me a giddy face over her shoulder while the doc grabs a treat and care instructions for Maisy.

Doc hands the leash to Evie as we cross the threshold so he can chat with the mom, and we're greeted with the trample of tiny tennis shoes and a whooping six-year-old before she crashes into Evie. I guess her shoes didn't have traction to stop, but the girl's not phased at all by her crash landing. She falls to the ground and engulfs the neck of her writhing dog who proceeds to bathe the little girl in slobbery tongue.

Ugh! Dog spit, my bear complains, making me fight back laughter.

"Maisy! My baby! Is yer tummy good, now? Please, don't eat no more Legos, kay." A whacking tail meets the kid's bossy pout, but I'm pretty sure this dog won't learn her lesson off one tiny toy.

Grinning, Evie passes the leash to Lizzy's mom who goes to check out with a pamphlet of care instructions and twenty questions from her mini-me. Evie is still grinning when Doc walks us out, her excitement at getting back to work is obvious.

"Why don't you come in around ten on Monday," Doc says, blocking his eyes from the glare. "There's a lull after morning drop-offs, so I'll have time to introduce you around and show you the ropes."

"Perfect!" Evie steps practically bounce, walking toward the truck. I hustle this time and make it to her door before Evie can open it. "I'm sorry. I'm not used to this gentlemanly thing," she says, humor dancing in her eyes.

"You better get used it, love." She blushes as I eye her like a Christmas ham. The wickedness rolling through my head for all the ways I want to care for her aren't sharable in public, especially in front of a clan member and my girl's future employer.

I summon every ounce of willpower to close her door and say goodbye to one of the most respected shifters on the mountain.

"Thanks for everything, Doc." I hope he can read the gratitude in my eyes since I can't say it out loud, but either way I owe this man for backing me up with Jax's story. He waves, but it's accompanied by a stern look that lets me know how he feels about my deceit. He still has my back.

I expect a call from Unc this week. Doc won't let this slide without a conversation in honesty. Too bad my uncle's going to take whatever I give him, because I am not giving up my mate. I'll have to convince him that his jadedness over never finding his own mate is just that.

Too bad. I got mine!

Once I climb in the truck, I blast the heat on high and find Evie watching me from her seat.

"Thanks for helping with introductions today. I feel better having the biggest thing on my to-do list checked off. Plus, it was nice being productive again," she admits, turning to gaze at the busy vet clinic where she'll spend her days.

"My pleasure, gorgeous. What other errands do you want to check off?"

"I'm good, I think. Researching a job was the biggest thing. Eventually, I need a place to stay so I'm not crashing in my childhood bedroom." She laughs, but it sounds strained, and I wish she didn't look so overwhelmed.

"I can help."

"That's sweet, but I'll take Kayah with me apartment hunting. I'm just tired this morning. Didn't sleep well... a lot to think about you know." That sad smile twists my insides. I desperately want to wipe that look off her face.

Leaning on the console, I pull Evie's hand to the middle so I can stroke the soft skin while I figure out the best wording for what I want to say. Electricity tingles every place our skin connects, like it does every time I touch my mate. Evie's drag of breath lets me know she feels it too, but I know she's not ready. As much as I want to stoke that fire, I can't.

"OK. Just promise me, if you need anything, no matter what... you call me. Alright?" She nods, looking caught in the same trance I feel.

I need her closer.

Listening to my bear, I reach out to brush under Evie's jawline, letting the low rumble vibrate the back of my throat when she tilts to give me better access. My hand slides behind her neck, pulling until Evie's face is a few inches from mine, her harsh breath teasing the air in front of me in anticipation.

Lightly, I brush my lips against hers, knowing if I give in to more, I'll have her pulled across this truck and in my lap without caring that the entire town could walk by and see.

Not good enough, my bear complains.

I smack that voice down and enjoy a few more tastes of her sweetness before resting my forehead to hers. I ignore my cock trying to blow out my zipper in favor of winning over my mate's heart. The fact that she lets me hold her while we breathe each other's air shows she feels connected beyond just lust.

Evie's eyes close in a peace I'm struggling to find. I can't wait any longer to tell her the truth. It's getting too hard. I'll sit Evie down and *calmly* explain about my bear. Then pray she doesn't run away the moment she knows.

"Baby, I want to cook you dinner... soon. Would you be OK with that?"

She giggles, "You can cook?"

"I'm a single man. Of course, I can cook." I feign offense, popping my dimpled grin just to add a little extra incentive. "If I didn't, I'd eat nothing but cereal and microwave pizza."

Evie's eyebrows crease, looking skeptical, but I hear her heart rake spike as well. My breath freezes while I wait for her verdict. Finally, she pulls back, judging my seriousness. "Like, actual food, right? Not frozen dinners and French fries."

"What do you take me for? I can feed my woman."

"Oh really." The challenge in her eye is at odds with the delicious blush sliding up her neck. But she likes my possessiveness, judging by the arousal scenting the cab of my truck. It's all I can do not to speed home and satisfy that need building in her. Stake my claim.

Needing to bring us both off that ledge, I go for levity instead, holding up three fingers in scout's promise. "I, Wyatt McAllister, promise you won't end up with food poisoning. I am not a stranger to the kitchen, and will try my best not to burn your meal."

Evie's giggle is music to my ears, but thankfully, she nods. "I'd like that. As long as you promise, no salmonella and I bring dessert." Her wink earns a growl of excitement from my bear and a bark of laughter from me.

"When?"

"Next Saturday," she offers.

"Tonight!"

She laughs. "Wyatt!" I shrug, not at all caring about my overexcitement. "Friday," she counters.

"Tonight." I grin, letting her know I'm joking when she slaps my hand exasperated. "OK, OK. How about Monday to celebrate your first day of work?"

She squints with play-judgment, but holds out a hand to shake on it. "Deal."

With a light heart, having made as much progress in my morning as Evie did in hers, I drive the woman who will be my future home. It's going to take some planning to figure out which meal will impress my mate enough to keep her after she knows my truth, but it's time.

That's a lot of pressure on one dinner.

Chapter 24

♥

Evie

It's *the* night… date night.

All weekend, I ran around town, rearranging my life to function in Talon. Something I never thought I'd do. But I felt productive. Like I was finally getting a handle on life.

Yesterday was a full load of check offs. Kayah and I went apartment hunting through town. I haven't decide on anything yet, but my favorite was a little one-bedroom bungalow behind old lady Beachum's house.

The *only* drawback—and why I didn't jump on the thing—is I would never have any privacy with guests. If I ever wanted to have Wyatt over the whole town would know by ten p.m.

If… hah!

After our search, my biggest surprise was Mom and Ama meeting us for lunch, like we talked about doing when I first got home.

I told them about shadowing Doc V today and working on a trial basis. Ama even sprang for a bottle of champagne to toast my homecoming. It was all very sweet! And after, we all tried on clothes at the little boutique across town. I picked out an outfit for my date—Ama approved—and got grilled endlessly for details about Wyatt.

My face turned fifty shades of red when Ama insisted I needed to 'hit that and lock it down' in front of Mama. *Yikes.*

Apparently, Wyatt cooking me dinner is a straight shot to walking down the aisle and popping out two point five kids. *In her mind.* My face is still red now, remembering how mama tried to hide her smile.

Gah! I go back to getting ready for my much needed shower, stripping off my fur covered clothes from the office today. Doc didn't need me for the full day, so I left after we did a pig spay—something I never imagined doing. But the day was actually a lot of fun. I just need to wash off all the animal stink, and allow time for a mini panic attack, before for my date.

It's all starting to sink in that I haven't been on a date for years. When Wyatt offered to cook, I was floored. No man has ever cooked for me. Let alone one who looked like that!

I thought guys only offered Netflix and chill situations. It just shows how different Wyatt is though. He's intense. I feel like his be-all, end-all every time he looks at me. That's hard to get used to after about ten years of loneliness with brief intermissions.

Smiling, I grab my robe and sit on the bed so I can remove my two-week-old nail polish. *Have I really only been home for two weeks? Holy cow!*

I'm almost done with my second foot when Ama blows through my door, all sashays and booming energy. My heart tries to pop out of my chest at the sudden noise, and I come close to screaming but thankfully hold it in so Ama doesn't laugh too hard. She's already giggling enough, perched with crossed legs on Kayah's bed.

"You know, you could knock," I suggest, without any venom in the words.

"Psh!" My sister waves away my annoyance. "I'm here for date prep. You're welcome."

Smirk, meet glare. But honestly, I miss this side of my sister. "You're welcome to stay, but there's not a lot to do. We're just eating dinner at his cabin."

Ama scoffs, stealing my nail file to touch up her own manicure.

"Have you trimmed? Or are you a shaver?"

Huh?

"You have to be ready, just-in-case," she says. At my confused look, she shakes her head. "In case dessert turns into chocolate sauce and whip cream in bed."

A shocked squeak rips from my throat, making Ama laugh again. "Dude! I wear granny panties on the first few dates, so I don't let my hormones make bad decisions."

"Hah!" Now Ama's doubled over laughing, her palm pressed to her forehead like I'm giving her a headache.

Yep, me and my sister are polar opposites.

"Fine! I'll trim when I shower. Can you stop laughing?"

She wipes at her eyes, sucking in deep, purposeful breaths like its an effort to calm herself. "Step one. But now I need access to your clothes tonight. I can't have you wearing something Gran wouldn't be caught dead in."

"Ugh! You suck!" I throw my tiny pillow at my sister so she knows I'm joking, but Ama doesn't look overly sensitive today. She pretty much ignores me in favor of rifling through the pile of clothes I laid out on my desk chair.

Underneath the shirt I plan to wear are my comfortable beige boy-shorts and the razorback cotton bra that goes with it. Ama shoots me a firm 'yeah right' side-eye before she tosses both items over her head.

"What? They match," I whine, knowing that argument won't work on Ama.

She chuckles all the way to my underwear drawer, where I *may* have stuck the flashy set I bought earlier at the boutique. My heart was momentarily optimistic for a few weeks from now and of course, they're exactly what Ama snatches. Her victory fist pump to the sky cracks me up so I don't argue with the change of plan.

"OK, you should be dry now, go exfoliate," she says, pointing at my nails.

"Yes, ma'am." I salute, feeling a happy return to normal with my sister as I head out the door.

"And don't forget to kitten-scape," she yells, almost as an after thought. I cringe. Please God, don't let Dad hear that.

Twenty minutes later, I'm done washing, exfoliating, and yes... trimming. It's closer to date time and there's nothing left to do for distraction. My stomach twists with worry, but Ama, who was still in my room after the shower, takes over. She sees my freak out coming.

"Sit," she orders, pressing my weight into the bed so she can brush my hair.

I follow blindly, happy to have someone take away my responsibilities, just for a moment. Plus, Ama's chatter is a great distraction. The only issue is her talking up Wyatt's positive qualities non-stop. It's not helping me.

I have very little hope that I can resist his temptation already. Especially without my safety blocks of unshaved legs and chastity belt underwear.

Hell, could I resist him, even with those things in place?

Wyatt is a living embodiment of the perfect man. The urban myth turned flesh, bone, and incredibly stacked muscle. Except, I don't think it's perfection that makes him irresistible. Under his sexy strength is a compassionate side, someone who'd take time out of their day to ride with a friend a few hours just so they're not alone. Someone who cares about animals and their community and making the world a better place, not just for themselves.

Ama blows out my hair for me while my brain is stuck in la-la land. I can't contribute much to my side of the conversation but she doesn't seem to mind. By the time she's done primping me, and I've dressed in the skinny jeans and sexy camisole I bought to wear under my button-up plaid shirt.

I hope I'm dressed OK. A home-cooked meal doesn't scream cocktail dress... neither does Wyatt. But, at least with Ama's beauty help, and her wise wisdom to *loosen up and embrace my wanton side,* I feel slightly calmer going into the evening.

An hour later, I'm centered enough to not hyperventilate when I knock on Wyatt's cabin door. Until he jerks it open before my hand even taps the wood.

His face splitting grin throws me off balance. So does his silly apron that says *'Right to bear arms'* with a picture of a bear underneath it. I crack up at its boyish charm, which also breaks the ice on our night.

You've hung out before. Just talk.

Wyatt bends to wrap me in a hug. "You look beautiful." His raspy voice warms the shell of my ear, making it hard to concentrate on holding my two soufflés upright. They're my contribution to dessert, but currently—annoyingly—keeping my hands occupied. I'd much rather wrap them around Wyatt.

Holy crap! How does this man short circuit my brain in less than ten seconds?

With a large effort on my part, I pull back, needing some self-control for the heavy dose of hormones swamping my body. My panties are wet just from the exhale off Wyatt's breath over my neck.

Yep, no reason to be nervous at all... I'm only about to jump the man and he's only said three words.

The only thing stopping said jumping is the idea of this hunk of a man seeing me naked. Immediately the tips of my ears burn imagining it and I know Wyatt sees that, even in his dim porch light. That smolder in those bedroom eyes say he not only sees my blush, but he can already see me naked... or maybe just read my mind.

What the hell, Evie! Get a grip. You're less than a foot inside the door and thinking about wrapping yourself around the man like a koala.

I'm teetering on unstable ground here. I can't convince my feet to move… until Wyatt decides he hadn't finished with his hug and circles my waist again. His powerful arms lift me into his chest, our full bodies connecting with the warmest explosion of sensation every place we touch.

"Come on in, love, relax." That deep voice offers the suggestion, but Wyatt doesn't let me go to make the choice. He turns both of us and walks into the cabin while I giggle in his arms.

His rumbling laughter matches mine, but after the door closes, Wyatt lets me slide down the front of his body until my feet touch the floor. Too bad my giddiness makes me feel like I'm still floating, completely overwhelmed with Wyatt's scent and the sight of those thigh-hugging jeans. He's barefoot and comfortable, but he made effort to iron his shirt and mousse those soft waves. Completely irresistible!

And now, I have completely uncomfortable wetness in my *non-granny-panties.*

Needing something to do other than stare at the gorgeous mountain man in front of me, I hand Wyatt one of the soufflés, so I can concentrate on putting one foot in front of the other. "Can we put these in the oven while we eat dinner?"

"Sure thing." Wyatt's smile beams as he guides me to the bulky leather couch. "Be right back," he says, taking the other dish from my hand with a wink.

I wait, semi-patiently, while Wyatt puts our dessert in the oven. The entire house smells of whatever mouth-watering dinner he's cooking. *Wow! It's possible Wyatt won't poison me, after all.*

Laughing in my head, I take in Wyatt's warm living space, fascinated by the peek inside his world. The walls and end tables hold tons of photos, some of him with his brothers, some nature shots. One of the larger frames captures a shot of three bears standing by a drop off. It looks like an actual portrait, with the sun setting behind them. Did Wyatt luck into that shot? Or is it just a piece of art he bought? Either way, it shows his love for those massive animals, if that wasn't already clear by all the work he puts into saving them.

I want to stand up and check out the other knick-knacks on the mantle. I just don't want Wyatt to come out and catch me snooping. It's hard though. I want to dig deeper. Even if the cabin screams bachelor decorated with the leather furniture and a lack of throw pillows. It's still warm, every accent personal, but still perfect for the rustic chic cabin. It all just fits Wyatt's personality... at least for what I know so far.

Plus, the place is spotless. *Hallelujah!* I don't smell a gym sock in sight. Either he cleaned up for our date, or Wyatt is one of the rare men who doesn't live in a pigsty.

Another point in his favor, dammit.

Speak of the devil. When Wyatt walks out, dripping sex appeal like his bucket overflows, he's holding two glasses of wine.

"I hope white's OK to start," he says, handing the glass to me.

"It's perfect. Thank you." I take a fortifying sip, praying I don't look as nervous as I feel.

I expect Wyatt to sit on the couch, but not immediately beside me, like he does. When his weight dips the couch cushion and he tucks his leg my way, that long arm stretching behind my head. There's not a lick of space between us. I'm surprised, but I don't exactly mind. Anyone who can make a tall girl feel extra small is really nice.

"I'm glad you came, tonight," Wyatt says, his dimpled smile ramping up my hormones. Without conscious thought, my hand reaches out to rest on his knee, while I take another nervous sip.

"I'm glad you invited me," I counter. "Dinner smells delicious." Wyatt's eyes darken when I pull my wine glass down. He doesn't look to be breathing.

Before I can ask if he's OK, Wyatt leans forward, setting his wineglass on the coffee table and angling his body into mine. *Eep!*

Immediately, my heart rate picks up, every pulse thumping through my temples when those callused hands cup my face, his thumb stroking the edge of my slightly gaped jaw before finally closing the distance.

I never expected Wyatt to go for a kiss this early, but no part of me wants to argue with it. Especially when that cedar cologne warms me up like a scorching campfire.

And then we collide.

All games are off. Wyatt samples like a starved man, licking and nipping at my lips before pulling me on his lap like I weigh nothing. He's shattered any restraint I had left. Our tongues battle and within minutes, I'm squirming against his growing bulge, trying to crawl inside his skin and vice versa.

Wyatt groans, digging his fingers into the fleshy part of my hip, and pressing me against that steel column straining his zipper. The friction of it fires lightning behind my eyes, pulling a frantic moan from my throat.

Desperation claws my insides, building a pressure inside me I fear will break me apart. I need Wyatt. That need drives my fingers into Wyatt's hair, pulling back until his head hits the couch. I want my own access to his mouth. He's had all the control so far to drive me crazy.

His growl vibrates under my lips, sending a new rush of wetness below, but he holds still, giving me freedom to drink in the magical scent at his neck. I nibble the tendon there, stroking my tongue up the side and biting every few inches. It's like my mouth has lost control. It has a mind of its own.

The tingling under my skin is a revelation, pleasure vibrating from every part of my body touching his. It's fire and light, connecting us with a shared need.

Wyatt hisses when my fingers scratch the scruff on the back of his head, his soft waves falling over my fingers as he moans, "Evie." My name falls from his lips as those deft fingers drag under my shirt, spreading wide up my back to hold me tight against his front.

There's barely room to breathe in his arms, the need taking us over... it's hot! I swear I could come from just tasting his neck. By the time Wyatt pulls me back to his mouth, I'm panting as hard as he is, my breasts flattened against his chest. I want to scream for release. Desperation doesn't cover it. I would trade my soul right now to melt into Wyatt, to have every inch of his skin searing me.

An animalistic sound fills the room as Wyatt's hands move to my ribcage. His massive hands spread across my middle, inches in either direction from where I need him most. The frustration has me writhing to get closer, but Wyatt holds me in place, jerking his head up from the couch to take control of our kiss. I lose the grip on his hair but have no urge to argue because a moment later, Wyatt is taking his own nips of my neck.

"God, Evie." His tortured groan fills the air, his one hand moving to wrap up my hair. It holds me still for the sensual press of his hips. Those bottomless eyes locking on mine, watching every emotion caused by the pulse of his cock. The seam of my jeans pulls a keening moan I have no chance of hiding as the rough fabric slides against my freshly shaved lady region.

Ama did not mention how sensitive everything would be.

Although it could just be Wyatt. The man plays my body like a fiddle, drawing moans and gasps from me that I'd be embarrassed about in my right mind. Too bad I'm not. Until the oven timer startles us apart before I'm ready—before I'm done.

Wyatt's pupils have blown wide, his lips swollen probably the same as mine. Instinctively, my fingers touch the heated burn, knowing already I'm going to have beard burn tomorrow, even with Wyatt's five o'clock shadow. I'd be annoyed at how easily I fell under his spell, if Wyatt's breath wasn't just as ragged as mine.

We're both panting, our rhythms matching up when I rest my forehead against his, both trying to collect ourselves. How did I go from determined granny-panty date a few hours ago, to wanton lap dance after being nervous as hell? *Because Wyatt is still too sexy for his own damn good, that's why.*

It's a small comfort that his lips are as red as mine. But when Wyatt drags his thumb across my tenderness, I almost pull away. It's too much. So why am I'm desperate for more?

When I lift to meet Wyatt's gaze, his eyes shine an unusual shade of gold, like our passion melted them into blown glass. It's an amazing color, shifted by passions.

"Now those are some mood eyes," I say, awed, but they shutter closed before I can figure out how the light plays tricks with his irises.

Wyatt's chiseled jaw twitches, grinding his teeth together painfully. He only releases the tight clench when I stroke along the muscle, willing it to relax. When it doesn't, I lean forward, running my tongue along that enticing scruff. Wyatt's hands dive into my hair, pulling my head back and flaying me open with those eyes again.

"Evie... baby. I didn't ask you over for this." His voice strains and it might sound mean, but I hope he feels the same torture I do. Like I'm boiling from the inside out.

"You sure?" I tease, wiggling against Wyatt's bulge to lighten that serious expression that's clouding his eyes. He pauses, but my sarcasm—

or the grind of my hips—work to loosen the stress lines marring his forehead.

Finally, my taunting cracks Wyatt's composure. Like a whip snapping, he's on me, nibbling at my collarbone. A total seduction of the lips that throws my head back. Some shocking part of me needs him to have complete access. I want to give Wyatt everything.

Shit! The sensation of teeth against my skin vibrates straight to my core and I wiggle, involuntarily making Wyatt groan. His nose nuzzles up my neck, his lips dragging right behind. I'm soaking wet by the time our mouths crash together... again.

Wyatt's slow seduction is painful, dragging my body under his spell until I'm dying for more. More of Wyatt's mouth, more of his taste... that exotic flavor of wine, toothpaste, and... man. It drives me up a wall. I can't get enough. But Wyatt's hand fisting my hair stops me from diving back in. We stay locked like that, our ragged breaths swirling between us.

I should climb off Wyatt's lap and let him take care of that timer, but I can't yet. Before I can offer, Wyatt stands in a jerk, and I squeak.

Holy cow, this man is strong!

It's impressive, but instinctively my legs tighten. My death grip on Wyatt's waist lifts me higher, trying to become as light as possible.

"Wyatt, I'm too heavy," I argue, panicked, but his masculine chuckle shows he isn't having a problem.

"Woman, you're perfect. It's taking every ounce of willpower I have not to lay you out on this couch and taste every delectable inch of your body." The rawness in his voice sends shivers down my spine, though no part of me feels cold.

In fact, I can't imagine getting any hotter... until Wyatt bends us over, dropping my back to the couch slowly, deliberately. His impressive bulk hovers, surrounding me in his intoxicating scent. Like a thick cloud of rich leather and dizzying masculinity.

I'm seconds away from combustion. The vision of tanned muscle and searing gold eyes as they loom over me, rushing a wave of arousal to my core. It leaves me panting, digging my fingers into thick biceps, feeling the strain along the one arm holding his weight. My hands stroke with a mind of their own. The sinful temptation of Wyatt impossible to resist.

Suddenly, he rears up to his knees, keeping those strong hands locked on my thighs. Seductive dark eyes rake over my body, burning a path that has me writhing against the couch. The new wetness below tortures my now uncomfortable lace.

Yes, please.

A whimper slips out when Wyatt's thumbs rub circles on the inside crease of my thigh, his cocky smile showing he knows exactly what he's doing with this torture. It's difficult to hold still, my hips struggling under his strong grip. But I don't want Wyatt to stop. And he doesn't until that damn kitchen timer buzzes again. *Ugh!*

Wyatt's rough exhale mirrors my frustration. "I'll go check on dinner," he says, his feral smile promising things later that have my heart quickening.

When Mr. Gorgeousness stands, his impressive erection stares me in the face. *Hello!* I swallow, amazed at how it jumps when Wyatt catches me staring.

Gah! I wish we could skip dinner and go straight to dessert.

"Ugh, woman! Curb your eyes or I won't make it through dinner." I love how pained his voice sounds, but something in that rumble of laughter says he wouldn't care and would jump at the chance if I just gave a nod.

There's only the smallest grain of sanity holding me back. It sounds like Mama's voice and I focus on that buzz kill. Mama would have my ponytail in a vise if she saw me wiggling on a near stranger like this. I didn't even know Wyatt a few weeks ago, though it feels like I've known him forever.

And no matter how abnormal this gravitational pull feels, I still pat myself on the back for channeling Ama's confidence. If a night—or a man like Wyatt—never happens again, I'm damned sure going to enjoy wherever it takes me.

Chapter 25

♥

Wyatt

Our dinner hits the spot, satisfying at least one of my hungers deliciously.

The baked barbecue chicken was one of my tastier meals. With roasted potatoes, green beans, and a side salad, it's easy enough to prepare, but impressive enough to show that I know my way around the kitchen.

Tonight needs to be perfect to show Evie I'm worthy as her future mate. And as my reward—and torture—Evie has spent our entire meal moaning her pleasure over my chicken and driving up the other source of hunger inside me.

Every time she compliments my food, I compliment her. She licks sauce from her lips and my cock twitches under the table. He's longing to be on the receiving end of that little tongue, and it's driving me crazy. Little does she know, every enticing sound from her mouth gets her one step closer to me clearing the table in one swipe and laying her on top for my dessert. I've never wanted anything more in my life!

Except, I'd never pass up those enticing soufflés she brought. The amount of effort she worked into her day for such a decadent dessert swells my heart with pride. And now, watching how natural she looks in my kitchen, bending over to check their doneness through the oven window… I'm questioning how much more I can take.

The entire room is a sauna of pent-up need. My bear feels the heightened arousal. He's circling, clawing to get at his mate, and it's driving me a little wild.

"Thirty more minutes," Evie says when she turns around, her eyes dilating when she looks at me. The waft of excitement through the air assures me I'm not alone in this desire. Even if she looks nervous, fiddling with the hem of her shirt like she doesn't know what to do next.

I do.

Standing, I top off our wine glasses, finishing the bottle of Cabernet we sipped through dinner. With glasses in hand, I walk to Evie, feeling pulled to her like a magnet. She reaches for her wine and takes a healthy sip, swallowing thickly. She's prey caught in my trap; her nerves written all over her face.

Sensing the anxiety, I lay a gentle kiss on her cheek instead of picking up where we left off earlier. That sweet vanilla fragrance of her hair soothes my bear's claiming instincts, her sigh a balm to his rough edges. It gives me the patience to enjoy the simplicity of having my mate in my home.

"Would you like to sit out back while we wait for dessert?" Evie's eyes flash with surprise for a second before she nods. Was her mind on the same dessert as mine?

Smiling, I take her hand and lead her to the swing on the porch. The blast of brisk night air on my skin helps cool my body that's been overheating for hours... first from the hormones, then dread of the talk I'm stalling with Evie. I need something to stave off both issues because no matter what, I refuse to give in to the pleasures of our hormones before Evie knows the truth. That guilt would eat me up. Not to mention the pain it would cause to claim my mate and have her reject me after. I've seen bears go crazy with grief in those situations. *No, thank you.*

But since I've never told a woman—or a human—about my bear, that the mystical creatures they see in the movies are real, I have no clue where to start. Evie needs to listen long enough to hear me out, for me to explain and separate the truth from the lies on tv. She needs to know I'm not a danger. Not to her. Not to anyone unless they try to hurt my mate. Then no promises.

But that's protective, not scary, right?

With my heart racing, I settle myself on the sturdy swing I built right after completing the cabin, pulling Evie right up against me so I can wrap her in my arms and share my warmth. She shivers, snuggling right up against my chest, pulling a contented purr from my bear.

Behind me rests a wool blanket I keep folded for non-shifter visitors, not that I have many. But, my foresight pays off with Evie's appreciative smile when I wrap the warm cover over her lower half and tuck it in.

"Comfy?" She needs to be for this shock…

Evie's head lolls against my shoulder, humming an easy agreement that tightens my arms involuntarily, savoring her closeness. Hopefully, not for the last time. I could spend every night of my life just like this.

"Can we talk about something?" I venture, squeezing her shoulders. "Something important."

"Sure." Evie angles her body toward me, her hand coming to rest on my stomach which vibrate the muscles underneath in anticipation.

I keep a tight circle around her shoulders, not trusting my hands to venture anywhere else. I have a feeling this would be a lot easier if I didn't have to look in Evie's eyes. I'm afraid of what emotions I'll see when I drop this bomb. Honestly, I can't think of the best way to open my mouth and start.

While my brain stumbles over what to say, Evie's fingers slide between the buttons, rubbing the soft line of hair just above my jeans. My breath hitches and I try not to move. I don't think Evie's aware of the movement, but her fingers have the blood rushing away from my brain, distracting my thoughts. It's impossible to focus with her nails scratching along the ridges of my stomach, like it's the most natural thing it the world. The swelling below says otherwise. Evie's hands on my body make it extremely hard—pun intended—to resist her temptation.

Blowing out a rush of air, I press her hand against my stomach, holding it still against the tickle. I brace my mouth against the top of her head, trying to regain control of my groin. Evie's melodic chuckle shakes her small frame against my side, but she doesn't fight my hold, just rides the wave of my breaths with happiness radiating through her energy. *She's enjoying my torture, the vixen.*

"Evie, do you believe in things beyond the human world? Things like your grandmother talked about... different from you."

That gets her attention. She sits up slightly, her neck twisting uncomfortably to hit me with confused chocolate eyes. The sudden change in direction throws her off, but now that I've started, I can't lose my nerve. No matter how uncomfortable the conversation feels. No matter how much I want to forget about honesty and wrap myself in Evie's warmth.

"What do you mean? Like fantasy stuff? Vampires and werewolves. Or are we talking about believing in God?"

Not happy to see Evie contorted so uncomfortably, I grab under her ribs and lift to position our bodies better. She laughs at my easy handling of her body, blushing sweetly as I stretch out on the swing with her on top of me, our legs tangled together. My bulk takes the brunt of the rigid wood under my back. I built this swing large enough for a big shifter body, but there's nothing I can do about the discomfort of materials.

Once I have us comfortable, Evie goes back to her thoughts, stroking a hand absentmindedly against my chest. "Well, I do believe in a higher power, I guess. I believe that there are spirits in the world that help us through life. Most of my people follow those beliefs." She pauses and I rub my hand down the sinewy line of her back, enjoying her thoughts.

I stop at the dip above those gorgeous hips I've been lusting after for weeks and open my mouth to push the other side, the more fantastical, but Evie's hands take away my words... again. Maybe having his conversation with her sitting on the opposite side of the table would have been better, maybe sitting *on* her hands. Not allowing any touch or tease.

Because right now, I cannot concentrate with the slide of Evie's hands rubbing through my clothing. Especially not when she purrs her satisfaction. My bear loves that sound! Wanting her to enjoy the feel of us, as much as we do her.

At this angle, my bear feels like she's rubbing his tummy while we lavish on our back like a young cub. He doesn't want me to fight it. By the time Evie's silky hand slides around my neck, my breath has gone ragged...heaving. My cock is granite, and Evie's glorious scent is calling my bear home.

Claim. Need our mate. Now.

His growl takes over my conscious thought. The urges of man completely overrun by beast as passion takes over. I've never been this out of control with a woman. Barely able to contain my bear, keep him below the surface to prevent a spontaneous shift that's guaranteed to scare the hell out of Evie.

All the good intentions I started with are tossed aside by fate, incinerated under my craving for this gorgeous woman... my mate.

I need Evie now.

With one arm locked around her waist, I cup my free hand against Evie's face and dip to taste heaven.

"Evie… do you know that you're mine?" I have to ask. Despite her cluelessness to the impact of her answer. I can tell our fated pull is getting to her by the way she's opening up, despite her normal shyness. And while I love it, I can't have hormones making all her decisions.

It's one thing for me to know from my first taste of those soft lips that she's my fate. And for every nibble after that to send her deeper into my soul. But I'm aware of what's happening… Evie isn't.

"I want to be yours." The quiet confession is an arrow to the chest, sealing our fate. Her vulnerability propels me off the swing with Evie in my arms.

"Hang on," I growl, chuckling at her delighted squeak. And when her legs and arms wrap me in a tight bear hug from the sudden change of position.

"Where are we going?"

Evie pulls back enough to look in my eyes, which I fear give me away with the shifter gold burning, so I don't answer, just dive in to nibble the slope of jawline in front of me.

Evie gasps, her arms squeezing to lift herself higher like she's going to fall. "Wyatt… I'm too heavy for this."

"Mmm, perfect," I hum against the soft skin of her neck, stopping to press Evie's back against the side of my house so I taste easier. I lift under the curve of her ass to keep her still, my gaze locking on the heartbeat thrumming wickedly along the line of her neck, on the heaving flesh exposed above her camisole. It's a buffet of Evie I'm ready to gorge on.

My cock throbs painfully seeing her pulse quicken under the tanned line of her neck. I'm dying for a taste and that is my biggest problem. My control is vanishing with every sigh—every moan—that falls from her lips.

"Wyatt!" She wiggles. "You're going to drop me."

Little does she know; her weight is no problem. I squeeze the handful of flesh in my hands, groaning before I cover her mouth with a warning kiss. Those negative words stop with the swipe of a tongue.

By the time I pull back, Evie's hands are tangled in my hair and we're both panting. "I'd never hurt you, Evie." The promise triggers a healthy dose of guilt as her eyes search mine. My secrets could hurt her though, and that's the last thing I want.

I'm supposed to tell her before taking this next step—I was going too —but my bear has stolen my willpower. He basks in the feel of our mate pressed against us, knowing we'll always protect her no matter what.

Evie gives a subtle nod, abolishing my last restraint. With my hand cupping the back of her head, I dive in for another kiss, pushing off the wall in favor of my bedroom.

I'm surprised I remember to turn off the oven on our way through the kitchen. Dessert will wait. I need time to enjoy my goddess, room to spread her out. It's the only way I can stay away from her neck and its official call to mate. This won't be quick. I need to show Evie how great we can be together. Maybe it'll make up for all that she doesn't know... after.

Chapter 26

♥

Wyatt

By the time I make it to the bed, Evie has taken over our kiss, her hands roaming my shoulders, my back, tangling in my hair. The roar in my head is deafening. Her enthusiasm unleashes the tight constraints I have on my bear.

Gathering my wits, I unwrap Evie's arms from my neck and guide her backwards until her upper body lays on my freshly washed blankets. *Thank heavens for foresight.*

I keep a firm grip on Evie's wrists, so they don't test my control. But her legs—still wrapped around my waist—try to pull me down as she wiggles to pull her arms free. *Not happening.* I need a second to collect myself, to slow down so I don't embarrass myself and end this way too early.

Our mate is beautiful in our bed, my bear pants.

"You're beautiful, Evie." Both man and bear are basking in our woman laid out before us, in the pink-flush crawling up her chest. Somewhere on the way to the bedroom, her plaid shirt fell off and now my eyes have access to the delicate curve of her shoulder, to the dip of her collar bone I want to lick.

When I reach Evie's shy smile, I realize she's stopped fighting against my hands and I let go, satisfied she'll behave. The backs of my fingers follow the lines my eyes just traced, over every inch of soft skin exposed. My brain still wars with my bear. Can we do this?

I bend, resting my forehead against hers, just breathing in her air to center myself. Evie's hands tenderly stroke my back, comforting me with her closeness, and I force myself not to thrust and ruin this moment. We haven't even mated, and I know she would break me if she left.

The thought pulls my head back, but Evie's thighs have me trapped against her heat. Her hands grow bolder, massaging the muscles in my lower back and sliding under my shirt... up my ribs. Stroking my chest, my shoulders. My fists squeeze the quilt so I don't take over. The look of awe on her face is worth waiting, even if that look brings me close to blushing. *Though I won't admit the heating of my face, even in my own head.*

Needing to curb the sensations burning under my skin, I shift focus, sliding one hand under the back of Evie's shoulder blades and lifting her further up the bed. Her eyes widen at the movement, but my own body follows close, distracting Evie from questioning my strength with the heat of my gaze.

One elbow braces my weight, keeping it from crushing her as I settle in, letting the fierce longing engulf me. I brush a stray hair from her forehead and try to gauge the certainty in her eyes. I pray that Evie has control of her hormones—unlike me. That she won't regret tonight the moment she steps away from me, from our hypnotizing bond, in the morning.

Clearing my throat, I stroke the velvety skin along my mate's elegant neck, unable to stop myself from touching her even now. My bear purrs when a delicate shiver rolls through her body. He's begging me to stop thinking and enjoy our mate.

"Evie... baby. I need to know you're sure... about me." Her head tilts, confusion clouding her eyes. "This isn't just about tonight." I have to make sure that's clear. Even if it means waiting. My head pulls back when Evie tries to tug me in for another kiss. I can't be distracted... yet. I need the words.

"Do I not look sure?" she asks, searing me with the passion firing from those dark chocolate eyes.

My bear growls and I tense, fighting past his urges. I need patience to make her understand what I can't say... not without ruining this moment. If I can't share my whole truth, I at least need her to know the finality. What she's choosing with me. Because even without our full mating bond, I'll never have another.

My voice firms, rougher than I'd like. "Evie, once you're mine, I'm not letting go. I need you to know that."

Her pupils dilate, the intensity of this moment creating a deeper connection between our souls. The world is near glowing behind my eyes, but I hold back, fighting the fire in my lungs until I'm sure.

"Yes, Wy," she says on the quietest whisper. I worry it's my imagination hearing what I want until she lifts her mouth to my ear, nibbling the lobe in a wet caress and nuzzling against the roughness I didn't think to shave. Every ounce of blood flows south, my body coiled tight, ready to take my mate. With Evie's mouth at my ear, she's clear as day this time... "I'm yours, Wyatt." That throaty whisper steals my breath, leaving me at her mercy and happy for it.

I groan as those tiny teeth nip at the tendon in my neck, love bites that fire straight to my loins. My hips thrust from their locked position at Evie's middle, pulling a moan from her throat that has my bear stomping, begging me to take control. I won't yet. I'm content to enjoy the wildness of Evie's hands, her kisses. She's grabbing everywhere she can reach, while I press her to the bed with my hips. It takes a Herculean restraint to not rocket out of my body from Evie's mouth attacking any exposed skin she can find.

Evie's legs clench my waist, her hips grinding up with a need that's driving me wild. The girl couldn't hold me still under lock and key, but those urgent moans as she rubs against my hard length are worth digging for the extra self-control I need to let her have her way.

Finally, when I can't hold back anymore, instinct takes over and I bury my hands in those thick brown waves, tugging Evie's head back so I can enjoy the passion swirling in my mate's bottomless eyes, those swollen lips parted with a desperation mirroring mine.

I watch the flush creep into Evie's cheeks, growing hotter with every pulse of my hips against her softness. Every push is slow and steady, letting her feel what she's getting into. My bear growls, reveling in the sparks lighting her eyes, in the guttural moan that falls from her lips when her hands fly to my biceps, squeezing her enjoyment of my possession.

It's music to my ears, sending a rush of blood to my groin I can't ignore. But... *I need more.*

I lever back, kneeling between those muscular thighs and let my eyes, and my hands, roam. My hand smooths across the length of her jeans, hating the barrier. But, I grip the inside of Evie's knees and spread them wider, enjoying the sweet access to her scent dragging me under a spiral of longing.

Her heart rate ticks up watching my hands move. I slide the bottom of her top up, exposing her flat stomach inch by inch to my hungry gaze. By the time I reach the bottom of her lace bra, Evie is panting, her own fist gripping my blanket now. With a grin, I lift the fabric over those gloriously plump breasts and leave it there. *A front clasp... nice.*

My mouth waters. A growl I have no chance of containing rumbles in the back of my throat as I lower my mouth to taste the olive skin peaking from those tight constraints of purple lace. Evie mewls, writhing against my cock when I nip at the swell, dropping love bites over every inch of flesh and marking it as mine. Her hands lock on the back of my head, but still let me move freely, not stopping me from taking more.

With every jagged inhale, more of her breasts press against my lips. I smile against her heated skin as I finish tugging the disheveled tank top over her head with as much care as I can muster, not wanting to rip the soft fabric with my impatience.

Having my present revealed, I trace the valley between her rounded mounds, itching to rip them free. "Did you wear this for me?" I ask, my voice rough, unrecognizable to my own ears.

"What if I did?" That answering pant has me grinning, flicking my tongue against her heated flesh.

With one snap of my fingers, that pretty bra releases, spilling beautiful handfuls into my waiting—way too keyed up—hands. I moan when I gain access to those caramel-colored nipples, but Evie's hands tense, seeming like she wants to cover herself. I cock my head at her. "Do not move."

She draws a shaky breath, gripping the hem of my shirt to help her resist and I smile with approval, sliding the backs of my fingers from Evie's sternum, between each breast, to her ribs, and make a trail down her quivering stomach. The way she bites her lip, wiggling to get closer to my groin as I slide further down her body is pure torture.

"What do you want?" I ask, encouraged by the embarrassed flutter of Evie's eyelashes. I still her hips, but give in when she reaches to tug my face for a kiss.

Dangerously close to the edge, I dive in, lifting Evie's head for more. More sucking of her lips, more swirls of her tongue. She moans on each breath, driving me to a desperation that spurs me to break our kiss to sink lower.

Sliding down those tempting curves, I nip at the underside of her exposed breasts, plumping each to my will as I slide back and forth, not leaving an inch of tan skin untouched except where she needs me the most. Every time I pass over her taut nipple and move to the other breast she whines.

"Please," Evie pants, trying to guide my head where she wants, her body trembling. *Victory*.

Finally, I give in, rewarding her with a circle of my tongue over one stiff peak, latching on when Evie exhales her relief. My bear is going wild. He loves how she tries to get closer, arching her back to push her breast against my mouth. I flick my tongue again and again, closing my lips around the tip in a sensual kiss.

My hand mimics the movements on her other breast, a pinch for a nip, a caress of my thumb to the caress of my tongue. Dragging out the pleasure until I hear Evie's whimper, then I switch. Each beautiful breast gets her turn. I suck and nip, building Evie's vocal excitement until her scent of arousal has washed across my bed, those voluptuous hips torturing my groin. I lock them to the bed while I feast on her breast, keeping them still to stave off my own release that's threatening too fast.

I need Evie desperate... begging before I let go.

She battles my hold, forcing me to release her breast before I'm ready, and I pull back, watching the determination, the mischief, dance across her eyes. Purposefully, Evie thrusts upwards and I lighten my grip, allowing her heated core to stroke against me in the best torture. *I need to get rid of these barriers.*

Swiftly, I tug Evie's furry boots from her feet, giving me better access to the few remaining items hiding my mate from me. My fingers make quick work of Evie's cock-teasing skinny jeans, peeling them down those long legs like I'm unwrapping the best Christmas present. When they're gone, Evie's spread like a buffet on the bed, flushed red in matching purple lace—the last barrier to having my mate.

A fissure of the tension knotting me up releases. *She matched for me tonight. She was ready.*

Every inch of bare skin comes alive with goosebumps. And since I'm not one to pass up an advantage, I stand from the bed and take in the buffet laid out before me. The dips and curves of her feminine lines, strong and lean, but soft—judging from her blush—bashful, too. She's fighting the urge to hide, but she lets me look my fill, and I reward her with a dimpled smile.

"You are beautiful."

"Too many clothes," she counters, nodding her head at my still fully dressed body. I chuckle but give her what she wants. With a playful smile, she props on her elbows to watch from the bed and I almost blush myself.

My bear isn't happy when I force my fingers to go slow, releasing the buttons of my shirt one at a time, instead of ripping the thing off. But the way Evie's eyes roam every new stretch of skin is worth it. When my shirt is gone, the lust in her gaze spurs my hand into high gear, unbuckling my pants faster. There's only so much strip tease I can take and hold onto my sanity. I say a prayer of thanks for my bare feet when my boxers follow the pants to the floor where I step out of them easily.

Standing in front of my mate, I feast on the desire in her eyes. My bear strutting with pride as her hungry gaze drops to my cock, sending a new wash of arousal through the room.

With my eyes set on Evie, I climb across the bed, stroking the soft skin of her calf on my way up. Her scent fires my blood, making it difficult to go slow, but I need her wet and pliant to be ready. I'd never want to hurt my mate.

Bending, I run my nose along her knee, dropping soft kisses on the inside of one thigh, then the other. Evie's legs drop a little wider. Her heavy breaths shaking her body when I finally reach the top of her thighs. She's squirming under my hands. My gaze follows as I slide the lace panties with its visible proof of her wetness down her long legs.

I dip my head for the first taste of her glistening folds so she doesn't see the happiness glowing from my eyes. "So sweet," I groan, earning a surprised squeak from Evie. Her body tries to slide up the bed, farther away from my exploring licks.

"Nuh, uh, my sweetness." I lock an arm over her hips, keeping her still for my enjoyment. *And I am not shy about enjoying.*

In no time, Evie's moans grow loud enough that I hear them through her thighs muffling my ears. I smile against her wet heat, giving in to what she needs for that final push. One finger smoothly slides in, then two, curling against her wall while flicking the bundle of nerves at the top of her mound. My fingers stretch her gently, preparing the velvety softness for my size. With every pump, her wetness coats my fingers, but it's the desperate screech of my name that finally snaps my tightly coiled control.

My mouth attaches, growling against her center as I suck lightly until Evie's body careens off the bed. Her fingers scratch my scalp as she detonates on the last stroke, her inner muscles squeezing tight. I can barely move my fingers, but I ride the wave, slow pulses bringing her down from her first orgasm of the night.

"Shit! You're gonna feel so good wrapped around my cock."

Evie's hoarse laughter is a light to my ears. I love that she let go; that she trusted me with her body to ride the pleasure I could give her. Smiling, I drag my chin scruff up her stomach, nipping at the soft skin all the way up until I'm settled over my mate.

"You're gonna kill me," she sighs, trying to catch her breath with my straining cock nestled against her wetness.

"But what a way to go." It's impossible not to grin when Evie drags me down for a kiss, her excitement evident. She pauses momentarily, tasting herself on my lips, her cheeks burning bright before I nip at the lower plumpness. My tongue swipes against the seam, pressing her to continue, to let me in. Evie's moan when she opens throws lighter fluid on my arousal. She doesn't mind getting a little dirty.

And I'm more than happy to oblige.

Thankfully, I have enough awareness to reach for a condom in the bedside drawer, sheathing myself quickly before I stretch over my would-be mate again. We can't fully mate until she knows the truth, but I'm damn sure gonna make her yearn for me the way I yearn for her. She'll have no choice but to understand when I explain my world.

"You still want this? I ask, needing to make sure, even though I'm seconds from imploding. *Please say yes.*

Seeing her nod, I drop my head to nip at the space behind her ear, breathing in her vanilla shampoo. "Words, baby. I need words." This is the only out she'll get.

My worries vaporize when her legs wrap tighter on my hips. "Yes, Wyatt. I want this." Evie bites my shoulder since it's all she can reach with me buried in her neck and tugs my head back to meet her eyes. "I want you," she says huskily, firing the starting pistol that shatters my doubt.

My hands cup the back of her head, locking our eyes while I tilt, burying myself in heaven. Evie's sharp intake of air stills my thrust. I'm only a few inches into her wetness but the pained sound freezes my muscles on the spot. Her sharp nails bite into my sides, holding me in place as she exhales, her body bowed tight under me.

"Baby, are you OK?" I brush the hair from Evie's suddenly clammy face, taking in those startled eyes, the scrunch of her forehead. Her jagged breaths blow against my chest, breaking my heart. I stroke the line of her jaw, holding my hips still while I dip for a soft tastes of her lips.

Slowly, she begins to kiss me back, her hands not quite the death grip against my stomach they were. Sliding my weight to one elbow, I drag my free hand across Evie's nipple, rubbing and pinching again to distract her into relaxing her lower muscles. Her body needs to be loose to open for me. "Evie? Baby, talk to me."

"I'm OK," she promises, clutching her hand against my hip for control. "Just... big," she pants. *Hah!* I can't help the bark of laughter, but stop when Evie groans her complaint at the flex of my cock.

"You're very good for my ego," I say, trying to make her laugh. "Do you want to stop?"

Watching her face, I withdraw and hold myself in place on the edge of Evie's tightness, teasing her with little pulses to the point of distraction. She squeezes her knees to keep me from pulling all the way out which is a good sign. When the anticipation becomes too much, she lifts her hips gingerly, trying her best to slide my cock deeper, though my hips stay still. I'll have finger-sized bruises tomorrow from her effort to move me, but I don't care.

"Wyatt... please." Her whimpering moan urges me forward. "Move."

I give in, sliding those few inches in again before pulling back. My hand slides lower to circle the bundle of nerves I know will give me access. My fingers glide gently through her wetness, rewarded when Evie tosses her head back, her thighs relaxing as she begins to writhe under me, and I slide deeper.

A new flood of wetness relaxes her core, easing my entry against those velvety muscles. My movements stay shallow, but Evie's thighs draw me in. I lock my mouth on hers as she tilts her hips.

Slowly, steadily, I work my way in, each thrust feeling like home. Each press forward, I slide in farther until I'm seated fully inside my mate. My forehead drops against Evie's, trying to cool my panting lungs, but having her soft muscles wrapped around me makes it hard. The sensual moan that rumbles from her when I bottom out unleashes my beast.

I lift to one arm, cupping her hips against me and grinding deeper, feeling the fire of electricity in my lower spine. Evie's mouth falls open, her head tossed back while her body revels in the magic of our connection. It's a glorious view of her pleasure from above, but this moment is dangerous for me. The temptation to give her my mating mark is primal. I feel my bear scratching for it now. But even without it, this moment connects our hearts. Evie will attribute her sudden attachment to me as a product of sex, being physically close to another person. She has no clue that fate intervened in our lives and now, even if she wants to, she won't be able to fight it.

Please don't want to.

With a gasp, Evie's eyes pop open, flying to mine. *She feels it.*

The flash in her eyes is the last straw. My willpower breaks and my hips stutter forward. Her erratic heartbeat matching mine. I test us both with one long, drawn out stroke.

"Wyatt," she screams over our desperate moans. The pulse of her velvety walls too much. I'm hanging on by a thread, my release threatening to end this all too soon.

"Evie." Thrust. "Mine."

My hips punish with deep, languid strokes that carry us higher, building the pressure every time I hit bottom. Evie drags me into a passionate kiss, her hands sliding to cup my shoulders as instinct speeds up my rhythm. Evie's face transforms into bliss as she nears the edge, her liquid coating me for a smooth glide into heaven.

My breath catches when my bear sees the pulse throbbing in her neck. *Mark her.*

No, damn it. She'll wear our mark one day—soon.

Then, the nails that score my back yank me out of my head in time to see Evie scream her pleasure. The squeeze of her inner walls milking my release as I flood the condom inside her warmth. I wish I could have held out for another, but Evie is too much.

After our breathing slows, I roll so Evie's on top, keeping our connection tight. I don't want to crush her, but I'm desperate to keep her close. Her delighted giggle every time she's man-handled would light me up if guilt wasn't sinking into my soul. *I pray I didn't just make a mistake.*

Tomorrow. I'll tell her tomorrow.

With her head on my chest, I caress the ridges along her spine, lost in my head until her deep breaths are the only sound in the room. Gently, I roll Evie to the pillow next to me and take care of the condom in the bathroom before returning to curl around her body.

I slide into a tormented sleep. Fear taking over my dreams, repeatedly showing me scenes where I lose my mate. In every single one, I'm too late to save her. I wake up throughout the night in a fevered sweat, relieved to find Evie's body still tucked safely against mine. Finally, at dawn, I fall into coma-like sleep, giving my body a respite from the nightmares.

Chapter 27

♥

Evie

A tickle on my neck pulls me from a slow baking oven.

When my eyes adjust to the haze of light streaming through the window, I realize the tickle is actually Wyatt's breath puffing across my neck. His heavy arm drapes over my middle, locking me in his very warm—very sexy—cocoon.

Holy cow! That was the best sleep I've had in years.

My brain's having trouble waking up. Of course, that could be because I had the best sex of my life last night. So good that I passed out before Wyatt had left my body. I pray I didn't do anything embarrassing like drool on his chest.

That sculpted chest that's currently the source of my overheating problem since there's not a lick of space between our bodies. And while I love the feel of his big spoon to my little, Wyatt's furnace of a body threatens to generate some very unladylike sweats.

Carefully, I extricate myself from under his fifty-pound arm, trying not to groan at the stiffness in my legs... and stomach. OK, also a few other tender parts that are extra tender this morning. My breath catches from the soreness.

When I roll, I'm suddenly grateful that Doc V wants me to start my hours just three days a week until I get settled in. There is absolutely no way I could function in the office today, and God forbid if we had a farm call.

I shiver at the thought, and from the loss of Wyatt's heat in his freezing bedroom, but still manage to climb off the bed without waking him. My jeans and camisole are tossed on the floor, the camisole's wrinkly but otherwise OK. Jeans, however, would not have been my first choice the morning after my re-entry into Wyatt's level of sexual games after spending so long on the sidelines.

With no other option, I tug them into place, cringing when the rough material squeezes my very sore core. My bra is going to stay on the floor. I do not want to play with an under wire this early. Maybe I should find a pair of Wyatt's boxers. They would definitely be more comfortable, but I don't want to go sneaking through his drawers either.

Wyatt still hasn't budged on the bed. His finely tuned body curling around my empty spot with a messy wave of hair flopping over his eye. The innocence makes him look like the sweetest little boy, if he also wasn't a Greek God carved of marble.

My stomach rumbles, breaking me from ogling Wyatt like a lovesick adolescent in favor of giving him a good breakfast when he wakes up. After the delicious dinner he made last night—and all the orgasms—I'd like to treat him to something good this morning.

I just hope Wyatt isn't one of those guys who only has stale cereal in his pantry. It didn't seem that way from his dinner, but he could have stocked up to impress me and normally lives off of cheese puffs and TV dinners.

After I use the restroom—clean, thank God—I go to scour the fridge, and realize I shouldn't have worried. The man likes to eat. Fresh meats and cheeses stack the shelves of his fridge, juices and waters, milk… everything I need for breakfast sandwiches.

I grab the eggs and a few sausage patties, hoping he doesn't mind me using his food. He doesn't seem like the type, so try not to stress over it as I gather the bread and plates, and down to prepping our food.

While the sausage cooks, I hum the Wizard of Oz song that's stuck in my head, toasting and stacking bread and cheese on two plates. Two glasses of orange juice, some napkins and silverware later, and it's time to put on the eggs.

Breakfast is almost done by the time Wyatt's sleepy form enters the kitchen... shirtless. His plaid pajama pants hanging loose, teasing me with the sharp cut of muscles leading to what I know is an impressive temptation below. I swallow thickly, sliding my eyes upward so I don't get any wetter in my already uncomfortable jeans.

Thankfully, the upper half of Wyatt is distractingly adorable. His normally smooth hair curls a bit at the end, sticking up at all angles of bed head.

Wyatt's eyes snap to the table, his face lighting up with a sweet smile. "You cooked?" he asks awed, walking over to wrap me in his arms. My face flushes.

"Is that OK?" *Crap!* I hope he doesn't mind me invading his kitchen. I worried about the underwear drawer, but maybe protocol is to crawl out before daybreak. The easy exit strategy.

His masculine laugh vibrates against my neck where he nuzzles. "I will never going to argue over a beautiful woman making me breakfast. I'm starved!" A rumble from his stomach interrupts, bringing us both to hysterics. "Besides, the only other thing I'd like to eat this morning is probably off the table for a few days."

A furious heat burns my ears at the insinuation and I smack Wyatt's shoulder, feeling his smile curve against my neck before he nips a bite there. I laugh, but stop when he breathes a big lungful of me in. That's when I have to push away.

"You better stop sniffing. I smell like sweat and sex. That's not a very fresh combination."

"You smell like me," he growls, the gravel in his voice leaving no doubt where his mind is.

Unable to resist, I run my fingers through the back of his hair, enjoying the softness while I have free reign to touch. Wyatt drains any urge I had to play cool the morning after, just in case he thought I'd turn stage-five clinger. He moans into my neck and I start to feel my weight lift in his arms.

I can't stop giggle around Wyatt, but I really like the feeling. Still, I pop his shoulder to break his hold, needing both feet on the floor to finish breakfast.

"Alright, big man. Food first, other stuff later."

Wyatt grins but carries our finished plates over to the table without further distraction. He sits right beside me instead of across the four-seater where we could chat easier. The giddy girl inside wants to squeal. Outside, I try not to laugh at how his hand stays on some part of my body whenever he can.

Right now, it's on my knee.

"How do you plan to eat a sandwich with one hand?"

Wyatt smirks, taking a healthy bite of his sausage, egg, and cheese to show me exactly how he can manage with those large hands. "I'm very talented in the eating department." I choke, the grin on his face and the memory of just how right he is warms my body.

Knowing I can't compete with his dirty talk, I take a bite instead, loving how Wyatt digs into my food like it's the best he's had. He's so comfortable, so easy to talk to. He's a pro at knowing what I need, when I need it.

Especially in bed.

I flush, and Wyatt smirks. "Whatcha thinking about?"

"Not telling you. Get off your ego," I say, hiding an embarrassed grin behind my orange juice glass. Even his little innuendos are exciting, not gross like I usually feel when guys talk about their prowess in the bedroom.

It's because he can back it up.

I watch Wyatt clean his plate, thinking about how he made me feel worshiped last night, cherished. Something inside me loosened when we connected. I trusted Wyatt not to judge my flaws, and because of that, I could let go and feel. I've never had an orgasm with anyone other than myself, but with Wyatt... that was definitely not a problem.

Wyatt sets his napkin on the table and turns, sandwiching my knees between his with a seriousness brooding in his eyes. It knock me off balance. "Last night was amazing, Evie."

I cock my head, trying to postpone whatever thought is stressing his shoulders. "Were you reading my mind?"

Wyatt's brows crease, but the front door slamming interrupts his answer. I startle momentarily when Caleb and Jackson barrel into the kitchen, bouncing shoulders in the doorway as they race each other to Wyatt's coffee pot.

"Aww, Jax. We missed breakfast." Caleb's whine earns a pop behind his head from Jackson.

"Told you not to take so long, man. You know Wyatt needs the morning after energy."

Shit, they knew I'd be here. My cheeks flame. I guess parking my car out front isn't exactly discreet.

"Enough," Wyatt barks, his voice surprising me and the guys when it bounces off the wall.

"Chill, man. We're joking." Caleb ignores Wyatt's outburst and bends to raid his fridge, moving things in and out to look for a salvageable breakfast.

"I can make you guys a sandwich," I offer, trying to ease some awkwardness from the guys knowing I spent the night. Not to mention that I'm bra-less and wearing last night's wrinkly clothes.

"No, you won't," Wyatt says, squeezing my hand to keep me in place when I go to stand up. The flash of excitement falls from the guys' faces at Wyatt's denial.

"Oh, come on, bro. We're growing boys." Caleb pats his flat stomach while Jax and I laugh at the growl that rolls off Wyatt.

I kiss his extra stubbly cheek and go to stand. "I don't mind… really. Just let me get dressed and I'll whip something up." I grin, wanting to soothe the stress wrinkling his forehead. I whisper, loud enough for the boys to hear, "besides, afterward, we'll guilt them into clean up so we can make out on the couch."

Jax snickers behind me while Caleb fake-gags, but it's Wyatt's smile that's my real reward. He pats my ass when I turn to go, getting a sarcastic *aww* from his guests.

"Don't be long." Wyatt's voice follows me from the room, as does the boy's ribbing.

In the bedroom, I tug on my socks and boots and snap my bra under the tank, wiggling it into place. There's not a lot I can do with my hair but after finding my flannel shirt in the hallway, I stop by the bathroom to wash my face with a rag I find under his sink.

Figuring there'll be at least a few kisses, I swipe some toothpaste and brush my teeth with a finger the best I can. It's not perfect, but passable at least. My elated heart isn't caring about a whole lot this morning, but I do love how natural the boys seem around me. Getting approval from the best friend can make or break a relationship.

Is this a relationship?

Not wanting to think about that too hard, I head back to the kitchen and find Wyatt trying to shove both men through his back door. His stress lines are back when he hears me enter.

"Everything OK?" I ask, lighting a burner with a side eye at Wyatt. From the look of it, he isn't too keen on feeding our morning intruders.

"Yeah, we're good." His strangled voice tells me he's lying, but I don't know why.

"I promised to feed them, Wyatt." Then I stop. "If there's something you guys have planned this morning, I can just go." I plaster a smile on my face, hoping it doesn't look strained.

Does he not want me around his friends? The idea sinks my building hope. *Maybe Wyatt just wants a casual fling?*

I turn back to the stove so he can't see the tears blurring my eyes. *Why does that thought hurt so bad?* Does it matter if he used all those pretty words last night. Guys do that all the time to get in a girl's pants... make promises they don't plan to keep. I got ahead of myself.

There's some tussling behind me and when I look over, Caleb is sitting at the table like he's dead set on being fed. I'll just make some excuse when I finish cooking and get out of here. If I ran out now, it'll look like I'm bothered by Wyatt's brush off. I can at least save that revelation for when I'm alone and not in a room with three gorgeous men.

Jax brushes by Wyatt's arm and plops in the chair across from Caleb.

"Thank you for your hospitality, *Evie*." Caleb's tease pulls a sigh of resignation from Wyatt that sounds like someone stuck a pin and deflated him.

"Guys, I need to talk to Evie this morning. We're not feeding you breakfast."

Yep, there it is. The *'talk.'* The no strings attached, not the right time in my life, *talk*. Hurriedly, I layer pieces of toast and ingredients on their plates while the other food cooks, doubling my speed to get out of this room before Wyatt utters any words that'll crush my ego.

Sorry, buddy. No, 'let's be friends' welcomed here. Nope.

My shoulders are tight, bracing for the brush-off when Jax's voice catches me off guard. "Come on, Wy. I just want to thank the woman who saved me."

Wyatt's sharp gasp jerks my attention to him, confused. I turn off the stove and walk to the table, plates in hand. Wyatt looks like he needs the Heimlich, or like he's gonna to puke. Not sure.

"Besides, man, would you deny a healing bear food?" Jax's face is the picture of appreciation, of admiration, but all sound has drained from the room. Only a buzz remains like the inside of a seashell.

Wyatt stands frozen a few feet away, his skin ashen as he turns in slow motion to face Jax, murder pouring from his eyes.

"I'm confused," I admit, my voice far away. As if on autopilot, my arm sits Caleb's food in front of him, but he won't meet my eye. I take the two steps toward Jax and stand in front of him waiting for an explanation. "What did I do?"

Jax shoots a panicked look at Wyatt, whose hands are in his hair, pulling the strands like somehow he can yank the right answer out of that frazzled head. My eyes meet remorse. The devastation radiating back at me before his head drops to the floor is upsetting, like he can't stand looking at me. *What the hell is going on?*

Caleb's chair screeches on the floor, startling me from my stupor. He's on his feet and halfway across the room in a flash. "You didn't tell her?" His guttural roar aims at Wyatt but I duck, the anger deafening to my ears in the small kitchen. Jax bounds between the two brothers, one hand pressed against each chest, holding them apart.

Oh my god! What's gotten into these animals? They're acting completely different than a few minutes ago. The threat of violence in the air is thick, suffocating the room. At least some of the anger is coming off me, realizing there's something that Wyatt is hiding.

Whatever he hid must be huge if these guys are acting like defensive older brothers... for me, not for Wyatt.

We slept together last night!

"I was trying to tell her before you assholes crashed in here." Wyatt's hiss is filled with venom when he glares at his brother. It pisses Caleb off enough to break free of Jax's hold and shove two fists in Wyatt's chest. He only moves his brother a few inches, but it seems feet with the walls shrinking in on the kitchen.

"You mated her without telling her!" Fury radiates off Caleb, turning the fresh breakfast sitting in my stomach.

Don't guys normally cheer a brother getting laid?

And who uses the word 'mated' anymore? What am I, a poodle?

Wyatt pushes around his brother, quickening his steps until he blocks my view of the men behind him. "Evie, we need to talk. Let me get rid of them so we can have some privacy.

"No!" I push back on his chest, tossing the dish in my hand to the table. The *thunk* of pottery mimics the snap of my temper. "You're hiding something," I challenge, fury radiating from Wyatt's deception. "If having these two here gets me the truth, they stay." My nails cut into my hand, guarding it from reaching up to slap Wyatt upside his gorgeous, lying head.

"Evie, come on." He reaches for my hand, but I jerk it away. "I didn't lie," he says. "I omitted. There's a difference, and I planned to talk to you about it... this morning."

Anger rises up as I go to walk around Wyatt. He grabs at my arm in desperation, his fingers gripping harder than I'd expect, and I yank it free, connecting my opposite fist against the firmness of his shoulder.

Ouch! The pain in my knuckles piss me off more.

"Fuck off, Wyatt," I snap. "What are you hiding?" My temper bubbles over, but I shake my head, realizing it doesn't matter. Scalding tears are inevitable when I'm this out of control. *Don't let him get to you!* "Actually, never mind. I don't care. Keep your secrets!" I jerk backward, freeing my arm from his hold when the tears become impossible to hold at bay.

I turn to the two men who turned my morning upside down and watch them hang their heads ashamed, like the guilt is eating them alive.

Jax looks like he wants to block my exit. He palm twitching, reaching out with the tiniest movement like I'm a cornered animal. "Evie, will you let us explain?" he asks, his voice thick. Apology dims his eyes when they shift to Wyatt behind me, and I cross my arms, waiting. A silent communication passes between the men, but not a word of explanation out loud.

"Great! More secrets," I seethe, tossing my hands in the air. *I've had enough.*

I move to slip past Jax, but his body swings in my path quicker than a big man should. My startled shriek pierces the air, his sudden movement making me dizzy. But Wyatt is there immediately, pressing his body against my back, wrapping those big arms around me for comfort—*I think.*

It's not comforting.

My mouth drops open. *How did he do that?* Caleb turns to the door, not meeting my eyes.

"Baby, I was going to tell you this morning. I promise." Wyatt sounds pained, his voice barely a whisper in my ear. That massive chest heaves against my back while his hands hold firm on my arms.

The problem is, those hands burn my skin after Wyatt's betrayal. I gave him my trust... all of it. A whole new rage ignites inside at his touch. "Tell me!" I screech, twisting free to yell in his face. My eyes plead for answers, but I'm not even sure for what. My gut says it's something huge.

"Evie, I-I was just trying to say thank you for saving me." Jax's voice pulls my gaze. His face is the picture of contrite, but at least this one's talking. My sweaty palms run against my jeans nervously. The longer I'm here the more I feel like a guppy in a sea of sharks.

"OK, that." I point at him accusingly. "When did I save you? We've only met twice!"

Wyatt sighs, running his hands through the dark waves I found irresistible just an hour ago. "When he was shot in the woods, Evie. On our hike."

A sharp whistle buzzes in my ears... hearing two plus two is still adding up to eight. Wyatt's body stoops toward me, lifting my frozen hand in his. He's bent to eye level, but I still feel swallowed in his presence and not in a good way. He's too big, too much. *This is all too much!*

"Evie." Wyatt squeezes my hands with a little shake at feeling no resistance. He lifts my eyes to his and my chin quivers. "Baby, we're bears," he chokes out. "All three of us. And there's—"

My ears block the rest of that sentence, filling with the sound of rushing water as my legs go numb. I open my mouth, but my throat is too thick. Nothing comes out. I hear Wyatt calling my name just before the feel of free-falling washes over me and the darkness moves in—fast.

Chapter 28

♥

Wyatt

Time froze in the seconds between revealing our truth and watching Evie crumple to the floor.

Thankfully, I caught her before she hit tile. But my heart is raw from watching the color drain from my mate seconds before her eyes rolled back.

I can't stop looking at her now. Can't stop brushing the hair from her forehead. Jax and Caleb stand a few feet away, but I won't look at them. They feel awful—I can sense that—but two people who mean the most to me in this world just dropped an H-bomb in my kitchen leaving my mate unconscious to pay for it.

"We're so sorry, man." I ignore Jackson, focusing on Evie, willing her to wake up.

"Why did you have to open your mouth?" I know the question's unfair; this is my fault. But he stole my chance to break the news gently and now I have no idea how I'll make Evie understand when she wakes up.

A wet rag appears over my shoulder and I snatch the thing a little harder than I should. I'm not exactly in a forgiving mood with Evie lying stone-still on my couch. Still, I rub the wet rag across her skin, needing to comfort her somehow.

"Why didn't you tell her?" Caleb challenges, his judgment knocking my air out. I cut my eyes over my shoulder, but Caleb steps out of my reach, expecting the swing I'd love to throw his way. My brother's contempt is obvious, but I don't need more guilt added on.

My head falls, anger bubbling just below the surface. "I was going to," I hiss at them. "If you assholes hadn't pushed your way in here this morning, running your mouths half-cocked, I would be having that conversation with her right now. Peacefully."

"But you mated! I smelled her on you the second I walked in!" "We didn't mate, dammit! I wouldn't do that."

"Well, you slept with her." Caleb crosses his arms defensively.

"This isn't as easy as you think, Cale!" Anger at myself spills into my voice, targeting the wrong person, but I can't stop it. The guilt's eating me alive as I hover over Evie's prone body.

What kind of Alpha am I? I chickened out, and it hurt my mate.

A thundering roar shakes the walls of my cabin, drawing a glare from Caleb. I bolt off the couch, unable to sit while my lungs try to drag enough air in to feel like I'm breathing. *Is this a panic attack?*

"Wy, you need to calm down, man." Jax tentatively steps forward, resting a hand on my bare shoulder where needles prickle the skin. He feels the raised hair and squeezes... hard. "Wyatt! Listen. If you turn and Evie wakes, you'll terrify her. Calm... now," he snarls, effectively snapping me out of my near shift.

Our bears don't usually press so close to the surface without us calling them. But right now, flames lick under my surface, alerting me to the possibility. My skin is becoming too tight, too fast. It's a feeling I haven't experienced since my first shift as a young cub.

With my eyes on the ceiling, I narrow in on a dot there, focusing my brain on something calmer than how pale Evie's face is sprawled on my couch. Her heartache is because of me. It slices a machete through the broken parts of me that are normally soothed by her presence.

When I feel a semblance of control, I squat down and rest my fingers against Evie's pulse point for my own reassurance. *She's breathing. She's strong.* But it's not enough.

"What do I do," I ask the room, feeling completely inept. Gently, I lay my head on Evie's stomach, needing physical proof she's OK in the rise and fall of her breathing. It offers a small comfort to my bear.

My thumb strokes the line of her neck, amazed by how soft the skin is there. The memory of kissing every inch of that skin last night torments me. *Will she ever let me touch her again?*

"Wy," Jax whispers.

I glance up to find Evie's eyelashes fluttering awake. I'm beside her in a flash, brushing the side of her face, wishing I could erase the stress there. *Come back to me, baby.*

I whisper the call out loud, my voice pleading in her ear, calling to her through our connected hearts. I wasn't brave enough to say it before, but if she comes back to me, I'll share everything. I'll make her understand —she has to.

Evie's eyes fly open, easing the two-ton weight on my shoulders. Until the unbridled fear registers in her eyes. My jaw drops…

No. No. No.

She jerks out of my touch gasping. The tiny splinters in my heart become canyons. She's fully alert now, scrambling back against the couch cushion as far as it allows.

My hand falls from those trembling shoulders, not wanting to feel the quake of terror running through her because of me. I don't want to see her legs balled in front of her, acting as a barrier to protect her body. With heightened senses, hearing Evie's marathon heartbeat is hard enough.

Glancing over my shoulder, I see that both Jax and my brother are making themselves small against the opposite wall. *Thanks guys.*

To give Evie some breathing room, I slide a few inches down the couch but draw the line at removing my touch completely. I need contact. Unfortunately, Evie's relief from our increased space is a knife to the gut.

"Evie, let me explain this... please!" My desperation is obvious, but I don't care. I hate the tremble shaking her body. I hate that my actions caused it. I hate the accusation in her eyes.

"First of all, I need you to understand. I would never hurt you! *We* would never hurt you." I motion to the men over my shoulder, opening my body so Evie can see them, too. That she could be afraid of me—of us—drives the nail in my heart a little deeper.

Caleb lowers himself in my recliner, his hands clasped between his legs. His stormy eyes focus on his boots while Jax picks at his fingernails with his back pressed to the kitchen wall. Both look heavily chastised by our situation, never having faced anything like it themselves.

Evie notices the three of us *unintentionally* blocking her in the room and her breathing doubles. "You're all bears? Did I hear that correct?" Confusion wrinkles her brows, her head shaking in a slow disbelieving manner.

Those captivating eyes that were so full of passion last night, waffle between panic and skepticism now. Like we're aliens dropped in from another planet. Hell... to her, maybe we are.

"You remember the stories your Gran told you? About protectors of the mountain," I ask, watching her eyes shutter closed. They squeeze tight before burying her face in her hands, like it hurts to look at me.

"I didn't believe her!" Evie's screech hurt my sensitive ears.

"Talk to her if you need to," I offer, wanting Evie to have someone she trusts, but who we can trust, too. "We *are* different, baby, but we're good people. We're good bears." Her mouth drops open. My level voice is more of an attempt to calm a wounded animal than a reflection of the chaos rolling through me. I glance at Caleb, feeling slightly comforted by his nod of support.

Evie's quiet... processing. Both of us watch my fingers stroke her ankle. I pray it gives her peace, that she doesn't find my touch fully offensive. I want nothing more than to tie her to the bed and talk until she understands.

Can I convince someone I'm good by way of orgasm? Is that an appropriate incentive?

"Evie, I'm still the same person. I have the same thoughts, the same feelings. There's just more to me than you knew."

She scans my face, looking doubtful. I hate seeing her scared when I had earned so much trust yesterday. Now it's... gone. My only chance is to capitalize on Evie's curiosity. That she's searching for some explanation, to figure us out gives me a kernel of hope.

Of course, that hope dashes the second she pulls her foot free, climbing off the couch with jerky movements. *Is she running?*

My heart stutters, but I stay frozen in place, not wanting to overwhelm my mate. But she stops in the center of the room, eying Jax and Caleb and finally turning to meet my eye. I catch the few feet of distance she keeps between the three of us.

Evie's shoulders straighten, rising to full height though her face is guarded. I see the slight tremor in her fingers and it twists the knot in my stomach, our breakfast threatening to revolt. "The thing is Wyatt... you didn't tell me," she grinds out hoarsely, a look of resolve hardening her gorgeous face. Evie's justified accusation cuts, but I'd gladly bleed on the floor if it keeps my mate here. I'll accept punishment for my secrets, for lying. I just need her to stay.

"Last night—" Evie starts, her voice cracking as heartache and betrayal breaks her down. I lose my resolve to give her space. The dire need to touch her rocketing me off the couch, toward my mate. When Evie reels back, blanching, my bear cries out and I don't move again. Those sad brown eyes have nailed my feet to the floor, breaking my soul. Evie shakes her head, tears cresting over her cheeks that she quickly brushes away. "Last night, you... you used me," she croaks, swallowing thickly.

"No!" I gasp, panic seizing my lungs. "I didn't, Evie. I swear."

She's giving up, my bear howls in my head. *She's running.*

Desperation moves me closer. I need to hold my Evie, at least until she understands that she's everything. "Evie, don't do this, baby," I beg. "I love you! You're it for me."

A shaky hand flies to her mouth, the agonizing sob that rips from her lungs tearing me apart. But Evie doesn't want to hear it. She shakes her head, the flood of tears sliding freely now. "Don't say that, Wyatt! You don't love me. You lied!" Evie looks at me with utter certainty. Her judgment of my betrayal coloring everything we've shared.

My knees buckle and I fall, letting a hot tear roll unchecked of my own. I want to grab her, to stop this pain from ripping me apart, but I don't. I clench my fists instead, watching powerless as Evie muffles her sobs a second before she turning her back and racing for her purse.

Her heart severs our connection, dragging my head down as I try to press my own heart to stay in my chest. It hurts too much. Watching Evie keep a careful eye on Jax and Caleb, though none of us have moved, watching her ready herself to walk out the door. She looks prepared for me to chase her, but I don't have the ability.

My bear's wailing, his angry stomping has zapped all the energy that could possibly chase down my broken mate. Every ounce of concentration is focused on pulling air inside my lungs.

Plus, I'd never hurt her like that. Not when I can taste Evie's fear. It's thick in the room. If anything, my need to protect Evie means I have to stay away from her. For now. No matter how bad it kills me.

When she pauses in the open cabin door, I look up from my spot on the floor, needing one more chance to memorize that sweet face. "I am so sorry." It won't change what's happening, but I have to say it. She has to hear it.

The words—or perhaps my pain—are enough to lock our eyes for one frozen minute, neither saying a thing. Until finally, Evie inhales, fortifying herself against the fear. Her heartbeat slows just a notch as she takes in my brother and best friend who haven't moved from their position. They've kept their heads down, listening to this soap opera of pain with regret mixing with their looks of pity.

My family senses my sorrow and I know they don't want to add to Evie's panic, or my distress. Caleb may judge my actions, but no shifter would wish a rejection from a fated mate on another... under any circumstances, deserved or not.

With hands vibrating at my sides, straining under the pressure to stay still, I bore into Evie, trying desperately to telepath what my mouth can't say. I pray some part of her still feels me.

"I need time," Evie whispers, regret flashing momentarily before she turns and runs out the door, taking my heart with her.

My fists slam the floor, bracing my body to keep from crumbling after losing all the strength to stay upright. An excruciating pain slashes my chest, shoving me into a darkness where I expect to live if I lose Evie forever.

The sane part of me hopes Evie's car is long gone so she won't hear the agonizing roar from my unmated bear. Especially when I snap, his pain knifing through every pore in my body.

I found my mate and you lost her.

The guys are suddenly by my side, laying their hands on my back, my shoulders. Jax drops to his knees beside me and pulls my hair back, helping to cool the seething rage erupting from my gut.

"I'm sorry, man! I'm so—so sorry," Jax says and I feel his remorse in waves. At this point it doesn't matter. Evie's gone. We may not have mated, but our connection solidified in my heart. If I can't get her back, this is my end.

Chapter 29

♥

Evie

It may not have been the best idea to leave Wyatt's house in this condition. Tears blur my vision so badly the double yellow lines spread and sparkle into one twisting yellow road. If I were Dorothy, maybe I could navigate that, but mountain curves need 20/20 vision, not a broken-hearted freak out.

My death grip on the steering wheel cramps my hands, but pain is a welcome distraction from my emotional turmoil inside.

When I think about sleeping with Wyatt last night, how magical it felt in his arms, how he surrounded me and stroked me, another stream of tears flood down my face. It felt real.

But he lied.

Sniffing, I reach for a tissue in my purse, having no chance to hold the tears when I was open with Wyatt in a way I've never been with any other man. No matter what he says, I feel stupid. Not that I can blame myself for not realizing my *kind-of* boyfriend was a domesticated wild animal. Still, I was only comfortable with him because I thought I knew him. *I didn't.*

Are they laughing at the silly human girl? *She's too stupid to realize we could snap her like a twig.*

Even as I have the thought, I push that one away. I may feel like a complete idiot for falling for Wyatt's lies, for handing over my trust. But not a part of me thinks the guys would hurt me. If any of them wanted to, they had plenty opportunity when I was unconscious in that cabin.

The tears slow thinking that fact. They truly could have hurt me any time this morning, but none of them did. If anything, they tried to give me space. Although Wyatt still had to touch me, which I don't get. Why bother?

A large delivery truck barrels in my lane, blaring its horn. The shock jars me from my thoughts quick enough to jerk the wheel. *Shit! I was in its lane.*

With my wayward car back on the right side of the road, I realize how badly I need to get myself together. I blink several times to clear the fog clouding my head, knowing it won't clear the jackhammering in my chest. I just wish I could blame my rapid heart rate on nearly becoming a bug on that big brown truck's windshield.

Grabbing another tissue, I swipe my face of the tears that have streamed since I first ran out Wyatt's front door. I know better than to drive this upset. But when I think about those lies... I get pissed again.

My foot presses harder on the gas, letting my little SUV barrel down the winding road toward nowhere. I just need to get out of Talon today. Somewhere I can clear my head. It can't be far because I have to work tomorrow and I can't miss my second day, nor do I want to.

Maybe Kayah. Her apartment is a thirty-minute drive and she's always been the most logical of us all. She's also the one I've bounced big decisions off her since I got a C in the sixth grade and she helped me tell Mama. Not that this level of screwy is close to the trivial crap of our childhood. This is a what-the-hell, kick-in-the-balls, hire-a-hitman situation.

Immediately, I regret that thought after my last two weeks. Getting upset over last night won't change what happened, or who Wyatt is.

That one I still can't wrap my brain around.

The memory of Gran's voice flashes in my head... *our family lands are magical, Bug. This mountain itself is alive, protecting us, shining its light on us. Never doubt its power to guide you in the right direction.*

She told me that right before I left for college, when I was extra nervous about going in a new direction, away from everyone I loved.

Fear of the unknown will only cast a shadow if you let it.

The comfort that only comes from Gran washes over me, drying my tears, until there's just an overwhelming sadness inside. My eyes burn from crying. It's hard to breathe through the excruciating pain in my chest. At least I can think through this morning without my brain wanting to explode.

The low fuel light dings to life on my dashboard. Ugh! I forgot to fill up this week. I've been so focused on transitioning to Talon and whatever was happening with Wyatt that I've lost sight of my basic needs. I should be at home having appointments with the cops or FBI, or whoever handles this level of criminal bad guys.

When have I ever lost focus for a man?

At some point, Wyatt took over my thoughts with his do-good qualities, that towering presence. I can't beat myself up when his intensity is so damn overpowering, a nun would question her choices in life. *Is there a woman alive who could resist that muscle of a man?*

My brain takes over, numbing my riotous feelings with curiosity. The vet in me questions how any of this is possible. What differences in our bodies allow them to become a bear and not the rest of us? How many bear-people are there? Do they have babies or cubs?

I saw Jax in daylight, so it's not a 'by-the-moon' werewolf situation like in the movies. I can't believe I actually had my hands all over a shifter person and never knew it. Do they have any other differences? Abilities?

The inquisitive kid in me wants to ask why. She wishes I stayed for answers instead of freaking out. If I hadn't been so mortified, ticked off, and extremely... hurt, I would have.

At least the mortification has eased away, though I'm still embarrassed for not knowing about Wyatt. Although... *Hello! Is my boyfriend a bear isn't normally a relationship evaluator.* I didn't notice anything odd because Wyatt and the others acted like normal thirty-something men. A little nicer than I'm used to, if I'm honest.

Should I go talk to Gran like Wyatt suggested? If I drive to Kayah right now, I don't know how I would explain what happened, or if she'd believe me. *Should* I even explain this to Kayah? The guys keep their existence a secret for a reason, I'm sure. Would telling put her in danger? Or them?

My mind flashes through all the times I've been alone with Wyatt: on the trails, in his truck... last night in his arms. If he wanted to hurt me, he had plenty of chances. If anything, I imagine the world finding out about a werebear—if that's what you call it—would be a lot more dangerous for Wyatt than for us.

I drop my head against the headrest, looking for places to stop. If anything happened to those guys because I opened my mouth to vent— especially over a broken heart—I'd never forgive myself. A searing pain lances my chest at the idea, making it hard to breathe. Instead, I focus on pulling calming yoga breaths into my lungs and grab my phone. I need to stop for gas, but maybe I'll call Wyatt, just to let him know I'm OK. *And make sure he is?*

The idea of harm coming to Wyatt, of never seeing him again, hits me like a ton of bricks. An image of Wyatt on his knees, his face shattered, pops in my head and I suck in a sharp breath. He wasn't angry when I left. He looked broken.

All of this is abnormal! Not just the bear situation but feeling so connected to Wyatt in general. I don't do drama or confusion in my life, up until the last few weeks. Until then, there wasn't much feeling in my life at all. My life had become predictable to the point of boredom. Now, seeing a man I've known only a few weeks hurting damn near stops my lungs.

All my earlier adrenaline from Wyatt's cabin washes away, leaving me with regret. I see my first run-down gas station and pull over, edging onto the gravel by the vintage gas pump. I step out and fiddle with the rusted-out pump. At least, it's been upgraded to accept credit cards. *Thank goodness!*

After inserting the nozzle, I fiddle with the lever that starts the gas flow, questioning how old the gas is I'm putting in my car.

Pulling my phone out, I check the screen. The only messages are responses from Mom when I told her I wouldn't be home last night. It was the typical parent response of *be safe, are you sure, and have fun,* all rapidly sent behind each other.

Self-doubt washes over me as I wait for the slow nozzle to pump my gas. The gas chugging through the line is the only break to the morning's eerie quiet. *Wow!* I'm about to crack if I'm listening to the *lack* of sound in the air. There's not a single thing around, but the creepiness of the vacant lot amps up my uneasiness.

Obviously, the store is functional since there's electricity at the pump, but the windows are dark, tinted to the point I can't see inside. A flashing beer sign is the only clue this place isn't deserted. My eyes scan the parking lot trying to find a soul in sight but there's no one.

Then, why do I feel that same sensation of being watched.

A drop of wetness hits my face. *Great!* Above me, clouds are closing in, dribbling a watery preview of the storm in the distance. Just what I need. I hate when clouds block the sun like this. Everything becomes more depressing... muted.

The dark green sign beside the road says I'm fifteen miles from Talon, making my decision for me. I think I will go see Gran and dig to the bottom of those fables she told. Although, I guess they aren't fables anymore. But if anyone will have the information I need, it's that brilliant old woman. I know I'll see Wyatt again, and I want to have my mind on straight when I do.

My God! I've entered a dream world where fairy tales are real, my life has flipped upside down, and, oh yeah... I've fallen in love when someone—something—over the span of a few weeks. Someone who makes me feel alive and completely terrified at the same time. *How did that happen?*

The nozzle in my hand pops off loudly, reminding me of a fired gun. I cringe that my brain went there first. It shows I need to crawl in bed and sleep off these crazy feelings. Especially with that unease creeping up my neck. My imagination is getting a little too vivid, like I'm channeling Alfred Hitchcock.

Shaking my head, I store the nozzle in its holder and try to figure out if this ancient machine can print a receipt. *Ah, screw it.*

Ouch! Something sharp pinches my hip. I jerk sideways wanting to get away from whatever mammoth bug decided to take a bite out of me.

Before I can turn my head, my brain fuzzes, my vision tunneling as I try to blink through the sudden nausea that hits me. It takes all my concentration to look down . Something's out of place. I swat at the oddity in my hip, stumbling when the blurry tunnel barrels in on me. *God, I'm gonna throw up!* Somehow, in my fuzzy state, I recognize a syringe sticking through my jeans.

"Wha—tha—" My words won't working either. My numb tongue is too thick. I try to spit the saliva building in my mouth, but it's numb to my brain. *God, someone help me if I'm dying!*

My head sits heavy on my shoulders, wobbling to the side and taking my body with it. A stumbling step prevents me from completely hitting the ground, but my hand slaps the metal of my car hard enough to sting. The impact twists my wrists under the bulk of my weight, turning the weak joint at an odd angle. The only brief benefit is, the pain bringing focus to my head. I hear voices as tiny as gnats, so close but so far away. My brain registers that people are near, but I can't do anything about it.

And then, I'm falling the rest of the way to the gravel below, hitting the ground which causes my hand to drop the phone I forgot I had. I grunt, but before I can scream, my body's flies. Someone's physically lifting me toward the rear of my jeep.

Help! Please! Subconsciously, I know the screams are only in my head. No one can hear me.

In a panic, I kick a foot out, the only part of my body working with me. It connects on something metal, and my ears register a clang, but the arms gripping me tighten. I don't think my body is moving as much as I want it to, but I have to do something. My other foot kicks out and crashes through glass… the gas pump. The success registers in my head and I send thanks to my boots for protecting my feet. Yelling curses, my chair lift tosses me violently across the backseat of my car, smashing my head against the opposite door. A sharp pain radiates through my temples. It doesn't help my concentration. Panic flows through my system, even as my head lolls to the side. *Fight the sleepiness! I can't let them close that door!*

Slam. *Shit!* A stench of tobacco and grease overwhelms the car. Smells that do not belong in here.

Using all my focus to keep my eyelids open, I watch the two rough looking blobs in the front seat. One is older. His limp mullet and hollowed out skin seem two steps from a meth-lab. The other one is young, wiry; he's practically bouncing in the seat with excitement over their catch, complimenting the mullet-man on his prowess.

My eyes try to roll back in my head, barely catching the sneer over mullet's shoulder when he turns the ignition. I don't get to hear what he says before I pass out, but the younger man cackles at his twisted face and a cold dread follows me under.

As I'm sliding under the fog, I wish I were still laying in Wyatt's arms. That I never woke up to cook breakfast. That this was all a bad dream. If I had only known...

Chapter 30

♥

Wyatt

My head hangs for the span of a minute before my bear's rage takes over.

How could she run from us?

She's human. The crazy thing is, as mad as I am, I understand. Evie trusted me, and I didn't live up to that trust. It doesn't change how I feel about her. Evie's my mate. Somehow, I will earn her forgiveness.

You have to.

My body pulses with energy. I jump up from the floor, needing to move. Jax and Caleb eye me like a ticking time-bomb as I pace. Anger and desperation have taken over, so maybe bomb is an accurate description. My fingers dig into my temples, but it doesn't relieve the pressure there.

"Sit down before you lose control," Caleb says, his voice grating. I turn on both men who're stretched across my floor where I just sat, eying my out-of-control movements.

"This is your fault!" I yell, needing to vent.

"Oh, no, no, no, big brother. I'm not taking that." Caleb stands but doesn't move to approach me. "If you were honest with her—especially before fucking her—you wouldn't be in this situation."

"Do you tell every woman you're with that you're a bear? Really?"

"Oh, I get it." He smirks. "I thought she was your mate. It's a different story if you were just trying to get some random. In that case man, I really *am* sorry."

My brother's faux innocent act ignites my fury and I launch, only to have Caleb sidestep and miss the impact of my hit. The moment my feet land, I flip and advance again. His hands lift beside his head, the mock defense and that smirk on his face, pissing me off more.

When an expletive rumbles low in my chest, Jax steps in the way of me jumping at Caleb again, his hands flattening on my chest and holding firm. "Wy, we'll figure this out, man."

I'll have to hit my best friend to get around him.

My bear huffs, frustrated that he can't take his aggression out on these two.

"What do you two know, anyway? Neither of you have a woman!"

Caleb lifts an eyebrow but keeps his mouth shut. *Smart.*

Guilt stabs through my anger though when I see the flicker of pain cross Jax's face. He's been desperate to find his mate since we came of age. He won't even be with a woman unless there's the chance she's it. Which makes me the asshole here and I know it. I just can't find the power to stop myself when I'm falling apart.

"Stop looking at me like that," I bark at them both, walking to the window and scouring the distance of my driveway for Evie's car. *Please pull back in.* My soul calls to her, begging my mate to have a change of heart. "I know I should have told her before last night," I admit with my back to the room. "Just because I hurt her doesn't mean I won't win her back."

Resolute, I turn to face the only two people who can help me now. "I'm sorry for blaming you. But I do need your help. To fix this." My heart sinks at the look of pity on Jax's face. He thinks I have no hope to win her back.

I walk to the couch and crash into the leather. "Guys, please. Help me fix this." My head drops heavy in my hands and Jax takes a spot beside me, putting a comforting hand on my shoulder. Caleb's footsteps leave the room. *He must have had enough of my pity party. Or he genuinely thinks I don't deserve Evie after this.*

The lead boulder sitting in my stomach gets heavier and I press my eyes to keep from breaking down like a baby. I can't think if I lose it.

A minute later, an icy chill taps my shoulder and I look up. Caleb stands over me with three of Jax's craft brews. I keep my fridge stocked, but this is a new one I haven't tried. "We need brain fuel if we're going to win your woman back," he says, pulling a grateful smile from me and the first hint of light in my grief.

"Thank you, guys." I grab the bottle and take a swig, letting the bitterness slide down my throat. My face must show my thoughts, because Jax chuckles from his seat beside me. "What the hell is this new brew, dude?"

"It'll put some hair on your chest, man." Jax's firm slap to my spine pushes a cough from my lungs that has me tasting his beer again. *Ugh!* I clear my throat, my eyes watering a bit which I'll attribute to the hops and not to my boys coming to the rescue.

For the next twenty minutes, they help me concoct a plan to prove to Evie—or shove it in her face—all my good deeds. All the proof that I'm a good person she could ever need. All the times we were alone together, and she was perfectly safe.

She shouldn't need that, my bear cries. *She feels us. She's ours.*

Mentally, I know our fated bond has me, but I have no idea what humans feel. I can't live without Evie. But can she live without me?

Without warning, a slice of pain rips through my chest. *Aagh…* I grab the couch as the air leaves my lungs, ripping the fabric to try to fight the sensation of being skinned alive.

"What the hell, man?" My brother jumps from his seat mid-sentence, running to my side. I'm doubled over, sucking air through a straw into my lungs while my bear tries to bulldoze out from the inside. It's a battle to stop the spontaneous shift in my living room, which would prove disastrous to my furniture and hardwood floors.

Bear, chill! If Evie needs time, we give her time and proof.

Go get our mate, he screams in my head.

"Evie," I howl, grabbing my stomach. My bear's using my voice to release his plaintive cry. *What the fuck?*

"What's wrong, Wy?" Jax lunges out of the way as my bear takes over, shoving me from the couch.

Our mate needs us!

The psychotic urge to run spreads through me, one I have no power to ignore. "Trouble," I growl, the barely human sound ripping from my throat and bouncing through my living room. Both men are by my side.

"Wy… dude. We're working this out. Calm the fuck down!"

"Can't," I pant, shaking my head frantically, I wave off Caleb's attempt to keep peace and throw my body through the front door. Insanity tugs at my consciousness. I'm only coherent enough to hear Jax and Caleb calling behind me.

Evie's in trouble. Go to her!

By the time I land on the front porch, bounding in a single jump to the ground, it's all paws hitting the dirt, not size twelve boots. Caleb's right behind me, shifting and throwing himself into my head.

Brother, heel. What's going on?

She needs me! I snap a growl to the open sky, shaking my head when I see Jax running toward his truck.

"I'm so sorry, man. I can't shift yet with the wound," Jax hollers our way before climbing in his crew-cab to follow.

Caleb and I gallop with heavy tread toward the main road, shaking tatters of clothing that hang off our fur. I have no idea what I'm heading into, only that I feel a terrible panic for Evie. It says get to her fast.

My nose follows her scent down my drive. She turned away from her normal route. *Where was she headed?* Even though Evie left by car, her sadness hangs in the air, grabbing me. Our connected hearts pull me toward my mate, helping to track the smidge of her scent in the air.

The spritz of drizzle on my snout raises a panic in my head. If wetness moves in, it'll wash away what small amount of Evie I do smell. *This is bad!*

With urgency fueling my limbs, I run faster, claws ripping through soft dirt. Terror pushes them harder toward my mate, electrifying my muscles. Our bears stick to the edge of the forest, following Evie's faint smell in the air.

About five miles from my house, my front paws falter, tripping to slam my snout and chest into the ground. *She's hurt.* A staggering fear rolls through me that doesn't even feel like my own. I peel myself from the ground and turn to Caleb, who nearly somersaults over me from the quick stop.

What are you talking about?

I growl at Caleb, snapping my teeth as anger swirls through the panic. I don't have time to explain. *Evie's in trouble.*

How do you know?

The beady black eyes of my bear glare at my brother, until Jax pulls to a stop beside us. He nods and I ignore Caleb, lifting to my hind legs and barking at the two men to follow.

My fear grows stronger the closer we get to the main town, but so does Evie's pain. Tracking her is harder than I'd like, given we didn't fully mate, and her smell tainted by a stench of car exhaust, but nothing's going to stop me.

When we come to a dilapidated gas station, I skid to a stop. A tornado of smells taint the air: fear, pain, cruelty, and... sulfur. It's the last smell, the one I scented through town, that worries me most. Caleb smells it, too. Adrenaline turns my stomach, the nauseousness threatening to return my breakfast.

I jerk my head toward Caleb. *Something happened here.*

I know, brother. I know. He stalks toward the pumps. *Be careful.*

It's a risk to be in bear form this close to people, though this little store is a ghost town, even in broad daylight. But tracking is easier in bear form and with my nose to the ground, I follow the tobacco and sulfur to where they're strongest before they mix with Evie's fear and disappear completely.

Caleb chuffs behind me and I look up, catching a pair of eyes peaking from behind a blackout shade. We only have a small time before the clerk gets nervous and calls the cops to remove the two massive beasts in his parking lot. I pray if he does, it's Graham that shows up because I could really use a bear in law enforcement right about now.

When I turn away to focus, I see Caleb's eyes locked on the ground. His meaty paw swipes rocks away from something, watching out for glass littering the gravel. Above him, the face of the gas pump is shattered, the hose torn from its holder and left dangling on the ground.

This is it. I smell Evie heavy here, but it doesn't calm me. Her fear is palpable. My eyes fall to Caleb, icy chills rolling down my spine. He's staring at the cracked shards of her phone lying in a puddle of dirt and glass.

We couldn't protect her! My bear's wail pushes me to investigate. I tuck my head and sniff, dread closing my eyes because I already know. One whiff of the vanilla-honey scent and it's confirmed. That durable tangerine casing with a lightning bolt of cracks splintering the glass is my mate's.

Despair pulls me under. My bear lifting his muzzle and a giant roar to the sky, bellowing our pain. *Someone got to her.* I push Caleb, regret hitting me hard in the chest. I know losing my shit won't help. If anything, it risks attracting onlookers, or getting shot.

Caleb's snout punches my shoulder, gathering my attention as Jax rumbles to park behind the building. *We'll find her, brother. I promise.*

With a nod of determination, I postpone the anger at myself in favor of finding my mate. I'll spend the rest of my life apologizing. I'll cook dinner every night and massage her feet—if she ever lets me touch her again.

Gathering Evie's phone in my mouth, careful not to cause further damage with my teeth, I barrel toward the tree line where Jax waits out of view of the street. He tosses Caleb and I a change of clothes from his cab. "I stopped for supplies and reinforcements," he says, his face as sober as ours when we shift back to human form and cover up.

"We need a plan," Caleb says, stating the obvious.

Jax peels out and I hang my head from the window, bargaining with anyone listening to let me pick up Evie's scent in the air or find some clue. It's harder without my bear but I'll turn over this whole mountain if I have to... I'm finding my mate!

Chapter 31

♥

Evie

Groggy, I wake up in a dark room, my hip stinging where it meets hard floor. I can't move my arms.

Realizing they're duct taped behind my back, I at least understand why my wrists are on fire. Even the smallest twitch rips skin as I fight my way into consciousness.

A cramp works through my legs, making them jerk straight before I have a full-on Charlie horse. *How long have I been in this position?* The numbness in my shoulder says it's been a while. My heart sinks. How can I get help when my family thinks I'm with Wyatt, and Wyatt thinks I stormed home?

The dizziness that rolls through my head when I turn over makes me wish for sleep again. *What in the world was I drugged with?* Although, that question isn't as important as who the hell took me or where am I at this point. It's not like I can get first aid or an antidote… wait, this is a warehouse. *I'm tossed in the back of a warehouse like a sack of potatoes.*

Everything around me is blurry.

I blink, fighting to adjust my eyes adjust from their drugged sleep. Eventually, rows of shelves and boxes become clear. A dingy, push-out window above brings frigid air into the cavernous space, but at least the rain stopped. I guess I was out long enough for the storm to pass.

Or they drove you somewhere far away, Evie. Given the dusky color in the sky, I'd guess it's about five o'clock so either could be true. *I've been out for hours!*

Somewhere in the building, a twang of accents joke and rib each other. Although, understanding their grumbled words and tobacco-scratched throats is near impossible. When a raucous noise up front brings all the men to hysterics, their sadistic laughter echo off the walls and I cringe.

Several of the animated voices talk fast, getting louder as their hyper words spill three sentences in the space of one.

"Da-umn, Skin. Dat's the best news I heard in years," the hyper one cheers.

Shouts and congratulations ring across the building, but I can only make out a few words. Something about a stash they jacked and some cursing for a braggart. Then, a bunch of back slapping. Their jovial chatter about what amounts to pretty nasty business shakes my nerves. These people are capable of anything.

My hands tremble. What if those rough voices come back here and find me awake?

You have to get out of here.

Gently, I roll to my stomach, giving my deadened limbs some relief. The angle and the numbness make working the tape binding my wrists harder. Hair pulls with each push and pull of my arms, ripping a sob from my throat. Tears pour down my face, but I try to squash them. *I can't let those men hear me!*

Thinking my feet might have better luck, I push back and forth with my legs, loosening their sticky prison in increments. My jeans save most of the pain, but not the fear. That spikes harder with every scratch against the floor. The sounds might as well be fireworks in my ears, but I pray those guys up front can't hear my struggle.

"Fuck, man. Why we stuck babysittin' stead of going out and roughin' some heads?" Hyper guy's voice is a lot closer than it was earlier.

Shit!

Boxes scratch across the rough floor. "Stop yer bitchin', JB." "Can we at least have a turn 'fore boss gets here?"

Bile sours my mouth. For a minute, I'm terrified I'll be sick, which will definitely draw attention. I can't break down. I force my brain to focus, though the frenzy of emotions threaten to take me under.

With my lips squeezed shut, I muffle my grunts while I wiggle the bindings. *Please loosen. Please loosen.* My feet arch against each other, bending in ways that would make my second-grade ballet teacher proud. I'm sending her a bouquet and an apology for quitting if I get out of here.

The pressure around my ankles give just enough to allow for bigger pushes, harder tugs. My arms aren't catching that luck. They're bare, the slightest movement pure torture to my battered wrists and they're still just as tight as before.

In the distance, someone's phone blares a noxious death metal tune that resonates through the warehouse. It stops my wiggling as my ear strains to catch clues in the one-sided conversation.

"Ya, Boss. Uh, huh... right."

Chains clang against metal, screeching with the opening garage door. All the men clatter around now, a flurry of activity upping the energy in the space. I wiggle the tape harder, eager to get free. The men's conversation dips low, but one sentence sends chills through my body.

"The boss said get 'er ready."

Oh, God. Oh, God. Oh, God.

I fight my restraints harder, desperate to get out of here before I find out what *'get 'er ready'* means. Problem is... the harder I struggle, the more damage I cause to my wrists, the more warm blood leaks into my hand. I bite my lip against the scream of pain. But the alternative is worse.

Sadly, my desperation only earns a small lax in the tape before two of the goons walk back to my area. I freeze. The little one's sneer is pure evil. My body trembles with the adrenaline coursing through it, from the fear.

As if he senses it, the creep's smile grows bigger. He gets pleasure from my distress... or my pain. I'm not sure which one.

When the kid gets closer, I recognize him from the car. That stringy blond hair is pulled in a man-bun now, an odd sight with the rest of his backwoods style. Like those tan, shit-kickers that stop a foot from my face. They reek with unwashed grime.

"Mmm, she's pretty, Slim. What should we do with 'er?" He moans, tugging at the waist of his slouchy cargo pants with a leer from where he stands over me. I'm not sure if that look means he wants to touch me or kick me in the face with that boot.

The fat guy he called 'Slim' walks around, slamming a rickety chair on the concrete beside me. The little one grabs my arm roughly and jerks my weight into the seat. I wouldn't have thought his skinny body could lift me, let alone toss me with so little effort.

So that weeds out direct fighting. Their strength advantage is clear, even if it looks like a strong wind could blow this guy over.

At least he didn't notice my feet have loosened. My hands and feet stay pressed together so that small advantage stays a secret. The only sign of my struggle is the trickle of blood dripping into my palms. That evil smirk when Mr. Stench-on-sticks hung my arms over the chair proves he saw the blood, although he must assume I wasn't successful.

Finally, the sicko steps back, his eyes tracking the length of my body. "We been waitin' for our princess to wake up," he taunts, rubbing a tobacco-stained bony finger down the side of my face. I jerk away fighting my gag reflex. "Aww, sugar... don't be like that." His leer turns nasty. "Slim and I'll take real good care of ya, once you get us some info for Bossman."

"JB, stop being stupid." The fat one's sweating. I can't tell if it's because of his weight, his nerves, or the sick pump of JB's hips. Still, his scowl at the one in my face makes me feel not quite as alone in my hatred of the man. Slim swipes a handkerchief across his forehead, cutting his eyes at the entrance to our back area like he just wants to run away. He keeps his distance from the creepy little guy, but warns him all the same. "JB, if Boss catches ya touching her 'fore he gets his info, he'll have 'yer hide. You know that."

JB scoffs. "Don't got time fer nuthin' now no-way."

"What info?" I jerk my head to *Slim*, worry and curiosity going against my better judgment to keep my mouth shut. The JB kid in front of me laughs with disgust, but we're interrupted by an engine rumbling that draws the men's attention outside.

God! If those tires crunching would only be the cops. Or anyone else coming to save me! I don't care who. I'd move home and vow to do good for the rest of my days. *I'd do Ama's laundry for a decade!*

When the approaching car vibrates the interior warehouse walls, I know it's not the cavalry come to save me. The car's pulling inside. Which means they were invited... welcomed.

A scalding tear slides down my cheek when the men leave me to walk to the front. I'm partially happy to be alone again, but worried about what's coming next. Especially when *Slim* shoots a final tense look over his shoulder, a small amount of guilt playing across his face.

I wait until his back is turned, but the moment they round the corner, I resume twisting the tape at my ankles. *I need to run!*

Unfortunately, they don't give me much time. The raspy voices walk closer, their whispers drawing my eyes just in time to stop wiggling before one fancy-suited goon walks around the corner.

His Italian loafers and manscaped beard stand out against the other rough-neck thugs around him. A few seem enamored by his presence, but at least half look disgruntled with his high-handed air. Either way, Mr. Fancy is oblivious. Or maybe he doesn't care if they sneer at his tacky, gold Rolex when his back's turned.

Despite the vibe of having a money-stick shoved up his ass, the fancy guy's dead eyes are sickening. The other men look like they'd beat you to death, but this one looks like he'd torture and skin you alive first. Their differences give off a distinct vibe of dissension in the midst.

Of course, Slick's rapport with his henchmen may have something to do with the condescension he's leveling at the mullet guy who walked up with him. *Wait! That's the driver who took me!* Pompous guy looks like he doesn't want to touch Mullet with a ten-foot pole and I can agree on that one.

"You get info yet?" he asks Slim.

"Nah, Bossman. She just woke up." He stands back and lets *Bossman* take the lead.

Sweat trickles down my back when those vacant eyes turn on me. *I've run out of time.*

Panic blurs my common sense, letting fight-or-flight instincts take over as I struggle against the confines of my chair. I'm fighting for a freedom that is so far out of reach with these three hovering, not to mention the others behind them.

"Tsk-tsk." His foul mouth cracks an evil grin over starch white teeth, so opposite of the brutish rednecks stationed as guards. They're littered with tobacco stains and gold caps. *Don't these guys believe in dentists.*

Manicured fingers lift the ends of my hair, while the boss studies my face. He leans in and sniffs, getting close enough that I can see the red hovering around his irises. *Is he a shifter too? Bears?*

"So, I hear you have a problem with my organization and how we run our business."

I shake my head violently, which tugs my hair free of his fingers. "No. No, sir. I don't know who you are." Sweat beads along my hairline. He rubs his fingers along the tips again, letting it strum through his fingers. I never brushed my bed head this morning—if that was this morning—he cannot like the feel of course tangles.

"You smell like bear," he spits, his sick laughter joining the guys behind him. *How does he know?*

My eyes fill with tears at the mention of Wyatt. I don't want this guy knowing anything about him… except, somehow he does.

I jerk my hair free this time, angry at his invasion. My rashness only makes the thug cackle louder before his eyes hollow out with venom. He snatches a full handful of hair in his fist and yanks backwards, my head tilting at a hard angle. Immediately, I slam my eyes shut, waiting for a punch or whatever's punishment is coming.

"Have it your way, Missy." His grip tugs harder, popping my eyes open with the sting in my scalp. "This can be as easy or as hard as you want it," he sneers, stepping forward until my face is unfortunately close to his waist. Tears flood at the insinuation, and at the way he maneuvers my head to his will.

Bile burns like acid in my throat, but I squeeze my lips together, not wanting to give him power over my fear. It doesn't stop the sobs though. Those tears flow freely down my face, no longer able to hold at bay.

"You, little lady, have been a distraction to the lesser beings in our organization lately. I've had enough of it. They aren't producing because of you."

"Weak management," comes piping from one of the voices in the background.

The boss waves the voice off like a gnat, continuing his spiel. "After all the trouble you've caused, there's just two things that are gonna make me happy. You're gonna tell me where your boss is." He pauses, that sinister sneer causing my body to shiver violently. Bossman uses the hand not mutilating my hair to stroke along my jawline, almost like he cares.

Uhn!

"After we settle that, you're going to make it worth my while for traveling all the way up here to clean up the crew's mess." I close my eyes, unable to watch the carnal excitement streaking through his gaze. Though I won't have to worry about step two, because I can't give him even part of what he wants.

Unease settles in, wondering what this guy will do when I can't remember the last conversation I had with Dr. Michaels. "The doctor hasn't called me in a week," I argue, the shrillness in my voice grating my own ears. "I-I don't know what you want." I can't stop the tremors working through my body, and they only grow stronger with the spread of his evil grin.

"Hah! I want many things. But you and your boss have pulled me away from normal business a little too often lately, and I'm gonna get my money's worth one way, or another."

"Sir, I don't know you or your business," I lie, needing to buy time. "And, I don't have a boss, anymore. I'm unemployed."

"She's a fuckin' liar, Boss. Michaels' been calling her fer weeks."

"No!" I try to shake my head but it's useless in his fisted trap. "I-I used to work for him. At the clinic. But I don't know anything about anything else. I only quit to come home again." *Or I went home to quit, whatever.*

Mr. Italian suit barks another laugh, slinging my head away from his grip with a shove. "How 'bout this, then? Where is your conniving, chicken shit of an *ex*-boss?"

I blink up, confused. *I thought Michaels worked for this guy.* "Did something happen to him?" I ask before thinking better of it.

"Yeah, something happened to him. That jackass ran off with a bag full of my cash." Spittle flies as he screams that last part inches from my face. Uncontrollable trembling has taken over my body in the face of this guy's rage. I can barely hold still in the chair, but I try my damnedest, not wanting to piss him off any more.

On a whim, I search the thugs behind the boss, wondering if any of them have a conscience. The fat one, *Slim*, is the only man who looks torn. The skinny one's face is a mask of glee, and the older guy with the dark-red mullet smiles in victory. His shoulders are tight, glaring at the other guys like he waits to pounce.

When I don't offer any new answers, *Bossman* grabs my lower jaw, no longer playing nice. His iron grip cuts divots in my cheeks from his fingers pressing against my teeth. Sensing my discomfort, he yanks my face harder toward those red, glowing eyes. *That sick bastard is taking joy in my punishment.*

Anxiety kicks my heart rate into overdrive, but the sickos in the room just laugh. I have to do something!

In a frantic attempt to escape, I bend my knees up and use them to push against his hips, pulling my head back for freedom. It only increases the volume of his cruel laughter. No matter which way I pull, I can't get free of this guy.

I taste blood in my mouth and try to scream but the sound is muffled by the boss's firm hand, a wicked growl rumbling low in response. After learning what I did about creatures on the mountain this morning, I'm afraid this guy's going to turn into something scary. The regret washing over me is debilitating. How could I have ever thought Wyatt was scary? This is the monster! Wyatt would never do something like this.

I stop fighting when my breath falters, my heartbeat pounding a staccato through my ears. Desperate sobs coat my lips in salt, but I go for honesty in hopes he'll finally listen. "Sir, I am so sorry, but I have no idea where Dr. Michaels is. I would tell you... believe me." My voice shakes from the pain, from the hopelessness taking over.

The pleading still doesn't work. Bossman bends down, seething. His fiery breath wets my face, anger raising his hand to strike. I brace. I've never been hit before, but if I get out of this with only one, I think I'll be lucky.

Time stops and I open my eyes. The boss must see honesty in my face because he instead of hitting, he shoves my face away. The strength and momentum tilts my chair away from his body and I squeal, preparing to hit the floor as it teeters on two feet. Thankfully, it doesn't topple, but my relief is short-lived.

In a howl of rage, he walks over to Slim, his back rigid as he pulls the man's gun from its holster. With a quick jerk, the gun aims in my direction before he stalks back over.

Somebody... help me! The scream is only in my head. It would do me no good out loud anyway.

Every mistake I've ever made rolls like a movie through my head. From taking the job with Michaels to staying away from home. For feeling like my heritage was suffocating and not understanding the love from my family.

And the worst mistake of all, walking out on Wyatt this morning and not believing in fairy tales.

I feared the unknown. And people who had never done a single thing to hurt me. Unlike the monsters here now, the ones who are actually planning to end me any minute. They'll go back to their business without a care and I'll never get to apologize.

"Please," I beg, shaking my head desperately. The weight of despair floods through me and I drop my eyes. I can't watch their twisted faces anymore.

A fresh floodgate of tears opens up and I silently send love to all the people in my life. *I love you, Mom and Dad... Gran. I love you, Ama, Kayah.* And with sobs shaking my shoulders, I pour all the love I can from my heart to Wyatt, praying he feels my apology for judging him. For not letting him explain.

I am so sorry!

Chapter 32

♥

Wyatt (Earlier)

Jax parks the truck at his brewery, giving us time to form a plan.

In my lap, I swipe Evie's busted screen, surprised to see no pass-code to enter. Silently, I scold her, but thank her at the same time. Caleb peeks over my shoulder and sees the same surprising number of missed calls and text messages as I do. *What the hell is going on with her?*

"Is that her boss?"

"Yeah," I grunt.

"That's a lot of missed calls," he says unhelpfully.

"No shit." My gut churns with dread as I click one of the voicemails. I need to know what Evie was avoiding so hard. I'll apologize for invading her privacy later—after I spank her until she can't sit for a week. *If I find her.*

No, once I find her.

By the third voicemail, I'm livid. Her boss is a sketchy prick. His voice is tight and screamy, until it slides into full threats. He's panicking and taking it out on Evie.

"She never told me she was in trouble…" *Why!* Bellowing, I slam my fist into Jax's dash earning his deserved glare.

"Calm your bear, man!"

I ignore him, but keep my fist clenched against my thigh so I don't cause more damage. My finger clicks on one of the missed calls before they can talk me out of it. Her boss's nasally voice picks up after two rings.

"Holy hell! Thank the stars you're OK," the boss yells into the phone. "I've been trying to call you all week, Eveline!"

"Excuse me!" I growl, interrupting the doctor's rant. "We'll talk about how you speak to my mate, but first what in the hell have you gotten her into?" Gritting my teeth, I focus on Caleb's hand squeezing my shoulder, using the distraction long enough to gather information. My bear aches to launch itself at the closest threat to his mate and right now we'd love to sink our teeth into this asshole.

"Excuse me, son. Who the hell are you?"

"I'm the boyfriend."

The doc's tone goes indignant. "Evie ain't got a boyfriend."

A curse rumbles under my breath at the man's challenge. "Evie's missing. In trouble," I grind out. "I found her phone. There—" My voice cracks. "There was evidence of violence."

"Leave it alone, man. If they have her, you're too late."

Jax's fists tighten on the wheel while Caleb grips my shoulders. They both hear this conversation easily and both pick up on my barely held control.

The plastic of Evie's phone cracks in my hands. My fingers fly open, letting the thing fall to my lap for safekeeping. I tap the speaker button, knowing I can't ruin the one lead we have with this phone.

"Listen, jackass. I saw your messages. You tried to warn her, and it didn't work. Now you're gonna tell me who has her. And where they might take her," I bark. "I don't give a shit *who* you're scared of… I'm scarier!"

Silence crackles through the phone and I cringe at the worried look that passes between my brother and Jax.

"In-for-ma-tion!" My roar vibrates the truck and I slam the heel of my palm against the dash again... repeatedly. Guilt pulls me back before I damage anything. I shoot Jax an apologetic look, hating this feeling of losing control. My bear is scratching and clawing behind my eyes. I squeeze them shut to fight against him. I'm about to snap when a pained exhale hisses through the phone.

"This ain't smart, kid. If you want to stay alive."

"Fuck alive. You give me information, or I *will* find you instead." I pause, letting my words sink in. "If I find you… your last thought before your closed casket will be how not protecting my girl was the worst mistake of your life." The threat must get through because finally the doc starts cooperating.

"Okay. Okay, man. Dixon got her." I almost don't hear his whispered voice. It's resigned, edged with fear. "I ran, ok. But I needed cash for a full get-away. I-I can't work for them anymore! But I'm in the hole in a bad way. They won't let me out." His plaintive explanation might earn him leeway in a court, but not with me. "They took Evelyn to get to me."

Problem—meet solution.

"Fuck!"

From the corner of my eye, I see Jax on his phone, firing off a quick succession of texts before jerking back on the road. His tires spin gravel as he heads in the opposite direction than where we came from.

"Dixon? Please tell me you mean some other Dixon than Dixon's Mafia?" I glance at the family beside me—blood and otherwise—and fear stops my heart. Evie is my priority, but this is big. I can't risk them, too.

"I wish I did," Doc sighs.

"Where would they take her?" Jax throws the question between us, not meeting my eye.

Silence.

"Listen, asshole. Tell me everything you know. Right now! If you want any chance to stay alive."

The doc's frustrated sigh comes through the phone just before an announcement pipes over a sound system on his side. *Boarding information.* He groans, knowing I heard his destination.

"Shit." *Yeah, shit.* "Look man, the only place I can think that might be close to her parents is the warehouses in Asheville."

He knew she was here all along. It infuriates me that chances are this scumbag gave up her location to save his own ass. A train horn blares in the background, followed by the sound of bags being shuffled. Michaels must be getting ready to board.

"Earl runs a stash through Blue Ridge from that warehouse. It's going to be the easiest place for him to put her."

"Stash of what?" My patience is running thin, but at least Jax is barreling down the highway. Toward what... I don't know yet.

"You name it... guns, ammo, drugs. They run it all."

My brain visualizes fifty scenarios of how armed these fools will be and I look up at the sky, begging for a little help from anyone watching over us. *Just please let Evie be safe. I'll deal with whatever else they throw me.*

Michaels clears his throat, interrupting my train of thought with a soul killing revelation. "Um—so lately, the whole gang's been split internally. Big rivalry shit. There's a sect going out on their own. That's who's causing a stink. They're makin' a play for the top. One of them tried to recruit me, but I ran." He says that like it's something to be proud of.

"OK..." I drag out the word, running thin on patience. There something the doc isn't saying.

"Yeah, well. I heard they've been running women too. Don't know if that's the outfits in Asheville though, or somewhere more remote."

"Address!" Panic burns my lungs. I need the address. I need my woman. And I need air. Michaels rattles off a general vicinity of the warehouse, claiming he's never personally been there. Before I can get more, he disconnects with an ominous *'good luck.'* That doesn't make me feel better.

We'll sniff her out. My bear paces now that we have a location.

One look at my fellow bears show they understand—the danger and the importance of getting my mate back. Grabbing my phone, I fire off a text to Uncle Mac.

Me: I know you're pissed but I need back up. My mate needs back up!

Mac: You mated?

Me: Not yet. I pause.

Me: We will.

When my uncle doesn't respond, I text him the address Michaels rattled to me... just in case. A mile marker catches my eye. Forty-five miles to Asheville. "How'd you know which way to go?" I ask, realizing we've been driving for fifteen minutes now.

Jax's hands twist the wheel, his face brooding. "We've had words before," he says cryptically.

"Dixon?"

"There's pressure rolling through the casino and bars in the area." He cuts his eyes to me while he drives. "Ama knows about them too." My gut churns the more I learn. I pull out my phone to text Graham, but Jax lays a hand on my shoulder. "We've known Dixon had a headquarters in Asheville for a while. I just assumed when you said their name, so I texted Graham while you were on the phone that we needed backup."

Feeling useless, and like my buddy is five steps ahead of me, I rack my brain for the best course of action. Jax shrugs, his pensive eyes meeting mine across the truck. "I'll text Ama to alert their dad. He can wrangle us some back up," I offer.

"Yeah, we need some talented hunters on this one," Caleb says. "Especially if things go south."

I nod, thankful that I have people who have my back, and because of that, have Evie's back. A response chimes from Ama.

Dad gathering tribe. Text address.

Mac's texts ding my phone immediately behind it.

Mac: Crew headed your way. Text updates. Run point.

Mac: Be careful. If this is who I think it is...

Mac: Ancient shifter. Not confirmed...

Okay. This is good. Back up is on the way so I can focus.

My bear's urges are hard enough to fight without my mind and my heart being split in two. His bullheadedness would have me rushing in and take down anyone in our way.

I won't take that chance if there's a way it would get Evie killed. My bear is not going to rule my head!

Caleb reads the text over my shoulder and slaps my back in support. "Let's go get your mate, Wy."

Chapter 33

❤

Wyatt

A surreal clarity washes over me by the time Jax pulls his truck behind the Asheville warehouse. Every building around us is dark, except this one.

Not bright, morons. But thank you.

In the distance, a litany of horns and engines create ominous music from the highway, pointing out how removed we are from the hustle and bustle of normal life. A few light poles flicker in sections of the empty lot, others are completely dark. The vision paints the air with a creepy vibe that sends a chill down my spine.

From the back corner of the lot, I'm alone with my two best men, at least the ones US bound. And we're about to rescue my mate... from the unknown. None of us have remotely been in this situation before. The anxiety creates a low hum of energy in the air.

She's close. My bear smells Evie the moment we step from the truck. He's ready to fight. I shoot Jax a pleading look while I strip.

"I'll wait for Graham and the rest," he confirms, opening his toolbox to arm himself.

Immediately, my bear takes over, shifting so he can hunt easier. Jax straps himself with his knife at his belt, rifle on his back, and pistol in his hand. Since he can't shift with the recent injury, he's the most vulnerable of us all. Thankfully, he volunteered to coordinate reinforcements for the group attack, so I didn't have to force him into it.

Jax isn't happy about sitting on the sidelines. His agitated pacing shows that, but I lied and said I'd wait for backup if I tracked Evie. It'll help him feel better, though I know there's no way my bear will have that. If we all get out of this alive, I'll thank Jax and apologize later.

He doesn't believe a word out of my mouth anyway. My best friend knows there's no limit to my stubbornness. When I put my head to the ground and sniff for my mate, all semblance of thought outside of Evie is gone. Her scent's close. I hate she's with these people, but my panic lessens to know we found her.

Relieved, I perk my ears, barreling in the direction of my mate while listening for threats. My paws thunder the ground until I'm outside the right building. There's enough darkness for my bear form to hide, but when I scent the pain and terror tainting her sweet vanilla, my feet pick up speed, not caring about being discreet.

Settle down. My brother pads up beside me. *We have to stay quiet.*

You smell that? I turn on him with a challenge in my growl.

I don't get any other thoughts out before my ears fracture with Evie's gut-wrenching cry. Her voice connects in my mind. *I'm so sorry Wyatt. I love you.*

The air freezes in my lungs. Her heart resonates through me, sending my bear rushing the warehouse door before Caleb can stop me.

He's on my tail when I skid to a stop. Four smells sour Evie's, but all are some variation of the one I smelled in town. The fact that my uncle couldn't nail down what type of shifter it is worries me. However, with only four men, I like our chances. Whatever they are, very few species can match strength with our bears.

I turn my head, making sure Caleb is set. *Take care of her if something happens.*

Worry flickers behind his eyes, but his head dips in confirmation. *I'll follow your lead, man.*

I nod, appreciating his back up more than I can admit right now. Although, these guys are either cocky as hell or complete idiots, because not a soul guards the entrance. Their oversight makes it easier for Caleb and I to sneak inside, using a rusted out blue truck to block our bodies while we scour the empty facility for enemies.

Luckily, all's clear except for a few voices in the back. But I don't think anyone has smelled our bears yet. The entire place reeks of rancid tobacco smoke, killing a shifter's scent advantage. It's a pro for hiding us, but a con as I struggle not to vomit.

My front paws falter when a jarring clatter draws my attention. It sound like crashing metal and puts an end to the jokes that were flying from the soon-to-be dead thugs. After the crash fades away, an eerie silence fills the space, punctuated by the muffled cries of my mate. *Sonofabitch!*

I toss my head for Caleb to follow, crouching my hulking frame to hunt our prey as quietly as possible. I make sure my claws stay retracted so they don't click on the warehouse concrete floor. Those small details ingrained in our bears predatory nature helps us stalk past racks of crates stealthily.

Together, Caleb and I move past the metal machinery up front, past racks of crates labeled conspicuously for shipping.

I got your six man.

I nod, my focus stuck on the growing anxiety in the air. Well that, and Evie's scent getting stronger the farther back we go. At the final row of shelves, I suck a lungful of Evie into my lungs before we round the corner. I need her calming effect, unfortunately any relief I felt is thrown out the window the second I spot one slimy looking thug in a slick suit standing way too close to my mate.

His back is the first thing I see. My bear snarls, but it's not until he angles a recriminating glare on the greasy one at his back, that I see it...

a gun. Pointing at my mate.

Evie's watery eyes widen, first at the gun. Then when she connects with my bear barreling in her direction.

My brother and I both unleash a deafening roar that rattles the closest shelves. The sound takes the men by surprise, giving us a few seconds advantage. Caleb rears on his hind legs, distracting the men closest to him while I plow snout-first into the front gunman. My mouth is open, teeth bared, ready to chomp the arm holding his gun. When the thug sees what interrupted his interrogation, his dead eyes transform into nasty red slits that throw me off balance.

Shifters! Unc was right. What the hell are they?

Careful! I yell to Caleb.

The gunman's skin pebbles a split second before the full force of my bear slams his chest and my jaw locks on his elbow. His screech of pain echoes through my blood and I snarl, swallowing my satisfaction at snapping his bone with my teeth. The shifter's skin tastes acrid... sour. But I keep my grip on his arm until the gun flies. *Then*, I cackle in my head as I shake his crying body with all my might, like a victorious dog winning his rope bone.

Six-feet of ugly gray suit hits the hard concrete floor, followed by the sickening crack of his head. Not a sound leaves the disgusting lump after that. The man is quiet.

Evie has tucked into a ball, pulling her bound legs up to protect her body. This sight makes me snarl at the other thugs beside me, ready to avenge my mate.

Caleb drops to four paws beside the youngest kid in the room whose skin has turned leather, transforming into whatever these repugnant things are. He grabs for a knife at his hip, forcing Caleb to swipe the man's face with his bowed claw. The snap of his neck tells me this guy won't be a concern anymore, so I turn toward Evie, watching her side for my next target.

A soft gasp falls from Evie when I step over the pool of blood spreading around Mr. Fancy-pants, but I don't sense a single ounce of remorse coming off her.

It's OK, baby. I coo into her mind, just in case our mental link is still working. If ever there was a doubt she's my mate, it would be gone the second I heard her thoughts.

Evie's head snaps to me when she hears my thoughts, those tear-filled eyes as big as saucers. "Wyatt," she whispers, her mouth falling open in amazement.

I nod my head down once before turning to help my brother with the other men who are painfully stuck mid-shift. Caleb has the fat man, his heavy paw forcibly holding the guy's stout—and wheezing—chest to the ground.

He's not armed. Caleb confirms while I turn on the last man standing, the one whose stench followed us through the town.

The lowlife has sharp talons extended and a red scaly hide covering the length of his body, even though his appearance is still mostly human.

The shifter's haggard face bares yellow teeth sharpened to fangs and a scraggly red beard that narrows to a point on his chin. Somehow the man is able to hold a half shift, which fascinates me enough to watch his movements and advance slow in case he has a trick up his sleeve.

Though the lizard man has red fire in his eyes like the others, but his hand trembles as well. He aim a Ruger at me despite his pointy nails and mostly shifted body... a true coward, too scared to fight someone bigger, even with shifter advantages.

Only like picking on the weaker, huh?

Rearing to my hind legs, I use my massive body to shield Evie and hope the nervous shaker will just pee his pants and surrender. My teeth snap in warning and I release a thundering roar that vibrates the old windows above our heads.

One shot blasts the air before I slam my colossal front paws down and barrel toward the coward. He tries to fully shift but I launch his body—mid-change—to the ground, his gun flying on the way down.

Grinning, I press over his prone body with my bear teeth on display and kick his weapon out of reach with my hind leg. In the back of my mind, I register fire burning through my shoulder, but ignore it in favor of striking that arm into the nasty man's chest.

A few ribs crunch which immediately stops his transition and turns his skin back freckly white. My bear snarls approval, lowering a single clawed nail into the human's weaker skin. Vengeance fuels us both, numbing my veins against everything except hurting the men who threatened our woman.

A gnash of teeth over my shoulder drags me from my trance. *Don't*, Caleb growls in my head.

My bear tosses his head back and forth, knowing I should use restraint, but protesting on principle.

I protect my mate!

He presses his paw down with more force until the man below groans and Caleb barks again. At the same time, I hear boots pounding in our direction and I sniff, relieved to smell bear and not more enemy fire.

I lock eyes with Caleb and lightly swipe a blow across my captive's face, claw retracted. *You happy?*

His bear shakes with animal mirth, since we knocked out the last threat.

Turning to check on Evie, I bow my head so I don't scare her, fully expecting to be on the receiving end of her terror, or anger, after all that trauma... the violence. But I'm shocked when I raise my head a few steps away... I don't scent any fear. Not like when we arrived. I only smell awe. And *excitement?*

My eyes dart to Evie's, finding her sweet smile shining like the most beautiful diamond in the world. Tears remain in her eyes, turning them glassy, but she's chanting my name over and over—the sweetest prayer of thanks I've ever heard.

"I knew you'd come," she chokes, a waterworks flowing around her smile.

Overwhelming relief at seeing her smile soothes my jagged edges. She's safe. With a sigh, I step forward and snuggle my head into her lap, nuzzling.

Evie's surprised laugh squeaks in my ear. "Careful, big boy." My bear purrs into her soft belly with affection until she wiggles, and I realize she's still tied. Anger tries to wash away my peace, from what might could have happened. I just can't think about that right now. Not with Evie so accepting under me.

I lift a paw slowly, showing her one sharp talon extended before easing its sharpness through the tape binding her hands. She unwraps the sticky prison with a wince, while I repeat the motion on her feet.

"Thank God," she moans with a gush of air.

The moment she's free, her body launches at my neck and my haunches drop to the floor, supporting her shaking body as it works through the powerful release of adrenaline. Evie's hands bury in my fur, holding on for dear life while sobs overtake her body. My bear face nuzzles her head, hating that she had a moment of pain.

Part of me wishes to shift back human so I can hold Evie in my arms, but the stronger part—my bear spirit—rumbles its refusal. He won't give up the joy of his mate stroking his fur. Not yet.

Not gonna to lie, I'd be rolling on my back right now if it wouldn't be weird. Caleb's voice in my head brings a grunt of annoyance from my bear. I forgot he was here.

Every part of me agrees with him though. I want to celebrate Evie's acceptance. Her hands gripping my fur like she'll never let go. It's heaven… pure happiness. Especially when her laughter replaces the tears, and her long fingers start to explore and stroke my coat with appreciation.

"I'm hugging a bear," she laughs, a little hysterically.

"Gentlemen." Graham leans against one of the racks behind me, chuckling. When I look over my shoulder, both Graham and Jax have lowered their weapons. "Couldn't wait for the big guns huh," Graham teases and I snarl in his direction.

I am the big gun, G.

He and Jax swagger through the room, taking stock of injured parties and bodies needing removal. These pricks can't go to a coroner. As shifters, that would bring a whole new set of problems to our world.

"Unc's on the way," Jax says. "You guys were too fast for reinforcements." He chuckles too, but I can tell he's annoyed I didn't follow the plan. I bow my bear head, hearing a flurry of activity heading our way: tires in the lot, doors slamming, and a parade of feet running our way to clean up any evidence shifters were ever in this space.

Metal handcuffs snick over the two men still left alive, though in pain. Trusting my friends have our alive threats under control, I turn my focus back on Evie, humming deep in my throat. I hope she finds comfort in the vibrations under her head.

Slowly, a sniffling Evie lifts from my pelt and I take stock of her injuries. The bruise on her forehead and hand-print across her cheek infuriate me all over again.

My bear whimpers, sniffing across inflamed skin and wishing we could wake the dead assholes and kill them again. Since I can't do that, my bear's raspy tongue licks at her forehead, wanting to heal over the wounds. He covers her face in quick swipes, but Evie pushes against me for space, her laughter ringing through the room. When she slides away, my bear moans in denial.

"I'm OK," she says. "I swear it. But you're freaking me out, man." That giggle rings melodic in my ears when I worried I'd never hear it again. "Come on, Wyatt! A bear's licking my face! Oh my God!"

Over my shoulder, Graham cracks up and I slow my obsessive cleaning of her skin, relieved that at least she's not running away. And not afraid of my bear.

When Evie straightens in front of me, an exhausted smile shines from a layer of bruises and I lower my nose to her waist, sniffing over the rest of my mate for anything out of place, any scent that shouldn't be there.

I need to be sure she's not hiding any wounds... knowing my mate, she would.

Thank heavens for the remaining criminals in the room that there's no sharp pain I can smell, just a dull tinge of it lingering on her scent.

Somehow, Evie understands my intention and holds still, snickering when my fur tickles the length of her arm. A hand comes to my head, stroking the soft fur between my ears, moving to stroke their length distractedly.

"I'm alright, Wyatt." Trusting Evie's assurance she's ok—physically at least—I rest my muzzle behind Evie's ear and revel in her hands taking their turn to explore my form.

"Nice to see we're doing the hard work here while you get a rub down, man."

Evie startles at Jax's joke. I think she forgot they were here, same as me. I snuff annoyance in his direction before nuzzling Evie's hand with my snout. A hint for her to continue petting. Her laughter joins the men behind me, although her cheeks pink at having witnesses to her displays of affection with a bear. Thank God it doesn't stop that hand from rubbing my fur again.

"Wyatt!"

The sudden gasp from Evie has my head jerking around the room, bracing for an attack from a straggling enemy. When I find nothing, I turn back to Evie confused.

Her laser focus is on my shoulder as she scrambles to her knees, rubbing along my muscle all the way down to my paw which is slowly starting to ache thanks to the adrenaline leaving my body. My bear nudges his nose against her chin, relieved to have our mate caring for us.

When Evie pulls her hand back it's coated with thick red. "Oh my God! Why didn't you tell me you'd been shot!" Tears leak from her tormented eyes and it breaks my heart. Hurts worse than the hole in my shoulder.

As quick as I can, I shift back to human form, grinding my teeth to muffle the pain in my muscles from contorting around an open wound. Evie startles when I shrink under her hands, my fur disappearing. But the moment I'm back, I forget the bullet-hole in favor of wrapping her waist and pulling my mate in for a crushing kiss.

My shoulder may throb, but the pain washes away with the pure happiness of holding my mate. Evie's safe. She's mine—or will be the second we're alone—and beyond anything I could ever wish for... she's not afraid of my bear. Especially after seeing me take out two of her captors.

"It's OK, baby." I kiss the silent tears rolling down her cheek... moving to that trembling lower lip. I need to prove I'm OK... that she is, too.

Eventually, Evie's head buries itself in my neck, her body releasing the stress in wracking sobs as the impact of our day hits. I shush in her hair, stroking a hand down her back. "It's all OK." Now human, her tears wet my skin. I wish I could take away the last twenty-four hours… have a do-over. But not the way Evie's fingers dig into my back, holding me close like she'll never let go. That has its advantages.

Her easy acceptance fills the hole in me that broke when Evie ran out of my cabin this morning. Her gaze snaps to my face, realizing she's gripping too close to the steady trickle of blood sliding down my arm.

With a furrowed brow, Evie presses me to sit so she can examine my shoulder easier. Her hands run the edges of my wound, mouth tight with worry as she inspects the front and back of my shoulder.

"This is crazy!" Her spine is stick straight, venom dripping from her tone. "You saved me… and you were shot! That is not ok, Wyatt!" It's hard not to laugh at the steely glare she sends the dead man over my shoulder, but I don't think she'd appreciate my humor at the moment.

"I'll heal. Don't worry." My hands work to assure my mate with soft brushes to her arms, her shoulders.

"You shouldn't have to." Evie's face crumbles and she crawls carefully to straddle my lap, though I'm buck naked on my knees. I chuckle and pull her sweet smell into my chest with my stronger arm, thankful she cares. Thankful for her faint sigh of relief when she wraps her arms around my neck and buries her fingers in the nape of my hair.

She'd better get used to this. *I'm never letting her go again.*

"You boys are gonna have to stop getting shot," she pouts, her voice flat as she takes off her outer shirt to use to stem my bleeding. "I think it went right through, though." My hands brace on Evie's luscious hips, keeping them snug against me now that I can. Her head shakes adorably, but once she's satisfied that I'm not bleeding out on the floor, she chuckles. "I guess I won't be bored in my new practice here."

I share her laughter as we stand, Evie making sure to help me even though I don't need it. Then what she says sinks in...

"You're staying." I bend my knees until we're eye level, our giddy smiles a mirror of each other.

Masculine chuckles roll behind us, but I couldn't care less. I wrap Evie up and lift her by the waist with a twirl.

"Easy, son. Don't need to see all that," Unc teases, having walked in during Evie's assessment with a few of our stronger military clan members.

Evie's face turns beet red now that our moment is now public spectacle. Clearing my throat, I set her down so I don't add to her discomfort. Plus, I need to make a good impression on my uncle.

"Unc, thank you for coming." I nod to the powerful bears behind him, unable to express my gratitude for their back up. He tilts his head in deference to myself and Evie before walking over to Graham for an update.

Too soon the sound of bones cracking pulls Evie and I from our euphoria. I know the sound of a shift, but she looks over my shoulder to what I assume is my brother transforming back to human form. Her surprised squeak as she jerks her eyes back to my chest makes it hard to hold back a laugh. Especially when they dart right back up to my face, just as quick. *I think she just realized I'm naked.* The thought makes it impossible to hold back because odds are, she just got an eye-full of my brother as well.

Instinctively, my bear circles, straightening my back to hide my brother from our mate's vision. He doesn't like her this close to another naked male.

"That's uh—pretty crazy what you guys are able to do," she says with amazement. I feel my uncle's eyes on us, watching our interaction, but Evie doesn't know he can hear every word she's saying... yet. I hope she doesn't freak out and give him the wrong idea. "Does it hurt?" Her eyes focus on the wound at my shoulder.

"Not unless we're injured," I admit and Evie's eyes water with regret. Her shirt is pressing hard against my shoulder.

I can tell she's still processing, not used to seeing an animal become a person, or vice versa. Though she's handling it surprisingly well. Just a slight blush from all the nakedness around her.

I smile down at my sweet mate, my eyes promising all sorts of distractions for her later, which I think she reads judging by that shy giggle that sneaks out. Evie lifts to her tip toes and plants a soft kiss on my lips, blushing harder when her feet are back on the ground and she sees that my uncle has walked up.

"How you doin, son?" His gruff voice thickens when he looks at my shoulder, but when he notices Evie protectively guarding me, he smiles... a warm, light up your eyes, grateful smile.

"I'm good, Unc. Flesh wound," I say, meaning to ease the worry tightening his features. We shake with my good arm, and I wrap the other around Evie with only a slight protest from my muscle. "Unc, I'd like you to meet Evie... my mate."

Both their eyes fly to me for vastly different reasons. Evie's curiosity registers from my formal introduction, and I haven't even explained the significance of the word *'mate'* in our community. Unc's eyes register surprise with just a hint of... jealousy? He's significantly warmed on the topic of mates since the last time we spoke.

"Nice to meet you, young lady." Uncle dips his head since Evie's hands are still wet with my blood. She returns his polite greeting but there's a noticeable up-tick of her heartbeat. *She's nervous.* Uncle must hear it too because he softens his tone. "I notice you didn't freak out back there." It's a statement, not a question and Evie peeks over her shoulder to see which part of her crazy evening he's talking about. She catches Caleb bent over the passed-out mullet man still buck-ass naked.

Quickly, her gaze snaps back to our circle, her brows halfway to her hairline. Uncle laughs at the wide pop of her eyes as she tries to make casual conversation.

"Oh yeah, naked men walking around a warehouse with half-dead thugs who kidnapped me… totally every day." Her voice gets a little pitchy at the end but that she's finding humor in an awful day shows promise. Who can blame her for being a little freaked out?

"Naked *bears*," Mac corrects, pulling Evie's eyes to him.

"I'm not going to say anything," she defends resolutely, not looking the slightest bit intimidated by our Alpha.

"No. But you didn't freak out," he repeats with respect aimed at her I don't usually see him give to humans.

Graham walks in, interrupting Evie and Unc's stand off to toss a pair of pants at Caleb. "Why do I get the fat one," he groans, bending to lift the cuffed man off the floor.

Jax slaps our friend jovially on the back. "Because you're the giant fucker," he says laughing. In response, Graham turns his shit-eating grin on Jax, flicking him off on the way out the door.

"Holy cow! How'd he do that?"

I glance to Evie not understanding what she's asking. "That?" I nod behind me where Graham has the four-hundred-pound man by the collar, shoving him into his squad car. "He's shifter too."

Evie rolls her eyes to the ceiling. "So, you guys are everywhere, basically?"

I lay my best charming smile on her. "Don't worry. You'll grow to love us."

Jax walks up with my clothes in his arms. "Got your stuff from the truck. Company should be here any minute." It's a hint that we are about to be mixed with humans.

Reluctantly, I let go of Evie so I can dress but Evie and Unc's snicker pulls my gaze where they turn to Caleb. I'm thankful he has pants on now, but I laugh out loud when I notice Caleb's aggravation. Our six-feet-six friend obviously gave my brother his off-duty warm-ups, and the things swamp my Caleb to the point he looks like a toddler playing dress up.

"Shut up," he growls as Graham and Jax walk back in.

My brother's sensitive about being a shorter bear. At only six full fee he's at least a few inches shorter than every male we know, but still, he's built like a tree trunk. I'd trust him to have my back in any situation... obviously. Appreciation washes over me for all these men.

"Thank you, guys... for being here." I say, trying to find the words to show exactly how much it means that they were here for me, for my mate. Despite the danger.

"Always, brother." Jax waves me off and turns to Evie. "I texted Ama to let her know you're safe. She was with your dad and the mini army he'd gathered. I convinced them to hold off for tonight since we had the scene under control."

Jax looks at me and I see the unsaid message, *so there's not so many eyes processing here.*

"Your dad threatened my manhood if I didn't have you call them when you got home." Jax looks somewhat perturbed and I assume he's not used to dealing with disgruntled father figures. His wide eyes aren't sure what to do with a man when family protectiveness outweighs common sense.

My bark of laughter lightens the situation. "I don't think you being a shifter—even if he knew—would stop a Papa bear, man." Jax grunts but my uncle wraps a beefy arm around his shoulders and walks toward the door, leaving our bear crew to try to figure out what sort of shifter mess they left.

Shaking my head, I turn to Graham, "How'd you get here so fast?"

"I jumped in my car the moment Jax texted." He chuckles. "With my siren, I can break a few speed laws. But headquarters has been tracking Dixon's activity for months... since they started getting too close to home and messin' around in the casino." Graham glances at Evie meaningfully and my throat clogs. They've been looking out for my mate and her family longer than I knew.

In a daze, we observe the chaos of clean up rolling through the warehouse. I pause, thanking my clan for their dedication to keeping our community safe. "They're shifters though. How do we process that and keep the public out of what we know?"

"Well, this warehouse has been on watch for a while. All legit, bad shit. Not even shifter bad. There's enough evidence on these guys they'll be processed with no parole."

"Do we know what they are?"

"Suspicions but I hadn't believed it until now. The fact that they weren't able to shift before you attacked means they're an ancient species..."

"I saw a tattoo," I admit, remember the dragon on the one's neck.

Graham nods. "Yeah... me too. I thought the rumors were all myth, but... it makes sense."

We all watch one of the triplets drag the unconscious one out by his arm. She tenses when he starts to wiggle against his cuffed restraints. "I'll turn these fools over to the SBI. They'll have questions for you, but I'll push them off 'til tomorrow." He winks at Evie and I tighten my arm around her shoulder with a warning growl.

Graham chuckles, shaking his head as he resumes his evidence round up. The radio squawks at his hip and Graham relays coordinates of our location.

"Your friends are cleaning up this mess," Evie whispers. I can see fifty bad scenarios rolling through her head, so I turn her in my arms, distracting my mate until she can't focus on anything but me.

I shrug and lift her chin for a taste of those soft lips. "I know how to delegate," I tease between kisses, earning the laugh I wanted.

With the kidnappers in custody and Evie safe, I guide her to Jax's truck behind my still-grumbling brother. He tugs at Graham's pant leg every few steps when it slides under his foot. He's making a beeline for Jax's truck instead of the circle of bears where my Uncle is working out how to process such an awful organization and keep shifter secrets. *Guess he's had enough of this drama too.*

A smile cracks my lips as the three of us climb into the warm cab. My bear has peace knowing our mate is safe and coming home with us. I haven't told her yet, but she is. And *after* she's rested, I'll talk to her about becoming my mate and all that means.

For tonight, I'll enjoy the sweetness Evie in my home, and later when I tuck her in my bed, safe in my arms. Evie tucks against my chest, and I rest my head on hers, letting that delicious scent soothe my soul.

My bear and I both heave a sigh of relief.

I finally have my mate.

Chapter 34

♥

Evie

I wake in a cloud of flannel. The soft fabric caresses my skin, protecting it from the crisp chill of morning air.

My entire body screams with sore muscles, but I'm so overcome with relief that I don't care. Like seeing a mirage in the middle of a hurricane tossed shipwreck. I'm safe. In Wyatt's bed alone, but still... a day ago, I thought I'd never see him again.

If I never have to think about yesterday again, I'd be more than happy. It took us a few hours to get through interviews with the cops and get home. Wyatt put his foot down that I was coming back to his cabin and given that I feel the safest with him after that ordeal, I didn't argue for one second.

I did however have to call my family on the drive and deal with my mom's tears and a whole lot of upset—but relieved—family members.

I thought Dad would put up a bigger argument for me to go home, not with Wyatt... especially after the kidnapping. But he surprised me staying quiet. He was almost resigned, but said he was happy knowing I was somewhere safe. I wish I could've reached through the phone to hug him. I figured I'd deal with easing my dad's pride next time I see him. Last night, there was no gas left in my tank.

By the time we got back to the cabin, Wyatt had to help me shower anyway. My eyelids voted for crawling into bed and sleeping for a week, but Wyatt knew before I did, how bad I needed to wash off the day.

He lathered and washed any trace of those monsters from my skin, without getting any other ideas about friskiness. I tried, half-asleep, to entice him, but Wyatt's kisses stayed soft, cherishing, and his hands behaved themselves... *dammit.*

After he had me tucked into bed, he left long enough to heat up some soup from his pantry, insisting I get something in my belly. Before I passed out, warm and full, I think I heard Wyatt whisper he loved me, but I couldn't open my eyes to ask.

Now, throwing Wyatt's heavy quilt back with a groan, I scoot out of bed really needing to ask that question. My body boycotts any activity outside Wyatt's pillowtop mattress.

Too bad for those sore muscles, because my bigger concern is finding Wyatt and making sure he's OK. The stubborn man wouldn't listen about getting his gunshot checked out after we talked to the cops. I cleaned it as best I could, but he wouldn't let me sew it up for him.

"I'm a vet, dammit. I know you aren't an animal right now, but you need to be taken care of."

"I am being take care of," he insisted with a dimpled grin. *"I have my mate."*

I still don't know what he meant by that, but it didn't sound bad.

"We need to go to the hospital," I pressed, crossing my arms while we were getting ready for bed. The maddening beast just let his eyes lock on my breasts like a mischievous twelve-year-old which distracted me.

"No hospital... too dangerous." Before I could offer another argument, Wyatt had me stripped of my bath towel and redressed in one of his oversized t-shirts. His strong arms lifted me to prove his shoulder wasn't an obstacle and tucked me into bed for his one-sided pamper treatment.

Out of bed now and worried, I go in search of the clanging pots, plates, and glasses, knowing with more energy this morning, I can guilt him into letting me take care of his shoulder.

What I find though is Wyatt at his stove, talking to himself and stirring eggs in a fitted t-shirt and workout shorts. They distract me into checking out his biceps instead of thinking medically.

The long dining table beside his kitchen is set with bowls of berries, biscuits, a pot of gravy, and a pitcher of what looks like orange juice. A square plate decorates the middle with an assortment of jams and jellies.

"What's all this for?" I ask, hugging Wyatt from behind.

"For you, my love." He shifts, placing a sweet kiss on my hairline.

"This is a lot of food for me and you." I smile, squeezing his waist while he plates a pan-full of sausages on a napkin.

"You needed to sleep as long as possible," he says, his face tight as he turns to hug my waist. "But—uh, your family will be here in a few minutes." Wyatt's lips touch my forehead fast, understanding he's about to receive a freak-out.

"What!" My panicked squeak makes him cringe, but my brain is flying. "I can't greet my father, at my boyfriend's house, in a shirt barely skirting my thighs," I push back from his chest, trying not to notice the hard muscles under my hand or the handsome grin that spreads across his face.

"You can just tell him you're moving in," he says, surprising the hell out of me.

"We haven't talked about that!"

His eyes grow serious. "I don't want you to leave." He bends to capture my face. "I will protect you here. I want you here."

I open my mouth to respond but the doorbell interrupts and I shriek. "They're here!"

Pushing off Wyatt, I run, my socked feet sliding down the hall to his bedroom in search of presentable clothes. Blood covers my shirt from the day before. Plus, the two-day old camisole is torn and not fit for sight. My skinny jeans are ripped, caked with warehouse dust, and if I never see those clothes again, I'm gonna be a happy girl.

"I'm gonna get you for this," I yell, annoyed when his laughter follows me down the hall. "You were going to let my *dad* see me wearing your shirt!" My voice carries from the bedroom, while I dig through his dresser drawers, no longer caring if I invade Wyatt's privacy. I tie his extra-large t-shirt at my waist with a twist, making it more presentable only seconds before voices echo from the front door.

Quickly, I grab a pair of running shorts and roll them over and over before cinching at the waist. I'm pretty sure I look like a middle school tomboy who hasn't grown into her confidence, but when I step out into the living room, all that is forgotten. My entire family crashes into me, my mother at the head, and nearly knock me over.

"Oh, my baby!" Mom's voice cracks. Her hands swarm, patting everywhere, every angle. Light fingers trail across the knot on my forehead before she breaks down in tears.

Wyatt stands back, his nervous smile making me laugh because I can't imagine this big, powerful bear being afraid of anything. I guess he is nervous about facing the girlfriend's family though.

From the look of Gran hanging off his bicep, Wyatt shouldn't be too worried. She's the picture of happiness, her glassy eyes looking up at Wyatt like her personal hero.

"We're sorry to disturb you so early," Dad apologizes to Wyatt, his voice choked. "We just had to see for ourselves she's OK." Dad coughs to clear his throat, waiting not so patiently behind Mom for his own hug.

"It's no problem, sir," Wyatt reassures, his cheeks taking a rosy shade of pink that surprises me. It makes him all the more adorable.

When my sisters finally let go of my shoulders, sniffing and wiping at their eyes, Dad steps in their place. His strong arms haul me to his chest.

"Thank God, you're safe, baby girl." He pauses, his voice cracking with emotion. "I-I don't know what we would've done…" Dad doesn't finish that sentence. He squeezes my mom into our hug, hanging onto both of us.

When we've all hugged until my ribs hurt, Dad pulls back, leaving one possessive arm slung over my shoulder. His watery eyes turn to Wyatt. "And that young man of yours…" *His faux whisper doesn't fool anyone.* "I owe him the world."

Wyatt scoffs, but Dad lasers him with firm dark eyes. "Anything you need, son, you ask. Our tribe—and our family—is forever in your debt." Dad walks over and pats Wyatt with a man hug slap on his back.

"Thank you, sir."

"Kota. Call me, Kota, son."

Wyatt nods, his warm smile aimed in my direction from Dad's easy acceptance. "How does everyone feel about breakfast?" A chorus of yesses and Hallelujahs ring up as my sisters and mom follow my sexy hunk to the spread he prepared.

Dad chuckles as well, a rush of air blowing out his stress from the last twenty-four hours. His head rests against mine, his eyes taking in all the women in his life happily smiling around Wyatt's breakfast table.

"Thank you, Daddy." I pull away, hating the strain around my dad's eyes, the tension in his shoulders. Now that the threats have been taken care of, maybe we can all relax again.

Dad and I join the others at the table, a ghost of a smile tilting his lips when he pulls out my chair, catching the fact that Wyatt is pushing in Gran's. His obvious sweetness toward my family swells my heart bigger. I think it resonates with Dad too. He purposefully sits across the table from me, leaving the head of the table open for Wyatt—a significant sign of respect from a country man.

My family's expectant faces turn to us… waiting. Ama's full grin matches Gran's when Wyatt takes my hand. He gave me permission last night to share his secret and I know how powerful that is, but this conversation won't be easy. Sucking in a deep breath, I brace my hands against the table to pull the Band-aid off… fast.

"Guys, I'm sure y'all can guess, but Wyatt and I are in a relationship." No one at the table looks surprised. In fact, they all look amused. I glance at Wyatt, hating to see tension tighten his shoulders as he waits for what I'm going to say. It's the love and trust shining from his eyes that solidifies my decision, though. "Well… since I can't live in my childhood bedroom forever, and I'm not going back to Tennessee… I, um…" I pause feeling Wyatt squeeze my hand. His face looks as nervous as I feel. "I'm going to move in here with Wyatt."

I scan the table, braced for a moral lecture from mom or some chastising comment from my dad, but nothing comes.

"Sir… ma'am, I need y'all to know, I love your daughter." They all nod. Happy smiles shining at us across, bright as the summer sun.

Gran slaps her wrinkly hand on the table laughing. "Well, come on now, Bug. Of course you're moving in here. You're his mate." A coughing fit hits Gran when her laughter takes over her ability to breathe. Beside her, Kayah gently pats her back looking as confused as I feel.

Mom and Dad smile knowingly.

"Gran, what do you mean?" I ask, nervous by the shade of gray on Wyatt's face.

Dad takes over the explanation. "Eveline, honestly, did you never listen to Gran's stories. There's a reason she's a respected seer, Punkin'." He reaches across the table to squeeze my hand. "Gran feels when changes are in the air. Sometimes things others wouldn't believe—or can't believe." He shrugs. "It's served us for a long time, helped our tribe prepare."

Gran's head falls, her eyes shadowed. "I failed you in this trouble, Bug. Something sour was in the air but it was so vague… and it was all swirled into the sweetness of your courtship. I assumed it was the stress." She shrugs at my blank look. "You know. When you'd have to face Wyatt's reveal. What that would do to your relationship."

"You knew?" Wyatt stares at my Gran, his mouth slack. She nods, love shining from her eyes at his handsome face.

"I told her the stories. About your kind. Our protectors on the mountain. I sensed her love would hold all kind of possibilities in the future."

"Yeah, Gran, but before two days ago, I thought they were fairy tales," I say, feeling out of control. Kayah suddenly looks like a light bulb has flashed over her head and her shoulders slump in relief.

Dad chuckles, his shoulders shaking at the look on all his kids faces. "Well, guess you know better now. Don't ya, kiddo?"

Wyatt coughs uncomfortably, but Dad's hand squeezes his shoulder. Supportive, fatherly praise radiating from his eyes as he toggles between the two of us. "I grew up with the legends of the clans too. Our fathers passed down the stories from the time we were old enough to join them on hunts. Until recently, I assumed, like you did Bug, that it was only to teach us to be conscious of our arrows. The elders talked of good men and women that grew special powers; that it would be disastrous to mistake one during a hunt because they protected our mountain."

A puff of air leaves Wyatt's chest, his eyes big and slightly panicked. It's my turn to squeeze his hand in support while my family blows his mind.

"How many people know?" he asks at the same time I ask, "How did you know about Wyatt?"

Mama grabs my hand from her seat beside me, calming this unnerving feeling that I'm out of the loop. "After meeting your young man at the Moon dance, Gran came to us and filled us in."

"I didn't want your dad standing in the way of fate with some Papa-bear, rip-roaring tantrum." She snickers at her own joke and Wyatt's cheeks flame. He looks shell-shocked.

Dad grins at us both. "I'd like to defend myself and say I wouldn't have gone Papa-bear anyway. I am the perfect picture of calm." He straightens his shoulders with a defiant grin before slapping the table. "Plus, I need another protector in our family. Especially a big one. I've got three daughters, man!" He groans, raising his eyes to the sky and I shake my head trying to hide my laughter.

When Dad looks back at Wyatt, he sobers. "Son, I already owe you everything for saving my baby." His eyes mist. "Besides, Evie, you're a big girl. You can make big girl decisions."

Mama huffs a laugh, and my dad smirks at her across the table. "See, I'm growing," he says defensively before grabbing the big spoon and scooping some eggs on his place. "I think we should dig into some breakfast. Nice meal, young man."

Wyatt grins ear-to-ear. Neither of us expected an easy acceptance on any of this. It's almost hard to swallow but looking around at my family's smiling faces I figure; we might as well enjoy it.

Wyatt looks immensely proud of himself watching my family dig into his food. "Thank you, sir." The women laugh outright at the men's shiny, happy faces, but my gaze locks on only one, smiling as Wyatt grabs his own biscuit and spoons some gravy into his plate.

The rest of breakfast passes with easy conversation, my family getting to know Wyatt. He's adorable, blushing when he's the center of attention. And when he tells them about his business, his voice is firm, like he's proving he can care for their daughter. No one remotely looks to question it. In fact, his conservation efforts and protection plan for Black bears on the mountain, the poetic way he describes everyone sharing the mountain in peace, earns him higher esteem in their eyes. As a tribe who honors nature, he's going to fit right in.

A few hours later, with full bellies and smiles on their faces, my family hugs us both in a death grip and walks out the door. Wyatt and I crash on his couch, my head nestled against his shoulder with contented sighs. Everything feels peaceful. The cops have the people who were following me. Wyatt is somehow a bear, but even that is sinking in as just part of him after the other stresses of yesterday. But there is one more thing we haven't talked about.

"So, uh, we didn't get a lot of chance to talk last night," I say, wondering how to ask these questions.

Wyatt presses his lips to the top of my head. "Yeah, you were exhausted, baby. It was better for you to get some sleep."

I tilt my head up to see his eyes. "I'm rested now." He smiles down, caramel eyes shining with love as he reaches to bring my lips in for a kiss.

"What's your first question?" he asks, conscious that my brain's working overtime this morning.

"Well... you've said a few times that I'm your mate. And Dad and Gran used the same word. What does that mean? Girlfriend? I mean I assume since you asked me to stay here." I feel the tips of my ears heat, but Wyatt just chuckles softly, laying another kiss on my lips before he pulls me in to straddle his lap.

"It means you're it for me Evie. There is no other and will be no other." He sighs, massaging under the back of my hair. "We shouldn't have... I shouldn't have slept with you before you knew the truth. It was risky." My hand goes to rest on his chest, hating the sad look in his eye.

He swallows. "When you decide for sure that I'm who you want—who you see yourself with for a lifetime—we'll complete the mating bond."

"Like getting married?"

He smiles at my question, but hugs me against his chest with an exhale. "Something like that. Just more fun." Wyatt's heart thumps under my ear and I'm pretty sure I know what he means.

One large hand rubs my back, the motion meant to be relaxing, but his quickly growing erection has quite the opposite effect.

I fight to raise my head again, realizing something funny in his tone. When I see the heat in Wyatt's eyes, I blush, realizing their definition of mating may be a little more literal than I imagined. I look down, stroking my hands across the hard planes of Wyatt's chest, avoiding the tender area on his shoulder where the man took a bullet for me.

"What if I'm ready now?"

Wyatt's fingers sift through my hair, his eyes locked on mine with such intensity it makes me squirm. The memory of Wyatt inside me is causing an uncomfortable wetness below while I wait for his answer. When I wiggle to help my discomfort, his eyes rim gold before he squeezes them shut and tosses his head against the couch like he's in physical pain.

"There is no rush, baby. You have to be sure because once you're mine—truly mine—I can't ever let you go." His gruff voice calls to me, begs me to take away the pressure he's feeling, whatever pain it is.

I lean forward in his lap, ignoring the slight pain from his fingers tightening against my scalp. My lips kiss along the soft scruff at his jaw, enjoying the scratch of it. I work toward the intoxicating scent of his neck, encouraged by Wyatt's ragged breaths and the deep rumble in his chest.

After a few biting kisses where I feel like I want to crawl inside his skin, I finally speak again. My voice is rough, barely sounding like my own as I grind out the words between nips under his ear. "I'm ready, Wyatt. I want to be yours."

His grip on my hair pulls me up, those golden eyes popped wide glowing just inches from mine. I'm panting, my heart waiting to be whole. "I want you to be mine."

Wyatt's jaw ticks, like he's battling a war in his head. I wait, every cell of my body on fire, trying to stay still and not press against his erection. "Are you sure, Evie?" he asks, his mouth pinched at the corner.

I smile. "Make me yours, Wyatt." I drop my forehead against his and cradle his face as I move in for another kiss.

"As you wish, my love." He stands with a groan, tugging my legs tighter around his hips and walking with a shocking speed toward his bedroom.

Right before he crashes through the door, a joyful grin splits his face, and he laughs. "You're stuck with me now, woman. You better be prepared to go wild every day of your life."

His happiness warms my heart, and with love shining from those golden-brown eyes, Wyatt finally carries me through our bedroom door and into our future.

The End

If you enjoyed Evie & Wyatt's story, *please* don't forget to leave a review and share the love for other readers.

Epilogue

♥

Outside my frosted window, a thick blanket of puffy white powder covers the ground. The icicles hanging feet from my face tempt me to grab a long spire for a popsicle. I resist the temptation, remembering how many times Kayah and I got our lips stuck as kids and had to peel them from the ice.

Not on my wedding day!

Never being one for romantic fancies, I couldn't imagine my wedding would turn into a fantastical winter wonderland. Snow blanketing as far as my eyes can see, the fields, the barn. Fluffy cotton balls cling to every tree and bush in our back acres. It's gorgeous, even if the sun sparkling off the top layer nearly blinds me.

My eyes slide to the finished wedding area with its dark, wooden platform and chairs that thanks to Ash are on solid snow. My best friend was kind enough to compact a large section for me before the sun rose this morning, allowing us to get to work setting out chairs and decorations first thing after breakfast. Those three feet that fell overnight made morning preparations akin to trudging through freezing mud, but the reward of seeing our backyard transitioned into a crystalized panorama for my wedding... worth it.

Since frost bitten temperatures plan to hang around all day, I'm ecstatic that we have torches flanking the maroon carpet I'll walk down. Tradition dictates there are only seven waiting to be lit with fire closer to the ceremony. No matter how many times I argued with my dad that the odd number wouldn't work, he insisted. Don't mess with the lucky number seven and a Cherokee man. I laugh remembering the frustration on his face trying to blend his traditional senses with my stubborn, modern side.

And that red carpet! Another of my dad's gentle demands. At least it matches the deep wine roses that'll decorate my bouquet around my favorite flower, the Calla Lily. Dad stood firm on needing the long velvet walkway, though. Although his argument that since I'm his first princess to get married, he wanted to treat me as such, softened my otherwise non-princessy tendencies. Eventually, I'll admit to him I love the red carpet… just not yet.

Tears sting my eyes for the millionth time today, but I shove them down. I can't have bloodshot eyes when Ama does my make-up. Having my sister as a part of today, making my wedding special, threatens to pull the plug on the waterworks despite my best efforts.

Sniffing, I turn my back on the snow-covered scene outside, enjoying the first quiet moment I've had all day. I fought—and won, thank you—for this lull between the chaos of food prepping and decorating. Hardest part was convincing my mother that I didn't need the presence of every female member in my family to help me wash up for the wedding.

Thank you, Mom. I've been showering successfully for years now.

Chuckling, I shed my fluffy robe and slide on the bedazzled sweats my sisters gifted me at the rehearsal dinner. My reflection in the dresser mirror cracks me up. Hair in rolling pin size curlers. 'Bride' emblazoned in silver beads across my back and butt. Very tacky fashion, but incredibly sweet of my girls. Do people need reminding that they're a bride on their wedding day?

A knock interrupts my inner mocking of these silly wedding day traditions.

"Come in," I sing song, expecting every woman in my family to rush through the door. They waited longer than I expected to attack me with wedding preparations.

When the door bangs open, my two sisters, clad in matching red sweats similar to my white ones, sing 'Going to the chapel' at the top of their off-key lungs. Both dance into the room with champagne bottles in hand, my mom and Gran following behind with four glasses held aloft... also in matching sweats. The four women turn around in unison—even Gran—and shake their butts to the silly 1960s song. Their backsides announce their titles as maids-of-honor, Mom-of-the-bride, and head-Gran-in-charge. It's adorable and sweet and hilarious at the same time.

By the time they're done, I'm laughing so hard it's difficult to breathe, the stitch in my side doubling me over. Eventually, no one in my family can hold a straight face anymore. They all crumble into a laughing hug around me, my mom's face blushing from going along with my sister's silly game I'm sure.

"I love you guys!" I squeeze them all tightly before my sisters pull away to pop our bubbly.

Mom helps Gran sit on the trunk bench at the end of my bed before turning to me and wrapping those thick, motherly arms around my neck. I melt into her warmth while my sisters pass out the glasses of bubbly. When she pulls back, her eyes are brimming the same as mine. Instinctively, Mom's hand goes to adjust one of my curlers, but a throat clearing behind her stops her efforts to fuss with my hair.

"Mom, leave her alone," Kayah teases, handing mom her own glass to keep her hands busy. Kayah winks when she earns a put-out look from Mom.

Thankfully, Ama's clinking glass covers my giggle. "I want to toast to our Evie today and that fine chunk-of-hunk she landed..."

Whack! Gran's hand connects with Ama's thigh, which she's eye level with thanks to her primo resting spot.

"Ow, Gran… jeez. I was joking." Ama rubs her thigh. Their antics make me laugh harder, earning a grin from my grandmother. "As I was saying… E, everyone in this room is thrilled to have you home. I'm a little jealous," she admits, pinching an inch in the air with her fingers. "We may be as different as the sun and the moon, but you're still one of my top people. I respect you. I trust you. And I love you."

"Wow, Ama… that was… amazing," I gush.

"Even if you stole one of the hottest men on the mountain." She grins at our mother, who's shaking her head. "But the sacrifice is worth it if he keeps you home with us." She lifts her glass. "Here's to love, laughter, and long-."

"Ama!" My mom screeches, interrupting my sister while the rest of us double over with laughter.

I'm the first one to calm myself in the group, so I take over, reaching my glass high. "To family."

The tings of five glasses mix with feminine chatter from the women I value most in this world. Only Kayah and my mom take their glasses slowly, the rest of us downing the first and going in for a refill… much to my mom's annoyance.

Gran waves away my mom's playfully chastising look. "Oh, you remember your wedding day, Ana. I practically had to tie you to the chair for your hair, you were so…"

"Drunk?" Ama exclaims. "Was Mama drunk?"

"I was relaxed… and a little excited." Mama hiccups into her glass with a smile, giving me a hint that maybe she and daddy have been celebrating their daughter's wedding a little early today.

Ignoring the questioning eyes, Mom steps forward and hands me a dainty, lace handkerchief she had tucked in her pocket. "This, my girl, is the hankie I used on the day I married your father." She chuckles when all of us cringe in front of her. "Oh, jeez. I washed it." Gently, she folds it into my hand with a smile. "I thought this could be your something borrowed," she says, planting a kiss on my cheek before Kayah steps forward for her turn.

"This, my favorite sister, is a blue chalcedony crystal to bring you calm and clarity going into your new journey." She ignores Ama's tut at the 'favored sister' comment. "It's rumored to ease fear and anxiety and promote communication. That's key for a happy marriage, right?"

Both Gran and Mom crack up, knowing the many lectures they've given us girls about sharing our feelings, even when our teenage hormones made us snipe and gripe at each other. I hug Kayah hard, grinning when I pull back and see her cheeks a toasty pink.

"Ok, Bug, this is your something old." Gran stands, removing the thin copper bracelet she's never without. "Your grandfather made this for me on our fortieth wedding anniversary. He said that on our first date he knew it had to be me, so he carved that line from our favorite song into this bracelet and I haven't taken it off since."

With a watery smile, she slips the bracelet over my wrist and squeezes my hands. "The first time I saw Wyatt, I knew he was yours. Gramps would want you to have this. And look at it when he bugs the piss outta you because it's gonna happen. Just cause two people love each other, doesn't mean the ride's always smooth." She gently pats my cheek before going back to her seat and holding her glass out to Kayah for a top off. I catch her dabbing the corners of her eyes, but my tough little Gran waves off any of us fussing over her while Kayah fills the rest of us up. Most of our circle sniffling before Ama steps forward, deciding to bring some levity back.

"Alright, my turn." Ama reaches under the bed and pulls out a bracelet-sized white box she must have hidden when I was in the shower. Without a word, she hands it over with that cocky grin Ama uses when she's being naughty. Lifting the lid, I flush hot at the racy, red garter belt nestled in white tissue paper.

"Show us. Show us," Gran claps, squealing like she didn't have us all in tears a few minutes ago. Her bark of laughter when I turn the box, showing the lacy garment decorated with tiny bows and little silver bear charms dangling from satin ribbons, turns my face into a tomato. "Ooh, your young man's gonna love that one."

"I know. I can't wait to get the picture of Wyatt's face when he pulls that thing off with his teeth." Ama's giggle matches Gran's.

"We are *not* doing that," I insist. "Throwing the bouquet is one thing. I am not tossing my undergarment at a room full of men in my family."

"So, you would do it if the men *weren't* from your family," Mom teases, cracking the ladies up further. Mom and Kayah join in on the teasing, much to my annoyance. *They're usually the calm ones.*

"We are *so* getting that photo," Ama whisper-yells to Gran.

Knowing I won't win this argument, I grab Ama's hand, tugging her over to the colorful assortment of products on my dresser. "Time for makeup, oh-wise-one."

Ama laughs as I plop my butt in the chair where I will transform from ordinary Dr. Eveline Amos, veterinarian bad ass, to the future Mrs.—although still Dr. because *hello student loans*—Eveline McAllister.

"Make me beautiful, sister dear." I grin up at Ama, fully ready to enjoy my sister's skilled hands in all things girly. "And thank you all for the sweet gifts. Ya'll are amazing!" I finger Mom's hankie, wondering if I'll need the thing before the wedding even starts.

Gran corrects my wording in her sweet way. "You're always beautiful, Bug. All three of you are."

"Thanks, Gran," we chime in unison. Ama, Kayah, and I turn to flutter eyelashes at our grandmother, giving her the look that used to earn us extra cookies after school.

While Ama does my makeup and Mom unrolls the curlers from my hair, Kayah entertains Gran with stories of our snowy wedding preparations. The whirling wind of early morning is long gone. But the dead calm outside doesn't stop Kayah's impression of Ash pushing a snow compactor against the wind any less hilarious. Her teetering walk and twisted face make me feel slightly guilty for how much work my family put into making this day beautiful for me and Wyatt, but it's quickly washed away by more silliness. Who looked like a deer on ice? And our growing need for hot cocoa and caffeine to survive the outdoor frost.

"At least you'll have Wyatt to keep you warm tonight," Ama teases, dabbing the finishing touches on my face. I cringe thinking about my wedding night with Gran and Mom in the room. I don't care how old I am, it's going to be hard to look my parents in the eye after I'm married.

They'll know I've had sex.

Chills run through my body, imagining telling my dad I'm pregnant one day. *Ick.*

Ama keeps up her embarrassing innuendos while we get primped and ready in my childhood bedroom. At some point, one of my aunt's delivers a plate of fry bread with more champagne, kicking our party— and our noise level—up a notch.

Finally, after two hours of pampering, all five of us have exchanged our matching sweats for formal dresses, updo's, and glittery heeled boots. Except, Mom and Gran, who chose glittery ballet flats, saying we younger girls were crazy for putting torture devices on our feet.

"You should try Spanx some time, Gran," Kayah jokes, squeezing her hands together to mimic choking our ribcages.

"Never gonna happen, young lady."

I smile at the face Gran makes, taking in both my sisters who are ready to go. If I didn't love them so much, I'd be a green-eyed Bridezilla for how radiant they are in their burgundy A-line dresses. Each dress's neck and hemline suit the girls' individual personality, but that color against their tanned skin... the wide silvery sash cinching their waist. It all comes together in a knockout package. Especially when paired with those silver, calf-hugging boots. They're dressy while still giving a nod to our southern roots.

Glancing down at myself, I'm glad I chose a simpler wedding gown so I can breathe, especially as the time looms closer to walking down the aisle. Fitted lace overlays my strapless sweetheart neckline, helping me not feel like I'm going to fall out of the dress. It plays peek-a-boo with skin across my collarbone and down to my wrist, enough to entice Wyatt —I hope—but keeping a little modesty and tradition as well for the occasion. My high-low hem will show off our custom footwear and a little leg for Wyatt too.

I can't wait to see Wyatt's face when he sees-.

Knock, knock.

Knowing gazes lock on me as Mom opens the door for my dad, who's sporting his traditional Cherokee suit with his thick black hair braided down his back. He's incredibly handsome, though his red-rimmed eyes make mine glass up again as he takes in me from head to toe, fully dressed for my wedding.

Gran walks over, dropping a kiss on both my cheeks before her choked voice whispers. "You will be as happy with that man for all your years as I was with your Gramps, Bug." Smiling, she grabs my mom's arm to usher her from the room before we all start blubbering and mess up my makeup.

My sisters give me a thumbs up and file out behind them. Then, it's just me and Dad left waiting for our time to walk into the snowy oasis. His smile lights up his entire face, despite his swimming eyes. Dad's presence eases my anxiety over this huge transition in life.

"We're so happy to have you home, Eveline. I'd say I'm gonna to keep that boy in check, but I'm pretty sure he's got me there." We share a laugh, knowing Wyatt's shifter strength is not something human men can match. That my dad can joke about it shows how much he truly trusts Wyatt after everything we've been through.

"You're always going to be my protector, Daddy." A few tears spill over for us both as he gives me one more solid hug as his little girl. Pulling away, I fan my face, worried about streaking but also about having frozen water tracks down my face if I step outside while crying. "Stop it! Ama will kill me if I have mascara streaks before I make it down the

aisle." Dad chuckles too, tucking my hand in the crook of his arm.

"Just remember, we are always here for you, Punkin'. Whatever you need." His callused hand covers mine as we walk out of the house onto our back porch. "But trust me... I wouldn't be handing you over to someone so quickly if that man hadn't saved my baby girl once already." Dad's deep brown eyes sear into mine with honesty I've always valued from him.

"I know, Dad. I know." Smiling, I pat his hand in return, lifting my head to my handsome savior waiting for me at the end of a fairytale walkway. Wyatt grins as my dad helps me navigate those last few stairs, careful of the ice.

As the bridal march floats through the air and everyone stands, I find Wyatt's molten eyes locking me in, his magnetism making it impossible to look away as I take that ultimate step. The crunch of frozen ground vibrates through my body, but I'm not cold or nervous anymore. I'm floating on a happiness, knowing my future is at the end of this walkway.

Thank you for reading!!

Please don't forget to leave a review if you enjoyed Wyatt, Evie, & their big, crazy family.

Up next in the
Big Paw Mountain Series...

Caleb & Kayah in *Beyond Expectations.*

He yearns to be good for her. She craves to be bad for him.

Up next... Unleashed

♥

If you're curious for a behind the scenes look at the criminal organization in Shattered Illusions, dive into the world of Dixon's Dragons. Read every nitty-gritty, dirty detail with of course, a hefty dose of steamy romance.

** *Unleashed* is mirror time-line of *Shattered Illusions*. Full behind the scenes, fill in the blanks, hot, sexy drama.

https://dl.bookfunnel.com/s2mej9w2l2

Dear Reader

♥

Dear Reader

I sincerely hope you enjoyed Evie and Wyatt's story. Fated mates are close to my heart. They're some of my favorite reads and frankly, the world needs more of their all-consuming love.

I may or may not relate to Evie in my younger self (wink). That struggle to become your own person in a small town, to grow and stay grounded at the same time. To build a future while honoring the past. Let's just say as a stubborn, Scorpio, sometimes it takes time to learn some of those lessons.

Don't forget to follow me on Socials so you don't miss a new release!

Happy reading!

Annie

P.S. I always wanted to be a veterinarian. :)

About the Author

❤

About the Author

Annie grew up in a small North Carolina town full of people who will help a neighbor with a smile, hold a door, say 'yes ma'am' and 'y'all'. She grew up spending time in Blue Ridge Parkway, visiting Cherokee and learning about her ancestor tribe.

Now, as a wife and mom, she lives in Texas with two amazing kiddos, a house full of pets, and the sexiest, suited, mountain-man a girl could dream to be her prince (beard included).

She loves being outside or on the water, curled up with a book or cheering on the kiddos in all their craziness. The self-proclaimed sunflower would love nothing more than to be on a beach, writing her day away, and only prays to one day make that dream come true.

Follow Annie for more fabulous book boyfriends and playful laughs.

www.AuthorAnnieRae.com

www.ingramcontent.com/pod-product-compliance
Lightning Source LLC
Chambersburg PA
CBHW021952120726
47898CB00001BA/113